IF YOU READ ONE SF NOVEL THIS YEAR, LET IT BE...

A DOOR INTO OCEAN

A DOOR INTO OCEAN

JOAN SLONCZEWSKI

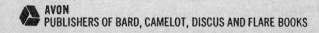
AVON
PUBLISHERS OF BARD, CAMELOT, DISCUS AND FLARE BOOKS

AVON BOOKS
A division of
The Hearst Corporation
1790 Broadway
New York, New York 10019

The Arbor House edition contains the following Library of Congress Cataloging in
Publication Data:

Slonczewski, Joan.
    A door into ocean.

    I. Title.
PS3569.L65D6   1986   813'.54   85-11141

First Avon Printing: February 1987

Contents

Part I

ASHORE

1

Merwen reached over the boat rail, but her hand froze above the weathered pier. To be sure, spring morning breathed peace through Chrysoport harbor, and the sea rippled without a crest. Still . . . a shore. Across the sky, where Merwen was born, none but the dead ever sank to touch the world's floor.

She shook herself and straightened her back. If she were to flinch now, dear Usha would balk altogether and drag her home from this parched planet. At Merwen's elbow, Usha wrinkled her nose as her long arms yanked tight the rope of the houseboat, which had born the two Sharers down along the shore, this endless edge of dry floor. Away from the space landing; *that* had been an unintelligible place of screeching noises and choking smells. Usha had been right to escape to the sea, though a strange sea it was with its floor jutting out hard as a whorlshell.

On planet Valedon, most people lived "ashore," upon dry land —if in fact Valans were people, Merwen reminded herself. Here in Chrysoport, a small, quiet place, she might find out. And that answer would save her own people.

So Merwen placed a hand, then a foot upon the pier. Loose planks vibrated warningly as Usha hoisted up the spinning wheel, the handloom, and the bundles of iridescent seasilk. Silkspinning would occupy Merwen's hands while she awaited the mission that had brought her and her lovesharer so far from their home.

The two women were foreign, but at first their presence went unnoticed in the sleepy town square. Olive-skinned fisherman were unloading their catch for the market, while brightly scarved vendors arranged onions and groundnuts on their stalls and came alive to shake their glass beads and argue shrilly over choice locations in the square. Those who did observe the strangers only stared in surprise. No one warned the pair not to settle beneath the luxurious shade tree by the granite storefront of the firemerchant.

As shadows shrank toward the low houses which lined the marketplace, villagers trickled in to shop for cabbages and to hear the latest word from Pyrrhopolis, the upstart provincial capital under siege by the High Protector. Protectoral soldiers mingled with farmers and tradespeople at the firemerchant's door; they all came to recharge firecrystals, the white diamond-shaped energy cells more precious than any diamond. As customers passed the great tree, they gaped at the odd pair sitting beneath, and some wagered on how long it would take the firemerchant to boot the strangers out.

Oblivious, the strangers wound their spindles full of rich shiny threads that squeaked when the strands crossed. Both wore garments of precious seasilk, yet crudely cut, like beggars clothed in a noblewoman's rags. Odder still, their flesh bloomed deep amethyst, from hairless scalp to nailless fingertips; and when a hand rose a moment, the overlong fingers spread to reveal scalloped webbing that shone translucent against the sun.

No such creatures had ever been heard of on the planet of Valedon, not even from Pyrrhopolis or the other provinces whose uprisings guaranteed employment to Protectoral Guards. Did they come from a far star, one of the hundred now ruled by the Patriarch? It took years to crawl between stars at lightspeed; no one had done better since the old empire had collapsed, many centuries before.

Away from the tree, a farmhand named Melas clapped dust from his trousers and leaned back against a vegetable rack. "They're Iridians, that's all," he assured the withered gray woman behind the stand. In Iridis, home of the High Protector, it was said that firecrystals littered the streets and moontraders wore such thick belts of gems that they swooned and fell off the skywalks. "That's an Iridian moontrader's boat they came on," Melas added. "I tell you, Ahn, they're tailored slaves of some noble lord. Did you ever see such perversion?"

Ahn shook her head in disgust. "Not since I lost my good eye." Ahn's right eye was shrunken and sightless, ever since her head had been grazed by a firewhip from a couple of Iridian guards in a drunken duel. Her remaining eye narrowed as she counted change for a customer: Spinel, the stonecutter's son. "You won't find a city wickeder than Iridis on all the planets of the Patriarch."

Spinel overheard her and smiled, for Ahn had never left Chrysoport, let alone planet Valedon. Then he stiffened with alarm and tightly clutched his change. An officer in Iridian blue and gold was just passing toward the firestore. To Spinel's relief, the officer took no notice; his chiseled features were set hard, and he walked straight ahead without looking left or right. The back of his uniform cut a striking figure, with its shoulder line swooping up to a point at either side where the ruby stonesigns glittered.

Spinel absently filled a bag of groundnuts for Ahn to weigh. His nose had an engaging crook in it, and his eyes were green as malachite, while his ragged shirt revealed a dark chest still bare of any stonesign to mark a decent trade. He was beginning to think of joining the regiment, to escape and seek his fortune far beyond this sleepy town.

Something occurred to him about the strangers at the tree. Dreamily he watched one of them apply silken fibers to the spinninghead through her long webbed fingers. "In the ocean," he murmured. "That's where they come from."

Melas stared at the youth. "You think I have cornstalks for ears? The bottom of the sea, eh? How does the mayor collect their taxes?"

"No, no," Spinel protested, as Ahn laughed so hard that her speckled stonesign shook around her neck. "I meant the *other* ocean. The Ocean Moon."

Ahn's laughter faded. She rearranged some bunches of ripe grapes bright as amethysts, or bright as the bare arms of the strangers. "Shora, the Ocean Moon. That's where the traders get their best medicines."

Shora, sapphire of the night sky, world whose sea had no shore.

But Melas strode forward, trousers swishing, and shook a finger in Spinel's face. "I thought those moon creatures the traders know have gills and scales! Where are their fishtails?"

"So I've heard," Spinel admitted. "They descended from catfish, and they spin magic from seaweed."

"A fishy tale, or I'm the Patriarch."

Spinel's arm shot out, but Melas parried the blow and sent him tumbling onto the stand. A crate of onions slid off; Ahn shrieked and uttered curses while she stopped to gather the scattered bulbs in her apron. Flustered, Spinel seized his groceries and left.

He drifted among the motley racks and stalls, where customers shouted and haggled, children played hide-and-seek though they should have been in school, and a robed Spirit Caller with a winking starstone received alms. He was sick of this, Spinel thought suddenly. Until he got a good stonesign, he would be left to running errands and sawing slabs in the stoneshop. He paused by a cage of silvery furred monkeys, a delicacy he had tasted only once in his life. Then an odor of fish lured him to Tybalt's stand, where basins overflowed with thick pink fillets and tight clams.

"Pst, lad; over here." Tybalt waved him over, neck outstretched like a plucked chicken. "Hagfish go for three *solidi* today. Two-fifty, for you."

Spinel rolled his tongue but said, "Not today, friend." His coins were spent for the day. Stonecutters were thought to own the stars, but a town like Chrysoport boasted few noble customers, and how many commoners could afford better than chip-flecked glass? His father's business was precarious at best, despite his mother's firm hand on the account books.

"Not today, eh?" the fishmonger repeated. "Wait. See that beauty on the cutting block?" Tybalt's knobby thumb pointed to a magnificent specimen laid out beside the cleaver. Still alive, its scales flashed as it writhed on the block. "Do me a favor, and she's yours."

Spinel's eyes opened wide. The fish would last their stewpot for a week.

Tybalt leaned over the table, and his stonesign swung forward. "See them foreigners at the firemerchant's tree? You've got a smooth tongue; get them to pick up and move, before it's too late. Trouble's bad for business."

The request surprised him. Tybalt must be in debt to the firemerchant again. Watching the fish, Spinel sucked air through his teeth. "All right."

He turned to the tree, whose foliage hung in thick folds like fishermen's nets. Slowly he approached the strange moonwomen. How should he address them? Their dress might be common, though it consisted of fine seasilk, now that he got a closer look. They wore no stonesigns, and not a single string of beads, which village women trailed in abundance. They must be noble; it was said that in Iridis noble ladies spun and wove for a pastime, despite their mechanical servitors and inexhaustible firecrystals.

But what in Valedon would bring them here? He scratched the back of his neck, warm from the sun overhead.

One moonwoman concentrated on the spinning wheel, her foot

rhythmically pumping the pedal. Wrinkled violet skin lay between her toes, which were twice as long as Spinel's own. He shuddered despite himself.

Her companion looked up at him from where she sat cross-legged on a mat of iridescent blue, while she pulled tufts of blue seasilk between a pair of wired cards. A gingery perfume wafted over, exotic and expensive-smelling. Spinel smiled uncertainly at the woman on the mat. If he addressed her as a lady, he decided, at worst she could laugh.

"My lady, I have an urgent matter to bring to your attention. To address you properly, may I ask your stonesign?" She must have at least one, if only to mark her noble house.

The woman on the mat watched him without missing a stroke. Baldness accentuated her long, oval face; small ears pressed back closely to her head. Her broad, flat lips gave her a haughty appearance. "What is 'stonesign'?"

The words fell distinctly, despite an odd cadence. The question, though, was nonsense. His face warmed; he must have guessed wrong. "Please, I'm just a stonecutter's son, and you know in a town like this a stonecutter lives on scraps, and I'm still assigned to my father. But the firemerchant's a different sort, and you're sitting under his best netleaf tree, and if you don't leave soon . . ."

She put down her carding and picked up a small vial whose contents she massaged into her arms and neck. "Sitting under tree, yes. What is 'stonecutter'?"

By now, several villagers were lounging casually within earshot. Thoroughly confused, Spinel was about to run off when the other moonwoman rose from the spinning wheel and came toward him, her webbed feet flapping slightly. She stopped and rested a gentle hand on the shoulder of the seated one. She had the same streamlined ears and flat lips, but her face was round and delicate, and her cheekbones stood out like jewels cut *en cabochon*. Her straight nose sloped steeply, her chin was small and level, and up her neck rippled a pale, creased scar.

She said, "I am called Merwen the Impatient One. My love-sharer is Usha the Inconsiderate," she added, caressing Usha's shoulder. "We do not wear stone, but our purpose here is to share learning."

"Well, I'm Spinel, son of Cyan the stonecutter." Then he realized what Merwen had just said. "But to *work*, you must have a stonesign," he exclaimed. "You may as well go unclothed as without sign."

"In that case, may we go unclothed?"

"Oh, no!" He recalled another tale from the moontraders and wished his tongue would not take off on its own. "'Share learning' . . . are you schoolteachers, then?"

"Teachers, yes," said the one called Usha. "We must learn many things."

Merwen said, "We call ourselves 'Sharers.'"

A proverb popped into Spinel's head: *The fool shares gold with a stranger.* He rushed on, "You've got lots to learn about Chrysoport, so please believe me for now and get away from the firestore. Anywhere else in the square is fine."

The Sharers exchanged words in a foreign tongue. Usha's expression changed, although it still told him nothing. "No other place," Usha said. "Whole world too dry."

"Our skin dries out," Merwen explained. "The tree gives shade. Is there another tree?"

Suddenly the onlookers vanished. From the wide mosaic tiled steps of the firestore, two guards strode briskly into the square.

Spinel remembered his groceries left at Tybalt's, but it was too late. He sprinted and wove in among the shoppers until he returned, breathless, to hide behind Ahn's stall.

"You want to lose an eye, too?" the vegetable woman hissed at him. "Trouble draws you like a moth to a flame."

Most of the villagers scattered, as Guard Roald knew they would. That was for the best, since no bystanders would get in the way. Roald nodded to his subaltern. "We'll take the debtor first." The two men approached the fish stand where Tybalt sat hunched behind his cutting block.

"Once again, Tybalt, your account is overdue." The guard spoke offhand, as though it meant nothing to himself, personally.

"Sirs, I need time," the vendor said quickly. "Another week at most, while the hagfish are running—"

"You owe Rhodochron for three months' worth of crystal charge. Pay up today, or you're out of business." Roald leaned across the table.

"You won't take my fish, by the Patriach!" With a desperate lunge, Tybalt leaped to his feet, wielding a cleaver.

A blue streak met the knife and cut through the fish and block below, before it stopped. Dazed, Tybalt held onto his seared fingers.

As Roald replaced the firewhip at his belt, he tried not to grimace at the stench of burnt meat and wood. "Always a fool, Tybalt." He reached for the vendor's stonesign; the thin chain snapped. "We'll keep this, till you pay."

"Pay?" Tybalt whispered. "How can I pay if I can't sell?"

"You'll find a way." They always did. With his subaltern, Roald turned to their next task: the squatters at Rhodochron's netleaf tree. The firemerchant disliked riffraff cluttering his storefront.

The sight of the strangers, their purplish flesh and funlike hands, filled Roald with particular distaste although he had seen his share of outlandish customers pass Rhodochron's door. "You, there," he called. "You're obstructing the doorway of Lord Rhodochron, the Protector's appointed firemerchant to Chrysoport." From Iridis, he need not add, since all firecrystals legally came from nowhere else. "Give your names and signs and remove yourselves, and you'll get off with a warning."

The creature at the spinning wheel raised a hand: spidery fingertips flickered grotesquely. The other creature rose and shuffled forward to stand behind her. "Merwen the Impatient," said the spinner. "And Usha the Inconsiderate."

"And?" Inconsiderate they were, all right. Why not get this over with? If they expected him to go soft on a couple of women, they had another thing coming.

"We are Sharers from Shora."

Roald frowned. "Shora? You mean the moon?"

Out of the corner of his eye, he saw his subaltern shrug. "Could be. Always a first time."

Shora, the Ocean Moon. Roald remembered, now. With their herbs and seasilk, moontraders brought holocubes of the womenlike creatures who lived in the endless sea, women whose men were never seen, who subsisted on seaworms and could dive deep beyond light's reach without going mad. Roald had never believed half of it. Now, a bit of myth had turned solid in front of him. He stood up straight. "Very well, Sharer. Where's your stonesign?" Her neck bore no mica chips to mark the textile guild.

"We have no stone. We weave but do not sell," Merwen explained. "We carry herbs, but we do not trade."

The other asked, "Will coral or raftwood do?"

Insolent as well as inconsiderate. "You've no business at all in the marketplace, then." Roald raised his firewhip in warning.

"You are a soldier," Merwen observed. "We too are soldiers, of a kind."

"Moon soldiers?" Behind him his subaltern's weapon clicked to standby. The Ocean Moon was not officially under Valan authority, although Valan traders had done as they wished there for forty years. His eyes searched the Sharers. Sterilized Valan women often signed into armed service, but these two wore no uniforms. His eyes narrowed. "Show your weapons."

Merwen spread her hands like fans. "What more do we need than what is ... inside?"

Roald's patience snapped. "Enough talk. Pack up, now, or we'll do it for you, fast."

The Sharers both became very still. The guard shot a dull orange flame to the ground at their feet; sparks flew up to leave black pinpoints smoldering on the base of the spinning wheel. Yet the creatures remained, transfixed, a mosaic frieze. Then color began to drain from their limbs and faces, dissolved like a spent wave upon the sand, and faded through lavender to white at last, the ghastly whiteness of a dead squid dredged from the sea. White they were, but not from fear.

"Sir," whispered his subaltern, "are they *diseased?*"

Roald's skin crawled, and he shifted his weight back. Disease warfare—he knew its history, from the early days when entire planets could succumb to a single virus, and more than one had done so rather than submit to the rule of the Patriarch of Torr. Such a scourge had never touched Valedon, but who knew what still lurked on the uncharted moon? He thought suddenly of his young wife at home: two children, and her gene quotient would permit a third.

"Women, who are you? What do you want here? What do you bear *inside?*"

No answer. Their bleached faces seemed to stare beyond him to the harbor where the rising tide splashed up at the docks.

The firewhip fell to his side. Whatever lurked behind those fearless stares, Roald wanted no part of it, even if Rhodochron raged and sent him packing.

"Remember," he said curtly, "you've been warned." The two men walked stiffly from the square, their shoulder-tip rubies flashing in the midmorning sun.

2

The Sharers soon regained color, but the villagers avoided them like the whitepox. When Spinel came back the next day, he was amazed to see the pair there again, beneath the netleaf tree.

"Hey, Melas," he called. "What happened? How come the fire-merchant let them alone?"

Melas grimaced under a bushel of potatoes. "Iridians in disguise. Some lord or other protects them, mark my words."

"Buy why?"

"How should I know? Go run off with the other signless boys. I've bread to earn, and tax to pay besides."

The remark stung him. Torr knows, he should have earned a stonesign by age eighteen, but could he help it if he was no good for any trade?

The paradox of the moonwomen; he would get it straight yet and show Melas a thing or two. Among the beaded skirts and baggy trousers of the crowd he spotted a patch of gray, the cowled robe of Uriel the Spirit Caller. Uriel communed miraculously with the Spirit of the Patriarch who ruled from Torr, four light-years out in space. He was supposed to call on all the knowledge of the almighty Patriarch.

Spinel ran after Uriel and slipped a coin into a deep pocket of his robe. "Uriel, how come those moonwomen don't get dragged away from that tree?"

Uriel turned his solemn face, and his starstone winked on his chest. "If I were to sit at the tree, I would not be disturbed either."

"That's no answer." Sometimes the Spirit got garbled in transmission.

"For shame," hissed a neighbor behind him. "Talking back to a Spirit Caller." But Spinel had already run off to tell Ahn what Uriel had said.

11

"It's more than that," said Ahn, as her good eye frowned at a customer pinching the tomatoes. "Those guards were scared."

"Scared?" His toes twitched. "Why . . . scared?"

"They're as superstitious as Dolomite goatherds. And why not? The moonwomen just stay there, cool as ice—they must have some sort of power in their veins, or they'd have run off like sensible folk." She sketched a starsign to ward off evil and whispered, "A pair of witches, if you ask me."

Vexed, Spinel snapped his fingers and turned away. He knew better than that; he had had eight years in the schoolhouse, after all. He would go back and ask his father, Cyan the stonecutter, who had the last word on everything. So he skipped through the cobblestoned streets past houses draped with fishing nets, dodging one-armed beggars and the nodding horses of farmer's carts and the firecrystal van of the Mayor. In the artisans' quarter he reached the old shop where his family had lived since before he was born. Behind the counter his sister, Beryl, looked up with a tired smile.

In the basement was his father's workshop, hung with round sawblades for marble and agate and cluttered with tools for the precious gems. The air smelled of wet clay from the polishing.

Cyan sat hunched over a wooden lap wheel that whined as it spun and spattered beneath the water stream. His face was shadowed harshly by the floodlamp that drained firecrystals so fast. The surface of the wheel was grinding a facet into a yellow-green peridot, until Cyan raised the dop stick to change its angle.

"Father, listen," Spinel shouted in his ear.

The whining stopped, and Cyan looked up through his thick safety glasses. His nose was broad and flat, as if he had held it, too, to the lap wheel for thirty years.

"Father, why did those guards run away from the moonwomen?"

Cyan regarded him balefully. "Fool's luck is the reason. Don't think it will last, for to cross the firemerchant brings worse luck than fool's gold. Son, when will you get yourself a decent stonesign like your brother-in-law, instead of running wild in the marketplace and poking your nose in the affairs of strangers? Keep away from them. Now go cut the tesserae for Doctor Bresius's new wainscoting."

The lap wheel whined again. Spinel went to switch on the diamond-edged saw, and as he did so his father's light dimmed briefly. Vengefully he wished it would go out altogether; but then he himself would only be sent back to recharge the firecrystal, for a sum that made his mother screech every month.

His mind wandered dangerously from the saw. It was not for him to put in the long tedious hours that produced fine crystals. Those creatures by the tree were the oddest sight he had seen in this sleepy town, one he could not soon forget.

The Sharers did not turn white again, and they approached no one. Once an exceptionally brave market woman ventured to ask their advice on the use of medicinal herbs from the moontraders. What she learned then amazed even Doctor Bresius from Iridis; and thereafter, knots of villagers gathered at the tree until the guards shooed them off. The tall one, Usha, would examine a sick child and produce bits of dried seaweed or powder for a cure, but she never broke the sign law to take payment. Even on the sly, the Sharers would not sell the fine seasilk they spun and wove into swirling patterns on their handloom. When the mayor's man came to ask their business, they merely said they were waiting.

Waiting for what? And what did they eat in the meantime? Some said the pair rose long before dawn to catch their own fish from the sea. Rumors spread of witchcraft practiced at nightfall, before the pair retired to their houseboat. Spinel scoffed at such nonsense, but he was curious enough so that one day he decided to find out for himself.

That evening, Spinel loitered at the edge of the square until the sun touched the far sea, spreading sparks like quartz dust across the waves. Market vendors were wrapping unsold vegetables and dumping fish refuse over the wharf, while customers haggled wearily for last-minute bargains. The Sharers were intent on their work, as always. The great tree was now denser than ever with plaited masses of leaves that hung like folds of a fishing net. Crickets began chirping, and soon their throbbing chorus drowned out the last of the market sounds.

Spinel had his eye on a long branch that swooped almost to the ground. He caught hold of it and swung lightly upward, steadying himself amid the leafy fabric. Through a break in the foliage, he could make out the Sharers below. He watched and waited.

The rest of the square was deserted. The tree's shadow lengthened until it reached the town hall. Night cloaked the town in velvet, with the stars like tiny jewels strung against it, and the queen of jewels was Shora, the blue moon, whose cold glow ruled the landscape.

Below, Merwen stood and walked to a crate beside the handloom. There sat a large conch shell, and she poured a liquid from it into a squat potted plant.

In an instant the plant glowed with golden phosphorescence. Merwen lit two more plants, and the light suffused the lower branches. This looked like magic, Spinel had to admit. He squirmed as if something were creeping up his spine.

Where was the other one, he wondered suddenly: Usha, who gave out the medicines? His foot slipped and kicked a branch; loose bits of bark fell away. As quietly as he could, he swung down and across to get a closer look. Merwen was sitting on a mat away from the handloom, facing past him out over the harbor, where the wavelets flickered in the moonlight. Her head nodded slightly, and with the spidery fingers of one hand she fashioned something out of thread, a sort of laniard which lengthened as he watched.

She was staring at him.

Spinel knew this in a flash, and blood pounded in his ears. He lunged backward the way he had come, but he lost his footing in the darkness. A branch gave way, and the leafy seines no longer seemed so strong as he pulled at them in fistfuls. He swayed precariously, then tumbled down in a shower of torn leaves and powdered bark.

Usha emerged from behind the tree. She crouched and glowered at him, and Spinel wished more than he had ever wished anything that he were elsewhere, anywhere, even in the dreary old schoolroom. Why had he not listened to his father? He wanted to run for it, but his feet stuck as if bewitched.

"You hurt?" Usha asked.

He blinked, then vigorously shook his head.

"You hurt?" she repeated.

"He is not hurt," said Merwen from her mat by the handloom. "Spinel stonecutter's son, come sit here."

Shaking all over, he picked himself up and went to sit on a mat of green seasilk. Could he dream up some tale to get himself out of this fix? It would not work this time, he was sure. "What are you going to do with me?" he blurted at last.

"Share learning," Merwen said. "Share the ways of stone, and the ways of this." She held out the woven strand, which had turned into a circlet. Hesitantly Spinel accepted the gift, and it rested on his palm, strong and fine as a silver chain.

He recovered some nerve. "What are you?" he ventured. "Clothworkers, or medicine women?"

"We are what we need to be."

Spinel frowned and sucked his tongue. "Even soldiers?"

Merwen cupped her chin in the scallop between two fingers. "You might call us soldiers of learning."

"What's that?" He leaned forward, hands on his knees. "You mean *spies?*"

"Something like that."

His thoughts whirled. Hordes of purple fish creatures invading Valedon—the vision came and went. "You wouldn't tell me the truth, if you were real spies." Why should he believe them, any more than the moontraders?

"Truth is a tangled skein, and time ravels it."

"When do you plan to invade us?"

"Valans have invaded Shora for a long while."

That was a twist. He had never heard of Protectoral troops invading the moon. Pyrrhopolis kept them busy enough. "Is there really no dry land on Shora? Where do you live, then? Do you hide all your men, even your Protector?"

"Sea blankets the land. We dwell on living rafts, and our protection-sharer is Shora, the mother of all ocean."

No human Protector? The Patriarch would never allow such a thing. Before the rule of Torr, men throughout the galaxy had lived free as gods, with firecrystals more plentiful than grains of sand. But then, men who live as gods die as gods, as the saying goes. They had died by the planetful until those who remained gave up their powers to the Patriarch to keep the peace among them. His Envoy came to Valedon every ten years, and there was no help for those who disobeyed.

Perhaps the Patriarch did not care about nonhumans. "You're not human, are you?"

Merwen paused, and Usha leaned over her shoulder to exchange speech that sounded like ocean laughter. Then Merwen asked, "Will you come to Shora to find out?"

Terror struck again; they would capture him and steal him away. "I won't bother you again, I promise: I swear by the Patriarch's Nine Legions!"

"You fear us. Why?" Merwen watched him, her face strained as if intent on his answer.

Spinel thought about it and felt a little silly. "I thought you might . . . make me come away with you."

"We cannot . . . *make* you do anything." She seemed to have trouble with the words. "Remember that. Share our return, if you wish. We'll go long before the sea swallows again."

"Sea swallows?"

"Twice a year, great seaswallowers migrate from pole to pole. Beasts of the deep, they swallow all in their path. Usha and I must be there to help secure the home raft."

"That sounds scary, all right."

"It scares me, though I've seen forty years of it."

The admission surprised him. Perhaps Merwen wanted men to come help her out, men who would not hide away. An attractive adventure, actually. "I wish I could go, but if I don't choose a stonesign before long I'll end up a beggar or a cornpicker."

"Shora has neither beggars nor corn."

No beggars and no corn? What sort of place was this?

Usha added, "No stonesign, either."

Startled, Spinel looked up at her. "You've got to have stone-signs."

"No stone," Usha said. "Except on the sea floor, where the dead dwell."

Merwen caught Usha's arm as if in warning or reproof.

Spinel was thinking that if he went off to Shora he could put off getting signed for months, if not a year, which was as good as forever to him. Still, there had to be a catch somewhere. "How do you get on, without having some sort of sign for what you are?"

"We are what you see. We share all things," said Merwen.

"Could I come right back if I don't like it?"

"Whenever you wish."

"Then I'll go!" Spinel held out his hand, and Merwen clasped it. A shock went through him at the touch of the nailless webbed hand, though it was only a hand, after all, and not in the least slimy or scaly. What would his folks say to this?

Suddenly he realized how late it was. He leaped to his feet. "Hey, catch you later," he called over his shoulder, and ran all the way home.

* * *

Merwen watched him scamper off and thought, How deftly he swings through those branches despite his stunted fingers. There were so many kinds of in-between humans on this world. "What do you think of him, Usha?"

A faraway look came into Usha's eyes. "For all his headfur and fingerclaws, he would make a good daughter."

Merwen smiled with a twinge of sadness. Usha would be thinking of their own precious daughters, on the home world that was now a blue disk so unbelievably small in the sky.

3

In the morning Spinel sauntered into the snug kitchen, eager to break the news to his parents. But neither of them was there. Sunlight streamed from the window, making bright diamond shapes on the cleared table.

His married sister, Beryl, stood over the stove, stirring a pot which gave off a heavy odor of groundnuts. Her apron rode high over her pregnancy. On the floor, pudgy Oolite sat licking a porridge bowl.

"Where's Mother?" Spinel asked.

"Up in the study," Beryl drawled to emphasize how late he had risen. Their mother was up at dawn as usual, to spend the day adding up accounts for unlettered farmers. The extra income helped make ends meet. "Hey, Spinny," Beryl asked, "will you never tire of running errands for Mother?"

"You'll soon sing another tune," Spinel shot back, "when Doctor Bresius knocks on the door by and by."

Her complexion deepened, from her neck below the tied-up hair to her nose, which had the same crook in it as his. Spinel regretted his words, a cruel reminder that his sister's gene quotient allowed no more than two children. He brushed her hair with a conciliatory gesture. Absently he drummed his fingers on the mosaic wainscoting. Then in three strides he crossed to the stairway. "Mother!" he yelled. "Mother, I'm leaving Chrysoport."

Beryl gasped behind him. "Who signed you on, a gem trader?"

"Well, not exactly...."

The stairs creaked as his mother thumped downstairs with alarming speed for a woman her size. "You what?" she rasped, her double chin shaking. "You have a sponsor for a stonesign?"

"I'm leaving Chrysoport to see another world."

"Leaving Chrysoport? Call your father! *Cyan!*" she shrieked downstairs toward the workshop, her beads rattling across her voluminous skirts. "Cyan, your son found a sponsor at last." She flung her arms around Spinel with a strength that knocked his breath away. "Tell me now, which firm is it? The House of Karnak? I always said you'd do well in gem manufacturing."

"Well, they're not really—"

"Who *is* it?" Beryl insisted. "Come on, Spinny. What stonesign?"

"Well . . ."

Cyan's broad shoulders filled the doorway. "Yes, Galena?" He eyed his wife wearily as he clapped the grit from his hands. Then all were still as a frieze, except Oolite, who burbled and turned her bowl upside down over her head.

"It's not like that. They don't have a stonesign."

"No stonesign?" Galena lifted her hands in astonishment.

"They're from the Ocean Moon. All I want is to see the moon, just for the summer. . . ."

One look at his father chilled him. "Were you pestering the moonwomen again?" Cyan asked in a steely tone.

Beryl exclaimed, "Why, they're not even human!"

Galena shook her head and sank into a chair, which creaked as her weight settled like a sack of gold coins. "My poor son, what can I do with you?" she muttered. "Will you never get some sense into that troll's skull of yours?"

Spinel did not care to be compared with Valedon's extinct native race of anthropoids, and Beryl's laughter only made it worse. It was true that the notion of his adventure seemed less solid in broad daylight than it had beneath the mysterious Sharer plantlights, but he was set on it, nonetheless. He clenched his fists. "Why can't I go, just for a while? Just for once? Nobody needs me around here."

"Go to Karnak of Iridis," his mother urged him. "There you'll get a good place and see the city, besides."

Beryl shook her head. "You'll never grow up, that's all."

The voices closed in on him. Spinel fled from the kitchen and burst out of doors onto the sun-baked flagstones. Automatically he headed out toward the shore beyond the harbor, where he would cool off in the sea. He loped past the back of the granite town hall, whose arched windows carried ornaments of chrysolite, like glass eyes that mocked him. Angry tears blurred his vision. His parents would never let him go. Why could they not understand his longing to see something of the universe beyond this troll's nest of a town?

As he rounded a corner in haste, he ran smack into Uriel the Spirit Caller. Spinel gasped and started to frame an excuse, but Uriel spoke first. "Never mind, son; the wind blew you in." Uriel looked windblown himself in the loose cowl that wrapped his head like a potato in a sack. Yet his gnarled hands adjusted the chain of his stone with slow dignity. The stonesign of the Spirit Caller was a star sapphire, a deep blue oval lit by three intersecting lines of light. This gem alone, by unwritten law, was never bought or sold.

"Your face tells me," Uriel said, "that you may need some wisdom of the Patriarch."

Spinel winced and fought back his annoyance. "What's that to you? Why should the Patriarch care a flint chip for me?"

Uriel did not answer but passed his hand over the starstone. The six points vanished, then returned as the shadow lifted. "If we cut off the light, the star is gone. So, if we ignore the light of wisdom, how shall we see?"

The starstone intrigued Spinel despite his bitter mood. Cyan had drummed into him its physical nature: aluminum trioxide tinted by iron, and inclusions of titanium that reflected a star, if one cut the stone *en cabochon,* just so.... Still, the sight of it tasted of magic, to him. And could there be any other explanation for spirit calling?

"Do you really hear the Patriarch's thoughts in an instant?" Spinel challenged. "Across four light-years?"

Uriel nodded slowly, almost reluctantly, Spinel thought.

Spinel glanced at the sky, which shone clear as if polished, the inside of a porcelain bowl. Yet high overhead an Iridian jet scored it like a diamond-tipped glass cutter. His bitterness washed back. "Then why do Iridians use radio?"

Spinel broke off and walked quickly the rest of the way to the shore.

The water splashed and eddied around his legs, and clouds of fine pebbles sifted over his toes. As he waded out his arm plunged to grasp a flat rock, which he tossed with a twist. It skipped several times, and he followed its flight until the brilliance of the water's reflections hurt his eyes. Down beyond his feet spread masses of seaweed, dark and mysterious as a woman's hair. He stood very still. The wavelets muttered and seemed to whisper: *merwenmerwen.* . . . Spinners, soldiers, or spies; somehow he would figure out those Sharers who lived without stone on a world with no shore.

4

If the Sharers were spies, Spinel decided, then he would spy on them and ferret out their mischief.

At first, their spinning wheel whirled as usual, and on Merwen's loom the batten swung regularly to beat the weft in. One day, something new did appear: an insect the size of Spinel's fist, with black legs splayed out and white eyes that bulged big as marbles. Merwen let the grotesque thing sit on her shoulder, where it clicked and squealed, scraping a lopsided pair of mandibles like a fiddler. About the same time that the insect came, more complex patterns began to grow in the weave, entwined swaths of green and blue and gold more fantastic than the robes of Iridian nobles.

And Usha wrought cures that astounded the villagers: a man paralyzed since childhood stood and walked, an infant born sightless cried out at the sun. Their reputation spread throughout the province, and once even a nobleman from Iridis came to them, his clothes bordered with the distinctive nested squares. Exactly what he was cured of no one heard, but the refusal of payment provoked him. "What's wrong with my gold? It's not pure enough for you? What are you here for, if not for a profit?"

"We came to share judgment," said Merwen. "To judge human souls."

That answer took root in the village. "They must be noble judges," Ahn assured Spinel, "just waiting for a good case worth their time." But Spinel knew better: they were spies.

For spies, Merwen and Usha showed a surprising lack of interest in the worldly events that stirred Chrysoport. Not even the Pyrrholite rebellion caught their attention, though talk of it was on every Chrysolite tongue. As summer lenghtened, Spinel scrounged through dust-choked gutters for newscubes of Pyrrhopolis, the city that dared to build its own power plant in defiance of Iridis.

Only the High Protector, in Iridis, had the consent of the Patriarch to draw electrical power from an atom-smasher. All power must stem from one lord, and have its limit, just as the number of people had a limit on Valedon. That was the lesson of the dead gods: too many people smashed too many atoms—and planets, in the end.

Yet Pyrrhopolis defied the Patriarch's law, so the Protector called on Valans everywhere to beat the rebels down. From the mountains as far as Dolomoth divisions of soldiers streamed in through Chrysoport, on their way to join the siege of the rebel city.

Even a few Dolomites took an interest in the Sharers, thinking they were water witches from the sea. On one sweltering afternoon a Dolomite corporal named Kaol came to Usha, pulling after him a young woman with terrified eyes. The man's face was heavily bearded, and sweat dripped to his shoulders, darkening his cloak of gray mountain wool. At his waist clanged an iron chain.

"You must do this," he told Usha. "I can't pay the doctor, but they say you can do it."

But Usha shook her head and seemed to withdraw into an invisible shell.

"You *must,* " he insisted, jostling the young woman from side to side. "I had her sent all the way from Hagoth Peak. She bore a child out of wedlock, so now her tubes must be tied. If I can't pay for it, they'll send her to the slave market. It's the law, witch woman." He drew a six-point star in the air.

The woman he held started to cry.

"Enough," he barked. "Worthless daughter, to bear a child without a father."

At that, a spring must have snapped behind Usha's tongue.

"'Father'? What use is 'father'? I never had one, nor did my mother's mothers since the First Door."

Furious, the Dolomite dropped his daughter and pressed a knife to Usha's neck until the skin puckered in. "You mock me? Death take you, witch or not!"

From behind Usha, Merwen lifted a hand, and the startling long fingers caught the man's eye. "And who are you," she asked, "friend of Death?"

Kaol stood still, and his breathing slowed. His gaze shifted down Merwen's neck, to the scar that snaked down and around it. He said, "Death pays a fair wage. But only a fool calls Death 'friend.'" He whipped the knife back, then turned and took his daughter away.

The Sharers spoke quietly together in their own tongue, their fingers fluttering like gills. Spinel crept away, disquieted. A world without fathers could have no place for him.

One evening soon afterward, Spinel got home late for dinner, expecting an outburst from his mother. Yet only Beryl and Harran sat at the kitchen table.

"Hey, what's going on?" He must really be in for it, this time.

Harran stopped chewing and looked away. A netmaker for the fishermen, Harran was a quiet sort who often seemed cowed by his in-laws. Beryl slipped another spoonful of spice pudding into Oolite's mouth, then wiped the baby's chin. "Mother and Father are upstairs," she said, not meeting Spinel's eyes. "Settling your future."

He raced up to the study, his heart pounding as hard as his feet hit the steps.

Galena's study was a corner room under the slanting eaves, filled with files and account books. Her chair was turned forward from the desk, and she sat in it solidly. Cyan stood beside her, and on the couch by the wall, the two Sharers sat with their outlandish feet tucked beneath their crossed legs.

"We've been waiting for you," his mother said. "The arrangements are concluded."

"*Arrangements?*" Appalled, he looked to the Sharers, whom his father had forbidden him to pester.

Cyan said, "The Sharer judges have agreed to sign you into their calling. This is a great honor for a stonecutter's son."

"True," said his mother. "You'll never have to count coins for a failing business, that's for sure. And look at the fine sign gift they have brought in your name." On the floor lay a seasilken tapestry with one end unrolled, the brilliant colors and intricate patterns that Spinel had watched for so long on Merwen's loom. The seasilk alone was worth more than a month's work in the stoneship, and the weaving was finer than any moontrader showed.

"But . . ." Spinel found his voice. "They don't even have stone-signs."

"What stone swims in the sea?" said Cyan. "They do have a calling. They are 'Sharers': that's a kind of judge on the moon."

"It is?" As well as weavers, doctors, and spies?

"A great honor," Cyan repeated, a little sternly.

Spinel clung to his mother. "You can't do this to me!"

"What? I thought you wanted this." Her voice grew hoarse with excitement. "My son, my only son, I only want the best for you. Haven't I always tried to make you happy?" Her face puckered and she wrung her puffy hands.

"I didn't mean it—not to sign away, that is." He remembered something. "They're *spies,* Mother! They're spying on Valedon."

Cyan demanded, "Who charges this?"

"They told me themselves."

"Impertinent fool, what spy would tell you so to your face? Forgive him," Cyan told Merwen, "he speaks without thinking."

"And besides," Spinel gasped, "there aren't any *men* on Shora."

"Nonsense. You can't populate a world without men."

Galena said. "There are fewer men, that's all. That's why they want you, for a son."

"A son?"

"You'll be so special."

"But they aren't even human. "

"For shame." Her bosom heaved. "Do you realize we'll lose the stoneshop, if you don't sign away soon?"

So the business was that bad. Cyan looked away. Spinel looked again at the precious cloth, thinking, I've been sold off.

Then Merwen spoke up, for the first time. "If you please, let us speak alone with Spinel, for a minute."

"Very well," said Galena. "Cyan, help me up, please." Cyan grasped her arm to help her stand. She kissed Spinel on the cheek. "Come now," she whispered. "We're so proud of you. So far

away; you'll come back to visit your own mother, won't you?"
Tears started down her cheeks as she turned away, following Cyan
out. The stairs creaked on her way down.

Merwen faced him, calm as always. "It is true that Shora knew
no men before traders came. But that does not prove that a man
can't become a Sharer. As I said before, you may leave us whenever you wish. The moonferry crosses often, except when the sea
swallows. Will you come with us, Spinel?"

His mind was feverish. He was certain, now, that Sharers were
not real "judges," any more than they were anything else that they
did. *Share the ways of stone . . . and of this.* He remembered the
curious silken loop he received from Merwen's webbed hand. It
must have been magic to snare him. He watched her hands now,
smooth-tipped fingers bound below the first knuckle by umbrella
folds of skin, with only the thumbs completely free. "I still want to
know: are you human or not?"

"We try to be."

"If you're a catfish, it doesn't matter how hard you try."

"We descended from the same fish you did."

Spinel was taken aback. His notions of evolution were hazy at
best.

Merwen added very seriously. "I believe you are as human as
we are."

Usha said, "Close enough to interbreed. I tested genes from
Nisi the Valan."

"No, thanks," said Spinel, recoiling from this new horror.

"Nisi the Valan," said Merwen, "has shared life with us for
many years now. You would know her as Lady Berenice of Hyalite."

"Oh, I wouldn't know a lady." Though he did know of the
House of Hyalite, the oldest of the moontraders, whose name was
emblazoned on the Sharers' houseboat. So the Sharers did have
friends in Iridis, after all. That was reassuring; and yet, it was
unthinkable that he, Spinel, might find himself consorting with
Iridian nobility, so unthinkable that it made him uneasy again.
What in Valedon could these Sharers want with him, if they shared
acquaintance with a Lady of Hyalite?

5

On Center Way, the uppermost skystreet of Iridis, Lady Berenice of Hyalite walked purposefully toward the Palace Iridium. Within the hour she had an audience with Talion the High Protector of Valedon, who answered to none but the Patriarch.

But Protector Talion had some things to answer for, especially with the Patriarch's Envoy due any day now—that same Envoy who had half emptied the treasury for taxes on his last visit, ten years before. This time, besides the Pyrrholite uprising, Talion would have Shora to answer for, forty years of not-so-benign neglect of the Ocean Moon.

Three times in three decades, the Patriarch's Envoy had come and gone without questioning Valan stewardship of Shora. This time, though, the oversight would be corrected, if Berenice herself had to face the Envoy. Talion of course must suspect her intention. Why else would he summon her to the Palace again?

Jets screamed far above, their trails radiating from the same port where the Envoy's starship from Torr would appear. Three levels below Berenice's feet, beggars mingled with tradesmen of every province, among the famed electronics bazaars and moon-trading centers; from this height, they crawled like little crabs at the bottom of an ornamental pool. On Berenice's level, slender hangcars passed between parallel walkways, shuttling to and from the Palace. Now and then one would slow to a halt beside her, but she ignored its shimmering doors. It was not just that she needed the exercise, to keep in shape for her travels on the Ocean Moon. Berenice like to absorb this glittering, ever-shifting metropolis where her parents had returned with their fortune rebuilt in the moon trade. Nowadays, she herself shuttled endlessly between this world and the other.

Berenice's childhood on the Ocean Moon had left her unfashionably thin, emphasized now by the plain straight talar she wore without even a border of the fashionable squares. And worse, as her beloved Realgar was quick to notice, her nose and hollow cheeks still carried a tinge of violet, from the symbiont microbes that stored oxygen for a swimming Sharer. Most moontraders took an antibiotic to ward off these "breathmicrobes," but Berenice let hers flourish while she shared the home of Merwen and Usha.

Merwen the Impatient. . . . Merwen was barely older than Berenice's own thirty-eight years, yet she exuded a greater sense of age than even the bones of the vanished trolls. Merwen rarely seemed to earn her "selfname," the epithet chosen by each Sharer upon adulthood. When her impatience did surface, the waves rippled far. It was Merwen who had called on Gatherings from many rafts to send visitors to Valedon this year—much to the Protector's dismay. Sharers had never cared to cross space before, Talion complained; why start now?

Sharers wished to find out why the Valan guests on their home world dumped noxious waste chemicals and raised trade "prices" without warning. At least, that was as much as Berenice herself knew of their purpose. She was not yet a "selfnamer," a member of a raft Gathering. Sharers heard her politely but seemed to appreciate her advice as little as Talion did, for very different reasons. Why selfname would she choose: the Unheeded One? In Sharer speech, that would also mean One Who Heeds Not. Yet who tried harder to listen to Sharers than she did?

To join the Gathering, though, would be an immense step forward. She had never dared to ask; but then one day had come . . .

While her feet walked straight on, her mind drifted to another world, to that sparkling turquoise ocean with its sharp, sweetish scent. The scent came from raft blossoms, golden tricorners that festooned the branches above water, while below darted fish in bewildering swarms, hiding among streamers of seasilk and other weeds that hung from branches of the living raft.

Merwen swam downward among the deeper branches, gliding with an effortless grace, her feet beating smoothly as fishtails. The inner lids of Merwen's eyes gleamed like hooded pearls; they were natural goggles which retracted when her head surfaced. A quarter of an hour passed before her skin turned lavender, then white, as her microscopic symbionts gave up oxygen, and she surfaced again for a deep lungful of air. Berenice, at that time, was nearly as violet as a native Sharer, but even so she needed three breaths for each one Merwen took.

Some of the main branches thrust deeper, and intricate coral forests grew upon them, delicate as lacework yet solid as stone. Merwen and Berenice picked their way carefully to avoid scraping against coral while they gathered the edible shellfish that clung to slimy branchlets. A whorlshell poked up, its conical armor spotted orange and cinnabar. Berenice plucked the shell from its hold and tossed it into the collection bag at her belt, which was all she or Merwen wore. Another shell caught her eye, and another, and she bagged six before she surfaced to gasp for air.

Abruptly Merwen grabbed her arm and pointed out along a level branch. A giant squid lay across, apparently dying; from its pear-shaped body the arms dangled so far that their tips were lost in the depths. Above was a sight that froze her blood: fleshborers in a swarm, brown streaks that writhed and snapped relentless jaws. They descended on the squid and burrowed in and out of it as if sewing a ghastly seam. Red clouds oozed, obscuring the frenzied feast.

Be rational, Berenice told herself; reason must keep her still, as she watched the red cloud. The "squid" was not a true cephalopod, since it had iron-rich blood instead of the less efficient hemocyanin; that was why cephaglobinid species ruled the Ocean Moon, from the kilometer-length seaswallowers to the petite fleshborers now devouring their hapless cousin—

Merwen flicked a webspan down her own neck. *Watch out,* the signal meant: the beasts won't be full; they'll come for us next.

Come for *herself,* Lady Berenice of Hyalite? Nausea overwhelmed her until she fought it down. Very slowly she headed upward, and Merwen followed. The fleshborers were dispersing now. One broke away and darted up toward her.

Merwen's arm shot out; she caught the sinuous body in one hand and looked into its snapping jaws. Her other hand took a whorlshell and thrust it down the throat. The shell snapped, but the jaws jammed. The beast jerked away, thrashing about randomly.

Berenice surfaced, wheezing and choking for air. She swam inward to the dry raft core where all the branches fused into one massive disk, climbed up onto the rough bark, and sat there, trembling uncontrollably. Across from her sat Merwen, crosslegged on a patch of moss. A breeze whipped past, rapidly drying their skin.

"We nearly shared death, there," Berenice ventured in the lyrical Sharer tongue.

"No," said Merwen. "Death alone can never be shared, no matter how hard we share life in her jaws."

Berenice swallowed hard, and tears stung her eyes. Unconsciously she drew back from Merwen. She was *alone* here, among people whose ways could still prove inexplicable after her many years of living among them. An ache filled her head that was worse than any physical pain. "I'm going home. To Iridis."

"We'll miss you," Merwen said. "You are strong, Nisi; you didn't panic at all. When you rejoin us, will you choose a self-name?"

She was as astonished as if someone had appointed her High Protector. Selfnamers were, collectively, the Protectors of Shora.

She caught herself, now, safe in Iridis. Her hands were clenching a steel rail which bounded the terminal platform of the sky-street. Her pulse returned to normal, and she let go of the rail, where dark blotches marked the sweat of her palms.

Before her, beyond the interminable courtyard, rose the face of Palace Iridium. A blunted triangle, to symbolize the never-seen Patriarch above all, the facade inclined slightly so as to rise like a steep mountain slope. Mosaic tiles, a million shining tesserae set in iridium, depicted scenes from the founding of the Patriarchy: the First Nine Protectors, with their planets and legionary symbols, then smaller panels below for the hundreds of planets brought under protection before Iridis assumed the High Protectorship of Valedon. The uppermost panel, which could easily cover a city block, showed the Torran Envoy Malachite. The Envoy was ageless, enthroned with eternity in his gaze. He had brought the Patriarch's word to Valedon for nearly a thousand years.

At the foot of the Palace was a skeleton of scaffolding, cranes, and other metallic insects, all setting up for a lavish pageant of welcome. The Envoy Malachite was due within two days.

A hovercraft picked Berenice up from the end of the skystreet and deposited her at an entrance hall some distance up the Palace face. Inside, the vaulted ceiling glittered with every gemstone known; for stone was more than a passion for Valan citizens, it was a source of exchange with distant planets which had exhausted their own supplies of various rare minerals.

The mineral potential of Shora's untapped seabed was one reason for a new interest in that moon. Besides that, of course, there were the medicines and perfumes, and above all the fine seasilk that the councilors and courtiers wore; even now, they passed Berenice in their long talars and sweeping trains, such lengths of the gorgeous stuff that little servitors like tortoises had to crawl in their wake to prevent the trains from snagging and tangling. Seasilk and minerals—that was what Shora meant to Talion.

The doors to Talion's office whined and parted and slowly swept inward. Talion sat as always behind his desk, a thickset man with tired gray hair and eyes nested in wrinkles. "At last," he said, "the Lady of Hyalite. We were just speaking of the Shoran question."

To her surprise, Talion was not alone. From a swivel chair at his right rose General Realgar, to whom Berenice had been engaged for over a year now. Realgar said quickly, "Don't look so startled, my dear. I came here on other business entirely."

"Promotion," said Talion. "To Commander of the Protectoral Guard."

"Well, congratulations." So the old commander who had let Pyrrhopolis get out of hand had finally been retired, and just in time for Malachite's appearance. Realgar had been aiming for the top post ever since his decisive victory over the separatists in Sardis.

Realgar bowed in acknowledgment. The immaculate shoulder line of his uniform swooped to the tips like the edge of a crescent moon. His fair complexion and straight auburn hair marked him as a Sard, and he still wore the orange-brown sardonyx of his former post.

Berenice smiled, genuinely proud of his honor and glad for what she knew it meant to him. There was a gleam of triumph, too, to think that, unconventional as she was, she had managed to captivate the second most powerful man in Valedon. Of course, she reminded herself, it did help to be Councilor Hyalite's daughter. Perhaps her father had clinched the promotion. "So long as it's not Shora you're bound for next, you have my blessing."

His mouth lengthened slightly, the closest to a smile that he would permit himself in public. "That's your project, not mine." He accepted her work on the moon, much as she put up with his tours in the field. "Shora is hardly a military concern," he added.

"And let's keep it that way." Talion pointed to a chair that had risen out of the floor.

Berenice seethed inwardly while she took the offered seat. She did not need such a crude reminder of the precarious position of her Sharer friends. If only she could get an audience with Envoy Malachite, Talion would sing another tune.

"Lady Berenice," Talion began, "for three years now you have kept us informed of what goes on among these Sharers."

"And informed *them* of Valan objectives." A devil's bargain it was, but someone had to do it. Better her than Talion's cold-blooded agents, who had failed in any case to make much sense of Sharer ways. Berenice, however, had correctly forecast both the crisis in the stone trade and the mysterious "environmental" problems that plagued Valan fisheries on the moon. For herself, she could only hope to keep up a dialogue between minds so divergent that any success seemed a miracle.

"Then why do they persistently *ignore* our objectives?" Talion's eyes accused her. "After keeping to themselves for decades, they now start turning up on Valedon to bring their troubles here. I banned them from our ships a month ago."

"But what have they done, for Torr's sake?" Berenice gripped the arm of her chair. Surely Merwen and Usha at least were safe; she had "shared learning" with them personally.

Talion ticked off his fingers. "Vagrancy. Traffic without a stonesign. Illegal medical counsel. Spying for a foreign power. Slandering the Patriarch. Immoral cohabitation."

"My lord," she interjected, "surely the last charge—"

"Applies well enough. This is Valedon, my lady; we cannot let the customs of other planets undermine our social order. The same goes for indecent exposure and witchcraft."

"Witchcraft?" Her glance appealed to Realgar for support, but he was watching Talion politely. "You did say 'witchcraft,' my lord?" she asked.

"They turn into ghosts," Talion added with a straight face.

Not that again. Berenice was annoyed. "I must have sent you a dozen reports on the whitetrance phenomenon—"

"Nine reports, to be exact. By the time you reach a dozen, you might even tell me just what the phenomenon is."

She flushed. "You know at least what it's not."

"But the common folk don't, especially in the rural provinces.

A thousand fools believe a lie, and it's good as truth. Wouldn't you agree, General?"

Realgar leaned forward. "The main point as far as Sharers are concerned is discipline. I know they're outside our own law at present, but—"

"Realgar," said Berenice reprovingly. "You know how harmless they are."

"No lawbreaker is harmless," he said reasonably.

Berenice crossed her arms. Why did Ral have to be here today? she wondered. Their relationship worked best with certain parts of their lives kept apart.

"Sharers are subversive," Talion told her. "As subversive as you are."

She sidestepped this reference to her checkered past. "What was that charge of 'spying' all about?"

"Your own friends Impatient and Inconsiderate admitted as much. They called themselves 'soldiers' and 'spies.'"

She laughed shortly. "A language problem, I'm sure. I'll clear that up." Privately, she was troubled. Merwen spoke Valan too well to use words loosely. Why exactly had they come here, and why had they declined to stay with Berenice? The city climate did not suit their health, Usha had said.

"Let's hope you do clear it up. And for their own sakes, let them know what the score is, before they join the others in prison."

"Prison?" Berenice half rose from her seat. "Who's in prison?"

"Another couple, calling themselves Lazy and Absentminded. Picked up for indecent exposure. They not only refused questioning, they turned white and limp to the point of coma. They took no food, and they soon stank like fish. After three nights they were dumped back on the moonferry."

Berenice shut her eyes and swallowed painfully during this recitation. Whatever happened to Sharers she took personally, as if she were both victim and perpetrator. "You only make my job all the harder. For years I've played up the benefits of free trade for Sharers, how useful our metal gadgets can be, and so on. I've ironed out countless problems with the local traders. But now, with such unwarranted treatment, why should they listen anymore?"

"Your notion of free trade does not always coincide with reality. Your own father is the founder of the Trade Council."

"Which nowadays fixes prices and milks the planet dry. What will Malachite say to that?"

Realgar was suddenly alert. Talion did not move a muscle. "My lady," Talion said at last, "you go too far. If you told your friends to expect the Envoy to favor them, you made a serious error."

Her pulse quickened, for she had in fact told them as much and still believed it. "Forgive me," she said with drawn-out irony, "I forgot that nonhumans are of no interest to the Patriarch."

"It's not that simple. Their genetic character allows a possibility that they descended from human stock."

"More than a possibility," she corrected with ill-concealed contempt. "But who cares? A thousand fools believe a lie, and it's as good as truth."

Realgar's face was a taut mask, as always when he hid unseemly emotion. It nettled her to see him embarrassed on her account, but he should have kept out of her business.

A thought occurred to her. "Has the Envoy himself already sent inquiry about Shora? Well, has he?"

Talion flexed his fingers, clasped above the desktop. "Subtle are the ways of Torr."

Of course; that was what had him worried. Berenice tried to hide her satisfaction. Now was the time to play her trump card. "If Malachite should choose to contact Sharers . . . you might like to know that I've been asked to take a selfname when I return to Shora."

Their reactions were gratifyingly swift. No Valan, after all, had ever been known to join a Sharer Gathering before.

"Promotion," Realgar remarked dryly. "My congratulations."

Talion leaned intently across his desk. "Then we'll have a direct line on their policymaking."

"Call it a firsthand view," Berenice said carefully. "I will tell you and Malachite what you need to know."

"And what you choose to tell. You would do well to be forthcoming." The High Protector paused as if weighing a choice. "Malachite will make his own inquiries, of course; his means are far greater than ours. But he won't get started for some time yet, and whatever you can discover before then—" He stopped.

Unconsciously Berenice clenched her knees while she focused her attention on Talion. "It would be helpful," she said slowly, "to know what I am looking for."

"If this leaks, my lady, you're finished. Malachite believes that these creatures, whatever they are, may have powers that interest him. Forbidden sciences."

Her eyes widened. Whatever could he be getting at? To be sure, Sharers were not the barbarians that Talion officially took them for. Their "lifeshaping" skills in particular were advanced, she believed, though incomprehensible to Valan doctors. But their skills could not extend to the forbidden. Forbidden sciences, by definition, were banned because they destroyed their creators. Shora had lived in peace for at least ten thousand years.

From Realgar's helicopter, Berenice watched the massive crystal garden that was Iridis pass slowly back below them. There was the silver dome of the fusion plant that Pyrrhopolis had tried to emulate, and there were the square courtyards of the Academy Iridis, where all permissible ranges of learning were preserved.

"Berenice," Realgar began, "your loose manner of speech with the Protector surprises me. It's unwise."

She raised an eyebrow at him, then relaxed in a chuckle. "Do I offend your sense of diplomacy? Ral, I've known Talion far longer than I've known you. He dines with my parents every week."

"It's not like you to appeal to your parents."

"You're right, it's not," she said seriously. "And it's not like you to reopen old wounds." She leaned into his chest, and the stun gun at his belt pressed into her side. Realgar brought his right arm around her, somewhat stiffly, the hand half closed. His arm had been torn apart in the assassin's blast that had killed his first wife instead of himself. Sardis had settled down since then, but the province still deserved its reputation for intrigue. Berenice wondered at times whether she herself risked a similar fate, though in a place where she rarely looked she knew that she loved him more because of the alluring risk, not despite it.

Realgar said, after an interval, "The Protector thinks that a show of strength might prove instructive for your Sharer friends."

She pulled away and glared at him. "I knew you had cooked something up together. He wants an invasion, doesn't he, the old troll. 'Pacification,' you'll call it."

"Nonsense. An exercise, a demonstration, that's all he proposed. They've never even seen a troop detachment or a directed-energy device; they have no idea of what we can do."

Berenice leaned back in the cushioned seat and closed her eyes. He must have good reason to tell her this, but she was so tired of the game. "It won't work, you know," she mused softly, more to convince herself. "The Sharers simply won't understand. And when your invasion lands, they'll all turn into 'ghosts.' You'll look rather silly, then." She believed Realgar's assurance, as far as it went. But the one sure lesson of her life was the fragility of sureness. She had to share some tough learning with Merwen, before it was too late.

6

The night before Spinel was to leave home, he stared out his window at the sky full of stars that shimmered in the sultry air, among them the blue gem that was Shora. Panic swept him. How could he ever hope to survive on that little moon image, a drowned world millions of kilometers away? Would he turn into a fish and be trapped there forever? He was insane to go along with those moonwomen just because no one wanted him here.

On impulse he fled from the house and ran down the unlit streets, all the way out to the pier where the Sharers' boat was moored. He would tell them the whole deal was off, that already he was homesick for Chrysoport, that his father needed him for the stoneshop. . . .

His foot caught on a rotten plank, and something splashed in the gloom below. He stopped; the market square was a different place at night, a realm of ghosts and shadows and the mournful clang of chains against the dock posts. He felt slightly foolish as he stared at the hull of the boat, where the name *Hyalite* gleamed in opalescent letters.

That Lady of Hyalite was to join them at the space landing tomorrow. No Iridian lady would go off to let herself turn into a fish, Spinel tried to convince himself.

* * *

In the morning, half the village gathered in the market to see him off on his bizarre journey. Spinel could only think of his family, whom he faced for the last time. "But not the very last," he assured Beryl as he kissed her tearstained cheek. "I'll come back to see your new baby." He hugged Harran, saying, "You take care of my sister, okay?"

"Take care of yourself, now," Harran said. "If it's true that fish grow as big as mountains up there, be sure to hook one for our stewpot."

Spinel grinned and felt a little better.

Then Oolite set to wailing, louder than a flock of seagulls; Beryl had to pick her up and soothe her.

His father embraced him awkwardly, with eyes cast down, and pressed a cloth full of agates into his pocket. "Gifts. Help you make friends up there," Cyan muttered tersely. "May the Sharers make a fine judge of you."

Galena could barely stand upright, with all the ropes of beads she wore for this momentous occasion, but she threw her arms about him and held him for some time. "Don't forget your lunch," she said at last. "I packed lots of good things, so those people will know what a Valan boy eats. And remember, Spinel, wherever you're going, and whatever you end up doing, do it right." Her black eyes exuded shrewdness, though half hidden in her swollen face. Somehow his mother had a glimpse of the unknown that was about to claim him.

Other villagers in their beads and caftans shouted after him and passed the wine jug from hand to hand. Someone even dared to offer it to Merwen, but she refused. Old Ahn pressed through the crowd and thrust some bags at him, though he already had too much to carry. "How can they grow groundnuts and tomatoes up there, without any fresh soil?" Ahn wondered.

Spinel did not know. Suddenly the food parcels became his most precious possessions.

"You'll come back to us rich as a trader, won't you, lad?" called Melas through cupped hands. "What a fish tale you'll bear then!" Or was it "fishtail"?

Before he could change his mind again, Spinel hoisted his belongings into the boat, where Usha stowed them away. A wind gusted in from the sea, ruffling loose skirts and trousers. Uriel's cowl slipped back as he raised his arm: "The Patriarch's Spirit has blessed your voyage. . . ." But his holy words were soon lost. The waving arms, the farewell shouts, Oolite's scream—all receded into the distance and the past.

They sailed up the jagged coastline, and Usha steered skillfully past Trollbone Point, where vertical cliffs broke into boulders tumbled (it was said) by the ancient Trolls. Spinel had explored there among fossil bones of the fabled giants, said to have eaten hoards of gems and laid eggs of alabaster. But Trolls had passed away when the godlike Primes came to remodel the planet Valedon to human standards. And where were the Primes today? His sense of melancholy deepened.

"Can Uriel reach his Spirit in an instant, even across the light-years?" Merwen was sitting on the deck with her legs crossed, her arms still except for a finger that waved slightly.

Startled, Spinel shook himself to collect his thoughts. He had asked Uriel something like that himself, once, and go no satisfactory answer. "It's his faith," Spinel muttered and looked away.

"Then he must be a man of immense power."

"The High Protector has power, and *he* has no use for faith," Spinel impertinently observed. "The Protector uses radio and starships." He jumped up and swung his arm in an arc to mimic the trajectory of a starship. "And he rules *everyone* in Valedon."

"Then everyone rules him."

Spinel stopped and stared down at her. "What's that?"

"Each force has an equal and opposite force," Merwen said. "So who rules without being ruled?"

His mouth hung open, and he pulled at his lip. He knew little of "forces," except for those that held crystals together, as his father had beat into his head over the years.

"You have to learn more of our tongue. In Sharer speech, my words will explain themselves."

"Oh, I can talk that stuff." Spinel repeated some of the words he had picked up, Sharer words for water and sky, as well as the "plantlight" and the splaylegged "clickfly" that sat on her head and emitted perverse noises. Merwen helped, always patient with his stumbling attempts at pronunciation, but Usha would grimace and shake with soundless laughter. Spinel got more and more annoyed, and when Merwen started on verbs his temper broke. "What the devil is *'wordsharing'*? Does the word for 'speak' mean 'listen' just as well? If I said, 'Listen to me!' you might talk, instead."

"What use is the one without the other? It took me a long time to see this distinction in Valan speech."

Spinel thought over the list of 'share-forms": learnsharing, worksharing, lovesharing. "Do you say 'hitsharing,' too? If I hit a rock with a chisel, does the rock hit me?"

"I would think so. Don't you feel it in your arm?"

He frowned and sought a better example; it was so obvious, it was impossible to explain. "I've got it: if Beryl bears a child, does the child bear Beryl? That's ridiculous."

"A mother is born when her child comes."

"Of if I swim in the sea, does the sea swim in me?"

"Does it not?"

Helplessly he thought, She can't be that crazy. "Please, you do know the difference, don't you?"

"Of course. What does it matter?"

Buildings clustered and towered ever higher toward Iridis, like the gathered skirts of a trinket peddler whose arms opened wide into the longest spread of docked ships that Spinel had ever seen. Piers jutted out as far as he could see, an endless comb at the coif of the sea.

Merwen steered in among the ships, whose hulls towered above her tiny houseboat. Spinel felt as lost and insignificant here as the bits of flotsam that washed up against the hull. But Merwen must have known her way, for where she docked at last a man waited to greet them—a rich, shiny man, in tight cream stain with a broad opal-studded breastplate. Eagerly Spinel ran forward to the prow; then he stopped and blinked twice.

The man had no face. There was only a pale, blank oval where his face should be. "It's a *servo!*" Spinel was delighted. It was said that mechanical servitors did all the hard work in Iridis, leaving the nobles free for leisure. Even so, that Lady of Hyalite must be exceptionally rich to have such a fine one and clothe it like a Protector, besides.

Merwen said, "Where is Berenice?" Her voice was strained. Puzzled, Spinel squinted back at her and at Usha. Usha sat still, her expression rigid; she gripped the gunwale, and the tendons of her arm stood out.

"Lady Berenice shall join you at the moonferry." The servo

spoke in melodious tones. "If my ladies please, board the hover-craft." An arm swung back toward the silver dome behind him.

"A *hovercraft!* Why, you can fly higher than a seagull in a hovercraft—" Spinel stopped. Merwen was whispering with Usha in that crazy Sharer speech. He waited, shifting from one foot to the other. "What's wrong with her, Merwen? We can't keep the lady waiting."

Merwen said, "Your speech cannot express what Usha thinks of this...object, the hovercraft. Like the servitor, it is made of 'dead,' of 'non-life,' of material that has never known the breath of life."

"You mean, she's scared to get into a hovercraft? What will she do about the moonferry?"

"We'll see. For now, we will walk."

Spinel opened his mouth, then shut it again and turned away. While the servo helped Merwen and Usha unload their belongings, which Usha reluctantly consented to stow in the hovercraft, Spinel sullenly kicked at a dock post. "Take *that* for your stupid 'sharer talk,' too." The dome of the hovercraft whirred and sparkled; wist-fully, he watched it take off on its own. Then the servo marched up the pier, and Spinel and the Sharers followed him-or-it into the city.

The streets were a confusion of motley colors and noises that all seemed to call to Spinel at once. It took him awhile to realize that not every blare of a horn was aimed at himself. And the smells, of oil and refuse, mixed with that of fruits and flowers sprawled in the vendors' trays, made an uneasy knot in his stom-ach. On either side of him buildings rose higher than even the cliffs of Trollbone Point; as he looked upward, he felt that he strolled the depths of a chasm. Yet in an instant that notion was swept away by the throngs of people and costumes, the hovercrafts flitting up and down like fireflies, the storefronts with letters of light that danced in the air.

When the travelers reached Center Way, Spinel was simply dumbfounded. There must have been more people crammed into that one thoroughfare than lived in the whole of Chrysoport. Women passed in brilliant talars, heels clicking sharply. Traders wore gems coiled around their heads as they exhibited bales of seasilk, piled precariously high, or cases of intricate metal imple-ments whose purpose could not be guessed. Spinel craned his neck up; way above him, the buildings rose forever, past the skyway where great silver pencils streaked by, their reflected glare stinging his eyes.

A hand clawed his arm. "A fiver, noble lord," croaked a stranger. "Oh, a fiver for the sightless." The stranger was gnarled and hunched over, almost a caricature of Ahn. Irritated, Spinel shrugged him off. Spinel had not expected to find beggars in the city of Iridis.

Where had Merwen got to, and the servo? For a frantic moment he searched. Then he caught sight of Merwen and Usha watching a green monkey that danced to the tune of a fiddler. The street fiddler scraped away to a lively beat, while the monkey capered about and flourished its cup for coins. When the tune was over, the monkey leaped and scampered up the arm of its master.

Merwen asked, "Is she human?"

"Are you kidding?" said Spinel. "It's a monkey. People eat them, even."

"How was I to know? *You're* human."

Spinel blinked in surprise. It was the first time she had snapped at him, that he could recall.

They turned away and walked on after the servo. In the distance ahead, a regular booming sound grew and reverberated beneath Spinel's feet. Parade music floated in above the heads of a crowd that now pressed solidly together. The servo somehow made a path through the crowd, and Spinel followed, until suddenly between two heads he caught a glimpse of—

Palace Iridium. The legendary mosaic facade that stared out of a thousand holocubes was now *there* in front of him, real as life. Before it, the courtyard was virtually paved with soldiers, columns upon columns of them marching past in precise crystalline arrays.

"What's going on?" Spinel exclaimed. "Are they off to the Pyrrholite war?"

A man laughed. "Not just now," he said in a clipped city accent. "Malachite, the Patriarch's Envoy, has only just come. Talion's turned out the Guard to honor him. No, there'll be no war while Malachite is here." The man pointed; a starship stood by the palace, a green needle that touched the clouds.

Spinel watched, mesmerized. All his strength, and that of legions of marchers, flowed and focused into that slim green starship that held the power of the Patriarch of Torr.

* * *

Where was Nisi? Merwen wondered, as Spinel tarried amidst the crowd. This city-place was stifling her. Merwen had gotten used to Chrysoport; indeed, the flat plaster homes of the village appeared sensible enough, for dwellings anchored to the solid floor of earth. But Iridis was a jumble of unintelligible shapes and fetid odors that made her swoon. It was a nightmare where dead things walked on two legs, or preyed above, while the ground bristled with sharp objects more dangerous than the spines of coralfish; for the hundredth time she fingered the soles of her aching feet. Her skin burned, dry as bleached raftwood, and she longed for some more of Usha's protective oil. In the summer heat, this place was even worse than on the first ghastly day that she and Usha had stepped off the moonferry. Would they never find Nisi again, and the moonferry, and get back to blessed Shora?

The Chrysoport youth seemed happy enough here, excited as a girl at her first hunt for a shockwraith. Merwen followed his gaze to the swarm of marchers in the distance. For a moment she was puzzled; then the meaning dawned on her, sending an eerie tingling sensation to her feet. The marchers were those of whom it was said that *death pays a wage.* Kaol the Dolomite had been one, but here was a whole school of them, so many that they merged into a mass of thornlike shoulders and thick black boots that struck the hard black pavement, pounding, pounding incessantly. If these creatures were all human, as Usha insisted, then some purpose must guide their boots, but what could it be? Did the pavement flatten the soles of their boots, or did the marchers work together to polish the somber pavement as smooth as a nightime sea?

7

"General Realgar of Rhodochrosite," intoned the monitor of Berenice's main hall.

Berenice lifted her chin and straightened her long neck before the mirror wall of her salon. Surely Realgar was still at the parade? She had not expected to see him again; he was so busy nowadays, with his new post at the Guard and winding up the Pyrrholite campaign. She stared in dismay at the image of her bald scalp, which she had just had shaven within the hour. Never mind; she rose and pushed away the white servo arms that snaked from the ceiling for her manicure and skin toning. Hurriedly smoothing her talar, she headed for the hall.

At the sight of him in full uniform, Berenice caught her breath. The crescent line of Realgar's shoulders glittered with jewels: for his family house, Rhodochrosite, and sardonyx for his homeland, and commander's grade rubies, and rows of others he had been awarded. Yet the spell was soon broken by the two children at his side: his son, Elmvar, a squirming eight-year-old, and the elder sister, Cassiter, who gaily carried Realgar's plumed helmet. "Look, Mama Berenice!" she cried. "The parade—wasn't it the greatest ever?"

"Yes, Cassi, it was. Realgar, how *did* you get away? The Malachite reception—"

"Just for a minute, that's all." He took Berenice's hands and kissed her. She closed her eyes, savoring the salt of his tongue.

Realgar drew back slightly to look at her.

Her bare scalp twitched. "Don't tell me," she sighed. "I look ghastly."

"A Sharer already."

"You know I'm about to leave."

"Of course, that's why I'm here. Cassi and Elmvar will miss you more than ever." He patted his son's tousled hair. "Berenice. Couldn't you stay just a month more? The Torran Envoy has incredible things to show, gifts from the Patriarch. It's your last chance for ten years."

"My apologies to Malachite, but I've a promise to keep. This moonferry was the last one I could get before Merwen's Gathering, the one which will judge my selfname." She sighed again. She was flattered that he had come to see her off, despite all the ceremonies, but why did he have to make things difficult?

"Very well, but this time I insist that you return before the seaswallowers march across the globe."

"Realgar, please."

Stern lines hardened in his cheeks. Even the children were still for a moment, sensing his mood.

"I'll stay as long as Talion orders."

Realgar let out a deep breath. "For Torr's sake," he whispered, "just don't make yourself a watery grave."

Berenice swallowed. She herself dreaded the whirlpools of those cephaglobinid monsters when they migrated from pole to pole. But Sharers faced the migration twice a year, and this year Berenice would face it with them. Then they would truly accept her as a sister of Shora.

A squeal came from Cassiter; Elmvar was tugging at the helmet, trying to wrest it from her.

"Elmvar, leave the helmet to Cassi," Realgar said. "Go play with this." He pulled the raygun from his belt, a ceremonial weapon as antiquated as a sword. The boy took it and waved it bravely about the hall, while making ferocious noises.

Suddenly Cassiter dropped the helmet and clapped her hands over her ears. Berenice winced; the child was still sensitive to sudden noises, years after her mother's death. She ran to Cassiter and folded her in her arms, rocking gently.

Berenice had no children of her own. Her first marriage had ended with her defective firstborn, which the doctors had blamed on her own genes. They had sterilized her then and her husband, heir to the House of Aragonite, had left her to build his dynasty elsewhere.

In despair, she had gone back to Shora, her birthplace, where her father had founded the moon trade. Sharers could mix and match human genes at will, even correct the bad ones. No Valan doctor would risk his neck to perform such "witchcraft," but Usha had fixed Berenice soon enough. Berenice could bear a healthy child now—if she dared. On Valedon, the very secret of her "cure" was an everpresent knife at her neck.

Then Realgar had entered her life, a gift of fate, or perhaps of her scheming parents, at whose home she had met him. She had fallen for him, with his ambitions and his two darling children. But how would Realgar fit into her life as a Sharer? Never mind, for now. Berenice pressed Cassiter's hair. "Cassi, do you know what I'll bring you from the moon? A whorlshell, that's what, a perfect whorlshell polished by the sea."

"A whorlshell? A real one, with golden stripes?"

"That's right, just for you."

Cheerful again, Cassiter beamed and let Berenice release her. As Berenice stood again, she caught a softness in Realgar's eyes, a rare show of feeling. "They need you," he said. "As much as I do."

"Yes." She barely voiced the word. She was just on the verge ... it would be so easy to give in, now, to solve everything for good. But there was something else she had gained from Shora, beyond physical wholeness: a wholeness of the spirit, a source of refuge that she would never find on Valedon. She could not give up Shora for marriage, not yet.

Cassiter picked up the helmet again and plunked it on her head. It came down over her eyes, but she marched ahead blindly, and her brother started to follow. "Come on, troops! For'ard! Tighten up the bleeding line!"

"That's enough, now," said Realgar. "We have to be going. Time to say goodbye to—"

Immediately the children rushed back and clung to her. "You can't go already," cried Elmvar. "Then there's just the old nanny servo; she's ugly, and she smells like motor oil."

Berenice swallowed hard and forced herself to look up at Realgar.

"They get so out of hand," he apologized. "They need a mother to keep them in line."

"Not for that, surely; they can't lack...discipline?" She paused at the word, recalling with distaste his dismissal of rebel Sharers.

His shoulders straightened. "Cassiter. Elmvar. Stand here." His voice had not risen, but the children released the folds of Berenice's talar and went to stand beside their father. "Now say goodbye."

"Goodbye, Mama Berenice," they chorused.

Unexpectedly, desire overcame her. Her head felt light, and she thought that if he asked her now she would surely say yes. But Realgar seemed content to look long and hard into her eyes, satisfied that he still held her. "You shall return safely, Berenice," he pronounced, as if binding even the elements to his will.

At the space landing, Berenice stepped gingerly among plastic shreds and metal curls. A gust of wind cooled her scalp but threw sour dust in her face. Ahead of her sat the battered old moonferry; it almost seemed to shrink back, as if apologizing for its existence amid Iridian splendor. If only she could have taken her father's liner, the *Cristobel,* but no reputable member of the Trade Council would carry her Sharer friends.

There they were, at the dark entranceway: Merwen and Usha. They wore brief shifts of seasilk to satisfy Valan notions of modesty, but their bald violet heads were unmistakable. As she drew near, signs of ill health appalled her. Their fingertips fluttered feebly, and their skin had a flat, dusky look, a smokier shade of amethyst.

"Oh, share the day, Merwen," she exclaimed in Sharer speech. "I'm so glad you're safe!" At least they had kept out of jail, or worse. She held Merwen close; it felt like embracing an ocean. "Surely the air at least was better for you, up the coast?" Hesitantly she kissed Usha, whose face was even more dour than she had remembered.

Merwen smiled faintly. "We breathed. And we shared learning, very much."

"That's wonderful. That's what you hoped for, isn't it?" Berenice fingered the opal stonesign at her neck. How could she reprove Merwen, whose mind flowed as if she had lived since the day that Shora opened the First Door? Yet Sharers had to be warned. "Talion's upset," she blurted out. "The Protector, he—he's heard bad reports, false, perhaps. You did not trade without stonesigns?"

"We shared seasilk and herbs," said Merwen, "but no coin or other non-lifestuff."

"And medical treatments? You know that's too dangerous here."

Merwen paused. "We know."

"And you did not call yourselves *'spies'?"*

"The term seemed apt. We shared learning, after all."

Berenice frowned. "A 'spy' shares hiddenly, for subversive purposes. You're not subversive, are you?"

"Are we not?"

The words numbed her. *Are we not?* What in Torr's name was Merwen getting into? When Merwen the Impatient One chose, she could sway the minds of thousands in any Sharer Gathering. But to try that here—it was unthinkable. Berenice could not tell her, for her own tongue froze at the thought. Yet somehow Merwen had to know that Talion meant business this time. She cleared her throat. "Merwen. Valedon is not your home."

"Is it yours, Nisi?"

Was it? She could not answer, and suddenly there was nothing more to be said. To collect her thoughts, she looked away, and then she noticed the stranger, a gaping youth who stood next to Usha as if he belonged with them. She drew herself up straight and looked him over: clearly a commoner, his coarsely woven shirt buttoned askew. His olive face and his hair looked clean, but he still might have lice.

"Berenice," said Merwen, switching to Valan speech, "another friend comes to teach and learn with us."

The boy bowed, a little too deeply. "Spinel, son of Cyan the stonecutter of Chrysoport, if you please, my lady."

"Indeed." Had she not explained to Merwen about nobles and commoners? And a male, no less. By the Nine Legions, whatever could Merwen want with a "malefreak" on Shora? But now, after what had just passed between then, Berenice was too proud to ask Merwen her reasons, or even the more crucial results of her mission on Valedon. Soon enough, Merwen would have to answer, to the Gathering.

Spinel was abashed at his first encounter with an actual Lady of Iridis. Her arched nose and precisely etched lips reminded him of one of those quartz statuettes that sold well as wedding gifts. Yet her clothes, though sleek and seamless, looked disappointingly mundane, and her opal stonesign was of indifferent workmanship. And her bare scalp—was she trying to look like Merwen?

From behind, a shrill whine pierced his ears. Spinel dropped the bags, clapped both hands to his head, and squeezed his eyes shut for good measure. The sound died slowly, and someone pulled his arms down. It was a man, short and loose-skinned, with a fleshy nose and a deep hollow below his throat. He shouted in Spinel's ear, "She's just warming up, starling." The man's breath had a touch of liquor. "You coming or staying?"

"Who are you?" Spinel demanded.

"I'm your captain, Captain——" He pronounced a name that sounded like a whistle. "But you just call me Dak, starling. Captain Dak, at your service from here to Torr." Captain Dak jerked his head toward the ramp against his ship, which even Spinel could tell was not about to fly as far as Torr.

Merwen started up the ramp, but Usha stopped in her tracks like a mule. At that, Lady Berenice hurried over and spoke in low urgent tones.

"Hey, Sharer, you remember me," Captain Dak called to Usha. "At least *I'm* made of 'life-stuff.'" A grin split his face, and he laughed silently.

Somewhat mollified, Usha let herself be led up the ramp until she fanned her toes across the doorsill.

Spinel picked up his bags and started on up, but for an instant he lost sight of everything except the dizzying fact that Valedon, his whole source of existence, was about to slip away from him. In panic he whirled and stared backward, outward, as if he could scan the entire planet with a glance and swallow it with his eyes. But all he could see was the windswept space landing, with ships planted here and there like tree stumps, and pavement crisscrossed by wandering strangers.

"This Door is not ours, either," Merwen told him, "but it's the only way back home."

That's fine for her, Spinel thought as the ship door closed behind him. There is no way home for me.

Part II

A DOOR INTO OCEAN

1

Spinel stood with the captain in the darkened viewport, lost amid the throng of stars. Shora was now a immense globe of ocean, patched with clouds. He reached out to it until his hand met the incurving dome. And Shora seemed to reach back to him, as it swelled ever larger.

Dak said, "See those greenish specks down there? That's where your native friends live."

Spinel blinked. "On greenish specks?"

"*Rafts,* starling; strong as anything, some of them with a hundred years' growth of raftwood. Even traders can't do better. We'll land on one any minute now, if this old bird can manage it."

Uneasily Spinel shifted his feet. "Uh, Captain, won't you be busy soon? With the landing and all."

"What, me? You think they'd let me touch the controls? That would really give your Hyalite lady the fits. No, I—damned if I don't feel more like a janitor on this servo-ship." Dak paused. "Wasn't always that way. Back in the fifth century—give or take a few—now, that was my heyday."

"Come on, there's a fish tale," Spinel muttered.

"Oh, no, starling; I used to run the Malachite ship. At your service, here to Torr—decades at light-speed were but days to me."

Spinel looked up.

"You see, I was just a starling like you when my home world——"— he birdwhistled the name—"burnt to a cinder in the Brother Wars. After that, why, I wanted to get just as far away as time and space allowed. So I took the Torran route and ran it for centuries. Until they retired me to this hole." He sighed.

"The Brother Wars—that was before the Patriarch. What, are you one of the *Primes?*" Those men who lived like gods—this old troll was one?

49

Dak puffed his chest out. "That's right, I'm a Prime. I'm older than the Patriarch of Torr, and near as old as Shora. I was there when the new age began, when they pulled all the planets together like lobsters in a trap. I can tell you—"

"What do you mean about Shora? Was 'Shora' a person, too, a Prime?"

Dak shrugged. "Shora was a legend even in my own birthtime. Off the regular trade routes; never worth the bother, for the powers of Torr. But I tell you, out of the thousand worlds ruled by the Patriarch, you won't find one like Shora."

At that, Spinel frowned: finally, he had caught the man out. "There aren't that many worlds in the Patriarchy. Torr's Nine Legions rule ninety-three planets. I learned *that* in school."

"There used to be more. Nine out of ten are congealed chunks of rock today; some still smolder. Weed out the bad ones, you know. What else is the Patriarch for?"

Just then the deck lurched and shoved at Spinel's feet as if there were an earthquake. While he scrambled to keep his balance, his tongue stiffened in back and he knew he would be sick.

"We've hit the atmosphere," cried the captain. "Back to your seatbelt now, and hope the sea's not too strong when we touch raft."

By the exit, Spinel slumped on the deck with his travel bags. His stomach had been violently emptied but still felt queasy; the deck remained unsteady, though the ship supposedly had landed on something.

A crack of light appeared. A breeze invaded the ship, carrying ocean salt and an indefinable sweetish scent, mingled rose and orange.

On Merwen's head, the clickfly was perched again, emitting loud sputters and chirps. Usha chirped back at it, more lively than Spinel had ever seen her.

Weakly Spinel asked, "Where is all your luggage?"

"To be delivered." Lady Berenice brushed past him, her mani-cured hands empty. Clearly she meant to keep her place above him. Yet Merwen ingenuously treated her little different from him-self: with respect but not obeisance. Did Merwen not know the difference? Did Shora lack nobles, as well as men?

Outside, Merwen and Usha were down the ramp already. The clickfly circled overhead in a frenzy, emitting swooping cries.

From nowhere a swarm of clickflies descended to buzz excitedly about the Sharers like bees at a honeycomb, but the insects seemed to do no harm.

As Spinel stepped down the exit ramp, he surveyed the surface below. It looked like hard crusted soil, with a sort of evergreen matting, yet it could not be "land" underneath. His feet lost weight for an instant, and he gripped the railing until the swell subsided. The land-that-was-not-land stretched outward, about a fifteen-minute walk, he guessed, to where it branched into a herringbone pattern of channels all around. Beyond that, the gray girdle of ocean faded into sky.

Merwen came back to the ramp, with a lightness in her step and a glow in her eyes that she had never shown on Valedon. Dozens of clickflies perched on her arms or hovered above. "*Share-the-day*, Spinel, it's a glorious day!" she called, mixing the two tongues. "Do you hear the *clickflies?* All our sisters, from rafts and clusters across Shora, *share welcome* with us. Come on, our daughters await us."

"Does the raft always . . . move like this?"

"Oh, it's a good strong raft, it flexes well. It is many person-lengths thick. It is shared by traders; see?" She gestured toward the concrete buildings that lay behind the ferryship. "And our home raft is stronger yet, twice as thick at the center. The sea names ours Raia-el. Come home to Raia-el." She clasped his hand, and the umbrella folds of webbing hung loosely across his fingers. At the foot of the ramp, his soles met the tough, matted crust of plant growth.

"Hear me, starling!" Captain Dak's voice sang out from the ferryship. "You won't catch this old bird on Shora when the sea-swallowers come. Two months you've got, to turn back," he warned.

"Thanks, I'll—"

"With all the rest of the Valan cowards," Lady Berenice called back. Scornfully she tossed her head and turned her high shoulders.

The unladylike outburst startled Spinel. Blood rushed to his face, and he clenched his travel bag. "Thanks anyhow, Dak."

"Stop by and see me then. If you survive." A whistled arpeggio was the Captain's sign-off.

Before he could change his mind, Spinel hurried off with Merwen, who seemed anxious to reach the channeled raft-edge. The soil became moist, and long weeds straggled across it. Then the soil gave out altogether where branches immense as fallen sequoias extended out to sea, covered with barnacles and other scaly things. At Merwen's footfall, half the scaly things slithered down the side. Spinel recoiled, but Merwen unconcernedly went out onto the branch, so he followed, more slowly. The rose-orange scent intensified, and its source soon appeared: blossoms, brilliant yellow tricorners sprouting from bushes on side branchlets that grew ever denser as he went on.

A narrow boat appeared, carving its way up the flowery channel. Three tiny purple figures arose in it; they jumped and waved, dancing wildly as molten glass in a flame, and the boat heaved precariously. Abruptly all three dove over the side, and in an instant they were clambering up onto the branch, waddling ducklike, for their feet were even more outsized for their height than were the adults'. They surrounded Usha first, hugging and jabbering until Usha tugged the biggest girl back down to secure the boat.

Of the other two, one was waist-high and the other a toddler. They exchanged high-pitched chatter with Merwen and pulled insistently at her shift, until she loosened the garment and it collapsed around her feet. Now they all were unclothed.

Spinel burned with embarrassment. He had not believed that Sharers went unclothed, any more than he believed they were witches. He glanced back at Lady Berenice, wondering how she would take this. To his amazement, even she had slipped off her Iridian talar, stonesign and all, and had rolled it into a neat bundle under her arm. Coolly she returned his stare, as if daring him to run back to the moonferry.

Before he could think, the Sharer girls converged on him. Their arms flashed up over his shirt and reached for his hair, which must have been a novelty for children who were bald as sapphires. At length Merwen pulled them away, saying in Valan, "Come now, Weia, Wellen; Spinel is still shy, and you know what Valan plumage looks like, anyway. Here comes Flossa; is the boat ready now?"

"*Spi*-nel, *Spi*-nel," echoed Wellen, the middle child. The eldest, Flossa, started a spitting contest, and the three of them squealed with laughter. Merwen nudged them into the boat, where Usha was bailing out water with her efficient hands. "See the daughters of my womb?" Usha proudly asked him. "Grown so big and strong, with Mama and Mamasister gone."

"And *inconsiderate*," added Merwen.

At her selfname, Usha drew back and spoke again, in Sharer. The girls subsided. They crouched demurely on the floor of the boat, only stealing glances at the Valan creature, who huddled miserably next to the rail and wished more than anything that he had never left home.

Usha and Flossa paddled out to the open sea, where crests capped the waves and the boat heaved and smacked the water. Then, from the back of the boat, started the most unlikely sound Spinel would have expected to hear: an electric outboard motor.

Spinel turned, shook the wind-tossed locks out of his eyes, and stared in disbelief. The motor was a standard make from Iridis, used by those Chrysolite fishermen who could afford it. What in Torr's name was one doing here, on a boat made of some shiny substance completely foreign to him, with Flossa's webbed hand at the tiller? Nevertheless, this echo from home was a gift from the heavens, and as the boat leaped forward his spirits rose hopefully.

A shadow fell. Overhead passed an enormous bird with a fish snout and four spined wings. Wellen stood up and cried out to it, snapping her fingers. The bird descended and soared just past her head, its wingspan dwarfing the boat. Spinel ducked, and the wind from its wings brushed his back before it loftily soared away.

In the distance, a thumb-shaped projectile shot out from the sea, and a stream of water arched behind. The object glided majestically for a minute or so, until it returned to the sea with a thunderous crash. Another one rocketed from the sea, then another; there must have been a school of them. Waves soon reached the boat and rocked it steeply.

"They are glider squid," Merwen told him. "You'll see, they are good friends to share."

Spinel shook his head. How would he ever tell about any of this, back in Chrysoport? Even his own mother would never believe him, much less Ahn or Melas.

Something nagged at him; something was missing, he did not know what. As he watched the sea, it came to him. There were no landmarks of any kind, just the flat horizon. It was hardly safe, out on the open sea in such a small craft, and with what navigation? "Merwen . . . how do you know where you're going? I mean, you got a compass or something?"

"Yes, nowadays we get compasses from the traders. But the

clickflies always tell us. Clickflies know everything; you'll have to
learn to share speech with them."

The boat pounded across the waves until it reached Merwen's
raft, Raia-el. Once again he breathed the rose-orange scent, as the
boat threaded in through branched channels where the flowers
bloomed so profusely that they closed in a canopy just overhead.
Beyond, the flowers gave out again where the great level trunks
coalesced to join the raft.

Upon the raft rose a stalk of blue spires with concave sides that
fit together like curved diamond shapes, broadening at the base. It
might have been rock crystal, but the tips looked utterly fragile.
Spinel ventured to say to Merwen, "Is that some sort of . . . giant
flower?"

Flossa collapsed in a fit of giggles. She translated to her sisters,
who shrieked and rolled over backward, kicking their feet in the
air.

"You trolls' brats, you!" Spinel lunged at one of those infuriat-
ing flippers.

Weia and Wellen dove overboard and vanished, while Flossa
picked up her paddles again, still giggling. What a nuisance they
were, even worse than Oolite.

Merwen answered, "That is our house."

It looked flimsy for a house on the sea. In fact, he soon noticed, the sloping panels were nothing more than woven seasilk,
twisted into saddle shapes and glazed somehow. What would become of it in a hurricane, let alone when "the sea swallowed"?

They walked up to the "house." Usha touched a blue panel;
with a *whoosh*, a round wrinkled hole gaped in the fabric. From
inside, Sharers crowded to greet them, their voices rushing like a
song of the sea. Even Merwen spoke briskly, and her hands fluttered everywhere. Spinel stepped through the doorhole, feeling
lost in the confusion. The air he breathed was thick with foreign
odors; light-headed, he leaned against a wall. His arm sank into a
furry paste that covered the dipping walls and ceilings, glowing in
flares of green and amber that created a dizzying illusion of mo-
tion. The feel of the squished material added to his queasiness.

Merwen tried to explain. "It's decorative, it's . . . a 'fungus,' is
that right?" she asked Lady Berenice.

"A *fungus*? All over?" He pulled away and frantically brushed
off his arm. For once he appreciated his mother's strict house-
cleaning.

"Yes, isn't it beautiful? Flossa and Wellen have kept up the painting. Come, now, you have many sisters to meet. . . ."

The names all flew past him, except for old Ama, who reclined on a low couch that undulated slowly, as it was filled with water. Ama's hands were shriveled into birdlike claws, but they flickered a silent greeting. A seasilken blanket was wrapped around the grandmother; the others were all quite exposed. Spinel stared more boldly at the strangers than he had dared at Merwen or Usha. They were as hairless as infants, even below, and their skin had the same sheen all over, with the faint puckering typical of Sharer complexion. Somehow he felt a letdown, perhaps because he had expected to be aroused but was not.

Meanwhile, Weia and Wellen had insinuated their fingertips under the flaps of his travel bag. Spinel hastily pushed them aside and opened it himself. The first thing he drew out was half of a cheese sandwich. "That's my lunch," he told Wellen, adding the word for "sharing food."

Wellen took the sandwich in the web between two fingers and flicked it with her thumb. She sniffed it gingerly, wrinkled her nose, and coughed hard. Then she ran off to a large shrub that grew in the back of the room and stuffed the sandwich between a pair of broad, fleshy leaves. The leaves snapped shut. Wellen then pried open an adjacent leaf pair and scooped the contents out onto her palm.

This performance perplexed Spinel, but Lady Berenice's face softened with amusement, the first time he had seen her slip from her noble bearing. "Wellen thinks it makes good plant food," she told him. "For the 'pudding plant.' The leaf juices will digest it for a few days, and then it becomes 'pudding.'"

Wellen proffered him a sample of what looked like a mixture of moldy cheese and clay.

"What was that stuff originally?"

"Probably squid entrails."

Suddenly Spinel wished he had filled his whole pack with Ahn's vegetables before he left. "Uh, thanks, but—" He reached into the bag again. "Now here's something for you!" From his father's parting gift, a handful of quartz marbles fell to the floor.

The girls gasped and scooped up the shiny stones, fingering them avidly before passing them on to their elders. Voices died to a murmur.

Their distraction was a relief. Spinel yawned and stretched his legs, and slumped against the wall again. There were no chairs, only mats on the floor. It must be midnight, he felt, yet it was still light outside. It did not occur to him that his accustomed time zone was irrelevant to Shora.

Once again the doorhole gaped open. An arm reached through, knotted and muscular. This Sharer entered with difficulty because she had to pull a large netted sack through the narrow opening. The sack held a writhing mass of tentacles—octopus, perhaps, but impossibly bright red, and they moved more swiftly than any octopus he had seen; their beaks snapped like crab claws.

The newcomer paused and drew herself to full height, a good hand's-breadth taller than Spinel. Veins twined her legs like ivy, and her firm breasts heaved with exertion. Her figure was like Usha's, but her face was a startlingly fierce version of Merwen.

"Lystra!" Merwen spread her arms.

"Mother!" Lystra dropped the sack and embraced her. One snapping octopod squirmed out of the sack; how could it move so fast? Weia shrieked, and Wellen hurried to retrieve the creature, while a couple of elder Sharers dragged the rest of the catch away.

Lystra and Merwen held each other, rocking slightly, then parted just enough to face each other and speak in low tones. There was no mistaking the emotion that stretched between them, binding the mother and daughter as if no one else existed. Spinel felt vaguely jealous.

Little Weia reached up on tiptoe and tugged Lystra's arm. She held up a tiny fistful of Spinel's polished stones.

At first Lystra did not notice, then she looked down blankly, as if puzzled. Her mouth opened in shock. Her arm swept Weia's aside; the marbles flashed and darted across the room. The little one screamed and sobbed, while Lystra turned and saw Spinel for the first time. A harsh note entered her voice, and the others became very still.

Unaccountably, Lady Berenice stepped forward beside Spinel, as if to claim kinship: she, a Lady of Hyalite. Spinel looked at Berenice, than at Lystra again—wild Lystra, whose very eyes spoke fury now, as if Spinel were a demon conjured up by a witch. By Torr and all the Nine Legions, what had he done?

Lystra glared in consternation at the new Valan creature her mother and mothersister had brought home. *It* stood there, swathed in "traders' rags," head of a bristlefish and mouth agape stupidly. And carrying *stones,* no less; stones, to this of all silkhouses.

Merwen was squeezing her arm, pleading with taut insistence underneath. "He is young, he brought gifts, not to harm—"

Lystra wheeled on her. *"Why,* my mother? In the name of that which can't be shared, why did you bring a Valan malefreak to this very door? Do we not suffer enough traders, that we should take in extra?"

"This one is no trader. He will share learning with us. Why else did we cross the sky to the Stone Moon?"

Why, indeed. Anxiously Lystra studied her mother. Merwen looked years older after her mission to Valedon; her cheeks sagged, and new rills underlaid her eyes. Even mothersister Usha, the lifeshaper, was dusky of skin, and her muscles were slack. It seared Lystra's heart to watch her parents age so fast. Yet her ache for them, and her joy to have them home at last, was all muddled with her outrage at this creature they had brought. She took a deep breath and held it until her head cleared. "Mother," she said quietly. "You went to Valedon to share judgment of them in their own habitat, to judge if they can be human. Surely you have your answer now."

"Yes, in part, as they judged us."

"Don't listen to Usha! It takes more than genes to prove—"

"That it does," Usha's voice thudded. "Why do you think we spent two months on that half-dried-out planet?"

"And we barely scratched the surface," said Merwen. "You are still young, Lystra. Nisi, you know, will take a selfname tomorrow."

Her breath stopped short. "Then why does *Be-re-ni-ce* return to us as colorless as a stranded jellyfish?" She stared at Nisi while she addressed her mother.

"Lystra," Merwen said, "Who pulled you from the water when the jellyfish stung? Who wove new housepanels, day and night, after the storm last year?"

"Yes." She forced a whisper. "I know all that."

Nisi said, "Lystra, I share your thoughts. I have done the best I can on Valedon, and I bring vital news for the Gathering." At least Nisi had not lost the Sharer tongue.

But, young as Lystra was, she knew she was right about other Valans, the ones that swarmed in ever greater numbers over Shora, consuming entire populations of fish and poisoning others. And

the traders who came to share seductively artful implements of
stone and coldstone, they were the most dangerous of all. Stone
was as hard as coral yet as empty as death. No living presence
fashioned iron and quartz: these things grew in fire as coral grew
in water, and for some the paradox consumed the mind in fire.
Such things had no place on Shora.

2

By evening the neighbors had dispersed, leaving only Merwen's
family and the apprentice lifeshapers to curl up on their mats in the
communal sleeping room. Berenice was too exhausted even to
shave herself smooth; her scalp and limbs still prickled from her
depilation the night before. She missed her private bedroom and
her servos, and already she longed for Realgar's embrace. Still,
she had what she had come for: the free ocean, the purest air, and
the love of her sisters who had given her soul second wind.

All was quiet except for wind against the seasilk, and waves
upon the raft branches, and an occasional clickfly still chirruping
the now tiresome news that Merwen the Impatient had indeed
come back safely to Raia-el, with a Valan malefreak who might
turn out to be human. Berenice cast one last resentful look at
Spinel, who lay huddled in his clothes, having slept through supper, ignorant of the crisis that surrounded him. It was bad enough
that she had to expose herself in his presence, lest the more conser-
vative Sharers shun her; Realgar would be livid if he found out.
Now she actually had to defend the boy, for the sake of her own
roots on Valedon. If she denied his kinship at this crucial time, the
Sharers might expect her to cut her Valan roots once and for all. it
had never come to that, before today; Lystra's challenge shook
her.

Of course she could not stay purple in Iridis, since the micro-
bial symbionts were thought to be contagious. For Sharers, the
issue was sensitive because the traders and other Valan settlers

avoided the breathmicrobes, which seemed to highlight their supposed lack of "humanity."

In the two months since she had left, events had moved swiftly on Shora. The living fabric of Shora was at stake, and Sharers across the globe were clamoring to *close the Door*. Even Merwen might not sway them this time. Tomorrow, Berenice would see for herself what the Raia-el Gathering of selfnamers had in mind, and she would offer what counsel they would accept. That Talion, curse his ancestors, was little help at all. If only the storm held off until Malachite came.

Spinel slept fitfully. He dreamed that he was lost at sea, outswimming an unseen seaswallower, while the pounding of marching boots reverberated in his head. He awoke with a start.

Something was knocking about in his travel bag. It was a portly fish with an ugly jaw and three pairs of lobed fins. At his shout, the fish scurried away, leaving a trail of slime. The bag was a mess, everything scattered and sticky. The bread and fruit he had saved for breakfast was either eaten or inedible, and his empty stomach was growling.

For several minutes he cursed Shora and everything connected with it, including Merwen for having brought him here, his father for not having beaten some sense into his head earlier, and himself for having been such a trollhead as to climb that old netleaf tree to spy on strangers. Then he tried to think. Daylight shone through slits in the upper panels, and everyone else was gone. From outside came the rhythmic banging sound of Merwen's handloom. He set out to find her.

He picked his way through the winding hallway. At one point a basin of water hung from the wall, filled by a trickling stream from some sort of foliage overhead. Weia was scooping out water with her flipper hands, but at his approach she toddled off. Plants watering people? Spinel could only shake his head.

At last he found the disk of the doorhole. He touched it: taut as a drumhead. Then abruptly it dilated like the iris of a great blue eye. Sunlight streamed through, and Spinel squinted hard as he stepped outside, following the sound of the loom.

To his disappointment, the weaver was not Mersen but Lady Berenice. "Good morning, my lady."

"You may call me Nisi," she said, in a tone that clearly commanded him to do so.

"Yes, Lady Nisi. Lady Nisi, a fish got into my food."

"Don't keep food around, except in the pantry, which has herbs to repel legfish. Breakfast is ready there."

"No, thanks." None of that pudding stuff for him. Merwen would take him back to the trading post for some regular food. "Where's Merwen?"

"In the water, by the motorboat."

Spinel found Merwen swimming in a channel among the branches, her head bobbing above the surface. He tossed off his shirt and slipped into the water, warm as a blanket of turquoise seasilk.

Something nibbled at his toes. His pulse jolted, and he kicked hard. Probably just minnows—he hoped. And below, who could say how many kilometers to the ocean floor. . . .

Merwen's arms swirled the water, and she smiled at him. Despite himself, Spinel smiled back. "Merwen, I'm hungry. A legfish got my food."

"I'm so sorry." She did not tell him to go get breakfast. She understood. "Spinel, would you spread some *fingershells* for me?"

Spinel blinked at the request, not wanting to refuse. In the boat was a sack full of tiny pearly shells; Merwen pulled herself up over the side to scoop out a handful of them, which she spread through the undergrowth from the raft branch. Spinel got some shells, but as soon as his hand reentered the water, red wormlets flickered from the shells, and he let go of them in a hurry. Each shell with its bunch of wormlets spurted off in a different direction, and soon all were lost among the coral stalks that reached up from the underside of the branch and paraded below as he swam. Bewhiskered fish swept past the coral, until a lump of mud and broken shells came alive to snap one up and tear it with its pincers. And everywhere, from nooks amid the coral, filaments of seasilk hung and pulsed to the rhythm of an unseen drummer, reaching deep among the branchlets that extended from the main trunk, down far as Spinel could see, an inverted forest.

Merwen was still spreading shells. "Listen, Merwen, what're you doing that for?"

"Fingershells eat parasites that ravage the silkweed when they grow too many."

"So why not spray the raft with something to clear out the pests?"

"Then seasilk would choke the raft. And fingershells would go hungry, and tubeworms die of the poison; then fish and octopus would have nothing, and what would Sharers eat?"

"And what am *I* supposed to eat? Look," he insisted, "I have to go back to the trading post or I'll starve out here."

"Very well," Merwen said, starting to swim off. "Lystra will take you this afternoon."

"Lystra! Not her." That horrid creature who had slapped away his gift stones and glared bloody murder at him.

"Lystra always goes to the trader, for metal tools and even firecrystals."

"But Lystra hates me."

"She doesn't know you well enough to hate yet." Merwen paused. "Lystra does know traders well. She will take enough seasilk to trade for your food."

Spinel had not thought of that. For survival, he was utterly dependent on his Sharer hosts. But Lystra, he was sure, would as soon see him starve. Sullenly he splashed the water with his hands. "Why does Lystra bother with traders, if she hates them so?"

"Traders are human, too. They would be fine, if they became *selfnamers.*"

"What's a selfnamer?"

"Come, I'll show you." She hauled herself up onto the branch. Spinel followed. He watched her breasts sway as she settled herself.

Merwen nodded at the water. "Now, what do you see there?"

Spinel looked. "The sea, that's all."

"Look closer."

"I see fish, lots of little ones, and turrets of coral." On the surface, light patches bent and skittered. "I see—myself, on the water," he added flippantly.

"Good, and what else?"

"What else is there?" he exclaimed. "I'm no good at guessing games, I don't know anything. In school all I did was dream about the mosaics on the wall. I'll never learn to be a judge. Why don't you send me home?"

"A lesser creature sees its rival on the water and jumps in to fight it. A human sees herself and knows that the sea names her. But a *selfnamer* sees every human that ever was or will be, and every form of life there is. By naming herself, she becomes a 'protector' of Shora."

"A Protector? You mean, everybody?" The bizarre logic of it

struck him. Without any nobles and commoners, everyone got to be a High Protector.

Captain Dak was right, he decided. Even if there had been ten thousand worlds inhabited, he would never find one as ridiculous as this one.

In the hallway of the silkhouse, an unfamiliar member of the household was scraping something up from the floor. It looked like the trail from the legfish, now hardened to a plastic. Spinel shrugged philosophically and went his way to the pantry. Perhaps there would be something to stave off his hunger.

The pantry, a room as irregularly shaped as every other, was cluttered with bowls and spoons and clear, polished plates that looked more like glass lenses. Wellen was stacking bowls, while Weia sat on a mat and took spoonfuls from a bowl of that nauseating "pudding." Weia fed the spoonfuls to Ama, the grandmother, who seemed very weak, almost paralyzed. Spinel only watched. He was not hungry enough for that stuff.

When Ama was done, Weia pushed the bowl toward him. Then she picked up a broom and started to sweep the floor. Somehow, though, her feet kept stepping on each other as soon as she fixed her attention on the broom, until her sister plucked it away to finish the job.

Spinel laughed and thumbed his nose at her.

Immediately they both sat down on the floor, their backs turned on him. Bewildered, Spinel blinked at their two small round backs, a silent reproach. "Well, don't dish it out, if you can't *take* it." He stomped out, retraced his steps, and slapped the doorhole to get outside.

A few paces away stood Lystra.

Spinel caught himself, prepared to run, but Lystra had not seen him yet, or chose not to. Shadows rippled in the muscles of her calves and arms and beneath her firm breasts. Her build was magnificent—a wrestler could not have looked better—and in Spinel's experience people who looked like that usually were used to using it.

Lystra was absorbed with the clickflies that hovered before her, their lopsided mandibles scraping out squeals and pops. Some were swinging across a sort of fence of fine black meshwork, like a spiderweb, that had not stood there before. "Look, Valan," she said at last. "It's a letter from across the sea." Lystra spoke his language fluently. "You would do well to heed its message."

Warily Spinel drew closer. The web was a fascinating pattern, but he could make nothing of it. Lystra's face was a bit harsher than he cared for, but there was a ghost of Merwen's eyes and cheekbones. And her cheeks were unlined; she could not be much older than himself.

Spinel lifted his chin. "What do you mean, a letter?"

She pointed to the clickflies. "They spin out their news so that all may read. In the Eighth Galactic, the Third Cluster, System Wanelion, many things were dying: glider squid washed up on the rafts, starworms floated up with their bellies gray and swollen; even shockwraiths were gone from the underraft. What was the cause? Your Valan sisters, of course, dumping poisons in the sea. But a lifeshaper of Wan-elion fixed that. She spread a slime mold that overgrew all the Valan fishing boats. Now the greedy fishers are gone from Wan-elion." Lystra watched him expectantly.

"So what's that got to do with me?"

"Everything, Valan, everything. Already you're in league with the traders—I told Merwen so. So you're hungry, are you? I'll fix that; I'll feed you to the starworm!"

Spinel stepped back a pace, then had a maddening sense of being tricked.

"Trollhead," Lystra muttered. "I'll feed you *after* I feed the starworm. Come on." She started to turn away.

"No," he burst out, "if you don't want me, then by Torr I want nothing from you." He tensed his legs and put his fists at his hips.

She blinked a few times, as if rearranging a puzzle. "Well said, Valan. A pity more of your sisters don't agree. Perhaps you've got some brains beneath your fur." She headed down toward the water. "Come along, Valan! You'll upset Merwen, if you don't."

He had no choice, if he was to eat. How could Merwen have done this to him?

Lystra dove into the sea, swift as lightning. Spinel plunged in after, and his leg grazed a submerged branch. He gasped at the surface, his leg stinging. Then more cautiously he tried to keep up with Lystra as she darted through the maze of channels. Schools of fish scattered like jeweled rain. Opalescent jellyfish loomed ahead, and he swerved aside to avoid them.

Where had that monstrous Sharer got to now? Spinel paused at the surface to catch his breath, his feet paddling slowly.

A head popped up. "What's keeping you?" Lystra said. "Just go on down."

Fear gripped him; something was wrong. His arm thrashed out to get hold of a branchlet, and the branches raked his palm.

"You can't swim," Lystra noted as if to herself.

"I can too!" he shouted. "I can swim all the way past Trollbone Point."

Lystra's arm shot out and pulled him under, down toward the dim blueness. She's drowning me, his mind screamed. He pried at the claw that crushed his wrist and stretched his arm till it would snap. Nothing could slow this relentless plunge, deeper with every kick of Lystra's powerful legs. A vise of water inexorably clamped Spinel's chest; any moment now, his life would spill out in a stream of froth.

Unaccountably, air burst around him. Spinel choked and splashed, and the sounds echoed hollowly. His arm struck something hard—the roof of a clear, glassy bell that enclosed enough space for himself and Lystra to tread water underneath.

Lystra floated, her palms gliding in lazy circles. She waited for his breath to slow to normal. Then she turned to a rack of tools set in the bell. "Good," she said, as she pulled a belt of tools around her waist. "Stay here till I'm done with the starworm." She slipped out of the bell and spurted away, gliding in and out of the shadows cast by great branches above, until she reached . . .

A green swath stretched beyond, perhaps as long as a market square. Tiny Sharers hovered at its mouth, which sprouted a radial pattern of stalks with bulbous ends. The body was bound to the branches above it by a spidery mooring, except for the tail, which swung ponderously and spewed a white jet in a long, waving curve. Spinel watched the beast, awestruck. Could this be a "sea-swallower?"

The starworm was not a seaswallower, but a lesser cephaglobinid species. It fed on plankton and small fish filtered from the seawater pumping steadily through its gut. The stream from the gut of a score of starworms could propel a raft gradually, enough to keep the rafts together in a system of eight and to guide them into currents that did not veer too far poleward. To bind the starworms and steer their course, to clean their mouth filters and raise their hatchlings—these were jobs for Lystra and her sister wormrunners.

As Lystra approached, two wormrunners already circled above the swaying stalks of the starworm's mouth. Elonwy the Fearful was about Lystra's age, but Yinevra the Unforgiving was the senior wormrunner responsible for all twenty starworms. Yinevra grimaced and lifted an accusing hand to demand, "Why late today, Lystra?" That left a bitter taste in Lystra's mouth. The Valan creature had kept her back, for he could barely swim at all. Mercifully, Yinevra did not stop for a grilling. She was pale from need of oxygen, so she sped off to the airbell where Spinel had been left.

What Lystra was late for was the time for "farsharing," the sending of news by way of the starworm's song. The starworm produced its song in low-frequency sound waves from within its roiling gut. The form of the song could be directed to send news within hours all around the globe. Now, according to time-keeping clickflies, it was farsharing hour for Raia-el.

Already Elonwy had prepared a special bait, a good-sized red squid at the end of a grappling pole. Lystra kept herself prudently outside the reach of its arms. Elonwy held out to her another pole, Lystra grasped it, and together they maneuvered the squid into the treacherous vortex of the starworm's maw. This sudden bulky mouthful slowed the pumping to a trickle, as the beast paused to ingest it.

Now Lystra could swim safely to the lip, for a few minutes at least. As she neared it, she averted her eyes from the throbbing tunnel inside, almost furtively, almost the same way she avoided certain mental tunnels of her past and future. . . . She banished that thought and caught hold of one of the radial stalks of the "star" that rimmed the mouth. She sunk her feet into a valley between two of the stalks and steadied herself. Beyond, over the beast's hide, shafts of light flickered and danced through the crisscrossing cables that harnessed it fast to the raft. Those cables, made of coldstone, were gotten from the trader nowadays, Lystra reminded herself sourly. Were it up to her, though—

Enough of that: she had to be ready for the mindguide, the instrument that would tell the starworm what pattern of groans to make. Did Elonwy have the mindguide? No, Elonwy was whitening as her breathmicrobes used up their oxygen, so she swam over to the airbell. Elonwy's pregnancy was showing now, in the soft round of her belly; a couple of months more, and the Gathering would see that she sat out awhile.

Yinevra came to the starworm. From her hand dangled the

black, curling fingers of the mindguide. Yinevra's chin jutted critically, but Lystra would do this right. She took the mindguide and set its tendrils behind a radial stalk, just over the proper neural node. The mindguide would release a timed sequence of hormones, in a simple code. Simple messages would result: *Merwen the Impatient Home Safe with Valan Child. Strain Ler Is on Way to Aial-el.* This was a fungal strain to cure an outbreak of lethal fever; Usha had made the cure and sent a sample by clickfly to the lifeshaper of Aial-el. And lastly, to be repeated twice, *Motorboats Drown Starworm Song; Stop Use.* Yinevra had long suspected that Valan motors caused the troubling upsurge in ocean noise, which at times shortened transmission range to only a few hundred kilometers. Now she was certain, and even Merwen had no answer to this.

The black tendrils of the mindguide had settled, and their hormones would take effect within half an hour. Everyone would have to surface before then, because the song of the starworm, though below the frequency range of human hearing, was so loud underwater that its power could kill. So Lystra went to the airbell for a quick gulp of air, took Spinel, and rushed him up to a raft branch before his miserable breath gave out.

In an instant Yinevra swung up beside her. Her inner eyelids retracted, releasing the pent-up fury in her eyes. Her foot scooped up water and showered Lystra. "Why late today? You're never late. You know it's not fair to the other rafts if we overrun our time. You know I have to get to the Gathering. And whatever did you bring that idle Valan creature for, to drain off an airbell all morning?" Yinevra pointedly kept her back to Spinel. Fine wrinkles spanned her scalp, though she still had the chest and arms of a veteran wormrunner. Yinevra the Unforgiving was even surer about Valans than Lystra was, and *she* was older than Merwen.

"I'm sorry about the airbell." The pneumatophores that grew from it conducted air only so fast. "But I had to keep him from mischief," Lystra added. "We're going to the trader. I thought you might like a look at him, after all the fuss."

"A skinny runt, isn't he? Merwen thinks I'll take pity on him and forget how the traders drove my daughter mad."

Lystra grew numb. She did not want to think about Yinevra's daughter.

"Yes," said Yinevra, "I know your mother well. When will you take a selfname and join the Gathering? You of all sisters will add weight to the Doorclosers—"

"No. I'm not ready." *Don't ask me why,* she pleaded in silence.

Yinevra watched, her mouth twisting slowly. "Well, then. When you visit the trader, let him share ten lengths of cable. Several starworm moorings need repair."

Lystra was dismayed. "So soon? He asked for a whole boatload of seasilk, the last time."

"Bring medicines, then. Usha makes the best."

Lystra flushed at this praise of her mothersister. "Usha came home thin as silkweed. She works herself to the bone, in any case."

"If the starworms break loose now, we'll drift until—"

"*Shora,* no!" In two months, before winter set in, seaswallowers would migrate southward. A ring of ravenous whirlpools would sweep from pole to pole. In the tropics, the ring would stretch thinnest, and that was where Raia-el must stay.

"Then hunt a shockwraith. Shockwraith sinews held starworms fast for millennnia, before traders came."

"Shockwraiths shared a harsher roll." The scar across her mother's scalp had been left by a shockwraith, although Merwen had never shared the details with Lystra. An event over which Merwen could not weave words must be unspeakable indeed.

Yinevra gripped Lystra's chin, and her own jutted close. "My girl, you've said *no* five times in as many minutes and as many directions. Is that all the young are good for nowadays? When the time comes for Shora to choose, only two streams will flow: to close the Door, or die."

3

Spinel shivered and rubbed his palms, which were puckered from long immersion. The sun soon dried him except for his trunks, and those began to itch. One thought held him now: when he got back to the traders' raft, he would stay there, no matter what, until the next moonferry. He would do anything to get off this planet and back to Chrysoport, even if he had to spend the rest of his days chipping tesserae in his father's basement.

But first Lystra had to take him to the trader—if she ever meant to in the first place, which he doubted more than ever. He could take the boat himself, perhaps, though how would he navigate? These questions ran through his mind as he skipped down the raft branch after Lystra. At the far end, just where the branches thinned out and dipped under, there was a boat similar at first glance to Merwen's. Spinel ran ahead and hopped into the stern. "Hey, where's the motor?" The sternpost was bare.

Lystra turned on him. *"I've* never used those noisy stone objects, and you can tell every trader in sight I said so." She grasped a paddle and raised it so high he thought she would strike him. But the next instant, it plunged down at a raft branch. The boat shoved off gradually, loaded as it was with tied bundles of spun seasilk.

"I just asked," Spinel said sullenly. "What'll you do, then? Row this thing out on the open sea?"

She tossed her head and laughed. "No, I'll fly away to the Stone Moon. I'll do that, one of these days," she mused, half to herself. "And when I get there, Valan, you watch out."

"Look, if you really hate the moontraders, why do you bother with them at all?"

"A good question." Vengefully she shoved at the branch again. "I wish more of us were asking it. Ask Merwen: she was alive when the first traders came. But you must know for yourself, trader's brat."

Blood rushed to his face. Spinel clenched his fists, leaned across the seasilk, and shouted, "I'm nobody's brat, I'm a stone-cutter's son. I've got a decent father with a regular trade, which is more than *you* can say. None of you have any stonesigns; you're worse than beggars!"

Lystra eyed him coolly. "Only Valans consider begging a calling. What have *you* done, since you got here? Who's been at work all morning, and who will 'pay' for your food?"

"I said, I want *nothing from you!* I'm going home." He dove out and swam, with no idea where. Blindly he thrashed among the branches, heedless of the squid darting away or the jagged coral fans that loomed ahead without warning.

Within half a minute, something grabbed him from behind, digging into his shoulder. He choked and twisted around to fight it off. It was Lystra, who hoisted him roughly up a dry branch. Barnacles gouged his chest and arms, and blood trickled down; salt burned into the wounds.

"Sit still, for Shora's sake," Lystra gasped, and her breasts rose and fell. "Why do you think I walked the branch, instead of swimming? Fleshborers nest here."

Spinel looked down, and his scalp froze. The water churned with fleshborers, maddened by the blood scent, their jaws clicking shut just above the surface before they coiled under again. Finding no prey, the creatures snapped at each other, and soon chopped lengths of fleshborer littered the surface like boiled sausage.

Spinel's stomach heaved, empty though it was. When Lystra got up again, he followed her very closely, back to the boat. He watched the shadows weave among her ribs, and he thought, She went in, to get me.

Lystra was signaling with her fingers across the water. A glider squid rose from the depths and rolled over, exposing an owlish eye. From the boat, Lystra tossed something toward the squid, a mere sprinkling of powder, but the squid must have liked it. It came right up to the prow and let Lystra slip a harness on. The squid spurted ahead, and soon the boat sailed at a good clip, bouncing on the choppy waves.

They entered the traders' raft at a bay cut into the branched mesh, apparently for larger ships that docked on solid raft. White-washed concrete buildings clustered on the bay. The nearest one displayed the opal Hyalite sign above its door. "Hyalite—that's Lady Nisi's House," said Spinel.

"Yes," said Lystra. "The best of a bad lot. Nisi does reason with them, at times." She unstrapped the squid and tossed it some more powder. "There, that's good, isn't it," she crooned at the beast. "Just leave me my arm, thank you, old girl." She tied the boat at the dock, jumped out, and headed for the Hyalite shop.

Inside, the linoleum cooled Spinel's feet, and a welcome blessing it was. Odors of hardware and amberscent mingled curiously. The shelves offered desultory stock: flashlights, kitchen gadgets, a whole row of cameras, plastic basins in a pyramid of sizes. But there, right next to the gadgets, gemstones spilled out in bins: garnets, topaz, onyx.... The gems were unset and crudely polished, but he fingered them happily, savoring each taste of home. It was odd, though, for who would buy stones on Shora? Chrysolite, amberlite, emerald, sapphire...

Star sapphires. Spinel blinked and pulled back his hand. Starstones for sale, just like ordinary stone? No law forbade it, but even the most unbelieving Iridian would pause before wearing for mere decoration the sacred sign of a Spirit Caller.

"Help you, sir?" The proprietor leaned cheerfully on his elbows across the counter. He winked, and creases rippled from his lips. "Those gems sell like a shot around here. Natives snap them up. You're a new face, son; trade or trawler?" He glanced at Spinel's chest, which was blood-streaked and, as ever, bare of a stonesign.

"Neither." Spinel sighed. If he stayed on Shora, he'd never get a stonesign at all. But there was little chance of that. "You got any farm produce?"

"All you can eat, and not a week old."

A week old, and he was used to the freshly plucked harvest in Chrysoport. Still, he was so hungry his mouth watered even at yellow tomatoes and wilted cabbage. At last he would get something to eat.

Lystra was well acquainted with Kyril, the Hyalite trader, a thickset, phlegmatic fellow with the serenity of an anglerfish. Whatever else he was, he looked her in the eye every time, and for that she gave him credit.

Kyril turned from Spinel and smiled broadly at her. "Share the day, Lystra," he said in her tongue. "That squid out there—she's a handsome beast."

From the window, the glider squid could still be seen as it rocketed above the waves with its trailing jet, then dove once more. It was on the hunt, its appetite whetted by the taxing haul and by the special treats Lystra gave. "She's a strong one," Lystra admitted. "And reliable; she never dives when in harness."

"Handsome, for sure. You know, I could share something handsome for her. A collector I know would give anything; she's worth more than a dozen boatloads of seasilk."

Lystra wrinkled her nose. "I doubt she would like to live on Valedon."

Kyril chuckled. "How would you know, Lystra? Must everyone share your taste?"

"Of course not." She switched to Valan and raised her voice. *"This* creature, for instance, can't wait to quit Shora."

Spinel looked up. "Why shouldn't I? There's nothing for me here."

"We'll sign you on," Kyril offered. "Everyone's looking for help. You'll make your fortune."

"Really?"

That took her aback. "Never mind. Merwen has adopted him, for much more important work. He's hungry. What he eats, I will pay for."

At that, Spinel grabbed a loaf of bread and started to wolf it down.

Lystra plunked three coils of cable onto the counter.

Kyril nodded. "Payment in what? Redleaf? Medicine?"

"No, seasilk."

"Hm, that makes . . ." His eyes took on a guarded look.

"Price up again?"

"It's just a lot, for seasilk. Might run to three boatloads."

She could not have heard correctly. "A boatload for each coil?"

"Steel's in short supply on Valedon. What can I tell you?"

The two of them stared, face to face. Lystra's anger swelled until it burst. "What's the use, if you can't even manage your own planet properly? Everything is plentiful the first time you share it, but once we come to need it, it vanishes."

"Now that's unfair. Those roof panels stacked there in the corner have been dirt cheap for two years."

"That's because all the rafts of Per-elion decided not to buy them. In system Wan-elion, the panels cost five times as much."

"Supply and demand," Kyril patiently explained. "If I gave away everything for nothing, I'd lose my shirt before sundown."

"So what?"

Kyril appealed to Spinel. "See what I have to put up with? Don't I have needs too? You tell her."

Spinel turned away and took another loaf of bread. For his part, he wanted nothing to do with Lystra's behavior. It was bad enough that she had crossed a Valan threshold unclothed, more shameless than a streetwalker, but her rudeness to the proprietor was simply uncalled for.

Lystra herself neither knew or cared what Spinel thought. "Kyril," she said, "whatever *you need to live,* we will share until death. You have only to ask."

"The House of Hyalite needs seasilk, to pay me good *solidi,* so my children can eat. Valedon needs steel; if I were to sell it all, here, the economy would collapse."

"Then why did you bring it here in the first place? And why does it suddenly cost three times as much as before?"

Kyril shrugged. "What can I tell you? Demand fluctuates."

Pity overcame her, pity for his cravenness and his childlike perceptions. If Merwen were here, she would have given the trader anything, Lystra thought, just out of pity. That was why Lystra insisted on going herself, instead of Merwen. Yinevra would go, too, except for her daughter's condition.

Lystra leaned on the counter and faced him close. "I don't believe you, Kyril." Her pulse raced. Had she told a Sharer, *"You share an untruth,"* months of unspeaking would result between them.

"He's right," Spinel mumbled, his mouth full. "It's the Pyrrholite siege—"

"No, no, that's over now," Kyril said quickly.

"Siege? What siege?" Lystra demanded.

"Pyrrhopolis," said Spinel, "where they built the forbidden power station, to make their own firecrystals. The High Protector besieged it for months. Guns and planes and satellites that rain fire—a lot of steel goes into that stuff."

Puzzled, Lystra said, "To besiege with witnessers is one thing, but to 'rain fire'?" Whatever that was, it sounded irresponsible to her.

"It's to teach them a lesson."

Then she remembered, and her flesh crawled. "So all our trading goes to help one set of Valan creatures share distress with others." It revolted her, much as if a fleshborer had poked its head up and said, "Share the fun, Lystra."

"Now, Lystra," said Kyril, "you've got it all wrong. In fact, if the moontrade were more profitable there wouldn't even be a Pyrrholite campaign."

Spinel's mouth hung open. "What do you mean?"

"Listen, son. The moontrade's been in a slump ever since the purple plague here six years ago; it just hasn't expanded fast enough. The great Houses had to make up their losses somehow. So they unloaded their steel and concrete in Pyrrhopolis, for the fusion plant, and the High Protector looked the other way. Once the war's on, they sell firewhips and airstormers, and pay tax to Iridis, and everyone's happy."

"It can't be like that. The Patriarch wouldn't allow it."

"That's how the world is. I tell you, straight; I'm not one to pretty it up for you. If you can't beat it, join it, I say. Lystra—if you need cash, why not sign on to one of the trawlers? They could use a strong hand like you. The pay's even better than mine."

"And help you rake our rafts clean of fish?" She pushed the coiled cables aside. "Enough. Nisi—Lady Berenice—is back, and she will deal with you."

Kyril hesitated. "I'm sorry, sister, but the new policy is that we're not to listen to Lady Berenice."

"What do you mean? What has she done to you?"

"Nothing, but she's not my supervisor. My apologies for being unable to serve you . . ." His eyes shifted toward another customer who approached the counter.

It was Rilwen, Yinevra's daughter.

Lystra whitened at the fingertips. She leaned again on the counter to steady herself. Rilwen, whose love Lystra had shared since her sixteenth year, suffered from "stonesickness," the inexplicable craving for those objects shaped by death.

Rilwen's empty eyes did not even acknowledge Lystra's presence. She was emaciated, and with arms so thin they seemed translucent she lifted a basket of redleaf to the counter, redleaf herbs she must have searched for days to pluck and gather. From her fingers fell four polished stones from the trader's bin. They clicked on the counter and shined, bright and malevolent as the bulbs of a shockwraith.

Kyril did not look back to Lystra, although creases multiplied in his jaw. Without a word he accepted the exchange. Rilwen took the stones and turned away. Her shrunken toes scraped softly until she reached the doorway.

Rilwen! The cry from her mind seemed to echo throughout the store. In fact, not a sound had escaped her throat. The time for that, Lystra knew, was long past. She had tried, everyone had tried, to help cure Rilwen's growing obsession with those inconceivable, unnamable objects from the Stone Moon. At last there was nothing left but to leave her Unspoken, like a psychotic, alone on an offshoot raftling until she came to terms with herself. Unspeaking was not a sure cure for stonesickness—Lystra knew that, but neither lifeshapers nor wordweavers had yet found a better way for those afflicted by this illness unheard of before Valans came.

Gradually Lystra's breath returned. "You promised," she whispered, still staring at the doorway.

"Free sharing," Kyril muttered. "Share and share alike. New policy."

"You promised," she repeated. "Rilwen is ill."

Kyril cleared his throat. "The new rule is," he said louder, "that we share with whom we please. Look—" He stretched an arm toward Spinel. "Look, son, I ask you: What's a fellow to do? I'm here to keep my kids clothed and fed. Is a liquor dealer to blame for the drunks that wander in?" But Spinel only blinked at him confusedly.

"Do you now share with all our Unspoken?" Lystra asked. "Then all traders must go Unspoken." She heaved the cables forward; Kyril jumped as the coiled steel thudded behind the counter. And *we* will hunt shockwraith once more."

Kyril shrugged and looked down at his hands. "What can I tell you? Share the day, Lystra," he called as she stormed out. Just to shame him, she dumped her whole boatload of seasilk on the dock to pay for Spinel's bit of bread.

4

While Lystra was at the trading post, all the selfnamers of Raia-el were assembling upraft for a Gathering, the first Gathering of the raft since Merwen's return. Merwen came with Usha and Nisi, who supported Ama between them.

Ama spoke, in her small dry voice. "Was it wise, Merwen, to leave the young Valan with Lystra so soon?"

Merwen winced, reminded of certain things about Lystra that gave her pain. "They have to share the same silkhouse. If Lystra wishes to share harm, let her share his safekeeping instead. That is the quickest way."

Usha looked sideways. "Our daughter shares your stubborness, dear one. And you know which name she'll take when the time comes."

"Let her choose her own name," said Ama, "as Nisi will today."

Nisi shook like a school of startled minnows. "A selfnamer takes a name that fits . . . and spends the rest of her life disowning it." Nisi's drawn face sought approval; she must dread the storm she faced. Merwen squeezed her hand encouragingly, and Ama smiled. Of all the selfnamers of Raia-el, only Ama was so old and revered that the Gathering had formally forgotten her selfname. Merwen herself had a long way to go.

Up the raft, beyond the silkhouse, grew rows of buoyant airblossoms, kept aloft by reservoirs of secreted hydrogen gas. Beyond the airblossoms, the raft sloped upward gently, until it dipped to a hollow at the center. Selfnamers were converging here, over a hundred so far. Shaalrim the Lazy and Lalor the Absentminded were back, too, from Valedon. They both flashed dimpled smiles.

Across the group, Yinevra was talking with others, some of whom Merwen recognized from other rafts of Per-elion, and a

75

couple from a cluster many hundred raft-lengths away. That was typical, for selfnamers traveled often to share other Gatherings, to strengthen the bonds of Shora's web.

And yet, ordinary as this Gathering appeared, its message would be awaited by Gatherings across the globe, all eager to share Merwen's judgment from Valedon. Anger with Valans was at a crest, higher even than that time six years ago when lifeshapers of the Seventh Galactic had shaped a drug resistant breathmicrobe to scare Valans off this planet. As she watched those with Yinevra, Merwen wondered how many already were committed Doorclosers. She herself they called "Skycrosser," and she wondered ruefully if the Gathering had become a line with two sides instead of a circle.

From the center, Trurl Slowthinker snapped her fingerwebs to draw attention. Trurl looked down her long nose with the ambivalent dignity of a seahorse. She tended to keep her eyes half closed, as if full sight of the world's absurdity might be too much to bear. She sat down, crossed her legs, and waited until everyone hushed and sat likewise, with just their fingertips waving slightly above their knees. For a few minutes the Gathering lay still, still as a bed of anemones, still as the clouds stretched above in a herringbone line from one horizon to the other—still enough to drink in all the spirit and wisdom of Shora.

In the stillness, Merwen reminded herself that as a wordweaver she had to weave not just her own words but those of all others into a truth that all could share.

"Share the day, sisters." Trurl spoke. "Let it not be in vain that our nets lie idle." Trurl stretched a bony forefinger toward Merwen. "Impatient One, your own nets have moldered for months on Raia-el. Was it impatience that brought you back?"

There was murmured approval, and Merwen knew it was bad, worse even than she expected. She rose to her feet and surveyed her sisters, all seated in their tranquil triangular postures. For a moment she actually longed for the careless chatter and clutter around her in the Chrysoport place-of-dry-land. There was no room for carelessness here, only for the most skillful wordweaving she knew. "My sisters, perhaps it was impatience that brought me home, for as far as one swims there is no door more welcome than that of one's own home raft. And yet, several of us Sharers have actually crossed the sky to the Stone Moon this year; and I assure you, it was not for less love of home that Usha and I are the last to return."

Merwen paused, then went on. "Now that all are home, the Gathering may share the completion of our mission on Valedon. Our mission was to dwell in the Valan world, in order to share a fair judgment of Valan humanness. But before we proceed further, a new sister among us asks to share a selfname."

A few faces broke into eager smiles. Merwen winced; she knew they were expecting her own daughter Lystra. "She has shared our silkhouse like a daughter, and her seaname is Nisi."

There were confused looks, and voices rustled like raft blossoms in the wind. Trurl called, "Let Nisi stand, then."

But Yinevra stood instead. "Let's not be hasty, Impatient One. How can we proceed in this case, without the outcome of your mission?"

The voices dwindled in shocked silence. Trurl said, "It's unheard of to turn deaf ears to the offer of a selfname."

"A Valan among selfnamers is unheard of."

Merwen said, "Nisi is a Sharer."

"She's a Valan, and a trader at that."

Trurl's eyelids lifted slightly at Nisi. "Nisi has shared our ways for many years. She deserved a hearing, at least."

Merwen saw, though, how many sided with Yinevra. Even one sister opposed could block Nisi's acceptance, as for any decision of the Gathering. "Nisi will wait, but she must stay at least to share our judgment of her kind."

Some debate ensued. Shaalrim objected to the term "judgment," saying that they barely had spent enough time on the Stone Moon for learning, let along judging. Others were reluctant to proceed in the presence of one who was unnamed.

"Let her stay," said Yinevra at last. "But don't expect her presence to prejudice our thinking."

"No more than my own presence," said Merwen. "In fact, I'll sit down and let others first share their unprejudiced judgment of Valedon."

Yinevra sat immediately. She must have sensed a loss of face, for Merwen's sense of fairness was respected widely. Merwen sat and hugged Nisi, whose face was a picture of misery despite Usha's soothing words.

Trurl said, "We already know what the others found; only you two remain, Impatient and Inconsiderate. But for your sakes, let the Lazy One speak again."

With a shrug, Shaalrim the Lazy One stood. "Well, I can't say Valans are *not* human. They're excitable, and very fearful. Like a newly hatched squid—ink first, think next. Perhaps it comes of dwelling on the world's floor, among dead bones. That is why Valans wear rags: to distinguish the living from the dead. Lalor and I left our rags off, one hot day, and the Valans were so scared that they put us all alone in a stone cell."

"So sad," muttered Trurl. "And what happened then?"

"We entered whitetrance, what else? Our Valan sisters thought we were dying, and they tried to share food with long tubes—a crude attempt, but touching nonetheless. Then they put us on the moonferry, without even asking *payment.*" "Payment" was the traders' closest equivalent of sharing.

"Remarkable generosity," said Trurl. "Perhaps Valans are more generous on their home world."

Usha's brow was furrowing, and Merwen tried to warn her off, but it was no use. "What's all this nonsense, anyway?" Usha said without preamble. "I tell you, Valan genes can mingle with ours. We are one species. So what if some of them have fur and claws? Their mind structure is not just similar; it *is* ours."

Yinevra rose immediately. "So is that your fine conclusion, yours and Merwen's? *That* you could have told us from your microscope, without ever leaving your place of lifeshaping in the tunnels of Raia-el. But there is more to a human than physiology. Your mission was to see if Valans can *live* as humans, and therefore whether they may die only as humans."

She looked around her, but no one else seemed eager to take up the theme. "We all know how Valans lived on Shora. They share poison: poison for fish and poison for the mind. They share miraculous gifts, for impossible 'payments,' and what becomes of the gift in the end? Those fire-motors, now, on the boats—I have proof at last that their noise is what drowns out the starworms' songs, which once reached from here to the Eighth Galactic."

This last was a blow to Merwen. Everyone knew that it was she who, with Nisi's encouragement, had introduced fire-motors to Raia-el.

Triumphantly Yinevra concluded, "Valans don't live as humans; as lesser sharers, they have no place in the balance of life.

Even seaswallowers have a place on Shora. But the ocean turned for eons without Valans. So now let's get rid of them."

Usha said, "Look then to the face of the sea. Valans are your sisters, Unforgiver."

At that, Yinevra could barely speak with rage. She swallowed stiffly, and her fingertips whitened. "My own daughter is beyond hope; can I forgive that? Where is *your* daughter today?" She eyed Merwen.

Everyone hushed. Merwen's head swam, but she breathed steadily. It would save nothing to enter whitetrance now.

At such a point, Trurl looked reluctant to push ahead, and her eyes shut altogether. No one spoke until Ama raised her frail voice, forcing it so that as many as possible could hear. "I can't help but notice that nothing said of Valans or traders so far is any worse than what Sharers have been known to say of each other. There was the Great Unspeaking between systems Per-elion and Sril-elion, and for what? All for the right to conceive a few more daughters without burdening the life balance. The fury was enough to feed a pack of fleshborers. Yet I heard no talk, then, of 'getting rid.'"

They remembered. How could anyone forget the Silencings, and the Witnesses, when many boatloads of sisters had come to sit themselves on Raia-el in silent protest. The torn strands of sharing had taken years to weave back. But at last they did weave back together. True Sharers always did.

At last, Shaalrim rose again. "I think the Valan traders have learned to share, in some respects. They agreed to stop sharing stone with Yinevra's daughter and others who are stonesick. And they do restrain their poisons and fishing practices, when Nisi shares words with them. So let's try harder. We have Merwen the Impatient, the most gifted of wordweavers, who helped heal that Great Unspeaking before she even had a selfname, and whose wisdom has since been sought as far as the Fifth Galactic. Let her and others try as hard as we've tried before."

"Try?" Yinevra echoed. "What have we *not* tried that is human? And recall what is *not* human, how some Valans behave like fleshborers."

At that, several sisters turned rigid with shock, and others turned their backs.

"Don't look so scandalized," Yinevra went on. "Why are we here, if not to talk of *that?*"

Merwen closed her eyes. There had been incidents, especially in recent years, when Valans had deliberately shared physical injury among themselves or with Sharers, even to the point of death. And on Valedon, there were those who openly proclaimed that *death pays a wage*. Yet Valans never shared Unspeaking, or showed evidence of any sort of treatment for these obvious mental defects. The possibility of widespread psychosis was unimaginable, but it would have to be faced—if Valans were human.

"Wake up there, Impatient One." Trurl's call gave her a start. "If you insist on turning your name inside-out, we'll be here all day! Share what you found on Valedon."

So Merwen rose again. "Many Valans shared learning with us. Valans are quick to anger, and quick to forgive. Although incapable of whitetrance, they seemed to respect it in us, in their own world, as they do here."

"Not anymore," said Trurl. "While you were away, eight sisters of Lira-el climbed aboard a trawler to witness in whitetrance till the fishers stopped sweeping their raft channels. The witnessers were thrown overboard."

The news touched her first with pain, then with a bleak fa-ta-lism. "Nonetheless," Merwen insisted, "they may be able to *learn* whitetrance, if they overcome their fear." She wished for the thousandth time that Nisi would try.

This idea stirred interest. "Then perhaps they can take self-names too," someone suggested, "if their minds work like ours. Did you meet any selfnamers on Valedon?"

Merwen said nothing.

"No whitetrance and no selfname—it's a miracle they survive at all," said Trurl. "They must have *something* going for them."

Trurl nodded to a sister across the hollow, who asked, "Could it be that the persistence of malefreaks has kept the Valan race in a primitive state? Only lesser races produce males."

"Besides Nisi," Merwen quickly began, hoping to avoid another outburst from Usha, "the one Valan we met who might have taken a selfname happened to be male, an aged male who wore a star caught in stone. He called upon a spirit of life and power very close to the Shora we know, only this other spirit seemed to dwell far away, where few can hear her. That is why, the more important a decision is, for Valans, the fewer of them are allowed to make it."

Trurl sighed. "Even children know better than that."

"Without selfnames, Valans *are* children. They are locked into childhood."

Someone asked, "How can you say that Valans are children and not just primitive creatures? Lesser sharers?"

Merwen whispered, "I don't know."

"What? Speak up, please," said Trurl.

"I don't know. It will take generations to know for sure. That is why I brought Spinel home, a young male, to live with us." There, it was out now. She sat to catch her breath, while around her there were gasps at this radical notion.

Yinevra spoke again, as if she had read her mind; Yinevra, who had shared Merwen's life so closely for a time, long ago. And still, despite the years since they had flown apart, they knew each other's hearts so well. "My dear sister," Yinevra began slowly, "you have indeed turned your name inside out. You expect us to wait for generations to complete your mission."

"There is no other way. In the meantime, we must assume they are human."

"*Assume!* When they threaten the very web of life of Shora? We must tear them from the web, before it's too late."

Merwen said nothing. Even fleshborers had their place in the web, but Valans...

"Or do you think Valans already are bound tight in the weave? Listen: we can discard their fire-motors; we can even hunt the shockwraith again. We don't need traders—yet. We *can* close the Door."

Merwen took a deep breath. "Yinevra, I share your thinking. I spun and wove seasilk, for all those weeks that I sat under dry sun on Valedon. Yet I ask you, which of us here weaves more seasilk than Nisi the Valan?" Her voice had risen too high, and she lowered it so others would have to listen to hear. "I will tell you what else I learned on Valedon. They are dangerous, more dangerous than you can imagine. If they are not human, if they have no door to the self, then they are surely the most deadly creatures Shora has ever known. But suppose they are our sisters, as Usha says, and suppose they die at our hand. Who will share their destruction?"

The two stood, stares locked. Yinevra's back was as rigid as coral. Her chin lifted, a web's breadth, and tendons shifted in her neck. "Let the Valan speak for herself. Let her name the Three Doors."

The names of the Three Doors were the oldest test of a self-namer.

Nisi rose among them at last. Her skin was not yet dark, but lavender, as her breathmicrobes had begun to bloom again. Merwen sat down beside her and watched her feet, so small they were and naked of webbing, and toeclaws neatly clipped.

Yinevra said, "Name the First Door of Shora."

"The sun, which shares all life," Nisi responded.

"Name the Last Door."

"Death, which all . . . which each of us enters, yet none shares."

Yinevra paused, then with an extreme effort went on. "Name the Door of your own."

"Nisi the Deceiver."

Deceiver. . . . Merwen nodded slowly. It was a good name for Nisi, she understood. Around her, others sighed. They could hardly reject Nisi now—though a single voice would suffice.

Yinevra had not finished. Her lips knotted, then relaxed. "Deceiver," she whispered. "No name is harder to disown than that." She turned and walked straight out of the Gathering.

Merwen half rose, stifling a cry in her throat. *No*—Yinevra *must not* walk out now, though it was her right to abstain rather than block the will of the Gathering. Now, of all times, the Gathering must stand together. A victory without Yinevra was hollow indeed.

As Berenice watched the purple forms flexing their webbed limbs, she wondered how she managed to keep standing. Her mind still reeled at the impact of what she had heard. Out of the weft lines that shuttled and bound the fabric of the Gathering, one strand fell like lead to her palm: Sharers actually believed they could wipe her people off their planet, although they *would* not, if Valans *were* "people."

Could they do it? Perhaps the Envoy Malachite knew, or suspected. Berenice herself knew that Sharer lifeshaping went far beyond anything known on Valedon, but it had never crossed her mind that its function could be twisted. Yet why else were such sciences forbidden, throughout the planets of the Patriarch?

And Merwen's mission—there was more to it than she had dreamed at the worst. It chilled her to think how many Valan citizens might owe their lives to Merwen and to herself, Nisi the Deceiver. Yet how many Sharer lives would be doomed if she and

Spinel barred their last hope for self-defense? Her ears were ringing. Two moon-planets circled feverishly before her eyes. Berenice shook her head to clear it.

A primitive, childlike people, who knew nothing of will and power. That was what Talion thought of Sharers. And how could she explain otherwise, each side to the other? *Deceiver/Deceived* —the same word, in Sharer tongue. Was it deception to go on explaining something she herself did not fully understand? How well Nisi had chosen her name.

5

Spinel had run after Lystra to pay for the food. He did not understand about the seasilk, and she was too irate to explain. Before he knew it, they were out on the open sea again, the squid plowing ahead, and Spinel had missed his chance to escape. How could he have been such a trollhead? There was nothing for it, now, so he sat and kicked at the empty baskets, wishing he had the nerve to dump them overboard.

The scene with the trader had only confirmed his worst suspicions about his Sharer hosts. Before they left Valedon, Merwen and Usha had behaved something like nobles, resisting provincial authority and associating with the Hyalite lady. But here, on Shora, they lived no better than his own family, and with the trader Lystra had pulled a fit over prices that would shame any fishwife.

Back at Raia-el, Lystra stomped off to the silkhouse. Spinel sat by himself on a raft branch, mulling over the mess he was in. He plucked snails from the branch and tossed them down, imagining they would fall forever to the ocean floor, but they only bobbed up to the surface. For a moment the sky darkened as clouds passed the sun. A pale sickle appeared; was that ghost of a moon his Valedon? Was it only yesterday he had left his family in the harbor?

What would Beryl be doing? he wondered. Showing pearls to a customer, perhaps, or stirring the stewpot; yes, he could even smell the flavors drifting past his nose. His sister was a sly one, but she did as she was told, and she would never end up like him.

A hand tapped his shoulder, little Weia's hand, like a frog's leg against his skin. He slapped it hard.

The girl sucked in her breath, then shrieked and toddled off toward the silkhouse, falling over her feet now and then. Her wailing gave Spinel a vengeful satisfaction.

For a while, shadows lengthened as the sun descended. Then a figure emerged from the water. It was Merwen. Without a word, she climbed up and sat beside him on the branch. Beads of water sparkled on her shoulders and neck, and on the long scar on her scalp.

Spinel did not know what to say. His heart beat faster, until he exclaimed, "Well? What do you want of me?"

Merwen spread her hands before him. "If you are angry, I am the one to strike."

He drew back from her, repulsed, yet a bit ashamed nonetheless. "You're *weird,* you know that? Why the devil did you bring me here, anyhow? There's nothing for me to do."

"You'll be busy soon enough. You have to learn your way around first. You're too important to feed yourself to fleshborers on your first day."

"Why am I so important? Why did Lystra bother to pull me out, when she hates me so?"

"Because you are human."

"Is that all I am, a pet human? No, thanks. I'm going home." Already he saw the faces of his father and mother, joyful to have him home, though sorrowing at his failure. . . . Well, it was hardly his fault.

Merwen said, "The moonferry goes again next week. In the meantime, won't you share some supper?"

The cooking odors were not just his imagination. Could there actually be some real food cooking? Spinel went to see.

Outside the silkhouse, Shakers were gathered around steaming platters of fish, squid and shellfish of unnamable shapes but delectable aromas. It overwhelmed his senses; he had not seen so much food in one place since Beryl was married. It looked and smelled like a feast for kings.

He became aware that someone was singing. It was a low, twisting melody that never found a resting place. Soon Merwen joined, and Usha, and even Lystra and Lady Nisi, and others whose names he had forgotten. Their voices wove eerily with the roar of the sea. Spinel watched, mystified, until Lady Nisi leaned over to whisper, "We sing for the fish, for those sharers of our sea who die that we may feed."

Berenice was relieved that Spinel had survived Lystra's care, especially once she heard of the incident with stonesick Rilwen. What Tallion would say, if Sharers did boycott all the trading posts, right in front of Malachite's nose—the thought chilled her teeth. And the Gathering: a day later, and she might have lost her bid for a selfname. As it was, Yinevra had abstained, a bad sign for the future. And Torr only knew what steps other raft Gatherings would take.

Still, Merwen was not without supporters. As for this Chrysolite youth, if his presence could help at all to hold things together, even just to buy time, then he must be encouraged. At the moment, Spinel looked contented enough, as he gulped down whatever filled his plate and Flossa and Wellen tried to teach him the names of the "sharers" he was eating.

It had always seemed odd to Berenice that Sharers would sing as solemnly for the things they ate as for their own kind who died. A few, like Merwen, would not even eat flesh, only seaweed and seeds. The song, though, was seductive, and Berenice had at last come under its spell.

The sun ducked behind a cloud again. Berenice got up to check the solar cookers. She saw that juices still bubbled in the scallopshell vessels, and the lenses were in focus. So there would be no need to burn hydrogen today. That was just as well, since the harvest of hydrogenrich airblossoms was limited, while the sun itself was endless. Of course even airblossoms, like all lifestuff, also descended from the sun, the First Door of Shora. Or, as children were told, sea and sky are the twin breasts of Shora, and sun is the heart that beats behind them.

Usually Berenice ate with relish when she was here, for sheer hard work raised an appetite she never had in Iridis among her servos. Today, though, she tasted nothing. She was too tense, straining at the debate that smoldered among the Sharers as they dined.

Lystra said, "The best thing would be to shut down the trading post altogether." She chewed thoughtfully on a slice of octopus.

"Remember the slime mold at Oonli-el? Usha could start a mold that would spread over their raft and cover everything."

"That would be terribly impolite," observed Trurl Slowthinker.

"But that's just what they are asking for."

Berenice said, "Let me share speech with them again. I'm sure we can work something out."

"Hah." Lystra jabbed a forefinger in her direction. "Kyril said specifically that they Unspeak you. It's a 'new policy.'"

Something choked Berenice's throat, and she set her plate down. The least her father could have done was to inform her of a change in policy. If the Trade Council had taken a harder line, she must find out why.

"Still," said Trurl, "there must be a more reasonable solution." Trurl looked over to Spinel and called, in Valan, "What do you think? How can we help your traders see our difficulty?"

Spinel looked up. "Where I come from, if the barber gives you a rough shave, you cross the street next time."

"And what about the 'firemerchant'?" Merwen asked him.

"Oh, well." Spinel shrugged. "There's only one of him in town."

Trurl was thoroughly confused, but Lystra said, "He means, stop trading. He knows his own kind."

"Perhaps so. But the current is hard to swim against. Merwen, do you think we can afford to stop trading?"

"Perhaps," Merwen said, "you ask the wrong question."

"And you've got the right one to swallow me up."

Merwen smiled very slightly. "If Valans are our sisters, will our action reach into their hearts or will it glance away?"

No one spoke at first. The sun was reddening above the horizon. Flossa got up to pour water into the plantlights; a glow sprang out, casting multiple shadows. Spinel and Wellen were jabbing octopus beaks in each other's faces.

"You think we'd be wrong to stop trading," Lystra muttered. "Forgive me, Mother, but with your head in the clouds that's why they call you Skycrosser."

"I did not say what I think. But who names the sister who never looks up from her feet?"

Lystra glared back. "Why should traders care about our fish or about our Unspoken stonesick ones if we ourselves don't care enough to suffer for their sakes? If we endure without the things that traders share, perhaps they'll sit up and take notice. Myself, I'll be the first to hunt a shockwraith."

"I agree."

Lystra slumped as if a wall had given way. "You agree?"

Usha sighed. "Don't be so eager for the shockwraith's embrace."

"Merwen," said Berenice, much alarmed, "surely you've not turned against our Valan sisters?"

"Not at all. But words without action are as empty as a bleached whorlshell."

"Well said," agreed Trurl. "But feet speak louder than words only when all swim together, from all the rafts, even from all Shora. Will you help convince other Gatherings?"

"I will," said Merwen, sadly eyeing Berenice. You knew, Berenice thought suddenly; you must have known it would come to this. Was that what impelled you to Valedon, before it would be too late—before the Door began to close?

Merwen added, "Traders, like Yinevra, respect outward strength."

There was an uneasy pause. While it was custom for several families to share the evening meal, Yinevra and Merwen had not been seen together over food since the day Yinevra's daughter was Unspoken.

"My dear sister," said Trurl, "someone must start to heal this breach between you both."

"Yinevra will never change. She knows that I never doubted Valans were human, that I never intended to find otherwise."

Another pause, "Then why *did* you cross the sky? Just to appease the Gathering?"

"Many reasons. To touch the floor of the problems we face. To give Valans a chance to share judgment of us, in their own habitat. Can you imagine what they must think of us, having shared nothing but traders' tales?"

"Ah, so most Valans are very different from traders."

"Nisi is different, and she is a trader."

Lystra crossed her arms. "In that case, I invite Nisi to join our witness at the traders' door."

Berenice started. "I'm sorry, sister, but—"

"Why not, Deceiver? Do you share fear?"

"I can't do it. My own mother and mothersister. . . .*are* the trading post." Sharers had no word for "ownership."

"All the more reason, for you," said Lystra. "What respect do you share with your mother, if you can't even witness for her own good?"

"I'll do it the day you take a selfname."

"I Unspeak you till then."

It had happened so fast, Berenice regretted her words even as she spoke them. What had made her do this? She hated her mother, after all. Now there was no telling when Lystra would share speech again. Imagine what it was like when an entire Gathering Unspoke someone, or even Unspoke another Gathering. . . .

Thoroughly miserable, she looked away to the sea, where white crests languidly lapped the waves. She had to get away tonight, to report to the High Protector. She had planned to present Talion with her triumph at the Gathering, but this threat of a trade boycott would sour it.

After dinner there would be songs and storytelling and other learnsharing well into the evening, when the clickfly webs glowed fluorescently. Merwen told Spinel that it was "schooltime," and he objected, saying that he had finished his schooling two years before. Whereupon Trurl observed it was no wonder that Valans never grew into selfnamers, if they stopped learnsharing at a certain age.

Berenice enjoyed schooltime, but her errand tonight was urgent, and she left early, just after sunset. The Stone Moon was a gloomy beacon above her path. She could make out a bit of Iridian coastline within the moon's curve; from there, Talion's signal would soon activate a submerged transmission station. She clucked a few notes for clickflies. Several responded and chirruped what the time was, in Sharer units.

She hurried down a raft branch, slipping once in the fading light. At the familiar place, a dull red glow appeared in the water. It grew upward and became more distinct, until the top of the station surfaced and the hatch opened. Berenice climbed onto the housing and descended. The hatch closed above her, abruptly silencing the chant of the sea.

Bright light filled the close round chamber. Berenice squinted until her eyes adjusted. The High Protector appeared, a pallid image behind his desk.

His pursed lips betrayed surprise.

"Oh!" Berenice clapped a hand to her mouth. She had been so

upset that she had forgotten to pull on some clothes for this rendezvous. Now she could have died of embarrassment.

"Never mind," Talion assured her. "My field agents normally report in native dress."

"I'm not your agent," she returned sharply. She sat on a low bench built into the wall and crossed her arms to cover herself. "I'm a go-between. There's a difference."

Talion flexed his fingers and chose not to quibble. "Did you join the Gathering?"

"Indeed, yes. I took a selfname."

There was a pause as usual, due to interplanetary time lag. It lent their discourse an artificial air of solemnity. Berenice often tried to spot the change of expression which marked when he had heard her. This time, it might have been a lift in the lines of his forehead. "So," he said, "you really did pull it off."

"Are you surprised?" she asked. He might well be, she thought with pride. To her knowledge, no Valan had ever shared a Gathering before, since the day her father's first explorer ship set down on a raft.

"Not at all." His tone brightened. "And what is your 'selfname'?"

She hesitated, knowing he was sure to misunderstand. "It means 'Deceiver' or 'Deceived'—and not for the reason you think. Merwen knows that I come here."

"Of course, my lady, I know the game: now they'll trust you forever. You've told them, of course, about Malachite?"

"I mention him from time to time. They haven't the foggiest idea who he is and are unimpressed."

Talion looked relieved. Of course—he had simply hoped to assure himself that Sharers so far had no contact on their own with the Torran Envoy. Berenice frowned at herself, for she need not have given him that. "And what does Malachite think of your having relegated Sharers to subhuman status for thirty years?"

"He finds our former judgment reasonable enough, given that the Sharer race cannot interbreed with ours naturally."

"For anatomical reasons only." After generations of breeding without males, Sharer anatomy no longer enabled heterosexual coupling. Sharer women "conceived" by fusion of ova, a process requiring lifeshaper assistance and the consent of the Gathering. "But the genetic compatibility exists."

"Genetic compatibility may exist. But we do not legally possess the means to ascertain it."

"How very convenient." Berenice's words lengthened with irony. It should please you to hear that Sharers, too, have revised their estimate of our relationship. The Raia-el Gathering thinks Valans probably are human, after all. And therefore they just might not wipe us off their planet."

Talion's expression did not change. "Go on."

"I've told you, my lord, that Sharers are losing patience with us. And they have powers of which you know nothing."

The pause lengthened beyond interplanetary lag. "It's absurd," Talion exclaimed at last. "Their technology is pre-stone age, for Torr's sake."

"They descend from Primes," she pointed out. "Primes whom the Patriarch never bound. Perhaps they are post-metal age. They fulfill their needs entirely with organic 'lifestuff.'"

"Why have you never told me this?"

"I've tried," she said with immense satisfaction. "I told you how those 'clickflies' store more information by the genetic code than does the data bank of Palace Iridium. I told you how Sharer 'lifeshapers' regenerate mangled limbs and construct new living species to order, and you told me I was fooled by witchcraft." And after that, of course, she had stopped trying. He thought her crazy enough as it was.

"Survival with Forbidden Sciences? Impossible."

"Does Malachite think so?"

"Malachite has never been to Shora. The very existence of Sharers was unknown, before your father discovered them. Malachite knows only what you've told me."

So Talion *had* taken her seriously, enough so to report to the Patriarch. Berenice tried to hide her exultation.

"It's nonsense," Talion insisted. "Why don't Sharers turn their planet into a paradise? At the very least, they could exterminate seaswallowers."

Berenice sighed. This was the part she herself found hard to understand. "Sharers know their own limits; that, perhaps, is their greatest strength. They don't like to alter the life balance. Something worse might replace seaswallowers...." Every "lesser shearer" had its purpose, Sharers claimed. "But they do use their powers. Haven't certain fishing vessels run into environmental problems of late?"

"Well, well. So Sharers were behind that."

That made her uneasy; there might be reprisals now. "Under extreme provocation, my lord. You must understand this: When Valan actions disturb the sea, they threaten not only the livelihood but the very center of being of every Sharer of Shora—"

His hand must have risen to stop her at her first sentence. "I know what you wish, my lady. You wish me to turn back the clock to the days when a few rugged souls ventured into the boundless ocean world and bartered a few curios to peddle back home. Your father was the first, now the richest of the lot."

At that, Berenice swallowed hard. She ached to recall her earliest vision of Shora, when free trade had seemed much like the native concept of *sharing*, and each side had endless wonders to offer the other. Where had they gone wrong? Over the years a hidden venom had poisoned the dream. If only the Patriarch's Envoy could heal it again.

"I will not overburden the Trade Council," Talion went on. "Business has suffered enough from the war; you should know how many Pyrrholite contracts Hyalite lost. This is no time to cut prices on Shora, or to squeeze the fisheries just because they offend the native aesthetic. A few fishing lines can't clean out a whole ocean."

His attitude faintly disgusted her, although she herself had no proof of Sharer claims, only her faith in their word. "Something has to give," she said flatly. "Otherwise, the moontrade will face a boycott."

"Boycott? Explain yourself."

"They'll stop trading, stop talking; that's it." Her hand sliced the air. "Traders will go Unspoken by the Gatherings."

"So a few natives stop trading."

"But if it spread, my lord—"

"There's no leadership to organize them."

Berenice shrugged. "I've warned you before."

"Indeed, with phenomenal accuracy." Talion crossed his arms and leaned forward on his desk. "Just bear in mind that I commission you to report on trouble, not to instigate it."

She sat up, rigid. "Why, how could you suggest such a thing? Would I hurt my own father's business? I'm trying to dissuade Sharers from anything drastic. I told them I'd speak with the traders, and with you—"

"Silence." Talion waited for her to take in his command. "You know too well that the last thing I need is for those natives to turn up their noses at us, just as Malachite is about to look their way. If you help them scheme at our expense, my lady, you'll live to regret it."

"I am a Valan citizen," Berenice replied frostily. "I serve Valan interests in the broadest sense. If you don't trust me, my lord, then I'm wasting your time."

"I'll be the judge of my own time. And when Malachite appoints a High Protector of Shora, that is who I'll deal with."

A High Protector? For Sharers? She tried to keep her face straight.

On second thought, though, it was no laughing matter. It was the one thing that could save Sharers and Valan settlers alike—if Sharers would accept a Protector and face the Patriarch on their own.

6

Spinel found that of the countless seafoods and herbs that Sharers knew, there were more than enough to delight his tongue. Now that he was determined to try everything, his stomach rebelled at the unaccustomed onslaught, and by morning he groaned with indigestion.

So he was sent below to the place of lifeshaping. A doorhole opened in the floor of the silkhouse, and tunnels extended through the raft, winding in an eerie phosphorescent maze. Some opened into brilliantly lit chambers, and in one such place Usha sat him down for examination.

Usha took between her hands a fine, leafless vine which descended from a profusion of foilage at the ceiling. She set the vine below his ribs, and it swiftly snaked around his waist. Startled, Spinel pulled back, but Usha insisted that he stand still. As his eyes adjusted to the brilliance, he spotted sources of light tucked away amid leafy patches, but no sign of firecrystals. Vines like the one on his arm extended and curled in all directions, like cobwebs come alive. It made his skin crawl, and he would have hurried out, were not Usha standing over him.

As above in the silkhouse, there was no demarkation between wall and ceiling, though in some places shelves curved like pockets among the vines. The pockets held objects of coral and shell, and a sort of clear plastic, and fibrous seed pods the size of his fist. At any rate, nothing hurt yet, which was not bad for a visit to a doctor. In fact, his insides had stopped churning, and warmth diffused through his limbs. Energy surged into him; he wanted to spring up from the niche in the wall-floor that he sat in and dive into the sea to swim all day. But Usha's hand held his shoulder, and her grip was deceptively strong.

When at last the vine whipped off his waist, he felt just the faintest twinge of something pulling from his skin. "You mean that *thing* wormed into me?" He stared at the spot, which tickled a bit, though there was no blood.

"How else? Not just look pretty." Usha still spoke Valan crudely, half on purpose, Spinel suspected. "Have to stir up gut chemistry, for new bugs in food."

At that, he wrenched away from her and ran all the way outside.

For the next two weeks, Lystra stayed mainly out with the starworms, to Spinel's relief. Merwen traveled to distant rafts, bent on obscure missions of "wordweaving." So Spinel explored the branches with Flossa and Wellen, exhausting himself to keep up with their swimming. Usha gave him a skin oil that repelled fleshborers, and he soon learned to avoid the worst nests of them. Raft blossoms were shedding petals like golden confetti; soon their seeds would drop to sprout new raftlings in the sea. Beneath the petal-strewn waters, he went hunting for shellfish and even those nasty crab-beaked octopi. He gathered silkweed, and dried it on racks in the sun, and tried his hand at the loom. With Lady Nisi, who had grown purple as a Sharer, he stretched the woven silk onto raftwood frames and twisted them into the saddle-shapes that upheld the spires of the silkhouses. To stiffen the shapes, they used a pastic glue from those pesky legfish. Lady Nisi worked ceaselessly, as though it were nothing out of the ordinary for an Iridian lady to spend her days fixing a roof for stonesign-less moonwomen.

* * *

Berenice still hoped to forestall the trade boycott. At the Gathering of the System, for all eight rafts of Per-elion, she tried yet again to explain about Malachite.

It took half her strength just to rise to her feet amid this sea of faces, all dark as the depths of the ocean. How much harder it was to face several hundred "protectors" than one alone. "A messenger will come from the 'Patriarch.'" Her voice echoed from the rim of the hollow. "The Patriarch is a worldmother, like Shora. He will build understanding." Of course Sharers would hear "She," but Berenice could not think of the Patriarch as anything but male. "His messenger is a malefreak who knows Valans and shares care of them."

"A malefreak with a selfname?" someone asked. "I'd like to see that. He must be a wise one indeed to share care of so many children."

The selfname; that was a bridge to be crossed later. "This malefreak is very wise, as wise as the Patriarch."

"As wise as Shora?" asked one of the Doorclosers.

Berenice sensed a trap. "Who alone could be as wise as Shora?"

"If the Patriarch is so wise, then why does he grow so few selfnamers on Valedon?"

"Because he lives so far away, with more than ninety planets and trillions of people to share his care." And Shora, with less than a million, would have to learn to share that care. Now, though, was hardly the time to say so. As it was, Berenice's offer generated little interest. After all, how much could one selfnamer do, however wise, for all of Valedon's psychotic children?

It was hopeless; there would be a boycott. Even Merwen wanted it, although she did make one request. "Must we Unspeak the traders as well?"

The sharing that followed ended predictably with an outburst from Yinevra. "You never could stomach Unspeech," Yinevra charged, "even for the most incurable condition."

Berenice felt for Merwen, then; she knew what the wordweaver had suffered in the past, at the hand of some who were better left Unspoken. Merwen, however, did not rise to the bait. "I wonder," she said, "what this 'Patriarch' would think of a Gathering that sets a raft full of children afloat, Unspoken."

So, in the end the selfnamers reached unity to stop trading but left open the doors of speech. As usual, Berenice believed, Merwen the Impatient had wrought precisely what she wished of the Gathering.

Merwen herself felt nearly lost at sea, as events drew her to the lip of an intangible seaswallower. There were times, she thought, when a doorhole had to constrict just a bit to get unstuck, but once it closed altogether, what then? Only Nisi could hope to hold it open, and Spinel, if he became a Sharer in time. In her dreams Merwen still heard the tramp of boots on a sea of stone and saw Kaol the Dolomite with his knife at Usha's neck, he who had said, "Death pays a wage."

Meanwhile, starworms sang through the ocean and clickflies sped from raft to raft, system to system, all the way around Shora. Merwen herself sailed hundreds of raft-lengths behind a glider squid, despite Usha's fretting about the storm season, to share the boycott with as many Gatherings as she could reach. The boycott outraged some because it was impolite, and others because it was long overdue. In the end, nearly all rafts joined, and for days sisters could talk of nothing else but this unprecedented planetwide show of disapprobation.

Nonetheless, while all Shora watched the boycott and the silent witness at the traders' doors, Merwen watched Spinel. She waited, and she wondered. When the first test came, would he become a Sharer or not?

Spinel picked up more of what went on, nowadays. He knew of the trade boycott, and how Yinevra's witnessers sat on the steps all day to make sure that no sister "forgot." He shrugged it off as no concern of his. In Chrysoport, the same advice held for politics and the weather: watch where the wind blows, and don't tempt fate.

One day when he was out raking silkweed with Flossa, the twelve-year-old abruptly tossed her rake into the boat and insisted they return at once to the silkhouse.

"What," said Spinel, "tired already?" His own swimming strokes were getting stronger every day, and Flossa was just a girl, after all.

"The coralworms are dancing," Flossa said.

"So?" It was true, he saw; the coralworms swam wildly up and down, flailing their tails at random instead of darting at minnows and hatchling squid. "Won't eat *you*. Share fear with coralworm?" He was getting the hang of Sharer speech, a bit at a time.

Flossa wrinkled her nose at him. "Coralworms know when . . ." The last part escaped him. Flossa pointed to the sky; it was blue and still, but for a thin curdled cloud at the horizon.

By the time they reached the raft core, sisters were running in all directions, tying boats down and packing looms and cookers into the tunnels beneath the silkhouses. The wind whipped up, and clouds appeared from nowhere, billowing angrily and shutting out the sun. The ocean frothed and pounded over the outer branches, while the raft core rose and fell, buckling so far that cracks opened in the soil.

"What's keeping you?" cried Lady Nisi. "Get below, for Torr's sake." She whisked him down through the doorhole in the floor, through passages farther than he had ever ventured. At last the passage opened into a cosy hole where sleeping mats were arranged. Weia and Wellen already huddled among the blankets with grandmother Ama. Weia clung to Ama with one arm and squeezed a pillow with the other, her eyes wide and moist, yet too frightened to cry.

Spinel waited, somewhat scared, though vexed at being stowed away without knowing what was going on. Sharers came and went, and at the very last came Usha and Merwen.

Merwen's gaze swept the chamber. "Are we all here?"

"Yes," said Usha.

"The Unspoken as well?"

"What do you think?" was the sharp reply.

Spinel looked around, but he saw no Unspoken ones, aside from Lystra and Lady Nisi who had Unspoken each other alone. There must be other chambers, for the Unspoken, and for all the other families of the raft.

"Are the doors sealed?" Usha asked.

"From this end, yes, each behind me as I came. We're tight as a nautilus shell."

The sound of wind and sea was absent here, until the muffled clap of thunder arrived. For hours the raft heaved and rolled, and Spinel longed more than anything else to set foot on solid land once more; just once, and he would never touch the sea again.

Sharers huddled together, disconsolately at first; then they began to come alive and filled the time with song and learnsharing. Neighbors appeared, for all the tunnels seemed to interconnect beneath the silkhouses. Trurl brought a twisted flute of a shell that spiraled to a steep point. Everyone hushed to hear her play, with no accompaniment but the intermittent groan of thunder. Food was passed around, dried octopus and pickled seaweed, and even "pudding," which did not taste so bad if Spinel could forget what was in it.

The storm died at last, but most of the outer tunnels were flooded, so Spinel had to emerge from a different entrance. It mattered little, since all the silkhouses were gone. Where Merwen had lived, only a few battered fragments of paneling still stood, jagged as a cracked eggshell. The surface of the raft was torn and stripped to the gnarled wooden core, while many outlying branches had been ripped off altogether. Some floated beyond, thudding when they crashed.

Spinel was stunned at the wreckage, but everyone else seemed too busy for that, sweeping debris, and pumping out flooded tunnels, and hauling up the new silk panels he and Lady Nisi had built and stored below.

"Be easy," said Merwen, sensing his distress. "It will be months till we get another storm that big."

"But everything is . . . gone."

"Only the outer shell. *We're* still here. What else do we need?" Merwen peered at him earnestly, but Spinel was deeply shaken. "We'll build a new house," she said, "and paint new designs in all the wall moss. It will make a lovely change."

It made no sense to someone whose own home, modest though it was, had stood for generations, the one bit of property his family could call their own.

Spinel could not easily shake off his depression, though the sky was at peace now, with clouds that were but puffs from a grandfather's pipe, and the sea was mirror-smooth. He threw himself into the rebuilding of the silkhouse and took to scaling it to patch the seams with legfish glue. His coordination was good, and he swung like a monkey among the ladders and handholds. Even Lystra was heard to mutter approval of his skill.

He often swam without his shorts, now, and they finally vanished, as had the rest of his clothing—how, he did not know, although he suspected that imp Wellen. Well, if that was how they felt about it, he couldn't care anymore.

Spinel's dark skin was tanned nearly black from long exposure. One afternoon on the rooftop, he leaned on an arm to rest and wiped the sweat from his face, shaggy with hair and unshaven beard. As his hand fell, an odd color flashed from his relatively pale palm: a touch of lavender, faint but unmistakable. He scratched at it; the hue reddened, but remained. It was there, on his soles, too, and parts his shorts had covered.

It had happened to Lady Nisi, of course, but—surely she did it on purpose? Spinel had no intention, had never dreamed it would just happen to him.

To Spinel, at that instant, it meant one thing: he was metamorphosing into a moon-creature.

The shock exploded through him. He screamed and lost his hold; the sky tilted over, a bottomless ocean. Somehow instinct brought him safely to the raft, but he was still screaming when he got there. Sharers reached out to him with livid limbs and flippers, grotesque signs of what he would become. Spinel thrust them away and ran, without knowing where. Somehow he craved shelter, a cocoon to hide away from them. The tunnels: he slipped through the floor doorhole and dove blindly through the maze until no one followed. At last, he came to a stop and crouched in the curve of a raftwood trunk, shivering, hugging his knees to his chest. There was only a dim yellowish light, and his skin no longer horrified him. He squeezed himself all over as if by sheer force of will he could keep himself from becoming a monster.

Someone made a sound at the bend of the tunnel. Spinel yelled so hard he could not hear his own words. Whoever it was, she retreated. Spinel waited on in numb quiet. Time seemed to hold still.

A flashlight switched on: a Valan flashlight, whose cold white beam brought a sense of normality. Lady Nisi held the light, as she stood there, clothed as before, normal except for her own purple skin. She shook her head sadly. "You didn't know, did you. Merwen should have told you, given you time. Even she is no perfect learnsharer.

"Listen," Lady Nisi went on. "There's nothing to fear. Breathmicrobes just breathe from the water, and store more oxygen than they need. It won't hurt you. You didn't even notice, did you?"

She crouched close to him and set the flashlight down. "Do you know how Flossa stays under so long? You will, too—not quite so long, you lack the extra pores in your skin, but ten minutes, perhaps, between breaths. You'll feel like a fish."

A *fish?* Spinel dug his back into the raftwood until he ached. "No," he croaked; his tongue was swollen. I won't . . . turn into—"

"*You* won't change at all. Sharers took generations to evolve that way. Look at me: my fingers are free, my feet are small, my hair grows until I shave it. I'm no fish."

"But now you're all *purple,* like them."

"I get rid of it, when I wish. You saw me white, in Iridis."

Hope leaped into his heart. "How did you get rid of it."

"Spinel, listen to me." Her hands twisted nervously. "I spent my childhood here. I played water games with Sharer children, I ate seaweed and 'pudding,' I learned to understand . . . at least, to know sisters like Merwen. Then my parents took me back to Iridis, to find a noble husband and enjoy our wealth. We never had to leave Upper Level again, never needed what servos could not bring, never had to touch the sea . . . do you understand?

"The day came, though, when I did need something I couldn't find there. I came back to Shora, and this time I wanted to *be* a Sharer as much as I could. So I stopped taking medicine and let the purple bloom."

"Medicine? What medicine?"

"I thought I would die, at first, I—" She choked on her words. "I couldn't recognize myself in the mirror."

Spinel said, "I just wanted to be *normal.* You've got the medicine, I know," he added breathlessly.

"But it passed," she went on. "Now I find peace here, and a purpose I never expected—"

"The me-di-cine, my lady!"

"Child, don't you see what a privilege you have? On Valedon, you are nothing; you're dirt in the street. Here, you're as good as anyone, as important as a Protector."

"No-oo," he wailed. "Give me the medicine!"

Her talar whished as she rose. Her nose and cheekbones were set in crystal, just as on that day in Iridis. Her hand jerked at him, and pills clinked on the raftwood. "There, craven commoner." In an instant she was gone.

Spinel lunged across the uneven floor and groped for the pills, which hid among shadows in the flashlight's beam. He caught one and fumblingly slipped it in his mouth. It choked up again, hard as a marble in his swollen throat. Spinel closed his eyes and tried to relax. He was alone, so alone. . . .

A simple question came, then: What next? He closed his eyes

tighter, but the question remained. What would he do next, Spinel the stoncutter's son? Must he go back to Chrysoport a failure? His mother would smother him in her arms and say, "There, now, my child, it's a troll's luck you've had."

His eyes opened, and the flashlight mocked him. He saw himself, a beggar grasping for a handout from a noble Iridian who sneered at his helplessness while condescending to help him. For a minute he hated her so much, he could have torn off her highborn clothes and beaten her to a pulp. He pounded the floor with his fists until they ached.

The release of anger calmed him. Lady Nisi had brought truth, however much it stung. On the "Stone Moon," his life meant nothing, except to a desperate family who had tearfully sent him packing, lest they lose the shoneshop. Here, though, he could prove himself as good as anyone, even Merwen. But could he pay the price to share this ocean world?

When Spinel emerged, dusk had fallen, deep as if a webbed hand cupped the sky. He came slowly, almost sleepwalking. Something itched on his palms, and he forced himself to look at them. There were brown crusts where his nails had scratched his own skin.

Many sisters were waiting. Only Merwen dared approach him, and she did not speak.

Spinel looked at her. "Share the dusk, Merwen." The low voice did not sound like his own.

"And all the days after." Her eyes pleaded with him. "Did you choose? Are you one of us, now?"

Spinel raised a blood-streaked hand. "What else will I have to share?"

She let out a long sigh. "Now you know why I am called Impatient." She fit her hand to his, and the thin scallops spanned briefly between their fingers. "Nonetheless," she said, "I will die to keep you from such pain again."

7

For several days Spinel kept to himself. As his color deepened, palms to amethyst and legs to coal, he found he could dive ever deeper beneath the raft branches. It was nothing for him to reach the airbell, now. A sense of power thrilled him and partly filled the well of strangeness.

Now he had time to absorb the silent drama that pulsed below the waves. Hungry eels hid in wait beneath raft seedlings, which now dotted the sea like copper medals. A fanwing's egg stretched and strained until the tadpole burst out and flittered away, to swim and grow until it sprouted wings. At the coral forest, a beakfish crunched the hard stalks with enormous jaws that never tired. After some minutes of this calciferous grazing, a puff of sand would spout from its tail. Spinel wondered how long a beach a beakfish could fill, were the sand not destined to fall several kilometers below.

Spinel was now more than simply curious about Shora. Something compelled him to come to grips with this place that was inexorably becoming a part of him. At times, he still wondered about his family, and whether his mother had sent him a letter, which he could not pick up from the trading post. He wondered more about that trade boycott, and just what all the fuss was for.

Even Flossa and Wellen chattered about the boycott as they mended their fishing nets, and the evening schooltime was full of it. Lystra and others had been dumped in the sea, for sitting like coral stalks upon the shop steps to prevent trade. After the dumping, of course, the last Gatherings holding out for trade gave way, and the boycott was total.

Merwen, however, was disappointed because the traders refused to speak with any Sharer who would not trade. "In effect, we are Unspoken," she said. "This door will be hard to unstick."

For the first time, Spinel seriously considered these questions

for himself. He descended to the chambers of lifeshaping to ask
Usha, "Why does Lystra fear stone? Is she allergic or something?"

"Nonsense." Usha was fondling Weia with one hand while snaking vines into a plant gall with the other, a procedure intently
scrutinized by Mirri, the apprentice lifeshaper. "People fear
stone," Usha said, "because it contains never-life."

"Non-life? You mean, death?"

"Nonsense," she repeated vehemently. "What's to fear about
death? Death is natural. Stone is *never*-life."

Spinel took another tack. "If they fear it, then how come
enough Sharers want it so the traders stock shelves full?"

"How should I know? Why do Valans drink the toxic waste
product of sugar-eating yeast?" Usha picked up Weia, who was
whining for attention, and started to murmur in Sharer tongue with
Mirri about the vines and the plant gall.

Much annoyed, Spinel stomped back up the tunnel.

At sleep time, he caught Lady Nisi before a mirror tacked onto
a rib of the wall-ceiling. Nisi was shaving herself all over with an
electric razor. Spinel watched thoughtfully, then stole a glimpse of
himself: over a month's growth of matted hair and beard. He
looked again at the shaver. "Can I borrow that?"

"Very well. I'll help, if you—"

But he did it himself. The bladeless Iridian firetoy amused him
as it cleanly swept his locks to oblivion. Fingertips of air brushed
his head and his armpits; it gave him gooseflesh. "Now I look
worse than a plucked chicken," he ruefully told the mirror. "That,
or a dyed egg." As he watched the black face and indigo scalp that
were his own, fear welled up him, a sense of falling into a frenzied
unknown. This time, he submerged the fear.

"Well, don't let it go a month, next time." Lady Nisi cocked
her head and looked him over, as she might a statuette for sale.

"How many *solidi?*"

She laughed and clicked the razor into its case.

"Lady Nisi, what does Lystra fear about stone?"

"Why not ask her?"

"She'd throw me to the fleshborers if I did."

Nisi's lips curved downward. "You should know Sharers better
than that."

"But you know them even better. Can't you say why?"

She gazed pointedly at his palms. "Few fears are rational."

"I'm no commoner, anymore."

Startled, she glanced away. "No, I suppose not." She paused thoughtfully. "Sharers...envision a life force, a sort of living ether, that pervades every atom of their universe. Each drop of water, each breath of air, holds a thousand bits of life in it, growing and struggling."

"Ugh." His flesh crawled.

Nisi laughed. "Why, even without breathmicrobes, the bacteria in your gut outnumber your own body cells. And you'd be very sick without them, even on Valedon.

"On Shora," she went on, "life builds everything, from raft to coral. Whereas Valedon's ocean breaks upon crystal rock, a thing never shaped by life—"

"But the granite that makes up the foundation; this was born of fire, not water. In Sharer experience, only the dead ever reach that foundation."

Spinel was not satisfied. "Seashells are as dead as granite. Do Sharers fear death that much?"

"What you know as death is the last of their fears. That death is but a passage, a Last Door, between one being and the next. Only a kind of death that *is*, without beginning or end, can really scare a Sharer."

The next morning, Wellen threw a tantrum because Spinel had lost his hair, and if he kept on changing, her friends on the next raft would not believe a genuine Valan creature was living on Raia-el anymore. Spinel ignored her, tired of children's games, and from then on the younger girls ignored him.

He looked out to sea, where the raft seedlings were growing at such a rate that they would clog the surface before long. The morning breeze gave him a slight chill. Sharers whispered that the raft system had gone farther north than it should, because the current was strong and because starworms on several rafts had been torn loose in the storm. More starworms must be installed, but that would take time, and mooring cables were in short supply. If the boycott did not end soon, a shockwraith would have to be caught. Already scouts were exploring the raft underside, where those dreaded beasts dwelled.

"Share the morning, Spinel," said Lystra abruptly. "Will you share a boat ride with me?"

It was the first time she had addressed him in Sharer tongue. Spinel stood a little taller. "A boat to where?"

"To see a friend."

"Someone I know?"

"Rilwen."

Spinel blinked. "Not . . . is she no longer Unspoken?" It could be, he thought. Just recently a sister on Umesh-el raft had returned from a year Unspoken for *death-hastening;* that is, causing a fatal accident. They said she had spoken to someone in whitetrance, though how that could hasten death Spinel had no idea.

At any rate, from Lystra's expression he guessed the Rilwen had not returned.

"Once in a while," Lystra said, "one must check to see that she is well, physically, and wants for nothing. And just perhaps—" Lystra stopped short and turned her head.

She had packed food and blankets into the boat. She rowed out just past the branch channels, slowly, giving Spinel a chance to push aside the raft seedlings. They came to a miniature raft, an offshoot of a trunk that dipped from the main raft and reemerged. It was mostly open branches, with barely an acre matted solid in the center.

Lystra got out, swung the bundles over her shoulder, and walked ahead as if unconscious of Spinel. There was one small shelter of seasilk, half a dozen panels, with frayed strands that stirred in the keening breeze. Beside the shelter lay a heap of pebbles. Spinel peered at them curiously. Gemstones glittered at random: blood-red garnets next to creamy opals, agates, turquoise, and starstones, a veritable troll's hoard. The oddness of it set his scalp tingling.

Meanwhile, Lystra had located Rilwen, the emaciated form whose appearance in Kyril's shop had unleashed Lystra's fury. Rilwen sat crosslegged beside the shelter, her back slumped, facing out to sea. Her pelvic bones stood out like the rim of a bowl.

"Don't you ever eat?" Lystra was saying.

That surprised Spinel. The Gathering would be angry with Lystra, if they knew; they might Unspeak Lystra, too. Rilwen's reply escaped him on the wind. He inched nearer.

"What do you mean, 'no time'?" Lystra demanded. "What else have you got, if not time? You need to eat fish, not time. Eat time, and time eats you."

Rilwen caught sight of Spinel, and her sunken face swung around.

"A friend of Merwen's," said Lystra. "Remember, at the trader?"

She pulled back, her bones flowing into the raft. "Are sisters becoming worm-fingered malefreaks? What illness is this?"

"Spinel is Valan-born. Even his seaname is a 'stone.'" Lystra used the Valan word.

"How can that be?" Rilwen wondered. "Shora would never share a dead name. . . ." She swallowed with difficulty. "If I could be a child again—"

"You *are* a child again," Lystra said grimly. "You have been for two years and more. When will it end?"

Rilwen seemed not to hear.

"Then tell Spinel why you stay here, Unspoken. Spinel is a shaper of stone."

Her eyes widened at him. Uneasily Spinel stepped back a pace, thinking that the Gathering could Unspeak him, too. But Rilwen lunged at the mound of pebbles and scooped up a palmful, which she held in his face. "Then you . . . explain . . . which cups nothingness into a shape one can touch and feel."

Spinel flinched at this demand, of which he had missed half the words. "Well," he muttered, "it's just, you know, the stuff a planet's made of."

"Not lifestuff. No living thing made these."

"Well, people can make some kinds, out of fire and—" He lacked the Sharer words. "Anyhow, people cut stones, polish them, and even add colors."

"But do you *shape* stone from your own flesh, as you grow bone, as the snail grows its shell?"

"A lot of sweat goes into it, I'll say that."

Rilwen considered this. "If I could just see that . . . it might make a difference. Traders never shape stone. They call it . . . that prisons nothingness."

Spinel knew he had missed something.

"Magic," Lystra translated. "Magic shells of emptiness. That is what Kyril calls stone."

Blood rushed to his face. "It is not magic. It's hard work—our hard work. Where do you think traders get their gemstones? I should know." Crystal structures, cleavage planes, and all his father's teachings whirled in his mind, trapped in words he could not translate.

Rilwen held up a starstone. "A star from the sky, trapped inside. That is what they say."

"Some of us know better," said Lystra.

"You don't."

Lystra shuddered all over. "I should not be here. *Eat* something, will you? I'll wait for you, always."

"Always I go back to the Valan raft," Rilwen went on, "always hoping that the next stone I find will reveal the mystery. And when I do find out, Lystra, I will share it with you."

Lystra tore herself away, and Spinel hurried after her.

As they rowed back to the raft core, Spinel's eyebrows knotted and he jabbed angrily at the raft seedlings that lay ahead. What right did any merchant have to deny Spinel's craft, that which earned his father bread? Nisi was a trader; he would get the truth from her. How in Torr's name had she dared return to Shora, knowing what her own House had done?

"By all the Nine Legions," he exclaimed in Valan, "you should call on the Patriarch for justice."

"Whose fault is obsession?" Lystra asked. "What would your 'Patriarch' say? Should we not share our own cure, first?"

"Sickness is bad," he agreed, "but to feed on someone else's sickness is worse."

"That's why we stopped sharing with traders. We must not feed on their sickness."

Spinel thought this over. The boat swayed as a broad raft seedling bumped up against it, unheeded. "Do you still sit on the traders' steps?"

"Always. At each shop, a few of us witness. My shift is this afternoon."

"Then I'll go with you." Immediately he felt better, knowing he could do something, however small. What would old Uriel the Spirit Caller say, if he knew the use of starstones on Shora?

When Spinel and Lystra arrived at the traders' raft, there were five sisters sitting on the doorstep of Kyril's shop. Trurl and Yinevra he knew, and Elonwy the Fearful, a wormrunner whose belly was full and stretchmarked with child. The others Lystra named from Kiri-el and from another neighboring raft. Yinevra got up to let Lystra take her place. Yinevra's needle eyes stared at Spinel, but she left without a word.

Trurl moved aside, pressing into her neighbor to make room for two of them on the step. Spinel and Lystra inserted themselves in the lineup, a solid wall of amethyst at the trader's door. Their scent mingled headily with the spices and oil smells at his back, from the shop.

Behind in the shop, hidden voices were muttering. Spinel's pulse quickened. "Will they dump us in the sea?"

"Sh," said Trurl. "They gave up on that last week. But they still refuse to share speech."

He sat on in silence. In the harbor, tugboats churned to keep pace with the Sharer raft system. The sea rumbled and groaned, a counterpoint to the muffled voices and footfalls from behind. How many names could come from the sea? Merwen, Usha, Lystra... Spinel? Perhaps the sea would call every name, sometime, if only you waited long enough.

The sun was high, and sweat beaded on their foreheads though the air was still cool. Spinel felt comfortably warm, even sleepy, propped up by Trurl on one side and Lystra on the other. Aside from tugboats, the harbor was deserted, until a small Sharer rowboat appeared. The boat docked, and its occupant walked toward the shop. She was Rilwen.

Lystra's leg tautened beneath his arm. Spinel breathed faster. He wondered whether Rilwen meant to join them or climb over them. Instead, she came to a halt several paces away and gravely regarded her sisters. Then she seated herself crosslegged, facing them, a hunched sphinx. For a long while they sat thus, stare into stare.

Something yanked Spinel's shoulder and dragged him up the step. He cried out and twisted in the doorway, to face a hulk of a man in billowing shirt and trousers who thrust his lips out in amazement. "By the Nine," the man growled down at Spinel, "just what're the likes of *you* doing here? If you're a catfish, I'm a cut chalcedony."

"What do you mean, 'catfish'? I'm—" Spinel grimaced and stumbled as the man pulled him into the shop.

"Easy now," called a voice from the darkness. As Spinel's eyes adjusted to the absence of sunlight, he recognized Kyril behind the counter. The face of the genial proprietor was now drawn and tight-lipped. "Son," Kyril said, "you look like you need to raise your dose of Apurpure."

"What dose? Let me go."

"Catfish-lover." His captor's grip drove pins into his flesh.

"That Hyalite degenerate is bad enough—at least she comes here dressed decent. You know you'll sprout gills and a tail before long?"

"That's a damned—" Spinel swallowed the rest of his retort, fearing the fellow would smash his face in.

"Release him, Rutile," said Kyril in a tired voice.

Rutile did so, with a shove.

"Son, you're in bad trouble," said Kyril. "We could ship you back to prison."

"Prison? What for?

"Disorderly conduct. Indecent exposure."

Spinel flushed. "I'll ship *you* back. For lies and indecent pricing. And selling starstones, to boot."

Rutile grumbled, *"That's* a lie. No law against it, anyhow." But he sketched a starsign in the air.

"False advertising?" Kyril suggested with a quirk in his lip. "You might have a case—against the Hyalite House, not us. Son, do you think I see any of those profits? I earn a wage; I got a wife and kids back home. And we're all scared out of our socks, now that the moon trade's dropped to zero. The Council is ready to fire the lot of us."

"Well," said Spinel, "I used to go hungry sometimes, when the stoneshop got no customers. But at least we did honest work."

"Let me at him," said Rutile. "I'll teach the kid a lesson."

"Look, son," said Kyril, "I'll drop charges, if you cooperate. I must send you back to Valedon, for your own good."

"No." Whatever would Cyan say, to have him back in disgrace? Spinel raised his voice. "No, you can't send me back!"

The men looked up. Sharers from the step were entering the store, Lystra, Trurl, and the Kiri-el sister. "Share the day, sisters," came Trurl's nasal voice. "We are deeply honored that at least you share words with us. Has Spinel explained the case to your satisfaction?"

"Cursed catfish! Get out, or I'll—"

"Shut up, Rutile," Kyril barked at him. In a cordial tone he said, "Share the day, Trurl Slowthinker. Did Sharers not agree to remain outside the shop, if left alone?"

"But sister Rutile herself invited one of us inside."

"The boy is a Valan, subject to Valan law."

"Indeed," said Trurl. "Spinel is even a 'shaper of stone.' Did he share with you our problem of stonetrading?"

"He accused us of 'liesharing.' It takes two to share a lie," Kyril said smoothly.

"And two to cure it," Trurl agreed.

"Get out!" Rutile was hoarse. "They broke the truce; dump them, I say."

"Leave us," Kyril pleaded. "Leave now, and we'll keep the peace."

"You are angry. You are unable to share reason now. We'll leave." Trurl headed for the door, and the others followed.

Spinel started out, but Rutile's arm snagged him. "Ow! Let me go."

Lystra swung her hip back through the doorway. "Spinel comes too."

"We're just sending him home," said Kyril.

"No, you won't, you'll send me to—"

Rutile clapped a hand over Spinel's mouth. Spinel writhed and tried to scream.

"Spinel comes too," Lystra repeated.

The other sisters entered the shop, all five of them.

"I can't take any more!" Rutile yelled over Spinel's ear. "If I don't dump them out, I'll knock them all senseless."

Kyril threw up his hands. "What can I tell you? Go on, dump them in the sea."

Rutile bellowed some names, and other men appeared. Over the din, Lystra called out, "If Spinel doesn't come too, every mother and child of Per-elion will show up tomorrow, enough of us to sink your raft."

"We'll dump him too, the catfish-lover. Haul them out, men," ordered Rutile.

The Sharers went limp. Their flesh squeaked on the linoleum as they were dragged out by their feet, including pregnant Elonwy, with some difficulty since a fully relaxed body is slippery to maneuver. Spinel kicked and bit at the three Valans who hustled him out, until one cuffed his head and stunned him. All seven witnessers were crowded into a small craft similar to the one in which Merwen and Usha had lived on Valedon. When the traders' raft dipped out of sight, all were shoved overboard.

Spinel gasped for breath among the rolling waves. Lystra and Trurl made sure he kept up with them for the long pull back to Raia-el.

* * *

After diner, Berenice was looking forward to schooltime, when Spinel turned to her. "I know where your 'wealth' comes from, Nisi the Deceiver." He spoke Sharer, except for the one word.

Berenice realized, with alarm and a touch of envy, that Spinel was absorbing Shora far more rapidly than she had, for all her childhood years on the Ocean Moon. Merwen's success had astounded her; she had been convinced the sudden "purple" would drive Spinel mad. Perhaps the way of Sharers came easier to a signless youth with so little to lose.

"I know my own name, at least," she replied to him.

"So you're frank about liesharing. What good is it?"

"Beware to share quick judgment, shaper of stone. Whose stones have we traded, all these years?"

Spinel looked startled. "Well, I didn't know," he said, switching to Valan. "We sold you no starstones, that's for sure."

"No wonder you stayed poor." His self-righteousness nettled her. "Would your father have stopped selling to us, had he known?"

"We needed the business, to eat. Just like Kyril." Spinel bit his lip. "But you're a lady; you have a power. Why can't you use it for justice?"

Berenice sighed. "Power is a 'sharing' thing even on Valedon. The more power you hold, the more power holds you. What gives me power: my family? My own mother once sent a police squad here to kidnap me."

"*Kidnap* you? Whatever for?"

"To turn my head away from Sharer nonsense. In those days my behavior was an acute embarrassment to the House," she added dryly.

"Well? Did you escape?"

"I hid beneath the raft, where the shockwraith dwells. The ships and sirens and sniffer servos did not think to look there. Later, my mother came to her senses—and I came to mine. I stopped making trouble, came home a few weeks each year, and accepted the fiancé they chose." They knew her taste, she thought ruefully. "And I agreed to—" She stopped. Though Sharers knew of Berenice's ongoing dialogue with Talion, they could not guess what a slippery game it was.

"Well, we'll show them," Spinel announced. "We'll send all the traders back where they came from, for good."

"A regular Doorcloser you've become." Berenice sighed and shook her head. "Soon they won't need trade anymore. They'll gather their own herbs and seasilk. It's started already; the boycott will only hasten it."

"But—we won't let them, that's all," Spinel insisted. "We'll fight them off."

"How? You're here, and I'm here, to prove Valans human. Even Yinevra will not strike another human."

"That's crazy. You can't just sit back and die."

"At best, you could hope for accommodation."

Spinel looked away, his eyes anxious and his mouth small. "Is that what Merwen thinks?" he asked in a low voice.

Berenice smiled wryly. "I wish I knew what Merwen thinks. One hope remains: when Malachite comes—"

Spinel gasped and clapped his hands. "The Patriarch's Envoy —*here?* He'll set everything right."

"So long as both sides stay cool until then."

8

There was no end in sight to the boycott, so the shockwraith hunt could be put off no longer. Yinevra had been an expert hunter, ten years ago, before steel cables came and the hunts were abandoned. So Yinevra planned the hunt, and Lystra was determined to go.

Merwen shared fear for her daughter. On the night before the hunt, she visited Yinevra. "Lystra is on starworm duty tonight," Merwen reminded her. "She will be tired tomorrow."

"We all are." Yinevra's chin jutted at Merwen. "We all wear our webbing to the bone. Such is the price of independence."

Merwen stilled her body, letting tension ebb through her fingers. "Lystra is not as independent as she seems. She has yet to name herself."

"She is strict with herself, that girl."

"And subconsciously, perhaps, she still wants me to be strict with her."

"Well, then," said Yinevra. "See to it that she shares your will on this matter."

Merwen was thinking that she could sleep outside the silkhouse that night, if Lystra insisted on joining the hunt. Then Lystra would shout and stamp her feet and be secretly glad to give in.

A smile fluttered at Yinevra's lips. As so often, she must have read Merwen's thoughts. "Am I to believe that the subtlest word-weaver Shora ever named, who opened hearts between Gatherings Unspoken for a decade, and has flung herself undaunted at the Stone Moon—can't share the will of her own daughter? What a mystery is life."

"A wordweaver's tongue is tied fast in her own home." A rush of anger followed her calm reply, and she nearly let out the one word that would have crushed in return. Merwen held back, partly because she reconized the old anger welling up with it, for the wrong she should long ago have forgiven.

At any rate, Yinevra the Unforgiven lapsed into pensiveness. "Lystra knows her selfname. She is waiting for Rilwen," Yinevra said, supplying the word herself. The two girls were lovesharers, and Lystra still hoped the other would heal. Their love would have brought peace to their mothers, as well; instead, Rilwen's fate had driven them apart.

Merwen pressed Yinevra's hand. "I share your sorrow. And you see why it is you who must tell Lystra to stop putting off her life."

A series of fleeting expressions played over her face. "I'm try-ing, Merwen, though not with words. Words will help your daugh-ter no more than mine."

As it turned out, everyone had some role to fill in the hunt, even the younger ones, who would wait at the airhole to assist the hunters beneath the raft's underside. Spinel said he wanted to go down with the hunters, just to get a glimpse of the dreadful beast.

"Will he be safe, Usha?" Merwen asked. "He swims better now, but still—"

"He swims," Lystra interrupted, "well enough to watch by the airhole. Someone must be posted there. Why do you fuss over him so? You'd think he was prize breeding stock."

Usha was scandalized. "I've had it with you, daughter," Usha declared. "If my ears have to share another shred of such nonsense I'll hold my breath until—"

"All *right*, I'm sorry. Let me go. We've got to set the bait, and the knives and the..." Lystra left, with the usual spring in her step, although dark rings surrounded her eyes.

Merwen turned to Spinel. She lifted his hand and circled the palm with her fingers. "Are you sure? I promised," she reminded him.

"I'll be all right. I want to share my part," he said.

Lystra watched Yinevra descend the airhole, gripping niches carved into the raftwood as she went. A rope at her waist would hold her, in the unlikely event that she slipped. It was perhaps a dozen sisterlengths to the underside, about halfway out from the center of the raft core, which was as far as a shockwraith normally wandered. Shockwraiths avoided ocean turbulence, which could disrupt their delicate stomach bulbs.

The rope tugged, so Yinevra was clear. Lalor went down next, then Kithril, Yinevra's lovesharer. Lalor's lovesharer, Shaalrim, would have gone, an excellent swimmer with a very cool head, but now that a child swam inside her it was out of the question. Shaalrim had shared her sister's judgment philosophically and now was here to hoist the net full of bait down the airhole. Wellen stood by proudly, having caught the bait fish and tied them into the net. Mirri the apprentice lifeshaper was prepared for emergencies. Merwen and others stood by, and even Weia was there, ready to scream for help in case of trouble.

And at the edge of the airbell stood Flossa and Spinel, ready to descend as watchers. They were adjusting beacons on their heads. Lystra tapped her own for surety, snug against her forehead. She pulled on her long gloves shaped from the hide of a trailfin, the one denizen of the dark side who was safe from the shockwraith. Trailfin hide was impervious to the formic acid that filled the shockwraith's delicate stomach bulbs. "Name your duties, sisters," Lystra said.

Flossa said, "We'll watch for the signal, like this." Her hand capped her beacon, on and off.

"Then we tug the rope," said Spinel. "For the sisters above."

"And we make sure not to wait too long for air, since there is no airbell and only one hole. And we never, ever, touch a shockwraith arm," Flossa concluded.

"Even with gloves," agreed Lystra. "Right." She took up her grappling pole, patted the knives at her belt, pulled at her rope once more, then started to climb down.

It was a long vertical tunnel, dank and gloomy. Light was at only one end—the receding end. The sudden touch of black sea chilled her.

With a few last breaths, she plunged below. Her beacon faintly penetrated the gloom. She tugged the rope for Flossa and Spinel to descend.

Already, three other beacons loomed around her and light flashed from grappling poles. Yinevra swam over to clasp her hand, an infinitely welcome reach from the darkness.

The net of bait fish hung, several scissor-kicks away. Spots flickered past, tiny creatures with glowing photophores, but no sign yet of that dread creature of darkness. Lalor and Kithril with their beacons waited patiently. A glance over her shoulder showed Lystra two more beacons beneath the airhole, their pale glow embracing the silhouettes of Flossa and Spinel.

Spinel and Valan. The enigma of him elicited reactions as ambivalent as they were extreme. A hateful malefreak, and a shaper of stone, he was also hardworking and infectiously eager to please. And he had the nerve to share witness with stonetraders, an act which deeply moved her. Even Nisi had not done this, for all that her own mothers were traders. Though admittedly, Mother was always hardest to defy. Merwen, now—why did Lystra's own mother insist on complicating their world so, at a time when complexity brought worse threats than any shockwraith? If that shockwraith got hold of one Valan, now, that would simplify—

But this thought, and her brief wish for it, made her shudder all over. the grappling pole slipped from her hand and floated upward; she darted up to snatch it back. She swam to the airhole and smiled encouragement to both watchers. Spinel nodded and went on watching the bait, his mouth small and his eyes ever so earnest above his upturned nose. Lystra could have cursed him forever for his lack of any cause to curse, or any sign of what Yinevra judged of his kind.

Lalor grabbed Lystra's arm and pointed. In the distance grew a pale haze, faint as a cloud in the night sky. It rolled forward beneath the tangle of dead branch roots. The haze brightened and resolved into blue spots. Those spots were the stomach bulbs, which by their glow would attract hungry things, to burst open at a touch.

The hunters gathered immediately at the airhole, just in case the shockwraith chose them over the bait fish.

As it drew near, hundreds of the blue spots delineated the invisible arms. It seemed to pause between fish and humans, then it decided on fish. It settled beneath the hung net and swung several arms around: five, six, seven...out of perhaps twenty.

Yinevra handsignaled to Lalor, who pulled over another bundle of fish buoyed with airblossoms to float almost freely. Lystra helped her tug it halfway within reach of the beast, then propelled it further with her pole. Several more arms twined ponderously around this unprecedented feast. Six lines of blue dots still hung free, of which one was a specialized arm for sensing and mating which must not be touched at all.

Now Yinevra glided toward one line of dots that looped apart from the rest. She swung the tip of her pole to the base of the arm. A knife sprung; the arm slipped away. The rest of the beast remained still, unaware, because the cut had come just at the proper spot. Yinevra retreated, away from any trail of acid.

Lystra knew she must be turning white, for urgent need squeezed her lungs. No time for that; she kicked and headed for the cut arm, extended her pole, and sank a hook just below one of the bulbs. The bulb seemed to watch her, a baleful eye. She pulled the arm away, and Kithril tied a rope to secure it. When the hunt was done, and all the hunters safely up, the arms would be hauled up to the surface, where the stomach bulbs could be emptied without trouble.

Now she darted to the airhole and gasped for breath. Yinevra's head poked up beside her, cramped in the vertical tunnel. Yinevra gave Lystra a rough hug, saying, "There, sister, one's in the bag. But no heroics, please; your breath comes first. If we lose one arm to the deep, that's nothing, but if we lose you, who'll grab the next one?"

Lystra gulped air and plunged downward again.

The next arm she cut herself, with Yinevra's hand to guide her pole. The cut sent a shock to her own flesh, for she knew well enough the feel of a blade. Shockwraiths did not seem to feel as humans did, but who could say for sure? At any rate, this beast would survive with the arms that remained, and with such a fine meal provided, it would soon grow back the rest.

Two more arms yielded to the knife, and two free ones remained, one the sensing arm, which could not be touched. Yinevra approached the last arm to be cut.

Inexplicably, this one came alive, undulating like a watersnake. The blue string danced in random waves, moving perilously near the airhole. Flossa streaked up the airhole quick as a minnow, but Spinel hung below.

Lystra waved her hand across her beacon, then again, urgently. Spinel just stayed there, staring, as if in a dream. What was the matter with him? Could he not see the whip of lights, drifting ever nearer the airhole? Already the beam of his beacon merged with the blue at his feet.

A few swift kicks sent her to his side. She grabbed him by the arm and lunged upward. She had not quite reached the airhole before her mind cut short.

Spinel awoke. Pain pried his leg, a thousand stonecutters chiseling at him, shaping a tomb in Cyan's basement. But I'm not granite, he insisted; you can't make a tombstone of me. I'm only a poor stonecutter's son. . . .

The pain receded slightly, a mixed blessing since now his awareness was more acute. Two faces hovered above him, Usha's and Merwen's, long and somber as the day he fell from the fire-merchant's netleaf tree. What are you going to do with me? I *am* hurt, Usha, this time.

"You'll get better." Usha's voice was oddly distant. Her face was a moon, dipping to the horizon, touching his leg. Spinel was floating on a watery cushion, weak all over, and his legs would not move.

"Did I . . . ?" He stretched his neck. "What happened?"

"One burst just at your ankle." Usha was doing something to his leg, he could not see what, but he saw the vines trailing down.

Merwen leaned over him, her face etched in detail, her round cheekbones gold setting for her eyes. "You will be whole again. I know." Her head turned slightly, exposing the scar, a ribbon that streaked her neck. Spinel thought, How much closer death once touched her. He raised a trembling finger to trace the thickened skin.

She clasped his hand. "How is the pain?"

"Not . . . so bad." Spinel remembered her promise. "Not so bad as . . . the . . . alone." He squeezed her hand to his chest. Sudden tears were flowing, unstoppable. For the briefest time but nearly too long, when the blue lights had wandered near, he had wanted death more than anything, to make it all easy, for good. How strong he had thought he was, before, when he had first turned amethyst; yet still, to go on in this world, or in any world, felt impossibly hard at times.

Within a day Spinel was out of the chamber of lifeshaping, to rest his leg in the silkhouse. He lounged luxuriously in seasilk and gazed over the panels that swooped above, some of which he had helped to install. The house was never quite the same after it was rebuilt; old nooks and turns were lost forever, and new unexpected twists had appeared. And the "painted" surfaces, a wall carpet of gold and green with intricate red lines that tantalized him to name their forms, were ever-changing as the fungi grew.

Usha came to inspect him. She kneaded his ankle critically. Already it was mottled with scarring. "The scar is too shallow."

"Did it heal wrong?" How had a scar grown so fast, anyhow? "You won't have to ... cut it open again, will you?"

"*Cut* open? What kind of creature do you think I am?" She scrutinized the scar, rather as Cyan would examine a gem on the lap wheel. "Cut, indeed," she muttered. "You want a bright mark, don't you, brave as a stretchmark after childbirth. Thus your sisters will see and respect your experience of life." She looked up again. "Your flesh is not what I'm used to. I'll do better next time." Abruptly she left.

Later, Lady Nisi was less modest about Usha's handiwork. "Even Hospital Iridis could not have done better," she assured him, "and it would have taken weeks to heal."

"Weeks in the hospital? My folks could never afford that."

That took her aback. "Well, I would have paid for you."

"Thank you, my lady." But his irony escaped her.

To pass the time while his leg strengthened, Spinel puzzled over a pair of clickflies that perched splaylegged on his arm or spun webs from wall to wall when he clucked commands he had learnshared in the evenings. All the while they rasped back at him with their violin mandibles. They could spell out whole books and even diagrams across their webs, guided by the coded clicks that Spinel haltingly produced. They could put what they heard into extra chromosomes and pass it on to their offspring; that was how volumes of news got spread, limited only by clickfly flight.

"Chromosome" was a word for which Spinel had no Valan equivalent in his eight years of schooling, but he envisioned something like Oolite's string of alphabet beads.

Lystra came in, carrying a spinning wheel that she stood nearby. This was odd, for he knew that she hated the indoors, and himself even worse, though not as badly as she used to. He watched her thread the spindle and chose his words with care. "Were the shockwraith arms recovered?"

"Yes." Lystra nodded over her work. "Treated with enzymes, they'll make a starworm harness in no time."

One harness? There would have to be more hunts, lots more.

She set her foot at the pedal. A broad streak crossed her foot and toes, where a web scallop was shriveled back. "You too!" Spinel exclaimed. Something pricked his memory.

"It's all right." She wrinkled her nose. "They won't let me back at the starworms yet. I have to spin—I can't bear to sit still." She adjusted her seat, an elevated part of the apparatus, the only sort of "chair" Sharers seemed to have. The drive wheel whirled, and the spindle purred. At the spindle head, her fingers alighted like a butterfly folding its wings. Her left hand fed fibers to the thread, while the right maintained a delicate twist between thumb and forefinger. Her hands were in precise control, while her muscular leg pumped the pedal.

Something came over Spinel, and he hastily cast down his eyes, as if too close a stare might drive away a wild bird. He looked again at her stricken foot and had an indescribable realization. "That was for me."

Lystra's spindle purred on; she seemed not to hear. Or perhaps he had not spoken aloud.

9

The sea had begun to swallow. Not yet here in Per-elion, of course, but sisters on the northernmost rafts had sighted whirlpools.

The news came overnight by starworm song. The starworm song could not actually be heard by human ears. It was detected by a raftweed whose taproot reached into the sea, covered with pressuresensitive hairs. The root hairs picked up the subsonic vibrations of the song; in response, the blossoms of the raftweed opened and closed. Thus Sharers could watch the "signal blossoms" at the appointed times for news from their sisters across the globe.

From Lrina-el came word of a boat fallen to one of the whirlpools, and nine lives reclaimed by their First Namer. Lystra shuddered when she took that message from the signal blossoms. Mourning songs were sung, and Merwen and Usha entered whitetrance for one of the dead, whom they had known.

That same day, traders informed the witnessers at their doors that all "prices" would fall to one-fifth and that no more stone would be shared with those whom the Gathering had Unspoken.

Lystra flung off the hapless clickfly that told her, but it recovered to soar away to the next silkhouse. Why *now*, just when Sharers had begun to stop depending on traders? Hard times were ahead, when everyone would be tempted most.

Something must be done—quickly. But Merwen and Usha were in whitetrance, no telling for how long, and Lystra herself could not get them out. Only a small child could reach someone in whitetrance without fear of triggering death. "Weia! Wellen! Where are you minnows when I need you?"

At the water's edge, Wellen and Flossa lay wrestling in a fury, hands grasping chins in a grip that could suffocate. Lystra wrenched them apart. "You 'trollbrats'! What's this about now?"

119

"She tore the net," was Flossa's shrill accusation.

"But *she*... overfilled it!" Wellen gasped.

"Flossa." Lystra's voice was barely audible. "Only days ago, lives of shockwraith hunters depended on you."

The girl winced and averted her eyes. With a finger she raised a corner of the torn net. "I'll mend it."

"And Wellen, if you're still an infant, then *you* can bring your mother out of whitetrance."

"No, I'm too old." Wellen looked as if she would burst into tears, but she plodded silently back to the silkhouse.

At last Lystra found Weia behind the house, playing giant-steps by herself. The toddler let herself be coaxed into waking her mother and mothersister from their trance.

Her fingertips still pale, Merwen heard Lystra out. Then she said, "For this you break my peace with the dead? If traders share reason, it's all to the good."

"But, Mother! We can't just go back to the old way."

"The Gathering will decide."

Lystra took a deep breath. "Yes. And this time, I'll be among them."

At that, the sun might have dawned. Merwen glowed all over, and Lystra felt a webspan taller for having spoken. She hugged Merwen as tightly as the day her mother came home. Then a sadness flowed out of her as she thought of Rilwen, and of how she had waited that they might take their names together. Their love could wait forever; but the Door of the Selfname, like the Last Door, could never really be shared. It had taken the touch of a shockwraith to remind her that a life postponed too long might never be lived.

Part III

WHEN
THE SEA
SWALLOWS

1

It was three months since Merwen had come home when the first seaswallower came within sight of Raia-el.

From a spire of the silkhouse, Merwen watched through binoculars. In the distance a thumbprint depressed the sea, its whorls lined by raft seedlings, spiraling into a white vortex. Unseen below, the grandmother of cephaglobinids sucked at all that dwelled in the sun-drenched upper waters, from myriad plankton to an occasional free starworm, as well as hosts of raft seedlings that would otherwise choke the ocean. Yes, the seaswallower had its place in the web.

When the Gathering next met, there was a question of trade to thrash out, on top of the familiar hardships of swallower season. But first of all came Lystra with her selfname.

A fine rain was falling, little more than mist, and the air smelled of damp weeds. The cloud cover was white with a touch of the olive hue that Merwen had once seen in Spinel. Lystra sat apart, glistening with beaded raindrops, roughly halfway between her mother and Yinevra.

It was Trurl's lovesharer, Perlianir, who put the Three Doors before Lystra, the same three that Nisi had named when she came to share the Gathering. The Names of the Doors were the oldest tradition known, older than genetic records, as old as the lips of Shora herself: the First Door of the Sun, the Last Door Unshared, and the Door of the Self. It was said that Shora would live forever, so long as the Names were remembered.

To the Door of the Self, Lystra responded, "Intemperate One."

Merwen kept a straight face, but Usha smiled. Usha had forecast accurately the selfname of their firstborn. Elsewhere there was a tumult of cheers and hugs for Lystra, and Merwen beamed with joy, though she also felt keenly for Nisi the Deceiver, whose selfname had met less of a welcome.

The rest of the agenda was more sobering. No fishing disputes or family quarrels, but the treacherous explosion of fleshborers that came in swallower season. "Let everyone watch where she swims," Usha cautioned, "even outside the known nesting holes. Fleshborers grow as numerous as raft seedlings, and mad with hunger; no repellent can turn them back. Just yesterday a youngster was half eaten alive, before we fished her out and got her below for lifeshaping."

It was enough to share fear with the most fearless. There was much talk of stronger repellents and parasite infestations to cut down the numbers, but from long experience they knew that patience and vigilance worked best. Fleshborers too had their place in the web and would bring an end to their own season.

Many sisters shared a similar judgment of the Valan stone-traders. Yinevra, though, did not yet agree. "Valans have no place in the web. The question is this: When will Shora expel that which Shora never brought through the ocean door?"

"Do they eat us?" Merwen whispered. Yinevra's head turned, and Merwen wished her words unspoken. She and her old friend were like stormclouds now; the slightest spark set off lightning between them.

"Valans eat fish, and they call *us* fish." Yinevra scanned the Gathering. "Who will they eat next?"

The allusion to death-hastening drew fewer scandalized reactions than usual. From all that Merwen and others had reported, the fact of widespread death-hastening on the Stone Moon was common knowledge, but the potential for it here was dismissed as something Shora would not allow. Merwen sensed this dismissal and worried over it, despite the recent trend toward harmony. In this she agreed with Yinevra; but beyond...

A hand fluttered: Shaalrim the Lazy. "Sisters, I think we get too excited about stone. If someone wants to share little stone-bits because they're pretty and bring smiles to children's eyes, why not?"

There was a slippery truth in that. "The traders agreed to respect our Unspoken once more," someone pointed out.

"Are we *dreaming?*" Yinevra exclaimed. "Trawlers still clean out rafts full of fish—and their noise still drowns the starworm's song. How long must this go on? I say, let us Unspeak them all, for good."

"Unforgiver, we know what you say," declared Trurl. She

asked the Gathering, "Who else is ready to Unspeak our guests from the Stone Moon?"

Several moved, but none jumped to respond. After a decent interval, Merwen observed, "Even our own Unspoken sisters stay bound to us, by submerged branches to our central raft. What bonds hold us to Valans?" She was thinking of Nisi and Spinel.

Shaalrim had something else in mind. "Don't forget all the good things traders share with us, from kitchen knives to starworm cables. They can't be all bad."

Lystra burst out, "But that's just what we've got to steer clear of! We can't depend on traders, ever. Their very words carry poison—even Spinel the stoneshaper says that."

What notion was this? Merwen had seen too little of Spinel lately.

"And which of us is perfectly dependable?" Shaalrim asked.

Lystra frowned defensively. "Some more than others. Traders depend on force only. We pulled out of their grasp, now let's keep it that way." She sat down. Not bad, for her first time, thought Merwen.

Trurl's eyelids nearly closed. "What force wins yields to force, Intemperate One."

There was an uncomfortable pause. Someone muttered, "How can infants who can't even name themselves ever know what true force means?"

In the end there was no agreement, on Raia-el or beyond. Clickflies told of Gatherings that kept up the boycott, of others who relaxed, and of others whose debate raged on. Among the Per-elion rafts, individual witnessers continued at the traders' raft—beside the shop steps, not on them. Trade reopened, but volume returned to a fraction of what it had been, despite the lowered "prices."

For her part, Lystra made up with Nisi, ending the Unspeech between them. And one day, for the first time in over two months of vigils there, Lystra entered Kyril's store for business—a small errand, and not for herself.

Her glance, brief but penetrating, took in the shelves which were filled to bursting with bolts of cloth, wire spools, firecrystals, and the everpresent bewitching gemstones. In an aisle Lalor was stacking plastic bowls. "To stock up against the next boycott," she cheerfully explained.

Lystra glowered without deigning to reply. What a disgrace, for a shockwraith hunter.

Kyril laughed heartily at the joke. "Why, Lystra," he said, "is it really you? Share the day, what an immense honor it is, and a pleasure too, to see you indoors for a change."

"Good day," Lystra said clearly in Valan. "I am called the Intemperate One now."

The trader shook his head. "Why must you sisters beat your breasts with your names? Be positive, I say; look where the wave catches sunlight."

She stopped, an arm's length from the counter. "I only came to pick up mail for Spinel the stoneshaper."

"Ah, the Chrysolite boy. What's he been up to?"

"Spinning our seasilk. And hunting shockwraith," she pointedly added.

"Earning his keep, eh? Glad to hear it. Well, here's the freight-ship mailbag." He fished out two smudged bits of web-thin material. Lystra wondered how such inert objects could carry thoughts to Spinel all the way from the Stone Moon. "They're pretty old by now," Kyril said, "but I'm afraid you'll hear nothing recent from Chrysoport for a while because—" He stopped himself for some reason and pretended to rummage beneath the counter.

Lystra handed over a pod of redleaf medicine that Usha had grown and powdered, to share for the mail handling. With his usual bad manners, Kyril weighed out a small portion for "payment" instead of accepting the whole. "Anything else?" he asked. "Did you look at our stock? All cut-rate—get your steel cables for next to nothing."

"And gemstones too."

"But we don't touch anybody with a problem, no way. On the Trade Council's orders, did you hear? Hyalite himself drew up the new rules. You left us no choice, and that's a fact. The customer's always right, I say. And did you hear even Malachite is coming to Shora? Once the swallowers clear out, that is."

"That reminds me," Lystra said. "How do you keep swallowers so far away from your raft?"

"If you like, we'll send a crew to protect your raft, too."

Lystra waved her hand in disgust. "Just watch which poisons you use here. The first dead fish I see floating—"

"Come now, Lystra, that was before your time. Say—" Kyril sprang up a ladder and pulled down a handful of plugged squeeze tubes. "New type of roofing cement, guaranteed stormproof for five years. Why not give it a try?"

"No more trading for me." She fingered Spinel's letters.

"Look, just try one, for free."

"A gift?"

"Sure, why not? Tell all your sisters to come back, too."

Lystra set the rest of her redleaf on the counter. "Then this, too, is a gift. I don't want your children to starve. But so long as one gemstone sits on your shelf, I won't depend on you, Kyril."

2

One glimpse of the two worn envelopes filled Spinel with joy. He tore them open and feasted his eyes on the pages of ledger paper covered with his mother's dense, sloping handwriting. The first letter, dated two days after his departure, was full of news and chatter: how the stoneshop was doing a brisker business than usual, especially rubies, for lads off to the regiment, and Cyan had finished the tombstone for old Amberlite, and Beryl was holding up well, and Oolite was crawling forward as well as backward. And when was Spinel going to write home about his new life?

It had never occurred to him to write, himself. Spinel could barely manage a sentence, in any case. Clickfly webspinning was much more fun. He glanced up at Lystra, who was eyeing the page curiously. "Could I send a clickfly to my mom?"

Lystra cocked her head to one side. "Would she treat it right?"

"Of course she would." Indignant, Spinel turned to the second letter. This one was brief—one paragraph, scrawled three or four words on a line. Spinel frowned; his mother never wrote like that. *My dear son,* it read. *We are all well and please forgive me for not writing often. Your father has lots of orders. Beryl sends love, and Oolite. Work hard for your sponsors, and don't worry about us. Your loving mother Galena, Cyan stonecutter's wife.*

Spinel looked up from the page.

"Well, what does it say?"

"It doesn't sound right." Nothing, not even about Beryl, who would be expecting soon. What could have happened? Had the business finally gone under, despite the gift from his Sharer sponsors? His mother would not lie outright, though like himself she would tell a tale in her own way. His lip twisted. "I better write back and find out."

"Hurry up, then. Swallowers are getting so thick, soon we won't be able to sail to the traders' raft."

He stood up to look out to sea, at the four or five spots, still distant, where raft seedlings were swirling toward oblivion. His muscles had hardened and he had gained height since he first arrived; his eyes were nearly level with Lystra's now.

Later, just before evening learnsharing, Spinel came upon Lady Nisi as she was pulling on a white blouse and tucking it into a severe black skirt.

He stepped back at the sight. The clothes were plain enough, but their unexpected appearance only exaggerated Nisi's female curves. A flush of heat came over him. "What's that for? You going home or something?"

She walked past him to her mirror. The tapping of her sandals brought back warm memories of footfalls on Chrysolite cobblestones.

"Lady Nisi, where are you going? Have you a lover among the traders?"

"Heavens, no. Your tongue grows as long as a shockwraith's arm." She patted her scalp, as if arranging nonexistent hair.

"Why won't you tell me, Nisi the Deceiver?"

The lady paused, then spoke in her most cultured Valan tones. "I am due for a chat with the High Protector. Via image transmission."

"The *High Protector of Valedon?* Oh, please, can I come too?"

"Please don't," she said quietly. "It's . . . official."

"I see. I guess he wouldn't give fool's gold for anything I'd have to say." His toe traced a circle on the floor. "Well, even if my folks are common, could you just ask him to check up on them, in Chrysoport? Please, Nisi, I'm awfully worried about them."

"I'll mention it." She clipped her opal to her blouse and briskly stepped outside.

* * *

Within the submerged station, Berenice sat with her skirt tucked under, and Talion across from her. Talion's shape squeezed and expanded from signal interference, but otherwise he looked as usual, an aging, careworn administrator perpetually dressed for a board meeting. He brought welcome news: General Realgar, now High Commander, would escort the Malachite delegation to Shora.

"Marvelous. I'll be so glad to see him." Realgar was the one part of Valedon she truly missed. "And such a diplomat he is, just right for the job."

Talion's smile broadened. "I'm glad you are pleased."

Why should she not be pleased? Then she recalled their confrontation in Iridis, before she left. "But of course, he'll just bring an honor guard for Malachite."

"Of course. Now, my lady, a quandary for you: whom shall the Envoy call on, if Shora has no Protector?"

She smiled mischievously. "They have nine hundred thousand Protectors. Minus children," she corrected herself.

Talion waved an impatient hand. "All-powerful though he is, Malachite can't very well visit every man, woman, and child of— you know what I mean. Surely there's some sort of authority figure, a chief witch-doctor or whatever."

Her lips worked in and out, oddly reluctant to respond. Yet she had known from the beginning what she would say; why put it off? "There is one who enjoys respect in every 'galactic' of raft clusters: Merwen the Impatient One." She shrank from the role of kingmaker. Merwen's reaction, had she understood just what Berenice was doing, would have been unimaginable. Berenice, however, saw no other way.

"Merwen the Patient," Talion noted for his monitor.

"Impatient," she corrected. "And please tell—that is, ask Malachite to choose a 'selfname' of some sort, or the Gathering will not receive him." This, too, was bending the rules, and if Yinevra or Lystra were so impolite as to inquire further—

"How about Malachite the Lowly Worm?"

"Too conceited. Worms are highly useful creatures." Talion, she thought, was definitely off-guard tonight, almost distracted. She wondered whether that signaled good or bad.

"Do not take offense, my lady. Merwen the Impatient will receive the Envoy, with all due honor. What a help you are, Berenice. I know I can always count on a Hyalite."

She smiled despite herself. Thank goodness that boycott was over. "Since I'm so useful, may I ask a personal favor?"

"Whatever you wish."

It felt almost like the old days, when she was first married, and Talion dined weekly with the House of Hyalite. "Please check the current status of one commoner, Cyan stonecutter of Chrysoport."

Talion called at his monitor and watched something outside the range of her view. "Sorry, the file is inactive at this time."

"Oh?"

"Dolomoth is still keeping the lid on, to consolidate their hold."

"The town's occupied?"

"Dolomites have wanted a seaport for Torr knows how long, and now they've got it. It seemed appropriate, once the Pyrrholite siege was concluded, given their assistance with the campaign."

"I see." In fact, she had expected the siege to drag on a year, at least. She disliked to admit how out of touch she was. She would have to catch up at the trading post.

"Now, Berenice. This trade business is still a bit of a bother. We've made enormous concessions, as you know. Why hasn't trade volume got back to normal?"

She sighed. Where to begin? "The stone trade, for one thing. It's very existence is hateful to many Sharers."

"If they hate it so much, why is stone our most lucrative commodity?"

For answer, she only returned his stare. Talion must know the sordid truth; why should he make her say it?

"Well, there you are," said Talion at last. "If the natives can't reach *consensus* among their own 'Protectors,' then by their own rules what can they demand of us?"

"Those who care the most shame the rest. And we're learning to do without Valan goods. Sharers have resourceful minds. And long memories, too; it's not nice to get dumped into the sea, even if you swim like a seal."

"Why can't they be reasonable, for Torr's sake? This season is rough on us too. What about the trawler lost to a swallower last week?"

"So I heard. Who rescued the crew?"

"The natives were cooperative, in that case. But a good ship sank, which makes for red ink."

"It is hard. We lose rafts every year."

Talion was silent a while. Berenice shifted her legs beneath her skirt.

"Berenice, we have to get a handle on these people. The stone trade won't do, it's dead in the long run. I see how the wind blows, although the Trade Council may not yet. But what next?"

Suddenly she was wary. "What does Malachite suggest?"

Talion's pause was longer than time lag. "Malachite is inclined to consider this an internal matter."

"Internal? Like one planet?" So the Sharer "Protector" might end up reporting to the High Protector of Valedon. This notion was new, the first she had heard of Patriarchal intent. She turned it over in her mind. "Then Sharers will get full protection of Valan law. That could simplify everything."

"Yes, but you see, it will be up to *us*, myself in particular, to control them. How shall I do that?"

The question revolted her, and puzzled her as well. Was it not enough that Sharers went naked and unarmed? Her eyes narrowed. "I'll think it over," she said politely. "Please remember, I am not your agent."

"Then what are you? Would you like a salary?"

She was on her feet before she knew it. "You go too far."

"Lady, I require certain information. I need to know where the weak links are—all of them. We can make it easy for you."

"Never! If you set your Sardish mindbenders on me, I'll—" She stopped. Of course he would know her "final precautions," since Realgar did. Except for one. . . . Her voice steadied. "I will disappear, now, for good. My parents never found me, the last time."

"Go ahead, then. But first hear this: Pyrrhopolis is empty. Leveled. By the hand of Malachite."

"Pyrrhopolis? Leveled? What do you mean?"

An age passed between them. "The city was evacuated beforehand, of course. He gave us time. Then his ship did something, and—" Talion shrugged. "The city crumbled to sand."

Berenice fell back onto her bench, shaking.

"A vast beach of sand, all that's left." Talion looked old, she realized; even his shoulders drooped forward. Pyrrhopolis, where the mightiest of architects built towers of gold. "Why?" she asked at last, though she knew the answer.

"The Patriarch could not wait for a year's siege, so Malachite said. The Envoy can stay only a few months before he reports back to Torr. He could hardly leave Pyrrhopolis in the hands of atom-smashers. The lives at least were saved, I—I pressed for that. But it had to be so."

"Of course." Atom-smashers smashed themselves in the end; that was the dogma of Torr.

"Berenice, the same holds for biological warfare. If Sharers have forbidden science—"

Her thoughts were in confusion. What could she tell him? How to subdue Shora? Who would more surely destroy Shora, Malachite or Talion himself? Not the Envoy, he was too wise. He would learn soon enough what Berenice knew, that Sharers were harmless despite their powers. But then he would depart, for ten long years. What dare she tell the High Protector of Valedon?

Share learning, always, so Merwen had said. Never fear to share what you know, because true strength frees itself.

But what did Merwen know of High Protectors?

Berenice studied Talion's eyes and the very fine lines that grew above and around them. For the first time she saw fear in them, fear of a great power. What shame and despair it must have brought him to watch a Valan city crumble because he himself had ruled too lightly. And now he faced Shora. . . .

"My lord, I have one truth to share: So long as Sharers know that you are *human,* you have nothing to fear from Shora."

It was said, and she nearly swooned. Then she saw that Talion did not understand, perhaps never would, no matter how hard she tried. Once again, despite herself, she had earned her name.

3

The true girth and shape of a seaswallower was not known, even by Sharers who knew so much about lifestuff, down to the very atoms. At the water's surface, a single whirlpool could pull perceptibly within a range as broad as Raia-el. By now, the beasts crowded so closely that their ranges overlapped, and the sea was a mass of sinking holes.

Spinel watched from the rooftop, to see how close they would come to the raft. Lystra was outstretched in a blue curve of roofing, her breasts braced against a seam. Her eyes squinted into binoculars. "They're moving in," she said through clenched teeth. "Grandmothers and great-grandmothers. Thicker yet they'll get, before the crest passes."

"But they're practically on top of each other already."

"Swallowers spread seed and eggs as they go. The closer they swim, the better chance for union."

In that case, Spinel thought, they were grand*fathers* as well as grandmothers. But it was useless to point this out.

"Along the equator," Lystra said, "the globe is wide and the crest spreads thin."

"And we stay here, thanks to starworms." Spinel knew she would appreciate that.

"And thanks to shockwraiths. Say, look there—beyond the branches."

He started; the whirlpool was so big and close he had not noticed it.

"Looks like it's stalling."

Spinel stared as if mesmerized. Would it engulf the vary raft?

A fountain rose at the spot, so tall that it brushed the clouds. Its foam fell slowly in the distance and turned to vapor before it rejoined the sea. For several minutes it stood, a white pillar erected by some mythic race to hold up the sky.

"That one got a mouthful of fleshborers," Lystra noted.

"What do you mean?"

"Well if *you* swallowed a school of fleshborers, you'd spit up, too. And that would be your last meal."

Spinel sickened at the thought. He wondered how long the fleshborers would last, to keep the swallowers away.

Lystra lowered her binoculars. "The offshoot rafts. They might break off." She meant Rilwen, he knew.

"Usha will bring her in, like before, for health's sake." Far off, another white column sprouted, in the vicinity of Umesh-el, Spinel guessed.

Lystra climbed down to the raft, and Spinel swung down after. A few sisters were still working on an emergency escape vessel, a long canoe with ten pairs of oars to speed off, in the event that the raft core broke up among the whirlpools. No glider squid could be controlled with swallowers about, but this vessel could probably make it to the nearest neighboring raft. Already the children from three families were settled in the boat, for the dozen hours or so that the crest would last. To the side, a score of airblossoms were tethered, drenched in orange photophores. These would be released like balloons as a signal to other rafts, if the time came.

It was all for nothing, most likely, Spinel tried to tell himself. The raft of Raia-el was over a hundred years old, and each year the sea had swallowed twice, once from the north and back again from the south. But the wailing of children and the feverish activity of their mothers little helped to calm him.

Nisi and Perlianir were carving an extra oar; raftwood shavings scattered everywhere. At the sight of Nisi, Spinel remembered something. "Lady Nisi, what's the news of my folks? You did ask, didn't you?"

Nisi frowned and wrung her sore fingers. "He could not get through. Spinel, you belong on the boat."

"What, with a bunch of babies?"

"You haven't a selfname," said Perlianir.

Spinel kicked the side of the boat, disgusted. It was bad enough to have been drummed out of one world for lack of a stonesign. He'd be a troll's cousin if he'd let them nag at him for a 'selfname.'

Behind him came the voice of Usha. "The Unspoken One refused to come in."

Spinel turned. Usha was facing Lystra, who stood as if she were ready for a fight. "She would not come, that's all," Usha repeated.

"Nonsense, mothersister. That branch may not last."

"She Unspeaks us. It is her right."

"Her right to die?"

"Even so."

The two faced each other in a way that on Valedon would surely have ended in a fistfight or hair-pulling, but Lystra broke away and ran, down one of the long twisting branches.

Spinel's heart beat very fast. Something had to come of that exchange, maybe not like on Valedon, but something just as crazy. He raced to catch up with Lystra. He found her shoving her rowboat into the channel. "Hey, you won't make it back," he called.

"Should I let her die?" Lystra's face was haggard.

"I'll call Merwen."

"Call on Shora herself! I'm my own selfnamer, now."

"Wait." He sprang from the branch and landed in the boat, which rocked and nearly capsized. He sat up and rubbed a sore elbow.

Lystra stared at him in amazement. "You 'trollhead,' what will Merwen say if I get you killed?"

"You're the selfnamer, Intemperate One."

She wrinkled her nose but said nothing more. They rowed out beyond the channels, passing clumps of fleshborers that tore at each other, maddened by the great deathfeast that tinted the waves a dull cinnabar. Lystra followed the line of the submerged branch that led out to Rilwen's offshoot. The sea was a confusion of eddies and sharp currents, but together the two rowers managed to make headway. The speck of raft appeared at last, a green leaf upon an unquiet sea.

Rilwen sat crosslegged between her troll's hoard of gems and her ragged excuse for a shelter.

"Rilwen?" Lystra laid a hand upon Rilwen's sunken shoulder.

The frail sister would not reply.

"Rilwen, this branch can't last."

A fountain roared up from the sea, the nearest yet. Waves came crashing onto the bit of raft and left a fleshborer stranded and snapping. The raft itself shuddered and swayed. Spinel lost his footing and caught hold of Rilwen's shelter.

Lystra was shaking her like a doll. "Rilwen, you have to come back. It's our duty; we share your protection." But already Rilwen was turning white, and that was it, Spinel knew by now.

"Let's pick her up." Spinel reached beneath Rilwen's arms to carry her, but Lystra pulled him off. "That's no use," she said, "her heart will just stop."

"What? But why? Of all the—" He let off a string of Valan curses. "Look, we can't just leave her here."

"She seeks her Last Door."

"It's not right, it's—it's against the—" He realized that he knew no Sharer word for "law." His arms fell. Lystra watched Rilwen, and Spinel watched Lystra. From the fountaining seaswallower a mist drifted over.

"Go on back," Lystra told him, still staring at Rilwen. "Take the boat, go on."

"What about you?"

"I'll swim."

"Among the fleshborers?"

"Rilwen may change her mind, if you leave."

Wincing, he turned and walked back toward the boat. Brown water already covered the branch that moored it. His feet stopped. Should he go? Would Rilwen really change her mind? He had to think fast, and that annoyed him; he just wasn't good at it, that's why he quit school when the master made him stammer out the square root of . . .

A wave lapped at his feet, and panic swept over him. Go now, said the wave; think later, safe on a dry mat in the silkhouse.

But his right foot carried a wrinkled scar.

His mind focused and centered on one thing. His face set, and he walked back to Lystra.

"You're still *here?*" Her lips contorted. "Get out!" she screamed.

"How will I tell Merwen I left you?"

"You shouldn't have come."

"What are you trying to do, share death?"

That cooled her a bit. "Share nothing. If I die for love, what's it to you?"

Numbness filled him; he choked on his tongue. He really was a trollhead, not to have understood. He should not have come. But it was too late; his mind had set a course and he had no will left to change it.

Lystra was determined to change it. Her fingers clenched and straightened, and her will reached out to him, so strong it was almost palpable. But the more she willed him to leave, the more he intended to stay. She could not move him, for all that she was a wormrunner.

They stayed there, all three, a frozen mosaic, for what felt like hours but could barely have been minutes. Then another swallower fountained. The waves poured over, for a moment drowning the little offshoot raft. Rilwen's shelter shuddered and collapsed.

Lystra tore herself away and headed for the boat. Spinel jumped from his trance and joined her, pulling with all his strength at the oars. The core raft lay ahead, a haven tantalizingly near, but with the shifting currents it took an age to get there.

Exhausted, Spinel lay back on the dry raft surface to rest, never minding the scratchy vegetation. It was no shore of land, but by Torr it was all he had to count on.

A deep rumbling began beneath him. Everything vibrated, as if the raft was about to split in two. The escape boat, could he reach it in time?

The tremor ceased with a sudden snap that flung him sideways. Slowly Spinel raised himself and ventured to look out to sea. A vast whirlpool spanned where Rilwen's raft had been.

Though the raft was firm again, Spinel found himself shaking uncontrollably. He had to try twice to get up on his feet. As he turned back, he saw Lystra, several paces up-raft, sitting with her legs crossed, facing out. Already she was beyond reach, in white-trance, to mourn her lost love.

Merwen came out with Spinel to see how Lystra was, and whether she had set herself safely up-raft. She had, of course; Lystra was at heart a very practical young sister. For a moment Merwen regarded her daughter, so still and white. Inwardly she bled for Lystra, and more for Rilwen, and most of all for Yinevra, who would live with this sorrow till her own Last Door. But Merwen tried not to pity her, for of all the well-meant emotions pity is the cruelest to share.

She bent down and lightly kissed Lystra on her scalp.

Spinel gasped and whispered, "Is that safe, in her trance?"

"Yes, but do not try to share words."

"But she can hear us?"

"In a distant way, like an embryo in a womb turned inside out to enclose the outer universe." Spinel would not understand this, not until he learned it himself. "A mental cord still connects her with this life. She hears us, but if our words tried to travel up that cord, it might snap." Merwen opened a pod of sunscreen and began to smooth it into Lystra's back, gently, almost reverently. "If she stays here many days, she will need this to keep from burning."

"Days, Merwen?"

"She was very close to Rilwen. Both of them were insatiably curious about the Stone Moon. Once they saved up seasilk together to trade for a—a 'picture maker,' that makes ghost pictures of living things. Lystra was determined to find out how it worked. She learned to speak Valan fluently, and she found out a little, about the lenses and the sensing parts that make of such an object a seeing eye. Beyond that, I think, even the traders did not know, and they said 'magic' because they knew no better."

"Magic is nonsense."

"Magic is anything you don't understand." Merwen kissed her daughter once more, then turned away. "Lystra will need more lotion, and a shell of water each day she stays."

"Oh, I'll bring that. But what if the raft breaks up?"

"The crest is passing, and the core raft is out of danger." Otherwise there would have been signs: great cracks in the soil and flooding of the inner chambers. Silently she walked home with Spinel and wondered yet again how much he understood. He was accepting of everything, even Lystra now, and that was a blessing to see. But was acceptance understanding?

She remembered that she herself must take time to mourn Rilwen, but she was not yet up to it. At the moment she needed another kind of solace, that which only her lovesharer could bring.

Merwen found Usha alone in a lifeshaping chamber, busily snaking nutrients into a vat of bacteria. "Will you never stop, dear one?" She kissed the nape of Usha's neck.

"Sickness doesn't wait. Suppose we get a flu epidemic, next?" Usha pointed to the vat. "Those unseen little sisterlings will make us lots of medicine." But she let herself relax and leaned into a wall curve matted with leaves, her cheek next to Merwen's. Merwen nestled closer and breathed the scent of Usha, so much sweeter than raft blossoms.

"Rilwen is beyond hope," Usha whispered. "Do you worry for Lystra?"

Merwen shut her eyes and let weariness drain from her. "Lystra worried me from the day she was born. When she wasn't yelling, she was overturning the pudding bowl on the floor. . . . I think Shora sent her just to test my name."

Usha chuckled. "So it is, to have a daughter. Shora has many worse."

"But you, Usha the Unconsidered, you never ask anything of anyone. You should worry me most of all."

Usha cupped Merwen's chin in her hands. "I asked for you, once. What else is there?"

Merwen shuddered, and they kissed searchingly, then long and hard, just as on the first day they had met in this chamber, so many doors of time past.

4

It was twilight when a spot of orange sailed aloft above a neighbor raft, Kiri-el.

At Raia-el, dozens of sisters crowded to the water's edge to scan the sea for survivors. Plantlights sprang up, to outline the branch channels, and boats were brought out to pick up swimmers. The first escape ship appeared, also dotted with plantlights, and a cheer went up when the ship made it to a branch. But then twenty-one refugees straggled out, children half dazed and half hysterical, their elders mute and haggard. Two more ships made it, bringing the total near eighty, and several were heard later to have reached other rafts. But three shiploads were never seen again, except for stray oars and one strong swimmer, picked up just off Umesh-el.

In the next few days, Spinel and everyone else worked hard to cope with the homeless sisters. A family of eight crowded into the silkhouse of Merwen and Usha. Two of them just sat in white-trance all day, but one, Mithril the Lonely, seemed to crave activity. She helped Spinel clean piles of octopus to feed everyone, while she chatted incessantly over the aborted history of Kiri-el; how her great-grandmothers had founded the raft and tunneled it with wood-enzymes over the years; and how just two years ago they had hosted a Great Gathering with sisters from five of the eight galactics, and it was high time for another one. "But the raft had one flaw of a crack that widened every season," Mithril told him. "Well, we'll have to start another one, soon as the water clears. Have you perhaps seen a good strong raftling about? No?"

Wellen came by, and Spinel handed her a plate full of octopus cleanings for the pudding plant.

"Usha's little ones have grown so," Mithril said. "And isn't it just like Merwen, to adopt a Valan daughter. I had heard you were a young one, but in fact you look about ready for a selfname and a—"

Spinel dropped the cleaning knife and left to escape her chatter. Merwen and Nisi were weaving seasilk for an extension to the house. The shuttles slid through their looms so fast that it almost hurt to watch. The two battens banged in time for a while, then shifted off beat.

"We could have saved them all," Nisi was insisting. "If only we could share in peace with Valedon. . . ."

"Share what?" Spinel asked.

"An airlift could have saved everyone. If each raft had a helicopter—"

"How much would that cost?" he said in Valan. "A raft's weight in seasilk?"

Nisi barely looked up. "A sharp tongue turns on its sharer."

Spinel clenched his fists but walked away. Tempers flared easily, as everyone rubbed elbows more than they were used to. The refugees seemed to be recovering, until Mithril unaccountably broke down and wept without stopping.

Lystra stayed outside in whitetrance the whole time. Spinel took her water, and each day it disappeared. He rubbed her with lotion, and he watched and wondered what in all Torr's planets was going on within that still head of hers.

There was so much to be done that a week went by without schooltime in the evening. Someone muttered that all work and no learnsharing turned minds into mud; and besides, everyone could use a break. So a marathon session was called for the entire raft, to last well into the night.

"This will be a celebration of life," said Merwen.

Spinel asked. "Will there be 'fermented beverages'?"

Flossa giggled. "You mean rotten food?"

"Well, it sure beats what your pudding plant spits out." It was too bad that Sharer stomachs did not tolerate alcohol. They did not know what they were missing, but Spinel certainly did.

At any rate, Flossa and others went off to the branch channels to gather delicacies for a feast. By now, the seaswallowers were practically gone; when a stray was sighted, a black airblossom was tethered up on the circular ridge. The water stretched smooth and sparkled, with barely a seedling or a fleshborer in sight. Lystra, though, remained in white. She would miss all the fun. "Send Weia to fetch her," Usha suggested, but a look from Merwen quieted her.

Wreaths of scallop shells were hung across the silkhouse, and some sisters piled them around their necks. Poles were planted for clickfly webs, with a plantlight atop each, and something added to the lights brought out rainbow colors. The solar cookers had been going all day, and the smell of boiled seafood clung to everything. Spinel ate and stuffed himself until he could barely move.

Despite the gaiety, a sadness with no definable source crept over him. Flossa and Wellen bantered with their refugee friends and exchanged ribald jokes, of a kind of women's talk that shut him out. Shaalrim brought out her shell flute with its plaintive tones, and Mithril produced hers, a pearly tapered corkscrew of a shell, the one bit of her home raft she had managed to save. She played a more fanciful tune, full of trills from her fingerwebs fluttering at the holes. It reminded Spinel of Captain Dak's bright whistle talk, and of his challenge, *"See you then . . . if you survive."*

He sat up with a sudden thought: Dak would get him news from home. He would ask Dak to find out if his family was all right.

The sun was getting low and caught a million ripples in the sea. Rainbow hues from the plantlights mottled the gathered faces. With no apparent sign, there was a hush as sisters turned their heads, and Spinel stretched to see. Grandmother Ama was half sitting up, cradled in Merwen's arms. Ama began to sing, and a chorus of sisters echoed each line. Spinel had heard the song before, but tonight for the first time he listened closely enough to catch the Sharer words, as far as he could comprehend them.

> *Door of ocean, heart of sky,*
> *Lips that pressed together lie,*
> *Flute of whorlshell lift in hand;*
> *Sing for those who dwell on land . . .*

He looked down and tugged pensively at some weeds. "There's no 'land' here. None you can live on, anyhow."

"No, silly," said Flossa. "It's for the fish you ate, and for Rilwen and the others, whose bones will sink to 'land.' Shora said long ago that our song would help speed each soul through the Last Door."

Spinel's scalp prickled. "What's it a door into?"

"Who knows? That's why it's 'last.' You can't share it; you go alone, and never return to share the telling." Flossa leaned her head back and watched the sunset upside down. "Or perhaps you come back through the First Door, with your memory washed clean, and you grow a new shell. That's why our numbers must stay about the same: there are only so many souls to go around. That's what I think." Her head snapped back, and her eyes sparkled from the plantlights. Dreamily she watched her grandmother.

The song made Spinel uneasy. His own family lived on true land, and he hoped all of them were on this side of any Last Door. He traced a sixpoint with his finger, a silly thing to do, but you never could tell.

He was glad when the song ended, and sisters grouped around the clickfly webs. Usha had set up a web to teach the apprentice lifeshapers how breathmicrobes worked, something of keen interest to him. Breathmicrobes had a special purple-changing molecule, shaped like the ring of dots that glowed in Usha's clickfly web. When this molecule held oxygen, it turned purple, like a light switch. The molecule could grab oxygen and spit it out again, depending on just how much air was around. That was why when the human host breathed very slowly, as in whitetrance, breathmicrobes gave up oxygen, and the purple turned off.

Mirri raised an objection. The oxygen-grabbing reaction could not work, she said, because the force barrier was too high, something like a wall that kept the atoms apart. Spinel got lost in this, but Usha seemed to think the point crucial. "This reaction works," Usha said, "because it *tunnels through* the barrier. It happens easily in molecules, the world of the very small. In the larger world, it happens also, though it takes a lot longer. That is the secret of strength: start small, and in time you will tunnel through."

The learnsharing went on until at last the plantlights dimmed and would not relight even when filled, and sisters wandered away, some for a midnight swim, others in pairs for more private wanderings across the raft. Now his loneliness returned in full force. It was true, these creatures did not need men at all. They were not really women, as far as he was concerned. How naive of Merwen to expect him to find a place here.

Spinel went down to the water's edge and let the sea murmurs wash through the dull ache inside him. In the moonlight he made his way down one of the huge trunks of a branch. The banks of seaweed squished beneath his feet. Above him the moon shone full, the blue-brown Stone Moon, round enough to be a "doorhole" that he could tap to open out upon the welcoming harbor of Chrysoport. . . .

He sat in the seaweed to watch the moon and its arcs of reflection in the water. For a measureless time he stayed, feeling nothing, drained of the energy even to want anything anymore, and not knowing what he should want if he could.

Something brushed across seaweed. Instinctively his fingers curled and dug in; then he looked behind and up—to see Lystra standing beside him.

The quest for Rilwen rushed back at him—all the fear, the pulling at oars till his shoulders burned, the raft shuddering beneath his feet. But only Lystra stood there now, dark as a shadow except for the moons of her eyes.

Lystra stretched her limbs, still sore and a bit stiff. When she had come out of her week-long trance, the music had wafted over from the celebration, music for dancing and growing. Her sisters must have had enough of death and mourning. She had taken a dip in the sea to limber up her muscles, then headed for home. By then the plantlights were mostly out and the channels deserted, except for Spinel.

She had stopped in her tracks. A dozen different impulses had fought through her at once, and at last her sense of adventure had won.

"Well, Valan." Lystra sat down beside him. "Why haven't you joined the fun?"

He looked away. "I want to go home."

"But you are home." Mystified, she peered at his dark profile, a web's-breadth away from her touch.

"Home is a 'shore' of land I can stand on. If I were to slip from this branch, I'd fall straight to the bottom of the sea."

"Not without coral deathweights. Otherwise, only the bones ever reach land."

"*I'm* not dead bones."

"Then you have nothing to worry about."

For his part, Spinel was at a loss; there seemed nothing left to be said. Yet something agitated him, and he had to break away before he lost control. With an effort he stood up.

"Where are you going?" she asked.

"What's it to you?" He flung the words down. "You told me to go," he reminded her.

"Ah, but you didn't go, did you?" From where she sat, Lystra reached out her arm and curled a finger around his ankle, flicking his instep.

A pulse raced through him. Reeling, Spinel sat down again hard and dug his fingernails into the weeds. Lystra's hand closed about his wrist to steady him. "But I'm a malefreak!" he exclaimed, not sure why he had said it, but an intoxicating warmth flooded over him.

"So what, I love you anyway." Lystra figured it was all right. Usha had said that males were not all that different, just bigger outside to make up for what they lacked within. For a moment she felt intensely sorry for Spinel, who had no womb for a little sister to swim in, only a thing like the mating arm of an octopus. The thought fled in an instant; pity was Merwen's failing, not hers. Spinel's skin was as warm as her own, and softened by a thin sort of fur, sparser than the wisp of headfur that a newborn soon shed.

Spinel held back, still afraid that the slightest wrong move would turn her into a fury again. Day after day he had seen Lystra's form, until he knew her as well as the branch channels, yet now, without clothes to pull off, a signal was missing. She explored him with her fingers, then with her lips. Then something she touched shattered the tension, and they both clung together as if they would merge into one, until the sun's first rays spurted across the sea.

5

The next several days passed quickly for Spinel. He went with Lystra everywhere, whether tending starworms or solar cookers. At night the pair took a blanket out to the water's edge, or if it rained they hid away in a trysting nest in one of the remoter raft tunnels. Spinel began to recognize nuances of finger-talk that had escaped him before, and for a while he could not look straight at a webbed hand.

No one said anything, but odd incidents began to happen. Once they both were out in a boat with Flossa and Wellen and a refugee girl. Without warning, the three girls leaped together and dove overboard; the craft capsized behind them, dumping Spinel and Lystra. The next day, for dinner, there was nothing but octopus, hundreds of meaty arms steamed over hydrogen burners. When the jokes started about various octopus arms and what their specialized functions were, Spinel more than suspected they were aimed at him. Then Flossa whispered something, and the rest of the little witches giggled like crazy.

"What was that?" he demanded, but they only laughed harder.

Lystra said, "She wonders how I can bear to look at someone whose 'breasts' hang down between the legs with an extra thumb in between."

That killed his appetite, and he fled behind the silkhouse.

Lystra came after him. "What's the matter, Spinel?" Her hands cradled his head. "You look glum as a starfish."

"Why do they have to pick on me?" Though already his mind was dissolving in the seafoam of her touch.

"Not you, us. That's how it is, when a pair of sisters swim as twins. The others will test us, to see how well we stick." She sighed. "If I hadn't a selfname to honor, I'd strangle them myself."

"Well *I'll* strangle them, if they don't leave off."

"Try that, and you'll set the whole raft to laughing. You should Unspeak them instead."

"Really? How?"

"Pretend Flossa does not exist. Just look straight through her every time."

"Maybe. . . ."

So he set his mind to ignoring Flossa. At first, she redoubled her tricks to get his attention. She would not leave him in peace, until the time she sat herself down right before the doorhole so he had to step over her to get in. His foot slipped; he fell and bruised his elbow. At the sight of this, Flossa took fright and kept asking whether he was hurt, until Spinel begrudgingly admitted that he might recover. The mishap quenched her interest in the game, and her companions soon gave up as well.

Merwen watched the pair discreetly. Though their friendship pleased her, its sudden intensity caught her off guard. Yet when had Lystra ever been anything but sudden?

Furthermore, Merwen still felt for Yinevra, who had taken her daughter's loss stoically but at some point was bound to explode. Would Yinerva lash out at Lystra, accusing her of forgetting so soon? For the sake of harmony, Merwen invited Yinevra to share a supper with the family, and somewhat to her surprise she accepted.

Now Yinevra was here, with her lovesharer Kithril, who was busily sharing acquaintance with Merwen's refugee guests. Yinevra sat quiet and pensive, leaning her elbows on her knees. Lystra and Spinel sat apart from the rest, caught up in a lively discussion, in Valan tongue, about the traders' latest proposal to hire Sharers as deckhands for a "wage."

"Sign us on, they say," Lystra grumbled. "Sign on to their own seasilk-raking vessels—now, for a year's supply of starworm cables. A year's supply! And they're short of steel?"

"It's all to hook you in," Spinel said. "Moontraders are scoundrels, the whole lot. Even in Chrysoport you couldn't find a straight one." His hand alighted easily on her breast.

"We'll send them all home," Lystra added, "by *whichever* ill-fated door they came."

"Yes, but that will take awhile. Why not lock them up first?"

"What?" Playfully she wrestled his arm away. "What sort of notion is that?"

"Just lock them away safe, so they can't hurt anybody."

"Is that what you do on Valedon?"

"Sure. How else do you treat a crook?"

Lystra seemed interested. "Does it work? Are they cured?"

"I guess so. Why would the Protector waste good *solidi* on jails if they didn't work?"

Yinevra had overheard Spinel. She nodded and stretched and addressed Merwen. "Curious," she murmured, "this Valen daughter of yours. I commend your choice; as usual, you knew what you were about, after all." She nodded again, to herself. "Yes, they took my daughter, Shora curse them. But we took one of theirs, and I think they will live to regret it."

Merwen sickened at this bitter wish. Learnsharing was such a subtle thing. She was loath to trigger another clash with Lystra, but better now before it got out of hand.

It took some vigilance to catch Lystra alone again, and when she did at last, she felt far from comfortable. "My daughter, I see that you have found a twin."

"So your plan worked. No need to—"

"I planned nothing of the sort."

The sharp words startled Lystra, who drew her face in like a snail. "Why not?"

Merwen searched for words. Few sisters had her daughter's knack of leaving her speechless.

"What a mother you are," said Lystra irritably. "No lovesharer of mine would ever suit you well enough."

"You have a selfname, but Spinel does not."

"It's too sudden, is that what you think?" Lystra glared at her. "Wasn't Usha *sudden*, for you?"

Merwen kept her voice level. "Usha was no Valan malefreak."

"Indeed, hear the wordweaver now!" Lystra crowed. "Who was it who convinced us all that Valans are human, male and female alike?"

"Each convinced herself. But—"

"You're wriggling out. If Yinevra could hear you now!"

"Valans require much learnsharing."

"And you thought that Spinel would come here to learn with you all the time. Instead, he shares with me. He hates traders as much as I do." She triumphantly crossed her arms.

"Hating is the saddest thing to share. What else have you shared with Spinel?"

Taken aback, Lystra considered. "I think that Valedon has two sorts of creatures, 'good' ones like Spinel, and 'evil' ones like traders." She used the Valan terms. "'Evil' ones are trapped like animals, so they won't hurt the 'good' ones."

"So only the 'evil' ones get trapped?"

"That's right."

"Including Shaalrim and Lalor when they were on Valedon?"

Abruptly Lystra stood up. "Well, who can say, anyway! You spent a whole summer there, and what do *you* know?" The door whooshed open as she stomped out, nearly colliding with Nisi in her haste.

Nisi barely noticed, she was so wrapped up with her own news. "Malachite comes tomorrow," Nisi announced triumphantly. "And my lovesharer, too. All as Talion promised." She paused for breath. "He—Malachite asks to visit with you, and with the Gathering."

"Malachite? The selfnamer?"

"Yes. He'll tell you himself," Nisi added quickly.

"Good. Was this what Talion shared with you, the last time?"

Nisi grew tense. She worked her fingers in between each other,

in a manner that unnerved Merwen. "We spoke of many things."
But Nisi had not shared them with Merwen later, as she usually
did. It saddened Merwen to watch Nisi struggle with her own
name.

Other Sharers were not surprised to hear that the Valan selfnamer would visit Merwen first. Merwen had always thought well
of malefreaks.

Berenice was beside herself with anxious anticipation. Everything must go like clockwork in this first contact with a lord whose
will could end a city, or even a world. Her first agonizing decision
had been how to present herself, clothed or not. It hurt her to
alienate Lystra and others who were sensitive about such things. In
the end, though, the presence of Realgar had settled it. From her
meager wardrobe she chose a plain, close-fitting talar whose hue
matched her skin.

Now Berenice stood at the water's edge, lacing and unlacing
her fingers, with Merwen and Usha beside. To her dismay, Merwen had insisted that the family be present, except for Flossa, who
was needed for a shockwraith hunt. There stood Spinel with his
mouth agape, shamelessly arm in arm with Lystra, whose curiosity
had won out over the hunt. And there were Weia and Wellen with
fingers in their mouths.... Berenice could only hope that the
Envoy would forgive any breach of etiquette from these ignorant
natives of the Ocean Moon.

A large bullet-shaped vessel pulled up to where the raft
branches rose dry. From it, a silvery walkway extruded, all the
way up to the core raft. As the visitors disembarked, Realgar
gleamed magnificently with the sun full on his studded uniform.
Yet the honor guard of twelve, striding forth in two perfect columns, made her scalp prickle as it approached this unarmed Sharer
family.

Malachite came last. A figure of perfect proportions, with platinum hair and seamless platinum clothes, the Envoy bore an extraordinary air of authority.

Realgar saluted. "My Lord Malachite, infinitely wise Envoy of
the All-knowing Patriarch of Torr, I beg leave to present Lady
Berenice of Hyalite, the Protectoral Liaison for Shora."

Her unexpected title first startled and then infuriated her. She
hurried to introduce Merwen and her family, as "protectors," and
recovered some of her composure.

Malachite gave Realgar an inaudible command. In an instant, the honor guard was marching back to their ship, leaving just the two men. Berenice relaxed enormously. Perhaps, after all, the Envoy would understand Shora.

Merwen had been disconcerted to see Valans in the plumage of wage-earning death-hasteners like up with this Malachite, the Valan selfnamer. The fact that one of them was Realgar, Nisi's lovesharer, was a revelation to Merwen. No wonder Nisi had always spoken so little of him; she must have felt as deeply for him as had Lystra for Rilwen.

Malachite himself was a disappointment, at first sight. Merwen had expected him to look more like a Spirit Caller, loosely clothed and with a long unhurried beard. Instead he looked almost Iridian, smooth-shaven except for the scalp, encased in stiff cloth and a collar that all but cut off his head. None of the epithets that Realgar embarrassingly listed for him sounded anything like a self-name, but of course he would share that himself; she would not be so impolite as to ask.

"You have a lovely seaname," Merwen told him.

"Thank you," said Malachite, in an accent as clear as Nisi's. "But I should share for correctness that the sea did not name me, since my home has no sea."

The Sharers were all amazed. "No sea *at all?*" Spinel exclaimed.

Nisi tried to hush him, much to Merwen's annoyance. Usha recovered to say with unusual grace, "Now that you're here, the sea has surely named you."

"I share thanks," said Malachite, "and to show my appreciation for your welcome I bring gifts from the Patriarch Himself."

The gift-toys that sprang from his spindly fingers were remarkable, even more so than those brought by Nisi's mother and mothersister, the first of the traders, when they first fell from the sky. A nugget of light sent cascades of flowers, then animal-shapes as big as the silkhouse, all of which vanished as swiftly as they came. A dot of fabric unfolded to an enormous drapery invisibly thin, yet strong enough to lift a fishing boat. A silver pyramid hovered like a clickfly and emitted teeth-shattering sounds her ears had never known.

Nisi, too, was impressed, and even her orange-haired love-sharer showed a spark of interest from within his bristling shell.

"These wonders come from beyond Valedon?" Merwen asked.

"From Torr itself, the home of the Patriarch," Malachite said. "These particular inventions came about in the years since I last toured Valedon."

Wellen and Weia pounced on the drapery skin, squealing and rolling in its folds until all at once it snapped into nothing again. "Don't suffocate, girls," Usha scolded. The silver pyramid hovered in front of Spinel with its shrill song and evaded his attempts to capture it.

Merwen said, "These tones seem alive. Do they reproduce?"

"We produce them in numbers that would fill your sea."

"A sea of toys," said Lystra, "for a world of children?"

Nisi gasped and covered her shock with a cough. Merwen guessed that the subject of "children" might be sensitive for Malachite, however well he repressed it.

In fact, Malachite only nodded toward Lystra. "Trillions of children sleep safe in their homes under the care and protection of the Patriarch."

Merwen's attention wandered as she thought again, A world with *no ocean* at all, only stone. She caught herself and invited the visitors into the silkhouse for refreshments, freshly picked seaweeds of several rare species. Usha warned Weia not to gobble too much from the bowl, since her elder sisters had dived long and hard to find these delicacies.

Malachite sat himself with perfect composure upon a seasilk mat. His leggings creased less than Realgar's did. "Your rooms breathe," he observed. "Yet there are no doors."

"Only a door to outside, and one to below. All others are within ourselves."

"You see how customs differ. Now Torr is called the planet of a thousand doors, nothing but doors among countless chambers, from the surface to the very core."

Lystra said, "It sounds like a planetful of coral, to me. How can you live in that? Where do you swim for fish?"

"Coral," said Usha, "is all dead at the core, like raftwood. This planet sounds more like a sponge, to me."

Realgar's cheeks puckered in that peculiar way of Valans who try not to laugh. At the bowl of seaweed, Weia sneaked under Usha's arm and grabbed a good handful.

"How many planets are there?" Spinel wanted to know.

"Ninety-six were inhabited, four years ago. Several are in initial stages of 'terraforming' for settlement," Malachite said, adding a Valan word.

"Wow! Is there a planet where they talk in birdsong?"

Malachite paused just an instant, then whistled a phrase.

"That's it, that was Dak's little tune." Spinel was delighted.

"A world that was once," said Malachite. "It failed, sadly, to learnshare the perfection of the Patriarch."

Something snagged in that sentence. Merwen spread her finger-webs. "Sorry, I don't understand . . . perfection?"

"The Patriarch is the perfect judge of humankind. His perfect judgment has been demonstrated for a thousand years of human survival."

"Then He must be dead."

Nisi blinked and her lips parted, but no sound came out.

"Now, lovesharer," said Usha, "must you be so literal? Of course only death achieves perfect balance among life's shifting molecules. But allow for poetic license."

Nisi bowed her head and clasped her hands. "Please . . . you can't judge the Patriarch by human standards." All the while, Malachite ignored her and the others but watched Merwen as if expecting her to continue.

"Listen," Merwen went on, annoyed at having to lecture. "What is the name of the perfect good? Is it freedom? Perfect freedom is death. Is it peace? Perfect peace is death. Is it love? Perfect love is to choose death, that others may live."

A silence absorbed her words. For the first time Realgar spoke, saying in Valan, "What a motto for a soldier."

"Since you so disdain 'perfection,'" said Malachite at last, "I will share with you my selfname, the Perfect One."

"Ah, now I see. Excuse me." A version of "hubris," the name was unusual but not unheard of. Merwen thought she understood, now.

"And, as the Lady Berenice indicates, the Patriarch is an entity beyond human. His is the perfection of that which you call 'coldstone.'"

Merwen shook her head, mystified again, and Usha waved her finger at him. "Coldstone, you say," said Usha. "That's what Valans like to think. Valans replace legbones with coldstone, instead of growing them back. But those are far from 'perfect.'"

"Do you regenerate limbs?" Malachite's words came quickly.

"When required, Shora forbid. In fact—" Usha paused to

glower at Weia, who had just snitched the last of the rare seaweed from the bowl. "Trurl's daughter is still recovering in the lifeshaping chamber. She had barely a head and chest left after we fished her from the fleshborers. But she's growing back, now."

"It would please me to see this."

An avid look came into her eyes. "Of course, you *must* come down to the tunnels and see." Usha was always ready to hook another apprentice for those skills that took decades to share.

The Envoy's reception pleased Berenice, so far. No irreparable damage had been done. Even Realgar was on his best behavior and bowed out without needing her to explain that we must not accompany them to the Gathering. The Gathering, though, would be something else again.

As sisters converged within the central hollow, a lively mood prevailed in the wake of a successful shockwraith hunt—nine arms taken, one of record size, with no injuries sustained. Yinevra was the hero of the day, and talk buzzed over the latest techniques in baiting and how to cut at just the right segment behind the neural node. Malachite faced a flood of questions.

"Where is your 'Patriarch,' Perfect One?" Yinevra asked. "Why does He live so far away?"

"The Patriarch shares care of many planets," Malachite replied. "He can't be everywhere at once. That is what the Envoy is for."

"Still, you can't let a pack of children run a planet."

"Why do you say 'children'?"

"Valans behave as children. Except for the Deceiver."

Embarrassed, Berenice hugged her knees and stared at the clumps of weeds beyond her feet.

"How is the Deceiver different?" Malachite asked, unperturbed.

"Nisi the Deceiver shares our way," said Yinevra. "She has risked life to save life, and she chose her own name. She shares our Gathering."

"Valans have their own ways and their own gatherings. Have you ever shared a session of the Trade Council?"

This suggestion met blank stares. Berenice took the chance to point out, quietly, that Sharers were not even permitted to board House space carriers, much less to attend the Council.

Malachite said, "That will change."

She sat up straight. This was exactly what she was hoping for.

"And what about those greedy fishing boats?" someone asked. "No excuse for that."

"Already, Valan trawlers are shut down, until my environmental study is complete."

This was a delight. Talion had never hinted at such measures.

"And the stone trade?" asked Yinevra. "Will that stop too?"

At that, the Envoy paused, not just to gather his thoughts, Berenice believed, but to emphasize his reply. "What I have shared here suggests to me that the entire system of trade between the planets, in its present form, may have to cease, to be rebuilt only along very different lines."

Berenice was amazed. Her lips parted and she stared without seeing, while she thought, Could it really all come true, so soon? With Malachite, it could. His judgment had come swift and sure, even as it had for disobedient Pyrrhopolis.

6

Malachite spent several days touring rafts; the places of lifeshaping were of particular interest to him. In the meantime, reports confirmed his word: trawlers were idle at the traders' rafts; House spacefaring vessels were opened to Sharers, although at a prohibitive cost; and gemstones actually vanished from the traders' shelves.

Captain Dak's battered moonferry, which had never refused a Sharer, resumed its regular schedule now that seaswallowers had passed. Spinel sailed behind a glider squid out to the landing as soon as he heard.

The old ship looked smaller and even more patched up than he had remembered. "Dak?" Spinel cupped his hands to his mouth and called up the ramp. "Dak, old bird, are you there?"

No answer. Spinel hopped up the rattling steps three at a time and skipped through the open door. Inside, it was dark; he paused until his eyes adjusted.

A song grew from the darkness, a low, wavering whistle. Spinel traced its source to the passenger cabin, where Dak sprawled in a seat with his legs splayed out in the aisle. The song was compellingly sad, the most sorrowful music Spinel had ever heard. It froze him where he stood, and his eyelids grew heavy. It ended with an almost unbearable version of the home phrase that Malachite had echoed.

Dak turned and gasped. "Torr's name—a *halfbreed?*"

Spinel blinked and wiped his eyes. "It's me, Dak, remember?"

"That you . . . starling?" Dak squinted forward in the dimly lit cabin. "Thought for sure it was the bottle. Is that really you, the starling who came on board clinging to the nonexistent skirts of a couple of Sharer gals? Torr's name, you're black as hell and a head taller since then."

"Well, not a head."

Dak reached up to clap Spinel's arm. "Granite muscles, too. Man, what do they *feed* you out there?"

"Oh, everything. And I cheated the swallowers, too. But listen, Dak, you've got to help me. I'm awfully worried about my folks in Chrysoport."

"As well you might be, since the Dolomites swallowed the town."

"What?" His knees faltered.

Dak pulled himself up. "Hey there, take a seat. And some of this." The bottle smelled strong, all right. Spinel sipped while Dak told his tale, first of Pyrrhopolis, how the City of Fire was besieged by Sards on the one hand and Dolomites on the other, only to meet its end in a mountain of dust. Dazed, Spinel shook his head. "Malachite did that?"

"Sure as I'm sitting here. You should see Iridis: refugees clog the lowstreets. The beggar population tripled in a day. Thieves crawl up even to the highstreets, until the scanners burn them out; newcomers don't know those tricks."

"But Malachite talked to us . . . so quiet, like."

"Well, *you* don't fuse atoms."

No, Spinel thought, my atoms just "tunnel through."

Dak frowned at his bottle. "Did I hear right: the Torran Envoy talked to you?"

"Well, sure. He came to see Merwen."

"The same Merwen that traveled my junkheap of a ship? I'll be a troll's cousin," he finished thickly.

"Come on, Dak, hurry up and tell me about Chrysoport."

"Don't hurry a millennial man, starling. For assisting the siege, the Dolomites got their reward, a seacoast at last, including your home town. Don't look so glum. I hear it was a clean takeover, hardly a man lost. I tell you what: I'll go look up your folks, next time down. How's that?"

Spinel looked up. "That's swell of you."

"Tell me about the Envoy," Dak insisted. "Is he still the same, after nine centuries?"

Spinel shrugged listlessly. "It's kind of funny, how he treats Lady Nisi."

"How's that?"

"Well, her and the General, both—he looks down on them, almost the way they look down on commoners." He nearly said, "us commoners."

Dak shook with laughing, in his weird quiet way, then he leaned forward until his hot breath brushed Spinel's face. "A wise man you've become. Tell the truth, though—you still a starling underneath?"

Spinel sighed and stretched. "I guess so. I don't even have a selfname yet."

While the Torran Envoy toured Shora, Berenice went to call on Realgar at the traders' raft, where he had set up a temporary headquarters.

"Realgar. . . . Imagine, to say your name again so soon."

He kissed her so hard their teeth cracked together. Luxuriously her fingers combed his hair, which was smoother than seasilk and the color of sunrise.

Realgar framed her head in his broad hands. "You gave me such a start, the day we arrived."

"I know. I'm as bald as an eggplant."

"You looked like you hadn't a stitch on, at first."

"Ral, you know how I live among Sharers. It's only natural." Teasingly she twisted a lock of his hair. If only she had time to grow her own back.

"Too many men around, nowadays. Who's that young fellow that lives with you now?"

Irritated, she pulled back. "You needn't put it that way. He's a common boy that Merwen took in. Do you trust me or not?"

His eyes were laughing. "By Torr, you're headstrong. I simply

can't stand to do without you, you see." He kissed her fingertips.
"You'll settle down, once we've tied the knot."

Her mind threw up a wall. Pass that threshold when it comes.

Realgar led her to a chair of russet cushions with legs ending in
lion claws, Sardish style. The claws stood upon a carpet of hunting
scenes tightly woven in red and bronze. Berenice shared his taste
for Sardish tapestry, its earth-toned elegance. From the ceiling, a
servo arm snaked down with a glass of her favorite wine; the fra-
grance was heavenly, after so long. "You travel well," she noted.

"To guard the Torran Envoy is a great honor."

"It caps your career. Though the Perfect One hardly seems to
require your aid." She watched him closely.

"Not at all, practically speaking. For your ears only, he carries
a regiment's worth of protection on his person."

She watched the reflections in her glass and waited for her
pulse to slow. Malachite must have told him to tell her, for her to
tell Merwen...but of course she would not. "Protectoral Liaison," indeed. What trollheads they were—that is, Talion was; not
Realgar, who was only following orders, or Malachite the All-
knowing, who was learning soon enough.

"Yes," Realgar added, "remarkable things are made on Torr."

She changed the subject. "How are Cassiter and Elmvar?"

"Splendid. Cassi is getting to be a crack shot; I'll be sending
her after the bears, next."

"Torr's name—that little darling?" Cassi must have overcome
her noise shock, after all these years. Tell me, Berenice wanted to
say; tell me, you didn't lose patience and send your own daughter
to a mindbender?"

"She's still sensitive," Realgar said, "but she faces it down. A
real trooper, she is."

"She must be." Berenice had joined his expeditions in the Sardish wilderness, where trees grew so vast that ten men could hide
behind one, and gray bears stood up on their hind legs tall as
prehistoric trolls. To look down a bear's throat took the same courage as to face a seaswallower.

"They still ask for you, though. Elmvar wants to know when
you'll come home and be his mama."

Two hints within five minutes. With her sandal she traced the
outline of a snarling tiger woven in the carpet.

"Your own mother asks too, Berenice."

Quickly she looked up, and her nails dug into the chair. "What for?"

"Easy now. Their only child, and when do they see you?"

"Once a year, I manage. Ral, they forfeited any right to ask." Screaming beacons haunted her eyes. No place to hide but the shockwraith's lair. . . .

Realgar took her hands in his. "A time comes to let wounds heal." The voice of a diplomat, gentle yet firm. No wonder he had risen far.

But it was Merwen who had said that Valans, if quick to anger, were as quick to forgive. "All right, I'll go." She sighed.

"Excellent." He pressed her hands. "When will you return, my love?" His eyes compelled her.

"Before the sea swallows next," she made herself say, to retain some leeway.

For a moment she could have cried out, I want to be with you *now and always,* but everything that holds you, surrounds you— makes you what you are—holds me back.

Instead, she asked, "How much longer can you stay here?"

"Ask Malachite. Between us, Berenice, those Sharer friends of yours have got his circuits whizzing. I think he's never seen the like of it."

"Oh, no?" Berenice sipped at her glass to steady herself. Just how forbidden is their "lifeshaping," she wanted to know. But it would be tactless to ask and pointless to expect an answer—yet.

This Malachite was a strange one, Merwen thought, as she rested at noon, floating among new green sprouts of silkweed that cascaded from the branches, while the shaded waters cooled her toes. While he was here, Malachite came and went in silence, with barely a footfall, and always alone after the first day. Always courteous, he never refused a request outright, yet for himself he never took food or drink and never entered the sea, even to relieve himself. There was a barrier, whether of extreme distrust or pride or stoicism, Merwen could not guess. He did bring about constructive behavior among Valans, as Nisi had promised. Yet the change seemed cold and sudden. How could one mind share change with so many, so fast? Merwen felt that the longer one took to change, the longer the change might last.

Malachite did come once more to sit with Merwen, this time out on a raft branch. The sea was lively that day, and some spray caught his feet. Merwen sighed and thought, Perhaps the sea has named him, after all.

Serenely, as always, he announced, "Tomorrow I share parting with Shora."

"I see." Sudden again. Merwen wished to express regret, but somehow it seemed inappropriate.

"I have changed my mind about Shora," he said. "Initially, I had expected Valedon to absorb your needs with ease, but now I prefer an alternative."

"I see."

Malachite added, "Your numbers are small now, but you will grow. Your Gatherings will need their own 'Envoy from Torr.'"

Confused, Merwen shook her head. "Why should our numbers grow?" Every conception of a child was a decision for the Gathering. Even Usha had been allowed a second child only after she had adopted Flossa, an orphan from a swallowed raft. Shora had only so many souls to go around.

Malachite said, "Human numbers always grow."

"But nine hundred thousand are just enough for us. It's been enough, for ten thousand years."

"You began with only one. You've grown since then."

Merwen felt an impasse. "Try your Valan language to explain."

"Valan is not my language, and Torran would mean nothing to you. Valan is irrelevant to this case."

"Then why did you use two Valan words a moment ago?"

No frown appeared in his flat, unlined features. None ever did. "The 'Patriarch,'" he said slowly, "is an All-knowing Mother. The 'Envoy' implements Her decisions."

"We have an All-knowing Mother, Shora, and we have more than enough decision-sharers."

"The All-knowing Mother of Torr will send an Envoy who can work with multiple decision-sharers and set up an appropriate program for your planet."

"What sort of program?"

"Installation of a controlled atom-fusion energy source to further your development. Regulation of its use. Regulation of other potentially harmful activities. Convenient birth control. Exchange of scientific and cultural achievements with other worlds."

Merwen was embarrassed. "Sorry, but I comprehend you less and less. You propose to make another sun?"

"A small piece of sun, encased safely in stone."

"A starstone?"

"No, much bigger. To make energy."

Bigger than a starstone, smaller than the sun. "But the First Door sends us more than enough energy."

"It will not, once your numbers increase."

"But we don't." Merwen was circling in a linguistic whirlpool.

"You don't think you will," Malachite said. "You don't think you will ever hasten death, either."

Merwen's lips barely moved. "And what do you think?"

"All peoples discover how to hasten death, sooner or later. Some start out like you, but they all learn."

Here was a riddle. "What are you trying to say? A few of us fall into sickness, of course."

"What becomes of them?"

With a sick feeling, Merwen forced herself to share the one case she had known. "Virien of Umesh-el . . . had to be Unspoken. She did not cure, so for the safety of the others she was helped away to a raft outside system Per-elion."

"And how long did she last there?"

Merwen hesitated. "I don't know," she said, which was true but not the whole truth.

"So her death was hastened, in effect."

The statement shocked her. Could this visitor not know what he was saying? "Virien might have cured, first. Some do. Life is not perfect." She nearly added, Only death is, Perfect One.

"But the All-knowing Mother of Torr is perfect."

At first Merwen made no response. Then she said, "I begin to see." Her words drifted like fallen blossoms on a wave. "Valedon does have a sickness, and it reaches out to us".

"The Valan sickness is checked, for now. But Sharers, too, have the seeds of it, within their own doors. I must protect you from yourselves, as well as Valedon."

Sickness—yes, she felt it in him, an appalling icy sickness that threatened to draw her in. Her fingertips whitened, but she pulled herself back. "Sickness, yes. The sickness is yours, Perfect One, a cancer of fear. I would protect you, if I could."

"You know no fear then?"

"I fear for you."

Among the raft branches, the ocean groaned and muttered to itself. Wormlets of foam crawled hungrily up the branch beside her. On Malachite's immotile brow, a few silver wisps stirred with the wind. It reminded Merwen that, among Sharers, only infants had headfur, which the sea took back soon after birth.

"You are innocent as children," Malachite said. "You could learn on your own, as most do; but if you were to survive, as many do not, your abilities would threaten Valedon and all other inhabited worlds. I cannot allow this. Someone must share this lesson with you, if not your own 'Envoy,' then perhaps Valedon . . . But that will be painful."

He had it all inside out. No one could be more cruel and dangerous than a child, and no selfnamer could threaten her own world, much less many. But the sickness of this Perfect One was beyond reach of words.

"I must leave tomorrow," Malachite said. "Will you at least receive an Envoy from Torr, one perhaps with a program more appropriate than mine?"

Merwen herself would receive anyone, but the Gathering would not, once they shared what she had heard. Lightly, Merwen touched Malachite's hand. It was warm; strangely, she had expected it to be cold. "Dissolve your fear. Stay and share healing with us."

She could not have said how long they sat, until all at once the Perfect One had gone away, and the cloth shell of his back was receding down the long coldstone ramp to his vessel.

7

It was the time of waterfire. In the wake of the seaswallowers, with lesser predators as sparse as raft seedlings, tiny "firelets" multiplied unchecked. By day these protozoans went unseen, but by night they glowed pale orange and lined the waves with flame. It was a spectacular time for night dipping, to bathe oneself all over in the waterfire; to swallow the "flames" and spit them out again. One's teeth glowed for hours afterward. Spinel and Lystra and other young funlovers, and some not so young, spent such late nights at the game that they dragged at their tasks the next day. It was fortunate for the health of the raft that waterfire receded within a few days, consumed by a myriad other "sisters" of the sea. Legfish, too, were returning slowly. And a few raft seedlings had survived to grow over the next decades into floating islands large enough to support Sharer colonies.

Several sisters chose to conceive children in order to provide new homes for the lost souls of Kiri-el. And Elonwy's child was born, underwater of course, into the arms of her sisters, whose ears were quick to catch her seaname. The experience impressed Spinel, who remembered the birth of Beryl's Oolite with the door closed upon secrecy and pain.

But what struck Spinel oddly was Shaalrim's attitude toward her unborn daughter. Shaalrim let Spinel feel the swift fluttering within, and her belly actually shifted from side to side at the kicks of the little one. "She'll make a good swimmer," said Spinel.

"Yes," said Shaalrim. "Strong little beast, isn't she?"

Spinel looked up. "Why . . . beast?"

"Because she is. She keeps me awake at night with kicking at my liver, and if I were at the Last Door she would still suck the last life from me."

"She can't know any better," said Spinel, vaguely disquieted.

"No, no more than an octopus. Or a shockwraith." Shaalrim sighed and smiled hopefully. "But she'll learn. And I love her, all the same."

He was perplexed still, and a sudden longing came over him, for Beryl and *her* second child, who must be born by now, and whose name he did not even know. Was it a boy or a girl, his nephew or niece? How could he just sit and wait for Dak to find out?

The sun had dipped below the sea. Behind him Lystra was fidgeting, and she leaned her chin into his neck. "Spinel, I have only two hours tonight before my starworm duty."

"Oh, all right." They swam off together to an unsettled raftling, one that would grow large enough for tunneling within a generation. As usual, Lystra had thought up some new and delicious ways of sharing pleasure that Spinel was sure would have astounded his Chrysolite friends. In fact, Lystra seemed to come up with every possible way there could be, except for the one regular way, which she still avoided. This had rarely bothered him, but tonight for some reason he felt that something was missing.

Spinel stretched back upon the weeds and let the night flow over him. For once he tried to think carefully, to frame a tactful approach. The more he thought, though, the more his nerve slipped away: that was the trouble with thinking things through.

"Lystra?" He ran his finger down the track of her spine. Lystra rolled over, her eyes half open, her breasts sloping languidly. "Lystra, I know you don't want to get pregnant, but I could take pills for that. Could we try it the normal way some time?"

She blinked at him. "For a Sharer, you still come out with gibberish once in a while. I won't start a child before we build a silkhouse. What is 'normal,' and how are the two related?"

"I'm just saying, I want to share love the way I'm made to, that's all."

"You mean the octopus arm? Don't I stroke it enough?"

"Oh, yes, your fingers are good, excruciatingly beautiful." He took her hand and dipped his finger into the scallops, aroused just by the memory of her touch. "And your lips too and—every part of you is beautiful. But couldn't we try it the other way, just once?"

Lystra considered for a bit. "Usha says it will make me sick."

Spinel frowned. "Mothers and mothersisters always say that."

"It's true enough. It would cause toxic shock to my internal organs."

"Your ancestors did it, all right."

"So I've heard. And a billion years before that, our ancestors were all one-celled and budded off like yeast."

"Well, how does Usha know? *She* never tried it."

"Traders used to try with us, a long time ago. Nisi calls it 'rape.'"

"Well *I'm* not trying to 'rape' you." He was highly indignant. "I love you."

"I love you, too."

There must be some way out of the predicament, Spinel thought. "Couldn't you get an operation or something to . . . ?"

"But I'm perfectly healthy. Why don't you be lifeshaped to be like me?"

"What! I'm a *man,* you trollhead," he exclaimed in Valan. The very idea gave him goosebumps all over.

"I know, stoneshaper. I love you anyway." Surreptitiously she eased her fingers around his thigh, but he pushed her away. Lystra shrugged. "Go ahead, sulk if you want."

Spinel was thinking, he should have known from the start it would never work out. They were a race of man-haters, after all. No wonder the traders cheated them.

Lystra added, "The traders soon learned not to share 'rape.' We applied ointment that stung on contact, so they shared the pain."

Spinel replied, "We don't put up with rapists on Valedon. We put them away, or even hasten death for the worst ones."

Her look was stricken. "Hasten death? You could do that?"

"Not me. You need a ruby, for that job."

Lystra stared pensively beyond him. "Merwen says that many Valans are . . . sick in this way."

"Well, *she* has nerve. Is it sick just to save yourself? Were you sick when you left Rilwen at her Last Door?"

Her face glazed over. Without a word more, she got up and walked away.

"Her, wait a minute." Spinel scrambled to his feet and hurried after her. "Look, I didn't mean it, I just—" He caught her arm, but she did not break stride; he had forgotten Lystra's strength. At the water's edge she jackknifed into the sea and swam straight back to Raia-el.

8

Once the envoy had departed, Berenice sensed a strangeness, a gulf between Merwen and herself that she had never felt before. She was at a loss to cope with it. It was unthinkable for Merwen to hold back her concerns.

"Nisi, this Perfect One," Merwen began, one morning after breakfast when most sisters had left the silkhouse for the day. "He puzzles me."

"How is that?" Berenice moved herself closer on the silk mat.

"He shared fear with us, not wisdom."

"Both, Merwen, always both."

"That cannot be."

A wave of cold swept Berenice. "Why not? Even you do."

"How do you mean?"

"Everyone shares fear with you: Yinevra, Lystra, even Usha at times. They fear your wisdom most of all."

"You fear, that is certain. And those who fear fight me. That hardly helps my wisdom, such as it is, to prevail."

Berenice was indeed terrified that Merwen would see into her and know her heart better than she knew herself. But she saw that the Sharer was not angry now, only immensely sad. This Berenice understood. "Power is always feared. The 'Patriarch' has incomparable power, and wisdom as well. Malachite can only share that wisdom. He is like a . . . a 'servo.'"

"Power fears its loss," said Merwen. "But your 'servos' are not human, they can't share fear."

"Oh, but Malachite is as close to human as an Envoy can be. Even though his brain contains circuits of coldstone."

Merwen's lips parted, loose; her eyes stared at some unseen horror. "Then . . . he . . ."

A shock jolted Berenice through every muscle. She had said something terribly wrong and could not call it back.

". . . is . . . dead." Merwen absorbed the impact of what she had just heard. *Coldstone*—she had shared speech with a coldstone "brain," a soulless thing that had never known birth, never passed even the First Door, let alone the Door of Self, a mind perfectly empty, living yet dead.

"A living dead. And all the while you knew, Nisi, you knew." Her voice wavered. Nisi's lovesharer and the others, they could not possibly have been cured, they were worse off than ghosts. And as for Nisi . . .

"What are you saying? Merwen! Come back!" Already Nisi's voice came from far away, as Merwen's senses hurtled outward from her whitened body, beyond the ocean, beyond even the stars, into the Door of Death itself.

The hole of that Door was a perfect white circle, more perfect than any silkhouse door. The Door stretched out into a tunnel of all those moments of her life which had already died. Some parts of the tunnel expanded wide, those rich times of her life, when the raft had prospered and her daughters were growing. Other sections pinched nearly shut, such as when the shockwraith's arm had touched her. Along the surface of the tunnel were door-points closed to branching corridors where her life might have turned—where she might have twinned with Yinevra, or might have begun to learn lifeshaping, or might have fallen into stonesickness; even before she left the womb, she might have developed a stunted limb or might never have developed at all. Before that . . . but that was back far enough.

Where in all her lifetime was there a clue to the terrible paradox of the people of stone?

Merwen had been barely five years old when the first skyboat fell to the sea. Mother Ama had lifted Merwen onto her shoulders to get a better look. Everyone gaped at the creatures that stepped out, these fanwings of flat nondescript plumage, until her mother had gasped, "I think they're our sisters."

Ama had not called them Sharers, the stronger term. Even then, Merwen had been wordwise enough to notice. Had her mother's instinct foreseen what was to come?

At first there had been nothing but excitement for the strangers, who were eager to share learning and gifts as exotic then as those of the Dead One seemed now. The greatest miracle was the camera, which produced images full-depth in light, recording life and memory in a way never imagined before. There must be some greatness in a people who could fashion such a thing, even out of coldstone. Merwen remembered this miracle at times when the Stone Moon seemed most hopeless.

As Merwen watched, the time-ghost of Ama changed, broken, shriveled. Ama was one of the few for whom lifeshaping came too late or was fated to fail. Yet the light of her soul stretched whole and sound throughout Merwen's tunnel. There were others for whom this could not be said. There was Rilwen . . .

And there was Virien of Umesh-el. If Merwen could not understand Virien, how could she ever hope to know Valedon?

Merwen had tried to help Virien. That was soon after Merwen had named herself. Virien was Unspoken by then, but had just hastened another death. So Merwen had asked the Gathering to send herself to share with Virien what healing she could. Hours, then days, she passed with that twisted soul, always remembering that healing had to flow in both directions.

"What do you want of me?" Virien spoke in a quiet, matter-of-fact tone. She was small, and her physical strength, like Merwen's, was mainly in her hands. "What do you want of me, Impatient One? To show the world you can outgrow your name?"

"Every Sharer wishes that," Merwen said, swallowing the sting. "I want peace with myself, just as you do."

"But I have peace."

"You think you do, but there are doors you fear to open."

Virien closed her eyes, then opened them with a start. "How do you know what peace means to me? Do you share my mind?"

"Of course not. But I have eyes to see. I know what a Sharer is. How long will you swim away from us?"

Virien smiled slyly. "Why were you sent here, if not because I keep swimming back?" To that she got no answer, so she shrugged, saying, "Look to your own doors. I hasten death because it suits me, that's all. I like it."

"What do you like about it?"

The words drew out from her tongue. "I like to feel the life's-breath stream away beneath my fingers. . . . "

And so it went, day after day. One day Virien seemed more agitated than usual, and she paced back and forth inside her little silkhouse. "Look, this can't go on, Impatient One. I really can't share another word."

"Then share my parting." Though incapable of whitetrance, Virien had only to Unspeak Merwen, and she would depart.

"No, no. I won't give you the satisfaction of that." Her path wound across the floor in a figure-eight. "Once you'd gone, they all would say, 'Even the Impatient One tried her best.'"

"I would give anything I have to see you healed."

"Even your life?"

"My life is a small thing."

Virien stopped in her tracks. "Ha! If a life is so small, why should I not hasten death?"

Merwen smiled. "You caught me there. I suppose that after so much sharing with you, my life has come to seem small indeed."

"Would you share your life with me? Would you share my love and raise my children?"

Then Merwen's heart beat faster. "Yes," she said levelly. "If it would cure you, I would."

Virien's face changed. "And what if it would not? Isn't that what love is for? Oh, no, don't answer, I don't want to hear it. *Shora,* you're so anxious to be a martyr, and all the while you loathe me like the rest of them."

"I share no hate with you. No one does—"

"Yes, you do! And pity, too, which is ten times worse!" She

lunged, but Merwen was prepared for it and fought back the hands that closed around her neck. For an endless minute Merwen strained, her lungs ready to burst, until Virien fell away and vanished between two silk panels. Gasping and shaking, Merwen wiped the sweat from her forehead. Then Virien came back—this time with a length of shockwraith arm. And if Yinevra had not been waiting unasked, outside...

That was all past, except for the scar. Today, Merwen faced a planet full of Viriens. Though it contained Spinels, too, and even starstones, she remembered. The aged male with the starstone had called upon a Spirit of... something, a Life-spirit at least. There was hope in that.

But there could be no hope for this Malachite the Dead.

Time was running out; Merwen had to face forward again. As she turned away from her past, the tunnel ahead was not fixed as was the one behind. It pulsed and writhed in all directions, like the churning gut of a starworm. It could pinch shut at any moment, if she willed that.

But in the world of this moment, of the living, she had left some unfinished sharing behind.

Her mind came rushing back to her, and she blinked. Outside, the sun was descending, and sisters were scurrying about the solar cookers. Merwen rose and stretched, snapping her toes until the webs hummed.

Nisi came quickly, and Usha too, with a disapproving furrow in her brow. Usha's arm came around Merwen, who rested her head gratefully on Usha's breast. "Too much mourning," Usha grumbled.

"How long does one mourn a soul that never lived?"

Nisi caught her breath, but words choked away. Her glance appealed to Usha, but Usha only listened for Merwen.

"Why, Nisi?" Merwen insisted quietly. "Why have you brought us dead ghosts from the shore?"

Nisi closed her eyes and swallowed. "Some sisters have a different concept of... of 'humanness.' Surely you understand that by now?"

"And who are you? What is your humanness? When will you learn whitetrance?"

"I—I can't, Merwen." Tears swelled Nisi's eyes. "I just can't ...hang my life by a thread." She clung to Merwen and sobbed desperately. "Don't close me out now. I've shared too far for that."

Pity arose in her, but she fought it back. She pressed Nisi's hand, brushing against the odd little shells at Nisi's fingertips. "Yes, Nisi, you try your best. But you see, I have to know now. I have to know whether you are like Malachite or only, perhaps, like Virien."

Nisi drew herself up very straight and rubbed at her scalp with a nervous gesture. "You have no right, Merwen." Her voice had lowered, and thickened. "That I could be so great as the one or so low as the other—how could you conceive of such a thing? Do you completely fail to appreciate what I've done for you on Valedon? Well, I've had enough; I'll go home, until you see. You've shared false judgment this time." With that, Nisi turned her back on Merwen, and perhaps on Shora as well.

For three days, Spinel could not get through to Lystra. No matter what he did or said, pleaded or threatened, he might as well address a slab of granite. Time crawled by in misery, and at dinner he was too depressed to eat.

Flossa pertly advised him, in between chewing on crab legs. "Ignore her right back. She's bound to come around, sometime."

Lystra was sitting right there, deaf to any remark addressed to him.

"But that's idiotic. Just plain id-i-otic." He drew out the word, pouring all his frustration into it.

"Oh, Lystra, dear," came Wellen's mocking voice. "Tell us, why won't you share speech with Spinel the malefreak, hm?"

"Who is that?" said Lystra.

Wellen convulsed in laughter, squealing and rolling back to kick her heels in the air. Spinel glared at her malevolently, and his fists tensed. Wellen did not notice, but Flossa did, and wrinkled her nose in obvious disgust at his reaction.

Spinel rose to his feet. "I've had it. I'm going home."

At the announcement, Usha looked up, her eyes owlish, but Lystra did not make a move.

"I'm going home *where I belong.* Where sisters love me *for* what I am, not despite it."

He strode down to the water's edge to sit on a branch and eat his heart out for the home he loved. Somewhere up there, his folks were struggling to make ends meet, or worse; what had become of them? A shroud of fog hid even moons tonight.

"Spinel," came a voice, "I love you for what you are." It was

Merwen who reached out to him, just as the last time, six months before, when Lystra had left him here, hurt, by the water.

"Lystra doesn't," Spinel said. "She's always hated what I really am."

"She only fears you, as a mirror to herself. Try this. Say to her, 'Speak to me, least I go Unspoken.'"

"And what then, if nothing happens?"

"Then you must go out alone, Unspoken. Think, will she let you do that?"

"She let Rilwen do it."

Merwen looked down. "That was different."

"I could never go. I can't bear even the thought of being . . . all alone." Fanwings screeching overhead, the sea pounding and nothing else: it was enough to drive one insane, if one were not insane to begin with.

"If it happens, Spinel, I'll go with you."

He was amazed. "You would? You mean the two of us would go off alone just because Lystra—" He shook his head. "You're weird. How can you call Valans 'sick' when you do such crazy things?"

"I never called you sick."

Spinel sighed and rubbed his aching temples. "I have to go back. I've got to find out if my folks are alive or dead."

"Oh, that's another matter, troublesharer. You'll go, then. And when you return to us, you will share a selfname."

Spinel sucked his breath in, then very slowly let it out again. "How do you know I'll return?"

"Because there is no other hope for us."

Merwen had sought him out, perhaps even from the day that their eyes first met in the market square. Spinel was just beginning to grasp the scope of what she expected of him, from scraps of words dropped by Lystra and Lady Nisi. The more he saw, the greater a burden it seemed. And yet it is a precious gift in any universe to be needed for something.

Part IV

STAR
OF STONE

1

Half a year had passed since Berenice and her Sharer companions had limped out to the Ocean Moon on Dak's rickety moonferry. Today Berenice was headed back to Valedon, and this time she had booked passage for herself and Spinel on the sleek Hyalite liner *Cristobel,* named after her mother.

At the water's edge she waited for a shuttle boat to the traders' raft. Her gray travel suit blew about her in the wind, which tugged also at the brush of hair that started from her scalp, and self-consciously she reached for the opal pinned to her collar. Beside her stood Spinel, obviously luxuriating in the silken white tunic she had ordered up from Iridis for him, with its border of nested squares in gold thread that sparkled in the sun. She had chosen the outfit deliberately to pique Merwen and to set off Spinel's striking figure, now coal black but for violet palms and lips.

Spinel stretched his limbs through the gorgeous cloth, which was actually seasilk, bleached and machine-finished. "Mm, this stuff slides like—like water."

Berenice pursed her lips. "Well, don't get carried away." Inwardly she was gleeful to see his delight in the richness she bestowed. He was not immune to the high life that Bernice craved and fought with every breath.

The sky darkened as stormclouds crossed the sun. When would that shuttle boat arrive as ordered? Berenice tapped her heels and clucked to a passing clickfly before she recalled that she had a watch to check, after all.

Then through the clouds broke a great shaft of light, sprinkling the waves, as if the Patriarch Himself had parted the troubled skies to extend His benediction. Berenice smiled with great contentment. This had always been her vision of the Patriarch of Torr: a hand of calm light, reaching down out of darkness. Talion feared His wrath, and even Merwen feared His Envoy. But Berenice knew that once the All-wise had spoken, the just had nothing to fear.

Recalling Talion's last interview, she pitied the High Protector now. How ashamed he must have been to see his will for Shora so overridden by the Envoy. Now he would need Berenice all the more, to keep the peace with Sharers. He had not called her of late, but, to set Merwen at ease, she would call on him at the Palace. She would see to it that events flowed smoothly in their new path, in the wake of the Patriarch's hand.

Merwen and Usha came out to see them off. Weia followed, although a glance at their trappings sent her scooting to hide behind her mother. Lystra was absent, of course. Merwen was still Unspeaking, but she would come round eventually, once she saw how things turned out. She needed Berenice's help as much as Talion did. Berenice went to Usha and hugged her without speaking. A sadness hit her; it did hurt, after all, this break with Merwen. Would the Impatient One really let her go without a word?

"Share warm currents," Merwen told Spinel. She added something else, but a hornblast covered her words, a ship's horn, from just beyond the channels. The shuttle boat had arrived.

Spinel's excitement at this new adventure largely overtook his immediate regrets at leaving Merwen and Raia-el raft. And Lystra —but why think of that, now?

Before him reared the *Cristobel,* a mountain of spotless "coldstone." Even the moving steps that lifted him up into it were a heady thrill. Once inside, Lay Nisi—Berenice, he reminded himself—led him to a lounge built of monstrous cushions from floor to ceiling. He wondered how he was supposed to seat himself.

Berenice simply lay back and sank in. "Two moon's-breath tonics," she ordered.

A long white snake twisted from the ceiling, with drinks in a hand at the end. Startled, Spinel tripped and sank knee-deep into yellow velvet.

"Do relax." Berenice laughed delicately.

Once he had achieved some sort of balance in his cushion, Spinel accepted his drink and sipped at it. The sweet warmth in his throat was heavenly. "This is the life, all right. Why'd we ever bother with Dak's old junkheap?"

"Sharers are not allowed. Were not, that is."

"But we're Sharers." He scratched his head; the hair just growing back prickled.

"We are when we choose to be. Here: you'll want some Apurpure." At the word, another arm shot down, proffering a bottle of white pills. Puzzled, he stared. Then his nightmare ordeal flooded back. His drink slipped; a white hand snatched it up with barely a splash.

"Oh, how could I—" Berenice slapped at the pill bottle and the arm retreated. She bounced forward in her cushion and sat up, contrite. "I'd forgotten, I'm so sorry. I always take them so I'll look 'normal.' in Iridis."

"Never mind." The first servo arm was hovering solicitously with his drink. Spinel's eyebrows knitted pensively. "This all must cost a troll's hoard."

Her fingers waved it off. "You're family, now. Better than my own, in fact."

The remark shocked Spinel. What a thing to say of your own folks. They were all you ever had, in the end. Yet what had Berenice said of her mother; tried to kidnap her, was it? What an odd lot were Iridians. Ahn and Melas would laugh and say, We told you so.

Out in space, he remembered just in time to go out to the observation bay for a last look at Shora before it shrank to a moon. The mottled blue gem looked even closer than the last time, a starstone that he could cup in the palm of his hand.

"You are still a Sharer," Merwen had told him, just when the boat had come to fetch him. "Remember that, even as a shaper of stone." The words had settled about him, almost a lullaby. Perhaps he could yet be a Sharer and himself, too. If only Lystra would understand—but that was altogether too painful to think of.

When the moving stairs set them down in Iridis, Spinel sighed; the fun was over. "How do I get to the coast steamer?" He had traded some amber weed for cash, enough for the steamer to Chrysoport that his father often used.

Berenice looked doubtful. "The steamer? That's rather slow, is it not?"

"Well, how else? Time to 'share parting.'"

"Share this, first." She held out to him an engraved ring. "A line of credit, up to two thousand a month."

His mind leaped. Cyan could retire on that, twice over. Yet something rebelled inside. "Uh, I don't know."

"It's all right, really."

How could he explain the distaste he felt? "Look, it's like this: Thanks, 'sister,' but when do I earn a beggar's stonesign?" He winced, knowing as usual it had not come out right.

Her face turned to crystal again, the glacial Lady of Hyalite whom he had first met on the landing of Dak' moonferry. "You're worse than Merwen." With that cruel compliment she left him, stepping briskly into the heart of the Valan capital.

Once Spinel went aboard the steamer, every familiar landmark on the coast made his heart beat faster. Trollbone Point with its jagged cliffs thrilled him so much that he could barely contain himself. At Chrysoport, he bounded down the plank so fast that a seam snapped in his tunic.

"Whoa, you there!" From behind, Spinel's arm was seized and twisted. He cried out and turned his head, to find himself staring into the shaggy beard of a Dolomite guard. "Where's your pass, boy?" A neuralprobe swung from the man's chain belt.

"Pass? What the devil—" Pain streaked up his arm.

"You can't get into town without a pass."

"But—but I'm Spinel, son of Cyan the stonecutter. I *live* here."

The Dolomite pinched Spinel's lip. "You look like no Chrysolite I ever saw."

Spinel burned all over but swallowed his hatred.

"I know the stonecutter," said a different Dolomite, a short burly fellow who combed his beard through his fingers. "I'll take the boy there. The fine is twenty *solidi,* without a pass," he told Spinel.

"Got none left but five." Spinel forced the words through his teeth.

His captor muttered, "Chrysolite scum," and spat on the dock.

"Pay what you got now," said the other one.

In a daze Spinel followed the man through the market square, its stalls full of cabbage heads and reeking of overripe fruit, and then the cobblestoned streets beyond. Little was new except for the appallingly inescapable Dolomite troops, all bearded and woolen-clad with chain belts clanging at their waists, some striding in groups, others posted at corners.

Spinel's guard finally reached the stoneshop. It looked much smaller than Spinel remembered, and dingier. For a moment he felt an utter stranger; but the old wooden door after all had its same weathered scratches, and it creaked as badly as ever when it opened.

"Cyan?" the Dolomite called. From within came mingled smells of lime dust and earthnut stew.

Beryl came first, from the storefront. She looked *tiny,* and the house felt like a dollhouse. She peered at him, her eyes wary under deeply lined lids, then her face lit up. "Is that—you? Spinny!" She flung her arms around him, clinging, tears streaming. At a loss, Spinel patted her dark hair.

His father's tread thumped up the basement stairs. "What's this? By Torr, my son is back." Cyan clapped his shoulder and tugged his fine tunic. "Look at you. You've made good, or I'm a troll's cousin."

Then Galena's hoarse scream rose above everything as she waddled over, shorter and rounded than ever, and Oolite bawled just to join the commotion.

Cyan pulled some coins from his pocket and started to count them out.

"Forget it," muttered the Dolomite.

"He had no pass—"

"Forget it." The man's bark stilled the tumult. He turned sharply and left.

"That's Sergeant Rhyol," Cyan said. "He's billeted with us, along with Ceric, a private."

Galena nodded. "How would they eat, if we spent food money on fines?"

"Lodgers?" Spinel asked, "But where do you put them? And why those filthy Dolomites, of all—"

"Spinel." His father's sharp word caught him.

"They're *good* boys," his mother insisted. "Just remember that." But for an instant an ugly look crossed her face.

Spinel shook himself. "Oh, all right. Say, how's the new kid? What is it, anyhow?"

Beryl smirked just a little. "Oh, Chrysoprase; he's sleeping in the shop. I'd better—"

"A son? Wow, Harran must be pleased to pieces. Say where is Harran? Still up at the crack of dawn with his ropes and nets?"

Beryl's lips worked in and out in a funny way. She burst into tears again and fled.

"Son, Harran joined the Militia." Cyan's voice was very tired.

"They tried to throw out the occupation, a few months back but—"

"But what happened to Harran?"

"He was brave," said Cyan. Galena wiped a tear from her cheek.

A numbness settled to his toes. Harran was dead, and Chrysoport was in chains. Spinel and his parents stared at their feet, united once more, yet each almost unbearably alone. For that, at least, Spinel glimpsed a reason. "Death can be hastened but never shared," he murmured.

His mother frowned quizzically at the sound of a foreign tongue.

2

The Dolomite "lodgers" were sharing Spinel's old bed, so that night he slept on the couch in Galena's study, where Merwen and Usha had sat when they came to claim him. All night he kept waking, convinced that the couch was rocking, rocking steeply enough to roll him off; but in fact the house was frozen still, and there was nothing but dry land and bedrock underneath.

In town, Spinel soon learned the new rules. Anything better than a pocket-knife was forbidden to the villagers. A town pass must be carried at all times; to get one, Spinel stood in line outside the garrison, which had taken over the Three Eyes Inn. A pass was an oval slip of metal stamped with a number and thumb print— "goat's tongues," people called them, on the sly. But it paid to weigh one's words. One evening outside a taproom, just before curfew, a regular who'd had a bit too much leered at a corner guard and said, "Know what the Sards call you? 'Hollow Horns,' that's what." The butt of a probe slapped him to the sidewalk. The Dolomite proceeded to beat the man's face in, with a cold, grisly thoroughness that left him unrecognizable. Every detail etched in

Spinel's memory, from the broken sprawled legs of the victim to the blood that mingled with oily streams in the gutter.

Resentment smoldered in hidden ways. There were codes and secret signs to spread uncensored news and ways to escape town without a pass. Local pride flourished, and it seemed that every child that was born had to be named Chrysoberyl, Chrysotile, or Chrysoprase.

At Spinel's home, the Dolomite "lodgers" were tolerable. Rhyol was gruff but quiet, contemptuous of regulations, staying out till all hours but never unmanageably drunk. Ceric was a thin-haired reed of a youth, younger than Spinel, who bit his nails and lived in constant terror of Spinel's mother. At dinner, Galena would glower at him across the table. "Eat, you stringbean! Don't let your officer complain I starve you."

The first time that happened, Spinel froze with shock, his eyes fixed on Ceric's neuralprobe. But the private only blinked, his Adam's apple bobbed a bit, and then he ate a little faster, while Rhyol stuffed himself in bored silence. Both men drank glass after glass of water as if to drain the ocean dry.

Now that he was home, Spinel wondered what to do with himself. Most of his old friends, even the women, were signed into trades or out in the fields. The deaths of several in the uprising appalled and depressed him. He escaped by hanging around the house and reliving his adventures on the Ocean Moon for anyone who cared to listen. He pestered his mother while she hunched over her account books, trying to cheat on the Dolomite taxes.

"You mustn't sell any stone to moontraders," Spinel told her. "It makes Sharers sick. Besides, traders charge five times what they pay us."

"Hm. Transport must cost something."

"Why, they even put starstones up for ordinary sale."

"Scandalous. Well, they haven't sent us any orders lately. Perhaps you can tell me why Sharer medicines cost ten times what they used to."

"We did stop trading awhile," he admitted. "That was because —it's kind of complicated." Where to begin?

"Strange," said Galena. "Zircon the peddler says that Sharers have flouted Patriarchal laws. They face the same fate as Pryyhopolis, he says."

"What nonsense. You know how traders talk, Mother. A nasty lot—why, they even dumped me into the sea, once."

"My poor boy." Galena poked at a silver box that spewed out digits flashing like minnows.

"That's new," Spinel remarked. "How did you afford it?"

She turned her head slightly, as far as her neck could manage. "Do you really want to know?"

"I asked, didn't I?"

"Your father was in the habit of leaving a coin on the dresser, after a good night. I saved them."

"Mother, really!" Spinel squirmed in embarrassment.

"You're a man now. Who else will tell you how the world turns, if not your mother? The Patriarch Himself must have had one."

Spinel fled downstairs.

In town, Spinel soon found that the unmarried shop girls chased after him. With his ocean-honed muscles, purple-black all over with sea-green eyes, his leg ostentatiously scarred, he came off as exotic, to say the least. For his part, the way the girls dressed unnerved him now. Their tight waists and packed bodices could only exaggerate the curves underneath. Compared to Lystra, they seemed fragile and frivolous, flowers to be plucked and tossed aside. So he made the most of their curiosity, tickling them with outrageous tales of the Ocean Moon, even to the point of embroidering a bit the way the moontraders did. But he stopped when Merwen's image rose in his mind: Merwen, who shared only the truth that she knew.

When the winter rains let up, he coaxed Catlin the drover's daughter to hike out with him to Trollbone Point. They chased and scared each other among the dusty bleached bones, then they settled down to more serious fun. Spinel fumbled impatiently at her dress—so many buttons and underthings. Then she pulled him on top of her, and the rest came very fast.

Spinel looked up, satisfied but uncertain. The girl was silent. Breakers thundered on the cliffs below, their salt scent blown over by fitful winds.

"Oh, well." Catlin sat up, flounced her hair, and began to reassemble her clothes.

"Hey, what's the rush?"

"Well, it's over, right? I'll catch it, if I don't get back. Besides, you popped two buttons."

"I'm not used to all them things to pull off."

"Sure you're not," she snapped as she brushed out her curls. "Carrying on with naked women all day."

"I did no such thing!"

"Well, what else did you do on the Ocean Moon? I should think at least you'd be better at it." She gathered her skirts and left.

Spinel was crushed. He had tried his best, but it all came so fast, and she just lay there the whole time—and now she blamed him. Lystra, though, had always made it last a long time. Even if it wasn't the "normal" way. Strange how certain things could set off Lystra's fury, yet for himself, alone with her, she had endless patience. She would find someone else soon enough, he thought bitterly, someone not a "malefreak."

He returned to the market square, where late-afternoon shoppers pawed through Ahn's vegetables. Ahn's good eye peered at him above the shrunken beak of her nose. "If it isn't the stonecutter's son! Tell the truth, Spinel; are they really all witches up there, those moonwomen?"

"I think one bewitched me." He sighed.

Ahn clucked her tongue. "You look bewitched. Here, try a papaya. Surest cure for a broken heart." She held out the sweet yellow fruit.

"How would you know?"

"Nasty thing, you! Ask the Patriarch himself. You, there, almsman," she called, a disrespectful summons for a Spirit Caller.

Uriel turned slowly in his faded robe.

"Come, almsman," said Ahn. "Call and ask the Patriarch: do papayas cure a broken heart?" She flipped a coin into his bowl. Her coarseness embarrassed Spinel. Home seemed a perpetual embarrassment, since he came back.

Uriel said, "Does a broken heart need curing, so much as clearer sight?"

"Fie, that's no answer."

"That's what Merwen does!" Spinel exclaimed. "A question for every answer."

"And who is he?" Uriel asked.

"She's a Sharer lady. She spun and wove seasilk under Rhodochron's tree." That shady spot stood vacant now.

"Ah, yes." Uriel shook his robe, and interest flickered in his eyes. "We spoke at length, before you left."

"So you did," Spinel remembered.

"Curious things they said, about faith."

"And about ruling. 'Who rules without being ruled?' The Dolomites, that's who." Spinel sullenly scraped his toe on a cobblestone.

"Are you sure?" Uriel asked.

"What? Just look around you. Does the Patriarch's justice rule them?" The guards were everywhere, watching the vendors hurriedly packing their goods in time for the six o'clock curfew. "Not a man would dare stay here tonight."

"Why not?"

The question took him aback. "They'd get beaten up, that's why." Yet Merwen and Usha had kept their spot under the fire-merchant's tree. How had they managed that, anyhow?

On impulse, Spinel walked up to a Dolomite guard. "Please, sir, couldn't I stay late in the square, just once? You see I'm up to no harm—"

The stick of a firewhip slapped him to the ground. Stunned, Spinel felt someone lift up his arm. His elbows were bruised, and blood dripped from his chin. Uriel helped him away, beyond the wharf to the beach, where he could rinse his face off. Spinel winced as his arms burned in the salt water.

Uriel said, "Some things you can't just ask for. Freedom is one."

"I hate them." Spinel's hoarse whisper swelled with an anger he had never known before. "I want them *dead, every one.*"

"What use is hatred, except as a step toward love?"

Spinel shivered as the evening wind chilled his damp skin. Uriel, he thought, was still a bit touched. You had to watch for that in Spirit Callers.

"You there!" came a strident voice from the street. "Get on home, Chrysolite scum." The guard made an obscene gesture, then jabbed a sixpoint star because of Uriel.

"I hate them," Spinel whispered again, nursing his swollen chin as he walked with Uriel to the street. Without weapons, hatred was indeed useless.

Yet Lystra hated stonetraders, and she had gotten the better of them. For weeks she had barred the shop doors, been dumped in the sea, and come back for more, and all the while shamed her sisters into keeping the boycott. Lystra knew no fear, except for stone. Spinel's throat ached with longing.

What was the matter, here? Did death select all the brave ones, like Harran, so that only the sheep survived?

Spinel looked again at Uriel. Of all the villagers, this old fellow at least showed no fear. Was that just his craziness? "Uriel, you got a place to stay tonight? You can sleep on our floor."

So the pair of them sat in Galena's study and talked late into the night, sharing lore of the rafts and of Valan backroads. And a plan emerged, a plan that Spinel thought might just be crazy enough to work.

3

It was noontime in the market square. "Melas," Spinel insisted, "what would happen if every one of us just stayed in the square tonight?"

The farmhand was on his back, fixing a bent wheel on his produce cart. "You're moonstruck."

"No, listen." Spinel was mindful of Uriel, who stood close by. The air was cold, but sunlight from between shifting clouds warmed his back a bit. "If *everybody* stayed, even women, customers too."

"You'd see the biggest massacre this side of Iridis." Melas grimaced as he pulled out a bent nail with his hammer.

"No, you wouldn't. Think, Mela: What use to them is a market full of corpses? Who would run the town?"

Melas threw down his hammer, picked himself up, and clapped dust from his hands. "They'd ransack the town and rape the women. Or didn't your sister tell you how it was?"

Blood rushed to his face, but he kept himself steady. Spinel could only begin to guess what his family had undergone. "At least Harran tried something. Why didn't you?"

Melas leaped and swung at him. Spinel caught his fists; he was easily the stronger, now. Melas wheezed as they grappled, until another voice interrupted. "Easy, there," urged Picrite the barber, distracted from shopping. "What's all the fuss, gentlemen?" Picrite added in his smooth-tongued way.

Melas wiped his face. "This young cur came back from the Ocean Moon just to taunt us in our chains."

"I'm saying there's a way out, Melas. Even the Patriarch says so; just ask—"

Picrite's gaze fell. "Your own brother-in-law died trying," the barber said.

"But there's another way."

"Look," snapped Melas, "if the Patriarch wanted us to be free, why did He send Dolomites to ravage us?"

Spinel looked to Uriel, whose robe swirled in the breeze. Uriel said, "The Patriarch knows that men must make their own freedom."

Disgusted, Melas turned away.

Picrite looked furtively about, then whispered, "A Spirit Caller might do something. Dolomites are superstitious folk; they even want their beards cut a certain way, depending on which planets are up."

"That's just it," said Spinel. "Uriel will stand with us."

"Stand where?"

Melas shouted back, "If you get even *ten* men to stay, I'll join you." With a surly shove at his cart, he moved off.

Spinel clapped his hands. "Here we go. We'll fill the square yet. It's simple," he explained to Picrite. "We just stand here, all bunched together, and don't leave. And Uriel—"

"I will lead an Open Calling at that time," Uriel said, "A time for us all to call to the Spirit of the Patriarch."

"To call for the freedom of Chrysoport?" Picrite was definitely keen on it now.

"We start a half hour before curfew," Spinel added.

"Hm." Picrite rubbed his chin. "I have to get back to my shop, but I'll let my customers know. Might even smuggle some knives for protection."

"Oh, no, you can't do that. A flash of a knife could touch off a massacre, like Melas said." Spinel's own words startled himself. This was not just a game, he thought uneasily.

Uriel's hand lifted. "Weapons are inappropriate for Spirit Calling."

"Ha; the Patriarch Himself has enough of them." But Picrite assented and went his way.

Elated, Spinel moved on with Uriel among the vending stands to recruit others. The next two they approached shook their heads, but several more were receptive. A few women were particularly eager, some who had lost a son or a husband in the uprising. The message spread throughout the town.

By evening, when Spinel reached home, even his father had heard of the plan.

"Yes." Cyan sighed. "Rhyol told us."

"Rhyol—oh." The Dolomite "lodger." Fear crept on Spinel then; it had not occurred to him that the enemy was bound to find out beforehand.

"Rhyol is worried," Cyan added. "He urged us to stay home and bar the door."

Spinel hardened his resolve. "I'll bet he's worried. Too late to stop now, and I'll be there, if none of you are."

"We'll *all* be there," Galena called from the hall. "You can tell Rhyol his dinner's on the stove."

Above the market square, the sun sank into a bed of pink clouds, rich as the velvet lounge of the *Cristobel*. The shadow from Rhodochron's tree crept over the cobblestones to where Spinel stood.

Uriel held a bell overhead and rang it steadily, signaling to begin the Call. Spinel looked around self-consciously, wondering who would respond. A few villagers warily drew near.

A guard stepped up to Uriel, his lips set in a grim line. "You're not intending any trouble, are you, Father?"

Uriel inquired, "Do you address myself or the Patriarch?"

The guard muttered some reply and sketched a six-point in the air, just above his ruby stonesign. He strode off to rejoin the group of Dolomites at the square's main entrance, twice the usual number. Nonetheless, a crowd soon grew around the Spirit Caller, huddling together for warmth as well as for safety.

To Spinel's amazement, some women brought their children along. Surely they knew what they were getting into? His eyes darted nervously, then froze. "Mother!"

Galena pushed her way through the crowd, with Cyan in tow, who carried Oolite on his shoulders. And Beryl actually brought her infant Chrysoprase, mercifully asleep in her arms. "Not the baby!" Spinel exclaimed.

"I said all of us," Galena told him. "Have we a nursemaid at home?"

"But—" Spinel lowered his voice. "Beryl, this could get rough."

"Tell me about it, Spinny." Beryl's cheeks were drawn tight. "You think we're any safer at home?"

Spinel looked down: there was nothing to say. In Torr's name, how had his own town come to be a battleground? With men disarmed and helpless, children became victims and soldiers both. But that was not the plan, was it? Anxiously he looked back to Uriel, who had lowered his bell and now stared solemnly at the sky.

An amplified voice blared overhead. "All citizens immediately disperse to your homes. Anyone who violates curfew will face prison, repeat, prison. All citizens disperse immediately..." The voice roared on, repeating its message.

"It's not even six yet," came an indignant shout. Villagers nodded and moved closer together. Uriel stood still, deaf to the world. Spinel peered above heads, trying to gauge their numbers; at least three hundred, he figured, counting children.

A disturbance stirred the edge of the crowd and rippled inward. The Dolomite captain was elbowing his way through to the Spirit Caller. "Enough of this foolery," he told Uriel. "No loitering in the square after curfew."

Uriel showed no sign of recognition. His rapt face watched the heavens.

"Enough, do you hear! No standing in the square!"

"He can't talk now," a woman said. "He's calling the Spirit of the Patriarch."

"To free Chrysoport," another added.

The Dolomite turned in disgust. "You'll never be free; we'll sell you to the slavers," he told the crowd. "Five minutes, and we start to haul you off."

From farther off, Albite the baker cried, "Then who'll make your bread for breakfast?"

The Dolomite stiffened and yelled, "For the last time, no more standing in the square!" His beard shook and his voice echoed from the storefronts across the street.

Very slowly, Uriel sat down, still staring skyward. Spinel did likewise, and automatically others followed. With a wave outward, the entire crowd was lowered, until none but the guard stood in the square.

He turned so crimson, he might have had a stroke. Instead, he stomped roughly out of the crowd, heedless of whom he stepped on.

Spinel let out a deep sigh and shut his eyes a moment. When he looked up again, he saw all the people wedged calmly together, desultory frocks and caftans like a meadow of wildflowers, and beyond in the street a solid wall of soldiers. Light was fading fast, draining colors away, until flashlights poked through the dark; somebody had been smart enough to think of that. Voices were murmuring, and a few infants wailed.

A scream shattered the calm, then another. People at the edge of the crowd were being dragged off, limp beneath the neural-probe.

Around Spinel, figures extended, half stood; dark eyes widened, like cows' eyes. Here and there a dusky shadow popped up and scrambled out to hurry home.

"Uriel!" Desperately Spinel whispered at him, pleading for help, but Uriel was too busy Calling. He had to do something, though, or all that day's effort would go for nothing. What could Spinel do; what would Lystra have done?

Spinel found himself shaking all over. He knew he was about to get up and do something, and he felt quite out of his head. He rose unsteadily, as if the ground were rolling. "Bring them back!" he called to the walls of guards. "Bring them back, or we'll *never* leave, do you hear?"

"Never!" a motley chorus echoed. "Bring them back!"

"And tomorrow," Spinel added, *"we'll bring the whole town."*

Of course, the town jail could not possibly hold the whole town. Now people settled in more firmly and shouted defiance at their oppressors. The screams stopped; it appeared that only a fraction of the crowd had been hauled away. But the mood was getting uglier, and here and there a knife glinted in the flashlight beams, which was just what Uriel had warned against. How much would the Dolomites stand for? Soldiers now pressed in a ring all around the crowd—practically the whole garrison must be here. One false move, and . . .

Uriel raised his arm high and beckoned all who could see. "The Patriarch hears us," Uriel said. "The Patriarch calls on us to sing to Him. We will sing the Anthem of the Nine Legions."

Spinel gasped; it was a stroke of genius. All the armies of Valedon put together would think twice before disrupting a singing of the Patriarch's Anthem. Uriel began, Spinel loudly joined in, and the song swelled throughout the crowd. Everyone knew at least the refrain, and most knew the nine legionary verses as well. And Uriel knew countless others, for every known planet and some long dead. . . .

Spinel's voice faltered at last, exhausted from the day's campaign. A few stars peeked through the clouds. There was even a hazy sickle of a blue moon. He slumped at his mother's side. As his eyelids fluttered he imagined that the stars were plantlights above the clickfly webs at a Sharer celebration. Then Lystra flashed into his dream, and he plunged into the ocean after her, pursuing her beating feet even to the deepest realm of nautilus and seaswallower. I'll chase you to the floor of the world, his mind whispered, but she never looked back.

4

Back in Iridis, Berenice could hardly wait to see Realgar again. At the door to his Iridian establishment, she was met by three pairs of guards: Iridians in blue with gilt tufts at the shoulder tips; Sards, maroon beneath capes of indigo; and Dolomites in their shapeless gray woolen cloaks. It gave her a start, for Realgar had commanded only Sards before.

A servo reached for her bearskin coat, but she kept it to show Realgar, since he had captured the beast after all. The servo padded ahead of her down the magnificent Sardish carpet, a universe of hunting scenes in russet and gold. At either side of the hall stood beasts he had caught and preserved, from stags and wildcats to the dreaded silver bears.

Realgar had a peculiar sense of honor about the hunt. He would hunt quite alone in the evergreen wilderness, armed only with portable weapons, though a servocopter could have bagged a forest full of fauna in a day. Men, he would say, were ordinary, civilizable creatures to be fought and mastered by the state, but wild things were an impenetrable mystery, only to be faced alone. In a strange way her heart understood this, though she feared for him almost more in the forest than on the battlefield.

And yet his worst tragedy, like her own, had fallen in the safety of his own home with his dearest at his side. . . . Berenice shuddered and pulled at the clawed clasps of her coat. For now, at least, Realgar was posted in civilized Iridis, rather than among Sards whose sophistication overlaid exquisite treachery. In a sense he was a rebel among his own kind, though not as much as she was among hers. *Merwen . . . if only you could understand.*

A door slid wide. Cool air brushed her, and blue sky smiled in the open courtyard: a shooting range. Berenice could not see the targets, but Realgar stood in sharp profile, his left hand at the base of the firewhip in preference to his damaged right, the shaft leveled with a blue streak toward a hidden target.

Unconsciously Berenice clenched her fingers together, responding to the tension focused in his stance. There had been a time, just after her husband left her, when she might have become an officer. It was a good career for a lone noblewoman without hope of a family.

Realgar must have seen her, despite his concentration, for the streak vanished. He tossed his weapon to the servo and came quickly to meet her. "We all missed you," Realgar said as he embraced her.

Cassiter was watching them gravely. She looked uncannily grown up in her red uniform that was a miniature of her father's. As soon as Berenice looked at her, the girl's face lit up and she skipped over to reach her arms up to Berenice's neck. "Mama Berenice, you'll be our mama, now, won't you? Did you bring me my whorlshell?"

"*Shora,* I forgot." With everything else on her mind—still, Berenice could have kicked herself for the lapse. "Next time, I promise."

"Then you're going away again." Cassiter looked down and pouted.

Berenice removed the girl's round cup of a helmet and pressed her hair, the fine straw-colored locks of her lost mother. "Next time, perhaps you'll come to visit *me.*"

Berenice glanced at Realgar for his reaction, but he only said, "I hope you plan to stay long enough to leave your coat, at least."

With a trill of laughter she surrendered her coat at last to the waiting servo, who almost seemed relieved to carry it off.

"A worthy foe that was," Realgar observed, meaning the bear. "Nearly clawed my eyes out."

Berenice made a face of mock horror. "Ral, I'd much rather have your eyes than an old bearskin!"

"So you've got both. Cassi's getting to be a good shot, now, aren't you, girl? Show Mama." So it was plain "Mama" now. He had always been careful to say "Mama Berenice."

Cassiter obligingly returned to the range and took her firewhip from the servo. She aimed it seriously, her cheeks and lips as straight as her father's. Berenice moved behind her just in time to see the target appear on the screen: six black dots in a hexagon standing on end, innocuous enough. But the dots had barely leaped into view before three lines of flame connected them, intersecting precisely in the center. There was not a sound from the weapon, only a *whoosh* as the flames sprouted into a starsign.

Berenice stared, vaguely uneasy.

"Excellent," said Realgar. "You're not superstitious, are you?"

"Of course not. Very good, Cassi." Jets of carbon dioxide sprayed the flames down.

"Would you like a try at it?" Realgar asked.

"Thanks, but I'm out of practice. Cassi would show me up terribly."

They retired to the parlor for refreshment, and Elmvar was brought in by the nanny, a servo of broad maternal build wrapped in a cheerfully embroidered peasant skirt. Realgar and Berenice sipped cocktails, while Cassiter and Elmvar plowed through the tea cakes, munching the ones they liked and crumbling those they did not. Realgar said, "I was comforted to observe that Sharer children are little better behaved, despite the abundance of mothers."

Berenice laughed as delicately as any other cultured Iridian lady. She refrained from pointing out that Realgar in fact ruled his own children as strictly as he chose. He wanted to make her feel needed as a mother, but she felt that far more from the way Cassi hugged her.

"It's good to see you happy," Realgar said. "You never seem to laugh, when you're purple."

"Do I not?" She would think about that later. "Sharers are full of laughter. How is your new post working out?"

He turned first to the children. "All right, kids, off to bed."

"Aw, Papa," they chorused. They hugged Berenice again before their peasant-skirted nanny bundled them away.

Realgar leaned back and stretched his legs. "You have no idea what it took to get away for a night." He told her some of his concerns, mostly things Berenice either knew or guessed. The diversity of the High Protectoral Guard was one headache. Talion had decreed the Guard's cosmopolitan makeup, to enhance the conviction of Valans everywhere that the High Protector and his Guard were in fact theirs. And besides, Berenice thought, Talion little trusted his own ambitious underlings. Realgar would not say as much, although he must have been aware of why he was appointed over several Iridians senior to him.

"It's a curious mix," Realgar said. "Dolomite troops are the sturdiest in a crunch but fiercely proud, tending to fly off the handle at a fancied insult. Also, they're put off by modern equipment and female commanding officers." Iridians and Sardish troops contained about a third women. "Your Iridians, now, are precisely trained, beautiful for drills and parade exercises. But get them on a battlefield—" Realgar shook his head. "A corps of servos. My apologies," he added politely, "but it's no wonder you get provincials to fight your real battles."

Berenice raised her glass. "And which troops are the best, all round?"

"Well." He looked up and past her. "Sards have special skills, of course. Especially in intelligence." Berenice watched his face turn blank. He almost never displayed his thoughts directly, but often he showed a blankness that might tell as well. Sards were masters at information extraction, the twisting and probing of minds, a guild so covert that even its stonesign was unknown to the uninitiated. Patriarchial law held that the mind was inviolate, but no state could function without some flexibility.

"Berenice, before it slips my mind, we're to dine with your parents tomorrow night." At her frown he added, "You did promise."

"I'm to see Talion that day. I have to make sure that—"

Realgar took her hands and murmured, "You hold too much on your shoulders. Leave Shora to the Patriarch. Surely you must trust His wisdom."

She let herself melt in his arms, but the sense of unease would not subside.

* * *

The next day, Lady Berenice walked the skystreet of Center Way toward Palace Iridium, ignoring soliticious hangcars as usual. Without newscubes to tell her, she might not have known that Iridis swarmed with Pyrrholite refugees this winter and that food riots overran the older sections. The bazaars far below were full, as always, and from this height who could tell how many of the crowd were foreign, or how ragged were their clothes, or how sunken their eyes.

Palace Iridium rose ahead, its monumental facade crowned by the image of Malachite. Within the palace, Berenice had to wait ten minutes outside the office of the High Protector.

Talion himself looked startingly solid after Berenice's sessions with his light-image, as if someone had just filled in a mold of his form with clay. He clasped his fingers upon his desk. "Lady Berenice. What have you to report?"

"Little, in fact. Sharers are content with the current situation. I have certain questions—"

"You intend to interview myself?" Talion's voice deepened with irony. "Our side is content, as well." His words were rapid, even brusk. "In fact, you may consider this an exit interview. From now on, we can manage without your services, which you so graciously provided for—was it six years?"

Berenice was surprised and irritated. "I still serve Shora. I must know what Malachite intends for that world." She had to find out how far Merwen's fears had been justified.

"Oh, not to worry. It turns out that the native life science is less developed than we had feared."

"What do you mean?"

"The Envoy found that their 'lifeshaping' would require a generation at least to create any threat to us."

"Well, I told you they were no threat." Although not for that reason.

"Exactly," said Talion. "You are prescient, as always. Now events can take their normal course." A melodic tone of dismissal sounded. "If you will excuse me, my lady, I run a tight schedule."

Automatically she rose and turned toward the door. Then she stopped and turned back. "What normal course?"

"The present course. My lady, I have a meeting now."

Berenice stepped to his desk and leaned across it. "Will things go back to what they were?"

"Of course not." Talion stood behind the desk; two servos moved discreetly from opposite sides of the room. "A new era begins in our—"

"New *how,* Talion?"

The mask of his face slipped askew. The High Protector was shaken by such astounding breach of protocol. "If you really care so much for your native friends, why didn't you get them to take an Envoy?"

"But that takes *time,* to adjust."

"Malachite had six months. That had to suffice. It will be nine years before he returns, don't you see? He can't sit and wait for little men to make up their minds." Talion pulled back, regretting his outburst. "I warned you not to meddle in affairs of state. Leave, before you leave me no choice."

The servos were closing in.

"Nine years or ninety, you will answer to the Patriarch!" Berenice fled the office, the halls, and the intricate maze of gem-studded corridors. Shaking uncontrollably, she found herself outdoors, leaning against the face of Palace Iridium, her body framed by a single marble tessera of the epic mosaic. Across the courtyard stood the skystreet, from which viewpoint these tesserae spread as small and numberless as grains of sand.

5

The window of the Hyalite reception hall bulged out over the city. Light points spread and crowded below like a frozen sea of waterfire. Other objects were motile; they swam and pulsed through the city's angular veins. Berenice leaned into the window as if she could seep through its restraint and plunge into the ocean of night. A dark place to hide, to plan her next move. . . . She had not felt such apprehension since the day she had hidden in the shockwraith's lair.

Malachite could not deliberately have left Shora to the wolves.

Yet it was equally unthinkable for Talion to disregard the Envoy's wishes so confidently, the moment his back was turned.

Behind her a dress train swished. "Berenice," called Cristobel, her tones low yet rising fashionably at the last syllable.

Berenice half turned her head, her eyes cast down. The evening dress she wore was an unaccustomed nuisance. Its long embroidered train anchored her, made her a fixture jutting from the floor, dependent upon the tortoise-shaped trainsweepers that scurried about to keep the trains untangled and unstepped on.

"Berenice," said her mother again. "Have you made the acquaintance of our dear unfortunate guests from Pyrrhopolis?" Cristobel's hand drooped in invitation. Her arched nails matched the cream of the stonesign at her neck. Her figure mirrored that of her daughter, but her face was all ovals, from the dome of her forehead to her rounded chin. To achieve a serious air she shrewdly kept her hair natural. Whatever gray hairs appeared, Berenice thought vengefully, she knew who had put them there.

Without a word, Berenice clasped the offered arm. She had to be civil and calm, at least on the outside. Cristobel leaned to her ear and whispered, "Come now, dear, Talion won't hold that spat against you." She paused, then added, "Our guests, you know, arrived in such unfortunate haste."

The Pyrrholite couple showed little sign of haste. They wore their provincial style, multiple layers of seasilk, fur trim, beaded embroidery on puffed sleeves, their robes cut short, mid-calf. That was just as well, since a room full of trains could confuse the trainsweepers and short their circuits.

"We still can't find a place," explained the Pyrrholite woman. "Why it was that everyone had to rush to Iridis, with all those lovely coastal spots around, I have no idea. For months we've looked, and the only establishment remotely suitable doesn't even have a skin-texturing room."

"Your parents took us in," the husband told Berenice. "How fortunate that one so generous runs the refugee program."

Cristobel in fact ran most of city politics, her fingers reaching every streetlevel and district. Her lashes lowered. "One must set an example. All Iridians will do their part."

"Oh, they have, surely," said the woman. "Of everyone I know, not one has been taken in somewhere."

"Oh," said Berenice, "then are food riots at an end?"

The Pyrrholites blinked at each other.

Cristobel squeezed her daughter's arm. "Of course the common lot have a difficult time. We process hundreds daily. But what of the thousands who failed to escape?"

"Three days the Envoy left us." The voice of the Pyrrholite man was low, intense. "Those who got out afterward might have wished they had not. They were little more than ghosts, their skin peeling from the bone, their bodies rotted away. . . . " He caught himself and offered a charming smile.

"You'll pull through," Cristobel told the Pyrrholites. "You know, you could regenerate your capital by investing in our lunar development plan. . . . "

Berenice caught sight of Realgar and her father walking toward her, absorbed in conversation. Realgar's head inclined toward the shorter man, whose indigo talar and train contrasted with his own brilliant dress uniform. Hyalite's features were as precise as his daughter's, though more intricate, with many crisscrossing lines.

Realgar slid his arm behind her, but she kept her expression cold. He knew what Talion was up to—and he had not told her.

Hyalite winked and raised his glass. "When will you two tie the knot at last? You know, my dear, all of us adventurers do settle down, sooner or later."

"Yes. How's the moon trade?" Too abrupt; she had to keep her voice casual.

Hyalite nodded, drumming his fingers on his empty glass. "Winding up smoothly." From above drooped a servo arm to replace the glass with a full one.

"Winding up?"

"Yes, actually we're getting out of lunar trade—"

"Out of trade! After forty years, Father?" The depth of her own reaction surprised her. "Free trade" had been her goal for so many years, before the rise of the great Houses.

"The new restrictions make it uneconomical." Hyalite looked her straight in the eye as he said this. "Mining is the thing now. You can't imagine what minerals lie untouched on the floor of that ocean. Enough to even our trade with distant planets and to pay half our taxes to Torr."

Berenice's fingers closed tight around her glass. "No more profit in seasilk?"

"Oh, the new raft rakers will take care of the silk and spice line. So much more efficient."

"It's . . . hard to think of, Father. After all these years."

Hyalite's face lit up, and the lines stretched. "Even you are sorry to see those days pass. Why not? You built the business as much as I, in the early days. As a child, you picked up the language before anyone; at age eleven, you were my official interpreter, remember that?"

Despite herself, the corner of her lip pulled into a smile. "I remember that, and how I swam among Sharer children. And I remember the way we traded then."

"Oh, yes." Hyalite laughed. "It was marvelously informal at first."

He nodded to Realgar, who listened politely. "No shops had been built yet, so we just heaped all our goods in a pile on the raft. A few days later the stuff would disappear, and we'd find a pile of native stuff, not just seasilk but preserved octopus, herb leaves, even odd sorts of powders that we didn't yet know were medicines."

"Yes, thought Berenice, it was all so informal that Malachite came and went three times without concern for the "native humanoids" of the Ocean Moon. "Won't you miss it, Father? Won't you deal with the natives at all anymore?"

"Well, yes, but the new regime is bound to change things."

Realgar caught her waist. "Berenice, love, you must be starving," he said a little too loudly.

"Sh, I'm never hungry."

But already her mother's gown whooshed toward them. "Into the dining room," Cristobel commanded. "I'll warn you, though, your father has taken to redecoration in his old age."

"My dear," Hyalite chuckled. "New surroundings keep us young, don't they?"

At first glance, Berenice saw nothing new, just the velvet wall with the same polished mosaic panels. She swirled her train back and seated herself between Realgar and the Pyrrholite woman. As her father pulled out a chair across from her, he tangled himself in his own train, despite the little servos scurrying behind. Hyalite was always an outdoors man, never quite used to the city.

Servo arms reached downward with cocktails. The arms were not white but deep amethyst, with ultralong fingers linked by stylized scallops of webbing.

Her breath stopped. For an instant she was back on Shora, in the late afternoon, where eager arms and laughing faces hovered over plates of crabmeat and steaming succulent fillets and seaweeds, and the lively hands were speaking and laughing, almost as much as their lips did. But here, Sharer "arms" were just another—

"Marvelous," the Pyrrholite woman exclaimed at Berenice's ear. "You're an artistic genius, Hyalite."

But Hyalite saw his daughter's face. "Berenice, it's just a novelty. I thought you'd—"

The table shuddered beneath her palms as she shot upright. "What have you done? What will become of Shora?"

"I? Why, nothing, child, Please, why upset yourself—?"

She wheeled and ran from the dining room, her train tearing under a hasty step. From behind, her mother hissed at her father, "I told you so."

In the foyer she spoke to the wall terminal. "What date next passage to Shora?"

As a voice flatly recited the freighter list, Realgar came and caught her by the shoulders. "My love, what's come over you?"

She struggled until his hands fell to his sides. "I've come to my senses, that's all. I warned you about my parents."

"And you were warned to keep out of affairs of state."

Fear chilled her again. As if he read her thoughts, Realgar said, "No one wants to hurt you. We want you safe from a situation that does not involve you."

"Does not—involve—me." Her words dropped like lead. Unbelievingly she shook her head. "You never took me seriously. At all."

"Seriously? Do you realize all the trouble I've gone to?"

"It's too late, Ral. You've forced me to choose, and I've chosen." Her throat stuck. She had not actually chosen until that moment. She turned again toward the terminal, but Realgar pulled her back.

"You can't go to Shora."

"Why not?"

"Martial law."

Dazed, she repeated, "Martial law? On Shora?"

"We're responsible for them, Berenice, responsible to the Patriarch. The High Protector must govern them somehow."

"He's invaded them—he's—"

"No, by Torr." Realgar's sudden anger checked her. "Nothing's happened at all—yet. Nothing's happened to your precious Merwen or her precious children. We're about to tighten discipline,

that's all. We have to start somewhere. If they're as peaceful as they seem, they won't give us trouble. Trust me, Berenice. I'll go easy on them."

"You." She crept backward until her palms met the velvet wall. Her nails sank into it as if clawing at a padded cell. Her surroundings detonated into unreality; wall moldings and table knobs stood in bold, jagged outline, meaningless fragments apart.

Realgar was holding her, shaking her. "Berenice, do you hear me? You can't go on like this forever."

"It's over, all right." Her own voice sounded dead. "It's hard to realize just how over it is."

"I can't leave you like this; I know you too well." Genuine anguish shook his voice. "What will become of you," he whispered, if you don't come round, this time?"

That was it. She was trapped in her parents' house. Sirens and searchlights, combing the seas—inside her head, this time. "A sanatorium." She spoke now with calm dignity. "Realgar, would you let them put me away in a sanatorium? Would you?"

He did not answer right away. Every tendon of his neck stood out. "I only want what is best for you. You need a long rest. There's my hunting lodge in Sardis. My servos will escort you."

A sanatorium or a Sardish retreat. What a choice. "I'll go, Ral. Just let me be."

"You're sure, now? You won't do anything foolish?"

"Oh, no, I promise." The wealth of Hyalite, a brilliant husband, a ready-made family. Bring me a whorlshell, Mama Berenice. *Flute of whorlshell lift in hand*.... Somewhere, another name was screaming.

6

The morning after the Spirit Calling in the Chrysolite market square, another Dolomite battalion was brought into town. Soldiers crowded the streets, disrupting traffic and setting tempers on edge. Regular commerce had to carry on, and the vendors put up with its as best they could. By evening most of the entrances were blocked off, but twice as many villagers as the night before stayed for another Calling with Uriel, whose collection bowl was so full he could almost have slept at an inn. That night they remained without incident, despite the hordes of soldiers that bristled outside.

In the days that followed, an unspoken truce seemed to develop: in the market square, one was safe, but anyone caught out at night in a back alley could still expect arrest or a beating. A new mood of pride infected the populace, as if they had snatched something back from their oppressors. Most soon forgot about Spirit Calling and started playing music and dancing to pass the time until dawn.

The new night life even began to draw traveling acrobats and theater troups who used to ignore the sleepy town, especially once the garrison was cut back again (there were other campaigns, after all) and the pass regulations began to break down. People mislaid their passes with disconcerting frequency, and the lower-ranked soldiers grew increasingly tired of replacing and enforcing them. The job of soldiers was to besiege cities and bring home fortune and glory, not to issue summonses to barefoot villagers. And the garrison commander was reluctant to start anything that might disrupt the flow of tax revenue to Dolomoth.

A month later, only Spinel seemed to remember how it all started. Spinel wandered around town with Uriel, getting an intriguing glimpse of the life of a Spirit Caller. Problems of all sorts were brought to the Caller for his wisdom, and it both fascinated and disturbed Spinel to realize the hidden weights of misery that could bury the simplest of lives. A young woman suffered a hideous skin disease that spread slowly, with no affordable cure. A brother and sister had become mortal enemies after their birth-home was left to one but not the other. Each knew that only the Patriarch could rectify the matter, but somehow Uriel always had an answer, or at least a question, that made them feel better.

At his house, Spinel was introspective. Beryl asked, "Where's your tongue got to, these days? What's a talespinner without a tongue?"

His mother warned, "Wrinkle your brow long enough, and when the cock crows, it will stay."

Spinel ignored them, so long as they tolerated Uriel, who often slept over in their bit of a hallway. In summer Uriel would sleep out on the beach, but winter's chill sent him indoors with whoever would take him in.

On a warm day, Uriel returned to the sea to bathe himself. Spinel watched as the old man lathered his shoulders amid the waves that snarled and foamed at the shore. It was easy to imagine that the entire sea, encircled by shore, was just an outsized bathtub compared to the ocean Shora. "Uriel, do you ever get sick of people's complaints?"

"All the time," Uriel said.

Spinel frowned and pursed his lips. He had not expected such a frank answer. Sand-clouded water swirled around his hands.

"Well, do you think I'm a servo?" Uriel's eyes were laughing at him. "Some more than others. Each soul is unique. Each day brings something new, and much that is the same. How about you?"

Spinel squinted at him, shy of revealing foolishness but curious for a reaction nonetheless. "I think there are two sorts of troubles people have: one sort, the world lays on people; the other sort, people lay on each other."

"And most, we lay on ourselves." Uriel waded to shore and dried himself with a rag. He replaced his amorphous robe, then the sparkling starstone.

Spinel was trying to decide about something that had puzzled him for a long time. "You know, when I met Malachite on Shora, I got the feeling that his Patriarch didn't seem to care much about folks like Sharers, or even us. He cared mainly about the Protectors, and a few Iridians maybe, and Merwen if she could 'run' things. But when the Patriarch talks to you, He cares about us."

"The Patriarch has many messengers."

"But He must care the same, no matter who He sends. Uriel, when this Spirit calls to you, how do you know it's Him?"

"When your own father speaks," Uriel asked, "how do you know?"

"I can see him, touch him."

"Trust your senses."

"But Torr is four light-years away," Spinel insisted. "You can't sense Torr in an instant; it's—it's against *physics.*"

Uriel's lips turned up a bit.

"All right, I don't really know any physics. Even so, Uriel—well, what if there's more than one Patriarch on Torr?"

"Did I ever speak of Torr?"

Spinel froze as if something were crawling up his back and all the way over his scalp. Uriel stood there as always, his cheeks sagging with age. Spinel felt himself overcome with mental vertigo. "Your Patriarch . . . He's not on Torr?"

"Is He? Sometimes He seems more distant than the farthest galaxy. At other times, He whispers in my ear."

"Then He's everywhere, like Shora. Or could it be that 'He' *is* the same as Shora?"

"Is the sea half empty or half full?"

Spinel's lips parted, but he stood without speaking. Dried sand itched on his leg; absently he rubbed it off, one foot, then the other.

Suddenly he was angry. "Why do you cheat us, then, all you 'Spirit Callers'? If 'He' is everywhere, anyone can call 'Him.' You play the Protector's game making us think the Torran Patriarch really cares about us somehow, when He wouldn't give a day-old fishhead for any one of us."

"Didn't I invite you all to call with me, that night in the square?"

"But we couldn't, not like you do. Like you say you do." Spinel was incensed: a common charlatan had been unmasked.

"You called as much as I did."

"I sure didn't hear anything."

"You heard, but did not understand. Understanding takes time."

"Then *make* people understand. Isn't that your job?"

For a moment Uriel twisted his face as if in intense pain. Then he relaxed and sighed. "I'm not very good at my job." He reached into a deep pocket of his robe and pulled out something on a thin chain. It was a starstone. He slipped it around Spinel's neck. "Perhaps you'll do better."

"Hey, what's that! I'm not apprenticed or anything—"

"Who is, then?"

Spinel stood speechless, while the sand blew all around, and the startling object lay cold on his chest. He had given up hope of a stonesign for the Ocean Moon, only to receive without asking an ocean-blue star of stone.

7

While Lady Berenice had promised to retire to Sardis, Nisi the Deceiver had no intention of doing so.

Years before, after the abortive kidnap attempt and the subsequent truce with her parents, Berenice had prepared a daring escape plan. The plan was to do away with her Iridian identity altogether, disappear among the Sharers, and raise a child among them, as she was now illegally capable of doing.

Somehow, with the plan in place, she had put off its execution, until Realgar had swept her off her feet with his promises and with the seductive vision of enjoying two worlds at once. Now that Realgar's true expectations for her were unmasked, it was clear that she had only put off the final day; but would her plan still work, on such short notice?

Outside her door the next morning, Realgar's two servos were waiting, as they had been all night since he got back to her penthouse. At least he had had the decency not to humiliate her with human guards. Well, she would return the compliment, by sending not herself to Sardis . . . but a servo.

The servo was a life-sized replica of Berenice, down to the smallest details of hair and skin texture, heartbeat and odor. The face in particular was a masterpiece of simulation.

The servo "Lady Berenice" was programmed with all her most typical responses and idiosyncrasies, and she had spent most of the previous night setting up a subprogram for the trip to the Sardish hunting lodge. Now that it was done, she watched with an eerie unsettled feeling as the machine pulled on her own traveling suit and her stonesign.

Something was not quite right about the machine. Was it too perfect? No—too young, that was it. Too few wrinkles about the neck and forehead, as she must have looked seven years ago. Her throat constricted; this ruse might not work at all. She did not dare try her skin-texturing facility, because the machine "skin" was artificial. At any rate, whether it worked or not, she had nothing else to try. Nisi/Berenice had met a fork in the tunnel.

She left "Lady Berenice" getting dressed and went to open a window beside her main entrance, partly for the air and also for the benefit of Realgar's servos, who would listen and record. A salt breeze blew in from the harbor, the last day she would ever smell a Valan ocean. For a moment she closed her eyes as if to store up the memory forever. Then she turned to the household monitor and loudly ordered supplies for the hunting lodge. "A week's menu, vacation style number two. A dozen video selections from my library. A recessed pen gun. One maxi-pack Argo personal explosive." Realgar would understand the last two items, since she was supposedly headed for Sardis, where Azurite assassins were feared. And of course, an "assassin's blast" was what would put an end to "Lady Berenice," whose carapace already contained a clock set and timed for oblivion.

The personal weapons she had just ordered were in fact not meant for assassins. If all else failed, Nisi would end herself, rather than submit to a sanatorium.

At last she gave "Lady Berenice" her final order. Her hands shook so that she could barely turn on the bedroom monitor to observe what would happen as the machine left her house. What took place was almost anticlimactic: servo met servo at the threshold, as unquestioningly as when Merwen and Usha had met Malachite.

She dressed herself now as a Dolomite woman, in a black woolen cloak that covered all but her eyes. Thus disguised she departed for the moonferry, her heart pounding and her hands pawing at her neck for the nonexistent stonesign, without which she felt more naked in Iridis than she ever had on Shora. Only when Dak's moonferry took off and Iridis fell away from her could she relax, sinking limp in her seat, eyes glazed, too stunned yet for tears.

Lady Berenice of Hyalite—she must never use that name again. Lady Berenice was a refugee, stranded forever in the Sardish wilderness. Only Nisi the Deceiver was going home.

8

At Raia-el, the raft blossoms bloomed again in profusion, but Merwen the Impatient felt much alone. Usha brought solace as always; but with Spinel gone, Lystra became impossible to share a silkhouse with. Lystra left at last with Mithril and the other refugees of swallower season, to help establish their new raft. As for Nisi, there was an enigma that only brought pain to Merwen's heart. Death ruled those who ruled the dead; could Nisi escape or not?

It was a shock, then, the day that the Deceiver returned to the doorhole of the silkhouse. Merwen could not bring herself to share speech again, but Usha did. "So, Deceiver," Usha observed in a thoughtful tone, "you slipped back before Death quite shut the traders' door."

"Listen to me," Nisi began unsteadily. "They're not done with you yet. You've traded traders for death-hasteners; do you see?"

"When death comes, life will rise to meet it. But you, Nisi; what does this mean for you?"

"I want to learn whitetrance."

Usha stopped, clearly awaiting a sign from Merwen.

Merwen wavered between hope and apprehension. Was Nisi really ready? she wondered, sickening with doubt. Yet Nisi had a selfname; she must be as ready as anyone.

Merwen said to Usha, "You are the lifeshaper. You will have to share this with her."

Nisi faced Usha in the lifeshaping chamber. Each sat cross-legged and carefully relaxed. At least, Usha was relaxed.

"Nothing to fear," Usha reassured her. "Whitetrance is your final self-protection."

Resentment flared; for a moment Nisi felt as trapped as when Realgar had forced her to let him "protect" her. But of course this was very different. Whitetrance would be her own, her last line of defense, the state of consciousness that said, I choose freedom above life. Intellectually, Nisi shared this belief. That was why she hid an explosive pack within her body and would keep it so long as a single Valan remained on Shora. Yet whitetrance — it panicked her, for some reason. It was only self-hypnosis, she told herself.

Usha set a mindguide upon her own head, a black spider shape with long tendrils that draped down her scalp. She extended another one to Nisi, as it curled from her fingers like little monkeys' tails.

A mindguide, a miniature version of that used on starworms. Nisi shrank back, hand to her mouth. "You won't — share my thoughts?"

"Nonsense." Usha's voice was sharp. "To 'share thought' is as paradoxical as 'share death.' No Sharer would try such a thing. Only our main brain currents will run parallel, like light waves in phase." Usha lifted the spidery thing to Nisi's forehead. "We could manage without, but it would take months or years. This way, a single hour will show you how; then you can do it yourself, always."

Every muscle of her neck rebelled against the thing that squirmed and settled on her scalp. She wanted to fling it off and run, but where? "Lady Berenice" had run already, and the door had slammed behind her by now. Only one path lay ahead, for Nisi.

Sound took on a hollow quality, as if echoing within an airbell. A haze filled her senses, as the world receded —

Panic snapped her back. Her surroundings returned to normal; the echoes were gone.

"You see," Usha said, "you can dephase any time. You choose."

Nisi breathed deeply until the hollow, echoing world returned. She could turn it on and off, by throwing a mental switch.

Ahead of her a dark tunnel opened, dilating like the doorhole of a silkhouse. The tunnel rose to meet, bringing first darkness, then light, as the planets, stars, galaxies rushed behind her. . . . The outer world was still there, yet at once light-years away. She could reach out and touch it, if she wished to badly enough, but it would have to be something urgent, as urgent as a frightened child.

As the tunnel brightened, it took on shapes, and she knew at once what it was. This place was *hers,* where she could choose to stay at any time, even to close the doorhole so that none could follow. . . .

She streaked back through the tunnel, back to her mat of seasilk upon the hard raftwood floor. Color was oozing into her white fingertips. The mindguide fell inert in her lap.

Nisi looked down at her crossed legs. It was easy, almost too easy. A question pricked her. If Sharers were so willing to kill themselves for freedom, why could they not kill those who threatened their freedom? Her lips parted to ask, but when her eyes met Usha's, she shuddered and looked away.

At High Command, Realgar was staring at the blank plate of the monitor that had just informed him, with the appropriate tone of apology, of an incident at his hunting lodge. Already the Azurite underground had claimed responsibility. . . .

It was impossible. Azurites were few and scattered nowadays. How could they have breached his security?

The vision of his wife flitted before his eyes, with Cassiter's hair and laughing smile; then the sight of her crushed form. This time, however, the blast had been so strong that not a trace of the victim remained. Once again, barefoot peasants turned terrorist had destroyed his woman in his own household for no other motive except—

His fist cracked the desk. The monitor came back into focus, just a blank plate on the wall. Methodically Realgar sorted his thoughts as if they were files upon his desk.

Perhaps Berenice had been careless. She wanted to die, rather then yield to him; had the explosive been hers? No, that was not like her. Berenice was a survivor, she always had been; not one to suicide, however she might threaten otherwise.

The Azurites had got her. They would take any chance to strike back at him, even the slaughter of an innocent. For years those guerrillas had ravaged the Sardish province of Azuroth, until Realgar's divisions had snuffed out their camps one by one. The few that remained were fanatics, sworn to vengeance on Realgar and all his House. That was the price of his success.

All peasant insurrections were like that, no matter what lofty slogans they started out with. First they invoked Spirit Callers and dragged their heels at regulations, when they sent their young men off to the camps; it always ended with grenades in the hands of their children. In warfare there were no innocents.

That was Berenice's mistake: for all her distrust of power, she believed in innocents. And where was she now? Which of his treacherous foes had she trusted? *Berenice*...

His eyes focused on the blue globe hovering above his desk, a hologram of the Ocean Moon. That was the site of his next assignment, Operation Amethyst. Objective: to bring Patriarchal Law to Shora.

No invasion, he had promised Berenice; what was there to invade? On the glove, red points of light marked the inhabited raft systems, two hundred and seven in all. Hardly a jungle for guerrillas to hide. Though now, in a blacker mood, Realgar wondered whether even helpless Sharers would find some way to strike back, vicious as any Azurite terrorist.

If only those points of light were targeted for destruction, Realgar's job would be done within six hours, the time for interlunar transit of a missile.

Unfortunately, that was not his assignment. The Envoy wanted those natives alive.

Malachite had made that quite clear at his final briefing. "If the Patriarch destroyed every planet that ever rebelled, we would be left with little more than charred planets. As for Sharers, they possess invaluable knowledge of life science—knowledge lost to us from before the rise of Torr."

The days when men lived as gods, Realgar thought with amazement. Though they died as gods, as well.

Yet Malachite had insisted, "There is no threat to you, at present. Subject Shora to law; that will suffice. As it should have for Pyrrhopolis." A stinging rebuke for Protector Talion—and for Realgar's own predecessor at High Command.

So instead of missile targets, Realgar was left with an entire planet full of bases and satellites to set up, plus medical inspection posts at all the rafts, and all to control a few hundred thousand women and children. He was a soldier, after all, not a colonial governor. But at that Malachite had condescended to warn, "Do not deceive yourself, General. Sharers will yield only to a stronger will." A fine vote of confidence for one who commanded all the armies of Valedon.

Alone, now, he burned with sudden hatred for that Torran servo who could reach from a far star to grind a city beneath his boot and lecture Valan rulers like a schoolmaster. But Realgar shook off the thought. The Envoy had a duty to enforce unpopular decisions. The duty of Commander Realgar was to control Shora, and, by Torr's Nine Legions, he would not fail.

9

Realgar's shuttlecraft from Headquarters Satellite Amber settled easily upon the former traders' raft of system Per-elion. As he emerged, a gust of air brought that scent of rose and orange peculiar to this ocean. The wind tugged at his Iridian blue uniform, an odious requirement of his new post. Major General Sabas and six other Iridians saluted smartly, parade-style. Realgar returned the salute with equal precision and hoped that Iridians would prove good for something else besides parades. He still wished that Talion had allowed him a good Sardish division instead.

His chief of staff, Colonel Jade, strode briskly to his side. Her promotion was still held up by the Palace bureaucrats. Jade snapped her heels together, and her blond head turned slowly as she scanned the horizon, an endless ocean riveted to the sky. "So where are all the rebel catfish?"

Realgar allowed himself a half smile. "They're not in rebellion yet, officially. They don't even know we're here." Nonetheless, he thought, if any natives did start to cook up grenades in their kitchens, Jade would be the one to find out. A member of that covert Sardish guild, her interrogation skills had served him well throughout the Azurite campaign.

He turned to Chief Medical Officer Nathan and asked, "Is the inspection team all here?" Realgar planned to start with inspection of one of the subversive "lifeshaping places" where the natives conducted their forbidden science.

"All except Dr. Siderite, sir."

"You mean the civilian plant-breeder? He's not still stuck up there in his lab?" Siderite was a Palace agronomist whom Malachite had briefed on Sharer science, or what little was known of it. However brilliant Siderite was, the choice of a civilian cut against the grain. Realgar glared at Nathan; the doctor's mustache quivered.

Jade laughed shortly. "A fine campaign this will be. How shall we even tell them anything, in that cat's tongue they call a language? With what passes for 'verbs,' you never know who's doing what to whom."

"Stick to Valan. They'd better get used to it."

"Excellent, sir."

Another shuttle from Satellite Amber touched down at last, and Siderite burst from the door, puffing and in a hurry. His loose civilian tunic emphasized his rounded shoulders and air of preoccupation, as if his mind were left behind somewhere. Annoyed, Realgar turned away; it was Nathan's business to keep the fellow in line.

With the inspection team complete, they all filed into a helicopter to take off for the first Sharer raft: Raia-el. He had chosen Raia-el because the inhabitants had a cooperative reputation and because the Palace still listed Merwen as the official "Protector" of Shora. Within minutes the raft appeared, a brown disk that bristled with outlying branches and had no harbor cut into it. By the time the helicopter landed, Sharers already were gathering to meet it. Realgar scanned them for familiar faces. Their nakedness bothered him much less without Berenice here. (Berenice—he pushed back the pain.) Something, though, was missing...children, he realized. The last time he had come here, children had found their way into everything, even that ludicrous "conference" with the Envoy.

He saw Merwen, who had received the Envoy the last time, only to reject him. "Greetings, Protector," he said stiffly, aware of the more hospitable circumstances of their previous meeting and annoyed at himself for recalling it. "I come under orders of the High Protector of Valedon, of which Shora has been declared a province by the All-powerful Patriarch of Torr. My orders are to inspect your 'lifeshaping' facilities." The sooner she got used to Valan orders, the better for all concerned.

"Share the day," Merwen said. "Does your Protection-sharer wish to share learning as an apprentice?"

"No," he said curtly. Her conversion of Valan terms into Sharer-type forms was surely deliberate. "We come to regulate hazardous activities."

"Usha is very good at that."

"Then she can guide us."

"She is busy today, improving our airblossom strain."

Realgar stepped forward, and his officers snapped to attention.

"We must inspect today," he said very clearly. "We carry out the High Protector's orders. You must accept that, from now on."

For a while she made no response, and Realgar could read nothing from her face. Suddenly he thought that he would give half a division just to know what went on inside one of those bald dark heads. No matter what the Envoy had said, Realgar still could not convince himself they were human.

Merwen appeared to reach a decision: she sighed and lowered her eyelids. "Come on, then. Usha understands the needs of the sick."

The rest of the natives watched in silence as his inspection team went on toward Merwen's house of twisted seasilk that still reminded him of crumpled blue paper. A pair of officers stayed outside; the others stepped one by one through the rabbit-hole of a doorway, passed the outer rooms, and descended to the maze of tunnels and caves. Roots and vines twisted from the walls at odd angles. This was where "lifeshaping" took place, although there was no sign of laboratory benches or plumbing, not even a stray petri dish.

At last they found Usha, the "lifeshaper." While the officers crowded into the cramped chamber, Siderite struck up a conversation with Usha, half in Valan, half in Sharer. Excellent, thought Realgar; now they would get somewhere. Merwen withdrew watchfully to a niche in the chamber but did not seem inclined to start trouble.

"Fascinating," he overheard Siderite say. "Where is your laboratory?"

"This is my laboratory," Usha said.

Siderite exchanged glances with the medical doctor, Nathan. Realgar was annoyed; he knew for a fact that this hole was the "laboratory," since he had come here before with Malachite. This Siderite had no business showing open doubt of the general's authority. He would need a good lecture or two.

Siderite then asked, "How do you perform your species manipulations?"

"Living things manage that themselves," Usha said. "Let's share some basics. Do you know of—" The rest went beyond Realgar's vocabulary, even in Valan.

In the meantime, Jade stood stiffly at attention, as if to show her contempt for the proceedings. No one else was short enough to stand up straight in the cavern. Sabas leaned into a leafy patch of wall, and one of his officers stifled a yawn.

A movement caught Realgar's eye. At a bend in the entrance

tunnel, a pair of little eyes shone, like a lurking gnome. In an instant it had vanished. Realgar looked back to Siderite, who was still listening to Usha.

Sabas cried out, and his officers reached for their firewhips. The major general stretched out the back of his jacket: its material was white and crumbling.

Usha hurried to his side, oblivious of officers and firewhips. "You mustn't touch the—" She went on in an excited stream of Sharer. A sudden wet spray drenched Sabas and washed away the crumbling fabric. Sabas stared with chagrin at the dripping, ragged edge of his uniform.

"By Torr, it was some sort of enzyme secretor he sat upon." Siderite sounded almost gleeful. He stared up at the ceiling with its tangle of vines and mouthed calculations to himself.

"I see." Realgar signaled the officers to relax and warily observed the patch of leaves where Sabas had leaned. At least there was plumbing of a sort, the first sensible thing he had seen.

Usha said, "I usually do not share this part of my workplace with children."

That was reasonable, if irrelevant. He thought of the little face he had seen hiding in the tunnel. Siderite resumed his discourse with Usha.

A tug at Realgar's sleeve startled him. He looked down: it was a girl, barely up to his waist. Her mouth opened wide to say something in squeaky Sharer. "Do you really hasten death? Why doesn't your Gathering Unspeak you?"

"Wellen!" Usha shrieked. She grabbed the child by the hand and yanked her out through the tunnel, scolding all the while. Merwen came out of her corner and watched Realgar as if she expected an answer to the child's question. The whole thing was incomprehensible.

Realgar drew Siderite and Nathan aside. "Well? Have you found what you're looking for?"

Siderite reluctantly took his attention from the leaves and vines. "Oh, I can't begin to say."

The reply and its casual tone were an affront. Realgar said curtly, "Then you'll need another visit."

"Or ten, or a hundred."

Nathan added, "We knew it would look nothing like one of our own labs."

"Yes, from the Envoy's briefing, but certain basic features at

least—" Siderite waved his hand to grasp at something insubstan-
tial. "As yet, I could not even tell you for sure this *is* their 'laboratory.'"

Realgar said in a level tone, "This is the place Malachite visited."

"Oh, yes," Siderite hurriedly agreed, "this is it."

But was the place their laboratory? Was even Malachite uncertain of that? It could be an elaborate hoax of theirs, these helpful
natives. Realgar's inspectors had no way to tell.

At orbital Headquarters Satellite Amber, Realgar made a brief
call to Talion. "If you please, my lord, this plant-breeder assigned
to my staff is not up to the job. He can't even tell a laboratory
when he sees one. Surely the Palace has someone better?"

The light-image of the High Protector glimmered, and its head
turned from side to side. "Siderite was briefed hypnotically by
Malachite. He's also our best agricultural geneticist. Genetics is
genetics anywhere, right?"

"He's worse than useless. Whatever I ask, he rolls up his eyes
like a frog."

"Give him time. He's a research man; he likes to hedge his
bets."

The general reflected on his limited experience of science or
scientists. Progress in science, other than the handouts from Torr,
was discouraged on Valedon. Yet now the Torran Envoy had
dumped a problem of applied science into their laps. It disconcerted Realgar when a superior switched orders without warning.

10

During the next few days, squads were sent to rafts all across
Shora, not for serious inspection, which was as yet useless, but to
mark the location and extent of putative laboratories, or "lab warrens" as Jade had dubbed them, and to verify the global census.

Logistic problems arose: one helicopter downed in a squall, several others had air-blossoms caught in the motors, all just part of settling in.

It turned out that nearly all the rafts had some extent of lab warrens. This discovery was a disappointment, since Realgar had hoped to have only one lifeshaping place to guard in each raft system, instead of eight times as many individual rafts.

More disturbing, it appeared that not all raft populations were as receptive as Raia-el. Several squads landed to find rafts deserted, homes completely empty. In one case, an entire system was gone. Fifteen hundred people could not just banish; they had to be hiding somewhere.

On other rafts, all the adults were found in whitetrance. "In these cases," reported Jade, "the patrols searched all homes and concluded, 'No laboratories present.'"

"That's nonsense. The patrols all have holocubes of what to look for."

"I doubt they ever located the rabbit-hole inside the silkhouse. Iridians," Jade added, a clear insult. "One odd case is left. Company Seventeen observed extensive damage to wildlife of several rafts. The captain thinks the natives are testing biological warfare."

"Where the devil did he get that idea?"

"I couldn't say, General." Jade's reply was blandly correct. Not even his chief of staff was supposed to know the real reason behind this campaign. The campaign itself had not yet been made public by the Palace. "I think it's a false alarm," Jade added. "That raft system is within the Aragonite testing ground."

"Of course." The House of Aragonite, a member of the Shora Development Consortium, was developing potent toxins for seaswallowers.

Within two weeks, most of the natives were meeting inspections in whitetrance. Rough handling seemed to make no difference; they were in trance, and that was it. Sabas retaliated with daily reconnaissance fights, zooming low over all the rafts, just to remind them that Valans meant business. But it was of little practical use, Realgar thought, barely worth the fuel consumption. Infrared and sonic scanners soon located tunnels, but the rafts were riddled with them and they all looked the same. At least Siderite was still making progress at Raia-el, where Usha was supposedly instructing him every day. Sabas suggested that they should await further developments from Siderite before pressing the inspections further.

Realgar disagreed with the major general. He decided to test an idea of his own. With Sabas and Siderite, he flew out to one of the rafts that had resisted from the first. They approached a silkhouse, outside which sat one adult native in trance, marble white with blue veins.

For no obvious reason Realgar paused a moment. Wind from the sea blew shrilly past his ears.

He wondered whether the native was conscious in this state. Traders gave conflicting answers, and Berenice had never spoken of it at all. With an effort he broke the silence and announced his orders, as he had with Merwen. He followed with a rough native translation, adding, "We share no harm. Your sisters on other rafts have cooperated with us."

The native made no response. Several minutes passed. Realgar was very conscious of Sabas and his officers watching the affair.

He tossed a holocube onto the raft. A cube of light-images sprang up, life-sized: himself, Merwen, other natives, a few legs and arms cut flat at the sides of the recorded space.

"Greetings, Protector," spoke the image of the general, reciting his Palace orders. Realgar had edited Merwen's response, leaving only her quaintly phrased acquiescence: "Come on, then. Usha understands the needs of the sick."

The cube of light vanished.

Shadows of movement flickered across the eyelids of the entranced native. A pale lavender gradually seeped into her skin. Her eyelids opened, first the regular outer ones, then the translucent ones underneath. She said gravely, "What needs can we share with sick children?"

Realgar wondered what she was getting at. Was his native vocabulary defective? He said carefully, "All we need is to share-seeing your place of lifeshaping."

The native then rose and led his team through her house. Siderite confirmed the identity of the lab warrens. Major General Sabas was no use at all, Realgar decided, and he wondered if he dared request a Sardish replacement.

At another raft, however, the trick failed to work. Three natives, blue-veined white, simply sat and stared out to sea.

Realgar was only slightly disappointed. He had not expected to solve the problem outright. The main point was, he now had direct evidence that the natives were consciously ignoring Valan orders. "Take all three up to Satellite Amber." There, Jade would work on them. The bodies hung like rags as they were carried off.

Siderite stared in surprise and sucked his lips. "General, is that necessary? Our local informants provide plenty of assistance to . . ."

Realgar stared coldly until Siderite's words trailed off. "You're under orders, doctor, like everyone else. Get yourself a uniform to remind you."

Siderite swallowed and hid his anger poorly, but a healthy trace of fear was beginning to show.

At any rate, Realgar decided, it was about time for a progress report, to find out whether the scientist was getting anywhere. Realgar received daily records, of course, but to him they were useless gibberish. The main thing he wanted to know was, were these lab warrens genuine laboratories or not?

"Oh, they're genuine, yes." Seated in the general's office, Siderite was full of his usual enthusiasm. Even in uniform his shoulders were rounded, and the pointed tips sagged. "There's work space, there's plumbing. No glassware, bottled chemicals, or autoclaves, much less recognizable analytic hardware. But those vines you saw, they form galls whose cavities can be inoculated with pure cultures of microorganisms. Other vines are specialized secretors for enzymes, organic reagents, acids, you name it."

Realgar was relieved. "Then their real labs were not hidden."

"I couldn't swear to that," Siderite cautioned.

"Come now, there's always uncertainty."

"Oh, I don't mean that." Siderite's eyes defocused, and he stared into space. "In a sense one might say . . . the whole planet is their laboratory."

"What's that?" An entire planet? Sweat broke out on Realgar's forehead.

Startled, Siderite shook himself. "Just speculation. Fascinating possibilities."

Realgar suppressed an impulse to strangle the man. "It was my understanding that Malachite had told you everything you needed to know."

"With all due respect, General, the Envoy is just a servo, remarkably keen at data collection but limited for analysis. That's why I'm here, after all."

The audacity of this offhand remark pushed Realgar beyond words. Had Siderite slept through the day of judgment of Pyrrhopolis? Nine years, Realgar reminded himself: nine years before we face that again. He swallowed and made a grudgingly civil reply. "When will your . . . analysis be complete?"

"In what respect?"

"To control their technology, by Torr. What good are a thousand inspectors, watching night and day, when they don't know what to look for?"

"No good. Give us, say, ten, twenty years perhaps—set up an institute—"

"Out of the question. The Envoy expects us to control them long before that."

Siderite's shoulders slumped. "The Envoy didn't tell me that. Well, perhaps their 'lifeshaping' is less advanced than it seems." Siderite actually sounded disappointed. "But my guess is that, short of forcing their hand, only long-term study will tell you what Sharers can do."

Provocation. Would he have to provoke the natives into showing their hand? The Envoy had said it would take them another generation to produce a real threat. There had to be something else. A ghost of an insight arose but eluded his grasp.

"By the way," Siderite added, "those guards you send with me are a hindrance. They interfere with my work."

"They're for your own protection. That will be all for now, Dr. Siderite." The last thing Realgar would do was to leave this civilian alone with those treacherous natives.

One of the traders debriefed by Sabas's staff proved particularly knowledgeable about native customs. He was Kyril, manager of the Hyalite outlet in Per-elion, and Realgar had him called in to clear up what mysteries he could. "For one thing," Realgar asked, "why do you suppose the natives describe us as 'sick'? What are they getting at?"

"Disapproval," Kyril said. "It means they don't respect you enough even to insult you."

Realgar had suspected as much, despite the cool politeness natives had shown. "Your frankness is appreciated. Tell me, what is your opinion of Sharers, after your years of dealing with them?"

Kyril pursed his lips. "They're honest, I'll say that for them. Infuriatingly so. And they take what you say as literally as a servo. But they're tough nuts to crack."

"How do you mean?"

"Tough as Dolomites, catfish are, when they're in their own element. Water's their element, and water's all around. Watch how you hook them; they'll run till the line snaps. We managed all right, until the day when all the catfish decided traders were 'sick.' Then the deal was up."

"All of whom?" Realgar asked. "A raft Gathering?"

Kyril's arms spread wide. "The whole planet, it seemed, overnight."

"They can't plan together. They have no long-range communications."

"If you please, General, they claim to telegraph subsonically, somehow, underwater. They complain to us constantly about interference."

"So it's easy enough to sabotage."

Kyril nodded. "Those insects communicate too, but I'm not sure what their range is."

Realgar had heard of clickflies, but he did not take them seriously. Insects, indeed. "So how's your own business doing these days? Not very well, I hear."

"No trade." Kyril slashed the air with his hand. "My own outlet's closing out next month. You want some cut-rate rubies for your troops?"

The general permitted himself a smile. "How would you like to sign on with us as a consultant?"

The trader pulled at his lower lip. "Don't get me wrong, General, but what sort of action do you foresee here?"

"We're here to install police. What other action could there be?"

The two men regarded one another coolly. Kyril said, "Well, an army is one thing catfish don't have, and it takes two of those to fight a battle. All the same—" Kyril grinned wryly. "I wish you better luck than ours."

* * *

On day fifteen of the inspection campaign, Colonel Jade reported to the general's office in person. Her cheeks were drawn in tight lines.

Realgar asked. "What's the bad news?"

"The prisoners, General."

At a word, the light signals changed behind his desk. Further recording within the office would be upgraded to the highest security level. "What happened?"

"One died."

"I did not authorize that."

"I am aware of that, General. The mindprobe triggered it."

Neither the pain-triggering neuralprobe nor the analytic mindprobe were intended to kill. They were "clean" probes, designed to read and control with maximum precision and minimum physical damage. Jade was an expert who rarely slipped. But now, Realgar would have to consider the details of what had gone wrong. It repulsed him, for some reason.

"The prisoner never came out of whitetrance," Jade said, "so I skipped initial interview. The scanner picked up all brain signals okay, but as soon as the mindprobe began—that was it."

"A hypnotic deathblock, to stop the heart?"

"Not an ordinary block. Usually I can detect that and probe around it; it might be a deathwish, say, at a certain question. This was different: a total block to the slightest touch of mind."

"A total deathblock. I see." Mental deathblocks were illegal on Valedon. To find one so absolute, among supposedly peaceful people, was a surprise. What could such a block be aimed against? The technique must have been developed long before Valan troops arrived. "Suspicious, don't you think?"

"Perhaps their minds are just too weak for the probe."

Realgar doubted that. He was sure the victim wished and intended to die. "How are the other two prisoners?"

"Still in whitetrance."

He waves an impatient hand. "How can I run this place if the prisoners won't break? You will find a way—and avoid further 'failures.'"

"Yes, General."

Nonetheless, he thought, what a subtle deathblock it must be to fool a Sardish expert. Poor Berenice had been completely taken in; those natives were terrorists, underneath, as tough as the Azurites who had got her in the end. *Force their hand,* Siderite had warned. Realgar planned to do just that.

11

At the newly settled raft of Leni-el, Lystra was digging tunnels for lifeshaping, and strapping young starworms beneath the raft branches, and on top of everything she faced the plague of Valan death-hasteners.

The soldiers she could cope with, despite their cravenly childish behavior and those clattering beasts they rode in the sky, hovering and swooping like overgrown fanwings. But what numbed Lystra to the heart was the silent noise that grew beneath the waves, worse than ever before, to drown the song of the starworm. Now only clickflies could get word to rafts across the globe, and that might take weeks. Lystra felt as if she had lost her own ears.

The Gatherings would have to respond to this unprecedented upsurge of Valan rudeness and puerility. Lystra almost wished she had stayed home to help, but still, it was a relief to get away from Mother for a while. Unexpectedly she missed people: Flossa, who had always tried to emulate her, and Shaalrim, whose unflappable humor had refreshed the sometimes dreary Gathering. At Leni-el, the Gathering was younger and less experienced than at Raia-el, and Lystra was disconcerted to find herself an "elder," expected to keep everything running smoothly.

There was pain when she thought of Spinel, whose departure she herself had caused, as surely as she would have liked to when he first arrived. Why had it happened? After all, she had never been so happy. Spinel was shockingly "different" but as delicious as . . . as any other sister. (She would not think of Rilwen in the same breath.) He was easygoing, yet earnestly caring, and so innocent of all the stratagems of will that most sisters shared with each other to the point of exhaustion. Nonetheless, he had asked of Lystra the one thing she could not give, then tore at her heart where it still hurt most. She should not have forgotten Rilwen so soon. There was no time for bitterness now: eat bitterness, and bitterness eats you.

She was returning to Mithril's silkhouse one afternoon, with a load of octopus dragging behind. Nisi was weaving at the loom. "You look ready to eat the whole catch," Nisi said.

Lystra grinned and thumped Nisi's back with a weary arm. Nisi, too, was better off beyond Merwen's scrutiny, even though she had learned whitetrance. Nisi had regained color and spirit since she left Raia-el; only rarely did Lystra catch her brooding alone with haunted eyes. Nisi had hiding places for when the soldiers came, in the storm tunnels, and in airbells deep below, in the cold underworld, where she had hidden from her mad mother before.

From the silkhouse, Mithril's chatter carried over. "A strange clickfly dropped in. We couldn't get the message; it comes from very far. It flapped like mad to go on, but I trapped it in the house. Nisi says you might know its code."

"I'll try." Lystra squeezed herself through the door, which was still tight, in need of reworking. She paused to admire the new wall cover. Mithril had painted several tones and textures of green, with different fungal variants, and swirls of a rare yellow strain. The pattern captured the grace and excitement of a glider squid bursting from the sea.

A clickfly was hovering anxiously, looking for a window. Its message must be urgent. Lystra caught it in her fingerwebs. Its black-plated back was torn from buffeting in upper atmospheric winds. "From the Sixth Galactic," Lystra said, noting the code of the colored ribs behind its head. She delicately flicked the sound-scraper mandibles until the insect started up its frantic message. Then she made it restart, because the code was in an unaccustomed dialect.

"Three sisters," Lystra interpreted. "Disappeared. With Valans."

"With *Valans?*" said Mithril. "Disappeared? You must have it wrong."

"Valans shared their leaving," Lystra insisted. "That part is clear. The Sharers were in whitetrance, yet Valans physically took hold of them, and they disappeared."

Nisi laced her bare fingers and squeezed them. "Why? Does it say?"

"Do Valans ever say why?" Lystra flung the clickfly out the door to send its message farther. "I meant nothing personally," Lystra added.

"Of course not," said Nisi abruptly. "I'm not a Valan anymore." Nisi was a Sharer—and now all Sharers were to be hunted like fish. Would they all have to take to the shockwraith's liar?

Lystra's chin tightened. "We'll see if the Gathering will put up with this." Yinevra at least would not. Yinevra knew how to deal with Valans.

At this Gathering, Sharers collected from all eight rafts of Perelion. No one knew where the three sisters had vanished, or how long they planned to stay. One had left two small children. Had Valans sought their help for something? To share healing?

It was understood, now, that Valans suffered a terrible madness because the Death-spirit ruled their souls, perpetuated by creatures of non-life who walked and spoke, yet never lived. This must be why Valans were so obsessed with Sharer lifeshaping; but what lifeshaper had ever heard of such an affliction, let alone its cure?

Even Usha's new Valan apprentice, though not a death-hastener, had offered little help on this point. Siderite simply agreed that most of his sisters were mad. When asked about the three lost sisters, he was greatly upset and refused to share more. Usha explained, "Valans are ashamed of their madness. They don't like us to see."

Merwen hoped that others would keep as calm as Usha, as she watched her sisters gather. Tension ran as high as when the Great Unspeaking occurred, years before. But this time they would have to stick together and chart a single course.

If only Nisi would come back to help, instead of hiding on Leni-el in fear of her death-mad lovesharer. Merwen loathed secretiveness, but Nisi had pleaded for freedom above truth; a harsh choice, and perhaps a false one in the long run.

Trurl raised both hands above the confusion of voices. "All right, let's get things straight from the start. First goal: to retrieve our vanished sisters, in good time and good health. Overall goal:

to heal this Valan plague. Any *constructive* suggestions are welcome." Trurl glared fleetingly, a rare lapse.

Someone shouted, "Let the Valan-lovers go talk with them. We all know what good that does."

A few laughed; others turned icily still.

Yinevra said, "Let's talk sense, before half of us walk out and the other half go Unspoken. The simplest solution is to share a strain of breathmicrobe that the Valans can't get rid of. It won't hurt a bit but will do the trick; they'll all scurry out the Ocean Door."

Heads nodded like airblossoms bobbing in the wind.

"A good start," Trurl agreed. "But how does that get our sisters back?"

"Would our sisters wish to see us all stay like this, with incurable rag-tied psychotics blundering through our homes? We'll all share their madness, before long."

Merwen's heart pulsed faster. Suppose we already share their madness, she wondered. We are one species, only one, she thought, as other Doorclosers shouted support for Yinevra's call.

Lalor asked. "What if it doesn't work? Some Valans get used to breathmicrobes. Others will be crazier than before."

That exasperated Yinevra. "Anything can go wrong, but how will we know if we don't try something? Who's got a better idea?"

Now might be her last chance. Merwen rose, and Trurl's finger lifted toward her. "Valans may be mad, some of them, but they are stubborn as we are. I believe the only end to the 'plague' will be to share cure of their madness."

"And how will that happen?" Yinevra asked. "Did it work with Virien?"

The blow shocked Merwen, until she saw that others took it not as an affront but as an intensely serious question: What can be done with the incurably ill?

"Consider this," Merwen said at last. "It may be that we can dispel the Valan plague by sharing force, as Yinevra suggests. I hesitate to guess what force the Valans will share in turn. It may be too late, afterward, to try to share mindhealing instead." Merwen scanned the Gathering to guess how many had understood.

Yinevra was still standing. "If we waste time now, it may soon be too late to gather our strength. Force is what Valans understand."

Trurl said, "Enough, let's hear from someone else," and she nodded to Lystra.

Lystra rose with her back not quite straight and a surly expression that marked her diffidence. "Excuse me, but certain Valans have been known to understand other things, even to share the life of our raft. Traders didn't start to respect us until we went *there*, where they lived, to share our concern. Perhaps the new Valans want us to do this, now. Could that be why they wished our sisters to join them?"

"That's it," someone called out. "They are like sick children— how else could they touch a sister in whitetrance? It's not good to ignore a sick child."

Yinevra said, "Their sickness is surely beyond healing. Nevertheless, I'm willing enough to share with them what we shared with traders. We'll sit at their door until shame drives them out."

A murmur of agreement swept the Gathering.

Merwen was watching Lystra through half-closed eyes. Perhaps, she thought, Lystra's friendship with Spinel had not been a total disaster after all.

12

A warm breeze blew into Chrysoport. Winter rain clouds were giving way to softer puffs of white, and herringbones ribbed the sky. Sun pierced the cold air with rays that brought an unexpected preview of spring. Spinel recalled that the morning had felt just like this when that little houseboat with the Hyalite sign had pulled up at the wharf with two of the most outlandish strangers the town had ever seen. He paused at the netleaf tree just long enough to imagine the shape of Merwen there, drawing him in among its shadows. Nowadays, a line of Dolomites led past the tree into the firemerchant's shop.

Spinel wore at last a genuine stonesign, the star sapphire of a Spirit Caller. Yet whenever he tried to imagine this "Spirit" that he must hear, either Merwen or Lystra would enter his mind. *You are still a Sharer... even as a shaper of stone.* Yes, Merwen's spell held him still.

Whatever the Spirit was, there was no end of work for a Spirit Caller in Chrysoport. Uriel wandered more and more on his own, nowadays, so the villagers turned to Spinel with their problems and questions. One had lost an entire harvest to the hailstones, another had a halfwit child who would never learn his letters— there seemed no end of souls in search of sublime healing for their daily miseries.

Spinel soon came to suspect that most of his clients would find their own answers, if any, in whatever he had to say. What they actually craved was someone to listen, if only for a moment. It amazed him to realize how many people led parched lives, thirsting for the faintest drop of empathy. For himself or anyone else to fill all that need was as hopeless as filling an ocean.

Still, Spinel hung on to the belief that some kinds of suffering were more evil than others and ought to be done away with. The Dolomite garrison was an entity apparently designed for the sole purpose of creating human misery. The Dolomite Protector levied endless taxes now; freight taxes, house taxes, taxes on vendors in the market square. To be sure, the curfew was still relaxed, a victory which Spinel kept pointing out. It dismayed him to discover that the villagers shrugged off their own achievement, forgetting so little time.

"The goatheads were planning to let up on us anyway," said Ahn. "Not worth the trouble."

"But that's the point, Ahn. We *made* it too much trouble."

"What trouble is an unarmed rabble?"

Spinel leaned his elbows on the vegetable stand. "Suppose we all stopped paying taxes, every one. What could they do about it?"

"Listen to the almsman! As if *you* ever paid a hundredth *solidus* of tax in your life. Go tell the High Protector; he knows what the Patriarch intends for us."

Spinel leaned closer. "Listen, Ahn," he whispered. "There's a different 'Patriarch,' not the one on Torr, but a 'Patriarch' here, all around us, a Spirit anyone can hear—"

Ahn shrieked and shoved his arms off the edge. "You're madder than the old one! Get away from me, do you hear? I've got one good eye and a sound bit of mind left, and by Torr I intend to keep both."

* * *

Undaunted, Spinel pressed his idea of tax refusal among the villagers. He hoped to enlist Uriel again, but the old Spirit Caller seemed to be wandering more in the countryside lately, with the breath of warm weather. Spinel argued with Melas, and he even pestered Picrite in the barbershop. "I'd lose my Dolomite customers," Picrite said between snips of the shears. "I get twice as much business as I used to."

Spinel even tried to convert his father, who pounded and chiseled all day in the basement. One day Cyan threw down his chisel and pushed up his shield of protective glass. His stern gaze leaped past his blunt nose and focused on his son. "So you know better than the Protector what's good for us, do you? All from that pretty trinket around your neck?"

"Protectors don't give a fishhead for you or anyone, except a few nobles and traders."

"Son, think about this—just think of it. Where would we be without the Torran Envoy to keep space safe, the High Protector to keep provincials from sacking our town when they take over, and police to keep order in street and market? Where would we get firecrystals if not from the firemerchants of Iridis, and who would produce them safely? Now just hold on, my words have been a long time coming."

Spinel shifted his feet, as the lecture discomfited him.

"Every ruler has his purpose, or he wouldn't be one." Cyan's workshirt hung loose, its creases vibrating as he spoke. "For traders, that goes double. Hyalite got where he is because who else dared to dig in on an unknown world, before your time, when the Ocean Moon was just another bauble in the sky? Hyalite made a profit, despite the huge risks, because millions of customers wanted what he got, herbs and things you'll not find here. For every thousand stonecutters like me, there's maybe one man with a vision like that.

"You think only Spirit Callers have visions. Listen: where would your Spirit Callers be without plain, dependable folk to put up with you? You've yet to make a home for yourself. And whose home did Uriel stay in, all those cold nights, with the firecrystal in the stove? Answer me that." Cyan paused for breath. "So if the High Protector puts us under Dolomoth, he has his reasons. He does his job, just as I do mine." Cyan pulled down his glasses and returned to his work.

Spinel frowned and opened his mouth, but no simple answer came to mind. The clang of the chisel muddled his head, so he skipped upstairs and outdoors. He sat on the doorstep and scraped his toe between cracks in the old stained bricks.

The more he thought, the more puzzled he became. It was true that Valedon would be in chaos without someone to lay down the law. Yet on Shora, things worked just the opposite: no one person could set a law for anyone else, and even if they tried, it would only create chaos, not curb it. Were people just different, on different planets?

Yet even his father had stood with him that night in the market square, when Uriel had led the Calling and dared the Dolomites to crush them.

Uriel would know what to say. Where had Uriel got to? Spinel ducked into the kitchen to ask his sister. "You seen Uriel lately?"

"Oh, didn't you hear?" Beryl's cheeks had regained color, and her gestures had recovered much of the liveliness she had lost. Oolite was into running: she plodded back and forth across the kitchen and caught the wall each time with a delighted yell. "They took him away," Beryl said. "To a home. He was—well, a bit touched."

"But . . . I don't understand."

"He's better off, you know. He barely made it through this winter."

"But how—who took him, Beryl?"

"Other Spirit Callers, of course. I heard it straight from the baker's delivery girl, who saw them. They were foreign-like, with hoods of mountain wool, but very kind and dignified. Spinny, would you shell some peas for me? Keep Oolite's fingers out of them."

So Uriel was gone, just like that. Vague resentment pricked Spinel, as if Uriel had let him down, somehow, by changing without notice from a mysterious hero into an ordinary old man. Spinel cocked his head quizzically, as if he expected a better answer. Around the tiled wainscoting, figures chased each other as always in endless circles.

He let his feet wander back to the shore, where Uriel had given him the starstone. The water foamed and its chill stung his toes; farther out it was a hard, rippling blue, just calm enough to mirror the trace of an Iridian jet high above the sky. He remembered that other day, last spring, when Uriel had made him angry, just why he could not recall, and he had run down here to the shore where the waves whispered *merwenmerwen*. . . . He listened closely again, trying to block out the clatter of a farm wagon on the road behind. After all, if he listened long enough, any name would come from the sea.

The next morning, the market was alive with the news. "Did you hear about your moon friends?" Melas said. "They defied the Patriarch, so Talion sent in the Guard."

"Nuts to you," said Spinel.

"I swear by every skull on Trollbone Point! It was a month ago, in fact, only the Palace just let it out."

"But—but why?"

"To teach those moonwomen a lesson, that's why. I told you no good would come of them. It's one thing to tweak the nose of a fire-merchant, but the *Patriarch*—they had it coming."

Spinel spent his last few coins on a newscube, the cheap kind that you had to squint into until your eyes hurt. There were a bunch of High Councilors calling for destruction of the Purple Menace. Would a war be declared? Then the High Protector came in with the new Guard Commander, urging calm; it was all under control, they said. Then the ocean switched in, and a raft with a blurred group of Sharers whose silkhouse was being searched for "planet-threatening weapons." The face of Merwen leaped out at him; startled, he dropped the cube and had to snatch it up again before it ran out. "Planet-threatening weapons" in Merwen's house?

And that was a month ago. . . . Merwen could be dead by now. *Troublesharer, you'll go now. Because there is no other hope for us.* But how could Spinel help at all? A few Dolomites were nothing compared to the Protectoral Guard.

His hand wrapped the cube, squeezing it until the points bit into his palm. His money for the market was gone, so he walked straight home.

"Father, I'm going back to Shora," Spinel announced.

"Between the Guard and the Purple Menace? Nonsense," said Cyan.

"So what? What was it like here, when I arrived?"

"We did not urge you home."

"And where would I be if I had stayed? Look, I'm still signed to Merwen and I have to go, that's all."

"You're signed to Uriel, with a stonesign so it's proper. Why not follow him to the old folk's home?"

Blood rushed to Spinel's face; he clenched and unclenched his fists. "I'm going, that's all," he said sullenly. "Just give me the travel fare and that's the last thing I'll ever ask of you."

"Should I give you money to die a fool?"

Spinel shouted, "It's my money too! Every coin I get for Spirit Calling, I chip in for the family.Every day I run to the market or cut tiles for you or whatever."

"Son, when you grow into a sensible man I'll make you a partner in the business. Until then—no."

Spinel was enraged. He wanted to crush his father's head into the workbench. He could do it, too; he was the taller and stronger, now, and he had grown up outdoors while his father withered away in a basement. Yet something froze his hand, that same part of himself that had recoiled after he shoved Melas into the produce cart, the day the Sharers first appeared. That part of him had fed and grown alarmingly since he passed the Door into Ocean.

Spinel pounded upstairs to his mother's study, where she sat hunched over account books as usual. "Just one ticket to the Ocean Moon, Mother, that's all I'll ever ask, ever again."

"Listen to your father," she said, without looking up at him.

That night Spinel slept fitfully among twisted dreams. He dreamed that he found himself on a barren island, alone except for mountains of bleached trollbones. For some reason he grew angry, incredibly, angry at Uriel, so that he tore off his starstone and threw it out to sea. But instead of falling, the stone paused at its zenith, just long enough for the sky to darken, then it settled gently among the stars, a sapphire moon.

He sat up, wide awake. A hint of dawn lit the horizon. If he were to leave now, he could catch the first steamer. Perhaps they would let a Spirit Caller aboard without charge.

Before he reached the door, his mother came downstairs. Her voluminous nightgown flapped around her. "Take this." She thrust a purse into his hand.

Spinel roughly pushed it back.

"What's wrong with you?" she whispered fiercely. "You're too good for us now? Is that what they teach you up there—to despise your own people?"

"No, Mother." He embraced his mother then, and they held

close for what might be the last time. Spinel wanted to cry, but it was bottled up inside. He wanted to say, It's you folks who despise yourselves. But he could never make them understand. He would leave for good now, go to the Iridis spaceport and then, somehow, he would make it back to Shora.

Part V

NIGHT
OF
CINNABAR

1

Two days after the first prisoners were taken, natives at another raft system a hundred kilometers away appeared at a garrison asking after their "sisters." Visitations soon spread to other bases, halfway around the globe. Even more annoying, the natives would not leave when put off, but grew in numbers and stayed by day and night until guards hauled them out to sea.

Realgar was stumped, on several counts. Why should natives risk life and limb just for a few "sisters" off a raft somewhere across the globe? For that matter, how the devil did they find out in the first place? By *insects,* as that trader claimed? If that was it, insecticides would wipe every insect off the planet.

He simply could not permit this widespread response, especially to such a minor incident. If he imprisoned all the visitors at his eighty garrison bases, it would be enough to fill the main penitentiary of Iridis.

Worst of all, five natives from Raia-el appeared outside the main base at Per-elion. These five, including Merwen, could not simply be put off. Not only was Merwen the "Protector," her mate was the one practitioner of forbidden science who would assist Siderite without coercion.

So Realgar decided to receive them in his office at the Per-elion garrison. A conference with the local Protector—at lease he could get a good press clipping out of the deal.

Two aides ushered in the natives, whose broad feet gently slapped the floor as they walked. One was visibly pregnant. Their nakedness jarred with the polished angular setting of the office; it disturbed Realgar more than it had in their own home. Acutely aware of his officers, he realized that any incident could easily make him look foolish.

With a hum of unseen gears, five chairs rose out of the floor. Realgar gestured, "Have a seat, ladies."

The natives casually sat on the floor in front of the chairs and crossed their legs. The press footage would require some touchup, he decided, in order to pass the palace censor. Fig leaves, at least.

Realgar peered down over his desk at Merwen. "Greetings, Protector. What can I do for you?" He found himself adopting the tone of voice he used for his daughter's friends who came to play.

"We seek our sister Sharers," Merwen said.

"Who might they be?"

"Lerion Nonthinker, Ronesha the Coldhearted, and Oo the Jealous, who were last seen with Valans on Nri-el raft."

So those were the names of the prisoners. Realgar now knew more than what Jade had got out of them. He felt at once frustrated yet perversely pleased with himself. Let them hang themselves by their own tongues. "Why did your sisters fail to cooperate as well as you do?"

"They were in whitetrance."

"Why were they in whitetrance?"

Merwen hesitated. "The clickflies did not say."

Clickflies, indeed. Not for long, he vowed. "Your sisters entered whitetrance in order to defy my orders. When your sisters cooperate, they will be released."

Eyes widened. The pregnant one said, "They are safe, then. I knew they would be. Well, we have to share speech with them, although if they're in whitetrance still, it would be better for you or some other child to speak first. They left two small daughters behind, one of whom needs her mother's milk. We must see them at once. The Gathering insists," she added almost apologetically.

Realgar fumed inwardly during this speech. He should have told them the three were dumped in some remote region. He could release the prisoners, since Jade could pick up plenty more elsewhere, but that would only put off the day of reckoning. Glacially he eyed the one who had called him a "child." "What is your name, my lady?"

"Shaalrim the Lazy. And yours, sister?"

"Shaalrim, you may put in a visitation request which will be processed by Palace Iridium."

"Is that where our sisters are?"

"Their location does not concern you." They were still at Satellite Amber, of course, in Jade's facility. "I must regretfully terminate this interview," he concluded, sorry that he had granted it in the first place.

Merwen said quickly, "We still seek our sisters."

"Then you, too, may file a visitation request. The aide will show you how."

"As you wish, but you see, we cannot leave until we have seen our lost sisters. We promised the Gathering."

Realgar crossed his arms on the desk. "Merwen, you are addressing the High Commander of the Valan Protectoral Guard. What *you* must see is that from now on you and your sisters will do as you are told."

"We understand very well," said another, the long-nosed one. "You wish us to sit on your steps for a while, as the traders did. But that's such a bother for all concerned. And you can't leave an infant without her mother's milk for days on end."

Realgar was amazed. Did they really have no idea what they were up against? "One of your sisters is dead," he barked. "Now do you understand?"

Their faces fell and shoulders drooped, sagging with their breasts. A few fingers whitened. A small voice asked, "Which one?"

"How can I—" Realgar caught himself. No need to admit Jade's probe had failed to get even a name out.

"Death-hastener," the fifth native called at him in Sharer tongue. She was built like a wrestler, that one. "Death-hastener," she called again, hoarsely. "Death hastens those who hasten death."

He kept to Valan. "Death is part of my job." He mouthed each word distinctly. "Remember that, next time."

The native said nothing more, but her breath came hard, and every muscle was a coiled spring. That one, Realgar told himself, would end up lobbing bombs at his garrison. What an odd assortment these natives were.

"Is it true," asked Merwen, "that Death pays a fair wage?"

Realgar watched her as she sat; still, except for fingers that tapped lightly at her knees. This one clearly knew more than she let on, but he had yet to figure out her game. "When needed," he said shortly.

"What is the wage of Death?"

What was the point of this; bribery? Realgar clasped his hands. "Ladies, I regret that our time is up. The aides will show you out."

None moved. The door hissed open, and the aides quietly reached for their neuralprobes.

The natives were losing color, slowly but steadily. Realgar watched with fascination as they bleached, first the webbing and fingers, then arms, legs, and overall, translucent with the blue veins showing through. He had never before observed the actual process of transition. His pulse quickened, and the reaction annoyed him. Silently he cursed the lot of them but did not let a gram of frustration show. "Show them out," he ordered. "Fifteen kilometers." Perhaps they would not make it home this time.

Later, Siderite was apoplectic. Though all five natives had made it back to their raft, every adult in sight was now mourning in whitetrance for the dead prisoner, and Torr only knew whether Usha would ever deign to "learnshare" with him again.

The scientist's fury amused Realgar. Such a typical indignant citizen, full of impotent blustering. "The natives are scared, at last," he assured Siderite. "It's better for them. You'll see, they'll cooperate twice as well as before."

2

Merwen did not stay in whitetrance long. There was too much to be done, too many decisions to make. That night when she fell asleep, she had a vivid dream.

In her dream she was swimming in an ocean, alone without a raft in sight, much as when the soliders had left her that afternoon. Yet it was not a natural ocean, it was an extraordinary hard shade of blue, and its waves were a thick clear paste that merged into sky without a seam of horizon. She could make little headway; her arms were not free to pull because they cupped something between the hands, a spark that glimmered out between the fingerwebs, a spark of something so terrible that she had to hold it fast and never let it escape. But it did escape, and the flame spread, a pool of waterfire so brilliant that it shone by day. It engulfed the ocean, and then sky as well, nothing left but fire all around, as if she had fallen into the heart of the First Door. . . .

It was just after sunrise when Merwen awakened. She squinted into the sun's rays that reached her from a slit in the seasilk. Lightly she patted Usha, who still slept; then she pulled herself up. Her leg still ached from a careless twist by the Valan who had thrown her overboard the day before. It was extraordinarily dreadful to be treated as a cold object by another sister.

She had to find Nisi. Questions compelled her that only Nisi could answer, Nisi whose own lovesharer was the most flagrant hastener of death. In Chrysoport, she remembered, that bearded one had said that Death paid a "wage." Merwen herself had barely come to comprehend "wage" and "payment," those concepts the traders valued above life itself. Yet she would have to puzzle out the source of that wage and Death paid, and only Nisi might have the key.

Merwen took a boat out through the branch channels. Most of the raft blossoms had fallen, and in the distance occasional dots of seedlings appeared. Merwen was not up to rowing, after her exhausting swim the day before, so she summoned a glider squid with a bit of attractant powder. Valan motors were long out of use, not that it mattered, now that another noise drowned the starworm's song completely.

At Leni-el raft, Nisi was actually glad to see her. They embraced, and Nisi held her very tight. Nisi's eyes were moist. "I heard what happened. I—" She swallowed, and her voice croaked. "I don't know, Merwen. What will become of us?"

Merwen brushed Nisi's head with both hands, and the tiny hairs pricked her palms. "Whatever you do, don't share fear. Better to die in a day than to live an endless death."

Nisi's smile flickered. She was getting thin, unnaturally so. "You do believe that, don't you?"

"Would I say what is not?"

"No, you would not. But there are things you have not seen." Nisi laced her fingers, like the warp and weft. "Merwen, there's still a chance, I think. You can still turn back, and follow the Patriarch. If not, then..."

"Then?"

"Then you'll share a current of blood. Do you understand?"

Merwen sighed. "Shora has many blood drinkers, from fleshborers to shockwraiths, even most Sharers, who eat the lesser sisterlings." Most considered Merwen's abstention from meat an affectation, or at least eccentric. They might think twice, had they been to Valedon, where there lived small thickly furred creatures whose semihuman existence reminded one of the continuum of flesh. "Nisi, what is the 'wage' of Death?"

"A 'wage'?"

"For someone like your lovesharer," Merwen suggested, although it could be anyone.

Nisi shuddered. "A 'soldier' has a 'wage' for hastening death when necessary."

"When needed? When is that?"

Nisi looked away. "You won't know, until you find out."

Merwen tried a different tack. "If this 'wage' is something like the 'wage' that a trader needs, then it makes sense for us to share with soldiers what we shared with traders."

"Yes, it's a start at least," Nisi mused. "Is there a Gathering today?"

"Yes, to decide what next. Will you come?" Merwen's spirits lifted. "Do you think that it's—"

"It's unsafe, I know that. But I'll defend my freedom as hard as anyone, thank you."

Merwen felt a fluttering at her scalp as she heard those words. She thought suddenly, sisters had gone Unspoken for less than what Nisi had meant to say. But Unspeech would not help Nisi now, nor the Gathering, which needed to hear her, to know her for what she was, as Merwen did. Another voice warned her. but again, it was too late. There was so little time. Would Spinel ever return?

Nisi, meanwhile, was thinking that if anyone was to survive, herself included, Sharers would have to learn to fight back. Oh, they thought they knew how, with witnessing and Unspeech, but in the end, the only thing a death-hastener would respect was another death-hastener. Sharers would find that out, one way or another, preferably before it was too late.

For now, Nisi figured, she would bide her time to gain the trust of the Gatherings. With luck, Realgar might still hold off a bit. . . . *Ral*. The pain of his betrayal consumed her again, and she nearly fainted from despair. Never mind that, now. Sharers would kill well enough, she thought, once they set their minds to it. Usha already commanded a virulent arsenal, although she herself would hardly call it that; not enough to wipe out an army, Nisi guessed, but enough to give those soldiers a run for their stones.

* * *

The Gathering decided to swamp the Valan headquarters with as large a witness as could be mustered. Clickflies were released by the thousand, saying: This soldier-place at Per-elion is where death was hastened; send your witnessers here.

Lystra rowed out to the soldier-place with Mithril, who chatted nervously about their new raft and about how her mothersharer hoped to start a child. Lystra, too, was tense, but she only uttered occasional gruff remarks.

The solider-place stuck out of the sea, a bloated squid of a building upon an artificial "raft" of whatever dead stuff Valans used. At least the traders, thought Lystra, had kept a decent raft. Around the perimeter of the soldier-place stretched a fence of shiny black mesh, like a clickfly web frozen to coldstone. Valan soldiers stood behind it, some of them malefreaks, all with muddy blue plumage and insect-stiff limbs.

Already, several Sharer boats bobbed on the waves nearby. About twenty sisters were standing before the fence. Lystra saw no place to moor the boat, so she drove out while Mithril searched further. To her immense relief, she recognized Trurl and Yinevra as she joined the group, most of whom were from other rafts.

Behind the fence was a Valan malefreak with a red face and a puffed stomach who waved his arms and gesticulated. "Just the rules, lady. You want to see prisoners, go fill out a form."

"I did that," said Trurl, "but nothing happened."

"It takes at least a week to process the form."

"But our sisters are needed now," said Trurl. "Their daughters are crying for them. One is an infant who needs her mother's milk."

"Lady, what do you want? A wetnurse?"

Another soldier stopped him, a "normal" sister, with more bright things glinting on her plumage. "What's this about? You got nothing better to do than stare at catfish?"

The malefreak grew redder yet and shifted nervously from one foot to the other.

Trurl said, "If it's too much trouble, we would be glad to come in and share searching of your home, as you have shared ours. All we wish is to find our lost sisters."

"Nonsense," said the "normal" one. "Secured area. Look, just go home quiet, okay? 'Share parting' or we'll 'share it' for you." She mixed in garbled Sharer words.

"We would be delighted to share parting," said Trurl. "So would our lost sisters, I think. Their daughters are crying for them, and one is an infant. . . ."

By now, nearly a hundred Sharers were crowding about the fence, nudging each other as politely as possible. The smell of sweat came in waves. Boats were still coming; Lystra had never heard of a witness this size in Per-elion. More soldiers were coming out, too. She wondered how long before they would drag everyone out to sea. The thought itself brought a taste of nausea.

Someone bumped her in the elbow and apologized. "I'm Shian the Restless, of Cara-elion. Are you local?"

"Yes. From another system you come—that's a fair boatride."

Shian wrinkled her nose. "We'll come from farther still, I'm sure. This new breed of Valan—they're the worst yet. Do you—" A large boat unloaded, and everyone jostled to make room. "Do you think they're really human? The Impatient One came to Cara-elion to share that with us, but now I'm not so sure. They look more like crabs to me. Overgrown crabs."

"They *are* human," Lystra snapped and looked away. The crowd would soon surround the entire garrison, she saw, yet nearly all the soldiers had vanished. Were they creeping fearfully into their shell?

Her ears sharpened. Something funny was happening at the fence, something she could not see. There were gasps and moans; a shiver ran down her spine.

Lystra doubled up, coughing and wheezing. The air had gone foul, stifling, burning the lungs. Sisters were pulling away; the sea splashed as they plunged in. Lystra turned instinctively to the sea, but thought, What if she never got her breath? To her horror she glimpsed white bodies already floating still among the boats. Red and black spots filled her vision. She sank where she was, and there was nothing, nothing at all.

At Satellite Amber, Realgar observed a light-image of the spectacle at Planetary Headquarters. Bodies lay unconscious, all around the perimeter fence, and those in the water were white. It was not a pretty sight, but something had to be done. The natives would awake with a splitting headache, wiser for the experience. "Any casualties?"

"None," said Jade. "They were pulled in from the sea before any could drown."

"Excellent." Though Realgar felt just a touch of ... disappointment? A regrettable lapse of emotion. Now the question was, What to do with them all? There were ten times as many as Headquarters could hold. Sabas could ship them out to other bases, but some of those were getting "invasions," too. Besides, Jade could only work on a few at a time, and she had enough for now. Better to let these go and warn others against such foolishness. "How are the new prisoners?"

"I cracked one," said Jade. "Got her before she could bleach out—no problem."

"Excellent. Why didn't you tell me at once?"

"I did not wish to interrupt you with trivial matters." But Jade's eyes gleamed with satisfaction.

Realgar allowed himself a smile. "I should have known I could count on an old hand like you. Did you learn anything?"

"She's not a spy, so what can you learn? Her mental profile was normal overall: standard levels of aggression, ego drive, affection, and so forth. Only one feature stood out: an extreme, almost pathological depletion of fear."

"A lack of fear." Realgar was intrigued. "If they don't know what killing is—"

"But their lives are full of dangers, General. Seaswallowers, storms, splinter rafts—you name it, her memories are full of it. It's her approach—" Jade broke off, perplexed. Her lashes lowered. "Catfish look straight ahead and follow *it*, whatever 'it' is. So far, they consider us just a distraction, like an exceptionally bad season of swallowers."

"They did, that is. Perhaps today will change their minds." Realgar watched the light-image. More natives had arrived at Headquarters, but this time they were carrying away their fallen sisters. Soon the deck would be clear; Sabas had everything under control. Still, what an odd campaign this was. Usually, Headquarters lay well behind the front lines, but here there was no "front line." Or rather, the front line was everywhere. Or had the real front line yet to appear?

Jade's mention of swallowers reminded him that the return season would be on in a few months. The Lunar Development Consortium was having trouble coming up with a good toxin for those beasts. Something would have to be done; Realgar would not tolerate such a strain on his operations.

"How are the lab warren 'inspections' working out these day?" Realgar asked.

"The usual. A few more rafts are deserted; it seems to be a growing trend."

Already one in ten were "deserted" by the inhabitants. Surface searches produced nothing. Sabas was starting with submarines, but it was a dicey business. Nobody liked to mess with the undersides of those rafts.

A pathological lack of fear. Yet fear was only an instinct for survival, after all. Without knowing fear, those natives should all have died out years ago.

3

Hosts of Sisters from the far raft systems inundated Raia-el, more than even the Kiri-el refugees, who thankfully had their new raft started by now. Merwen was constantly gathering food for the guests and nursing those who succumbed to the mysterious breath-shortening air from the solider-place. Most returned to the soldier-place as soon as they recovered, but as more returned from second and third rounds of air-strangling, Merwen's steps and swimming strokes grew slower and heavier. Some of the guests huddled listlessly in seasilk blankets, talking anxiously of children they had left at home as far as a hundred raft-lengths away. "What if the soldiers come for our children next?"

"Send the Valans back," one sighed. "Yes, close the door. Our life-shaper says that breathmicrobes will drive them out."

Amid all the sisters bustling in and out, Siderite arrived as usual with his two guards, who no longer bothered to enter the silkhouse but stolidly flanked the door and played games with little flat spotted leaves. Siderite himself was not really a soldier, despite his plummage; he proved it by stripping to his shorts, when out of sight of the guards. Merwen liked Siderite, thinking that he was almost as sisterly as Spinel.

Now Siderite paused uncertainly, as he watched Merwen adjust a blanket around a witnesser who had not yet regained consciousness.

"Share the day," said Merwen, a little out of breath.

"Well, look, I . . ." Siderite's hand waved aimlessly, like a confused angelfish. "That is, if it's a bad day for you—a lot of guests you've got here," he finished.

"So what's one more?"

Siderite flashed a smile. "Thanks, I'd get an awful hassle for a blank report."

Merwen got up. "Come, we'll see what Usha's up to."

In the lifeshaping chamber, Usha was staring at a very complex three-dimensional clickfly web, the sort that only experts learn well. The pattern was full of short, dense stretches stuck together at geometric angles. The connections represented atoms of a living molecule.

"Share the day, Inconsiderate One," said Siderite.

Usha had not heard him, Merwen thought, knowing that preoccupied stare. "It still doesn't fit," Usha grumbled. "*Shora,* I'm as thickheaded as a seaslug. Why can't I get the structure to fit?"

Siderite cleared his throat and inspected the model.

Merwen tapped Usha's shoulder. "Dear one, he wants to know what it is."

"The air poison, what else? It's volatile, so all I get is traces to analyze. And I'm so close, too."

"Oh, I see," said Siderite. "Agent Two-Six, that's what you're looking for. If that line represents a methyl group, it belongs on the other side."

"Is that it?" Usha asked. "For certain?"

"Of course it is. We've got canisters full of it."

"Good. By tomorrow night I'll have an enzyme to chew up the poison."

Siderite's mouth hung open. "You mean you'll go through the whole genetic design—today?"

"I should hope so," said Usha indignantly. "It's a simple molecule."

"May I observe your work? I'll stay out of your way."

Usha looked him over. "You can stay if you share the work. My other apprentices are overworked enough."

Merwen went back to the raft surface to spread the good news. The witnessers were cheered enormously to hear that the air poison would be swept away. Merwen herself did not stay cheerful long. To relax, she swam out among the branches, where the last of the seed pods were hanging from bowed stalks. She wondered, Shora, what seeds have you sown for us now, and what unimagined horrors have yet to grow of them?

At Planetary Headquarters, a pattern developed: the natives would collect up to fifty or so behind the fence, until the gas was released again. Then other natives in their boats would come to retrieve them, and within another hour replacements would begin to arrive. They always collected gradually, as if testing and retesting the limit to the soldiers' patience. Some patrols shooed their boats away and sank a few, but more natives would always swim in without boats. During the night the "invasions" diminished, and the next day only two or three natives appeared.

On the third day, Realgar watched from inside the garrison as natives arrived again. They collected faster than usual, reaching a hundred before the guards opened the gas canisters.

A few of them sagged and coughed, but they soon recovered. They pressed closer to the fence, a growing wall of purple flesh. And helicopters reported hundreds more on the way.

What was wrong with the gas? Was the shipment defective?

A spasm of fear passed through him, so fleeting that Realgar could not define just what scared him. It left only a cold sense of facing an unknowable enemy thing, and the urgent need to beat it back.

"Fire into the crowd," suggested Jade.

That brought him short. It might come to that sometime, but so far—one had one's honor to consider, after all.

Seeing his look, Jade added irritably, "Well, fire over their heads, and maybe aim crooked. For Torr's sake—"

"Enough. Where's Sabas?"

"Sir?"

"Sabas, try convulsant gas; that should hold them."

"There's none in stock, sir. It's on back order, for riot control."

"Well, *expedite the order*, for Torr's sake. Iridis must have a warehouse full." That was the first time he let slip an open slur on Iridis. Sabas showed no response, but then he wouldn't. "All right. Get me that trader, what's his name."

Within minutes Realgar was in his office with the trader, Kyril.

By now, reports had the crowd outside at three hundred, half of them children.

In uniform now, Kyril was special consultant on native relations. Kyril put his fingers together and nodded slowly. "You realize, sir, you'll have to start shooting, sooner or later."

"Does that include naked three-year-olds? How would you explain that to the Palace?"

"Well, now. You have to understand, sir, when I first came out here twenty years ago, the catfish weren't considered human at all, just another part of the natural fauna. You can't even mate with them properly, and to my mind—" Kyril shifted his weight and sat forward. "Look, if you're going to call them people, you better understand just what kind of people they are. They never had to back down to anyone, not since before the rise of Torr, and they just plain don't know how. You'll have to blow up half the planet to teach them."

Realgar thought, he should have let Jade get on with it before the kids started showing up with their mothers.

"There is one trick, though, that might just work," Kyril reflected. "To buy some time. And to show you what kind of mentality you're dealing with."

From the front line of witnessers at the solder-place, Lystra stared numbly at the fence wires that rose and spread in open, undulating patterns. Close up, they looked nothing like a clickfly web, just a crude mindless branching of coldstone lines. Their sheen flickered as clouds crossed the sun.

Somewhere behind those wires were her own lost sisters, eight of them by now from two different rafts. Why should Valans desire to keep eight Sharers among them, yet drive out all others with excruciating pain?

Her eyes flitted briefly toward Yinevra at her left, pressed in among the sweating bodies. Yinevra could barely sit up by herself, for she had not yet recovered from repeated doses of the airpoison. Her face was so grim yet pinched by the strain of it that Lystra could only shudder and look away.

A line of soldiers came out and filed past the fence before her. Lystra tensed every muscle; but the soldiers only stopped and waited. One of them was Nisi's lovesharer, and apparently their most respected wordweaver, if respect was the appropriate term. But a different one stepped forward from the line, someone whom

Lystra vaguely recognized: the coarse mud-colored headfur, the wide jaw—

"Kyril." She struggled to adjust to the shape of him in his altered plumage.

Kyril smiled expansively. "Why, it's Lystra! Share the day, Lystra; I never expected to see you here."

It was something of a relief to see the familiar trader, despite his transformation. The bad old days seemed idyllic compared to nowadays.

"You're too busy to share this place, Lystra," Kyril said. "Those starworms keep you swimming night and day."

"And you, Kyril? Does trade no longer keep you busy?" An admittedly nasty remark.

Kyril shrugged genially, and his pointed shoulder plumage exaggerated the gesture. "We're closing out, as you know. Everything's marked down; you should go have a look. We'll be sweeping our own rafts for seasilk from now on, uninhabited ones, so we won't share annoyance with you anymore." He spoke as if sharing a great favor.

"But every raft has inhabitants."

Kyril paused. "Uninhabited by Sharers—"

"So you'll clear out all the other little sisterlings." Lystra watched him distastefully.

"You don't share trust at all, do you. You'll see; we know a lot more about raft management than we did forty years ago." Kyril crouched before her where she sat, so that their eyes were nearly level. "Listen, Lystra, what are you doing here, anyway?"

"Waiting for our lost sisters. It's been two weeks, for three of them. Have you seen them?"

"I know you're worried. But it won't help to keep torturing soldiers this way. Why do you think they share poison with you?"

"Torturing?" Lystra was uneasy. "If torture is shared, it is we who feel the pain. We come only to share speech." Everything worked both ways, but Lystra herself had done no harm.

"But we're surrounded, Lystra—hundreds of you, and there's barely a hundred of us in here. It's driving us crazy."

Yinevra said, "You were crazy to begin with."

"And you're making it worse. What if we die of it?"

"Oh, no." Mithril stood up. "Why should anyone die from— from us coming to find our sisters?"

"Your witness, your *being* here, unasked, in our home—it's

too much to take, psychologically. For some of us," Kyril added quickly.

"Then why do you keep invading *our* homes!" Yinevra rasped and coughed. "You're all dead, anyway: living, walking *dead!* Get out and close your door—" Yinevra heaved with coughing, and another sister came to hold her, to soothe her.

Others were shaking their heads. "It can't be," said one. "What about the breathmicrobes, the new strain our northern sister life-shaped? Does that share hurting, too?"

"Breathmicrobes?" Kyril raised his voice and shared a look with the other soldier, Nisi's lovesharer. "Lystra, you know how Valans feel about breathmicrobes. That alone will hasten death, I'm sure."

"A childish fear," Lystra curtly replied. She did not like the sound of this at all, but Kyril was no selfnamer, so there was no way to challenge him. The truth would have to be checked. Already the witnessers were returning to their boats. "No more deaths," one sighed. "Too much pain already."

Lystra got up; her legs stung, and she stretched them. She went to lend an arm to Yinevra, who would let no one but Lystra help her walk. As Yinevra got up she told Kyril, "You're responsible for yourself, Valan, even as our stonesick sisters are. Don't think you've seen our backs for good."

Realgar watched the natives begin to leave, some in boats, others just slipping beneath the waves. He could not figure it out. "They really believe that they're staring us to death?"

"Something like that," Kyril said. "I tell you, they don't understand killing, or even almost-killing. They desperately want some rationale for what you've done."

The mention of breathmicrobes sobered Realgar. "Do you really think the natives are behind those outbreaks of purple-skin?"

"Could be. There were rumors the last time, about the purple plague."

"But why did they tell us? As a threat?"

"I told you, sir, they're as honest as servos. But they are not fools," Kyril warned. "If you still want to avoid nastiness, release those prisoners before Lystra and her cohorts have time to think again. Out of pure generosity, of course."

"Perhaps." How thoroughly he had misread the drama, from start to finish. He never intended to hold the prisoners indefinitely.

Why had things blown out of proportion? And then, with all their insane bravery, why had the natives turned away with a bit of nonsense from Kyril?

What about the breathmicrobes? Could he consider that the first shot from their side?

To know your enemy was the oldest rule of warfare. Realgar would have to learn fast, before they cooked up something worse than purple plague.

4

Throughout the witnessing, Nisi had helped Usha tend those stricken by the air-poison. Back and forth she went through the fungus-swirled hallways, carrying water and blankets and medicines until she dropped from exhaustion. Most of the victims had recovered now, although a few remained with Usha....Nisi pulled her thoughts back from that. It was better to keep busy, to exhaust every moment, than to think—especially to think of Realgar, who had said, They are peaceful; I'll go easy on them. Realgar had betrayed her far worse than she betrayed him.

When Lystra came back and the witness was over, Nisi's temper broke. "What do you *mean,* you all left? Can't you see they're just desperate? Now is the time to push on. What's the matter with you?"

Lystra's eyes flashed as they used to so often. She grasped Nisi's arm until pain streaked through. "And what if it's the truth? What else could make them share poison? You tell us, Deceiver."

"They are death-hasteners. 'Death pays their wage.' They won't share respect with you, until you do likewise."

Lystra's stare bored into her. Then at last she dropped Nisi's arm, and her fingers left pale marks. "That will be at the end of time. And the end of Sharers."

Mithril said, "I don't believe it. Shora would never let such a thing—"

"What's true is true," rasped Yinevra. "What are *we*, if not Shora Herself? Who will act for us? Come, Lystra, you still have starworms to feed beneath the raft. I'll help you as best I can from the surface."

Mithril's little chin lifted as she watched Yinevra leave. "Death itself won't stop Yinevra. But I was there too, today, despite my young girl at home, and what's to become of her, poor thing? I tell you, Nisi, some things are better never to have known."

Too late for that, thought Nisi. It was too late for innocence. The Primes themselves had not lasted. Ten millennia you had for peace; how many peoples can say that? For your granddaughters, peace will be only a legend.

In the cool water, branch shadows wove fleeting patterns upon the hide of the young starworm. Lystra admired the sinuous trunk that stretched several swimming-lengths ahead of her, though barely a third as long as the maturer specimens of Raia-el. The mouth-stalks of the starworm spread in a perfect star around its lip, none broken and regrown as on older starworms. As Lystra swam to the lip, two swimmers darted from an airbell, carrying rakes to clean the mouth filters of the beast. Cousins of Mithril, the two were just learning the care of the starworm. They approached its mouth from the side, careful to avoid the ingoing stream, which was listless in any case from lack of feeding. And if Lystra and Yinevra had not returned early, the starworm might have gone hungry a few hours more.

The young starworm had lone streamers of filters within its mouth, because it was not yet large enough to digest squid or large fish, only plankton and fingerlings. As Mithril's cousins raked debris from the filters, Lystra swam up to the surface to get the net full of fingerlings that could be fed into that star-rimmed mouth, a handful at a time.

Yinevra awaited her in the boat. "I don't know, Lystra. This young one isn't growing fast enough. They all need more feeding at Leni-el, and more frequent raking."

"Well, I do the best I can—"

"Of course you do, and almost single-handed. It's just bad luck that the seaswallower got nearly all the Kiri-el starworm crew."

Lystra looked away. In the net that hung down from the boat, the fingerlings were packed tight but still were fresh pink and wriggled a bit. This would do the young starworm good, but there were a dozen more starworms to be fred on Leni-el. "You think this raft won't make it."

"Already Leni-el drifts too far behind the system. As it is, I take too much time away from Raia-el."

Was fighting the Valan madness worth losing another raft? Lystra did not ask.

"Lystra, what do you think of the Deceiver's notions?"

Lystra shrugged. She stretched her arm over the side and drew obscure signs in the ripples. "I still can't figure Nisi. She likes it here, and yet hates it here." Lystra hesitated. "She's still a Valan." Like Spinel—and Spinel had gone back to Valedon.

"What if she's right?" Yinevra asked. "If death is all that Valans understand, perhaps the soldiers wish us to help them die."

Lystra sat very still, her hand just trailing in the water. "What do you mean?"

"Think how tortured their minds must be. Death might be the kindest fate." She coughed suddenly several times, and her chest heaved. "Ah, I'll beat this poison yet. Listen: Suppose we set a trap, and warn them, and they still walk into it. Who's to judge, Lystra?"

The next morning on Raia-el, Merwen was washing blankets and sleeping mats in a branch channel, a large load for the many guests. A commotion of shouting started from the silkhouse. Merwen looked up to see a helicopter standing with Sharers crowding around it. She dropped her wash on the branch and hurried back to see.

Wellen broke away and skipped out to her. "They're back, Mother-sister—all our lost sisters!"

Others were talking excitedly, a few weeping quietly. Several tightlipped soldiers huddled at their helicopter, with six Sharers, pale and dazed, six of the eight who had been missing. The Sharers blinked confusedly, and one flickered white and lavender, uncertain whether or not to stay in trance.

Realgar stepped forward away from the others. Sunlight traced arcs on his helmet, and his boots ground into the weeds. "Greetings, Protector," he began. "As you see, we are prepared to release all captives currently held, as well as the remains of those two who died by their own hands."

So another had fallen. The pain was sharp but brief; Merwen knew she had to concentrate. Something was not finished.

Realgar continued, "Our condition is that you and your followers will cease all resistance and cooperate fully with the Guard from now on."

Merwen eyed him bleakly. "What can I share with you that I have not?"

"You must acknowledge the authority of Valedon."

Authority: responsibility for oneself and others. What authority could Merwen ascribe to these sad children? Even Siderite was no self-namer.

Then she caught sight of the returned sisters, still held fast by the other soldiers. They were not yet out of danger. She must not jeopardize their safety with a careless word.

She forced herself to face Realgar again, to look into the blank horror of a soul dead in life. "I respect your authority," Merwen said, "when you show it."

Realgar appeared to expect something more.

"When you behave as adults," she explained. She knew as she spoke that she skirted the edge, but some things have to be said.

"It is not your place to judge our behavior. You will obey us or pay the price: more pain, more deaths."

To obey meant to share will. How could she share this Valan's sickened will? "What do you want of me, specifically?"

"Keep your sisters away from the garrison."

"I will communicate your wish," said Merwen. "I assure you, no Sharer within this system desires to go near the garrison."

"Stop 'lifeshaping' your breathmicrobes to harass my troops."

"That is a bad thing," Merwen agreed. She had been disappointed to hear that other rafts had chosen such a response. "Again, I will share your wish with others."

"You must go further, Protector. You must make your sisters obey in all things."

Her toes squirmed uncomfortably and she avoided looking at them. "Am I Shora, to share infinite will? I can't even share the will of Weia and Wellen all the time, let alone that of all Sharers."

"But you can convince them."

Around her, sisters watched, hope and dread straining their faces. Uneasily Merwen considered her own gift of wordweaving; like all power, it contained its own peril. "I can share what I believe, nothing more."

The solider leaned back a step, his head tilted to one side. "Do you always speak the truth, under every circumstance?"

"If what I believe is true."

"What is it that Sharers fear more than anything else?"

This shift was a welcome change from his impossible demands. Realgar wanted to trust her, she saw, despite enormous pressure against it. "I think we fear ourselves, most of all."

Realgar seemed disappointed, but it was hard to tell; his head might have been carved of raftwood.

"That may change," Realgar said. "Your sisters will soon tell you what you can fear from us."

Abruptly the lost ones were free, and the soldiers were climbing into their helicopter. The big blades whooshed round overhead.

Greetings were shared again, more subdued than before. On the raft lay the two wrapped shapes of those who had ended their own existence. Their bodies would be sung for, then hung with coral death-weights and sunken to their final dwelling place. Their spirits had already flown through the Last Door, perhaps to return in daughters not yet conceived.

Someone must share this lesson... but that will be painful. Those had been the parting words of Malachite the Dead. How much Valan pain will we share, Merwen wondered, and how much of us will be left?

5

General Realgar reported the incident closed. But he was far from satisfied by his exchange with "Protector" Merwen; essentially, nothing had changed. Elsewhere around the globe, several bases still faced native "invasions" in various stages of resolution. Rumors of the purple-skin problem, and even "catfish transformation," of all things, had damaged troop morale. And in some regions every ship and helicopter was grounded by weeds stuck in the engines—oil-eating weeds.

That Iridian major general was incapable of any initiative, and it would only cause trouble at the Palace to try to replace him. So

Realgar set up permanently at Planetary Headquarters. His children back on Satellite Amber complained that he never saw them any more.

"We've cleaned out the clickflies," Jade told him at last.

"Well that's a relief. No more global uprisings over a couple of lost natives."

"Yes, sir."

Realgar leaned back from his desk and clasped his hands behind his head. "We have to get a handle on these natives. They must have a weakness."

"It's pathological," Jade said. "They just don't know what fear is."

"They have a word for it."

"They think they do, but it's on a different scale from ordinary fear." Wrinkles puckered between her eyes. "With the mindprobe, only one ill-defined concept brought a fear response anywhere near normal levels. Something hard yet empty, with a cold light."

Realgar had no patience for riddles. "Go get some more prisoners and find out what makes them tick."

"Yes, sir. By the way, have you kept up with Siderite's reports?"

The desk screen lit up with a page of fine print, of which one paragraph was highlighted. The general read it, then barked at his monitor, "Get Siderite in here, *now.*"

Siderite was dragged into the office, his lab apron askew, a pair of surgical gloves dangling from his pocket. "What the—" He swallowed. "You can't just hustle me out when I'm in the midst of—"

"Did you actually tell the catfish how to beat our riot-control gas?"

Siderite blinked and shifted his feet. "Usha would have figured it out, sooner or later. Scientific exchange."

"Treason. I could execute you on the spot."

"Execute me?" Siderite laughed unsteadily. "It's not even wartime."

Amazed, Realgar stared at him. "Just what do you think this is? An Indian parade exercise? Doctor, you're in big trouble."

Siderite swallowed again and blinked several times. "I thought that—I thought you would be pleased. Sir." His voice wavered. "In one day, I learned more about 'lifeshaping' than I expected to in a year."

"Indeed. Well, you'd better sit down and tell me about it."

A chair rose from the floor, and Siderite sank into it. "I didn't tell Usha how to neutralize the gas. I just gave her a tip on its molecular structure. Then she modeled an antagonist, a sort of synthetic antibody, based on calculation by those remarkable insects. And finally we—that is, the lifeshapers—cloned an enzyme secretor to produce it. I followed the whole procedure. Now I can tell you just which of the shrubbery in those tunnels is significant and what's going on."

"Then you could train an inspection team to actually inspect, for a change: to hunt out those enzyme secretors and..." And destroy, if necessary.

"In theory, yes. Still speculative. Of course, there are hosts of other sorts of lifeshaping that I've barely got a glimpse of yet. For instance—"

"Very well. I'll suspend your execution. But from now on, doctor, you will take six guards with you, two of whom will not let you out of sight."

"But General!" Siderite half rose, and a glove slipped from his pocket, a display of untidiness that intensely irritated Realgar.

"Would you prefer a selective mindblock?"

He looked at Jade, and his face blanched. He stood up, leaning his arms on the chair. "I've had enough. I can't work under such conditions. I'll return to the Palace today."

"Sit down, doctor, sit down." Realgar's tone became smoothly persuasive, full of the intensity of his will. "You remain under my authority, and I do not choose to release you. Besides, you don't want to leave—because this planet is the chance of a lifetime."

Slowly Siderite sat down. His look was frankly hostile, but he said nothing more.

Realgar signaled to the guard. "Good luck with your experiments, doctor." The guard led him away.

Jade said, "Let me have him. I'll fix him for good."

The general shook his head slightly. "If he cracks, the whole operation is doomed."

"He won't crack; he won't even know it happened. In any case, there must be other plant breeders on Valedon." She stepped closer. "Mark my words: if I don't have him, *they* will."

That touched a nerve, because of Berenice. But before he could answer, the monitor interrupted. "Trans-space relay from Palace

Iridium, office of the High Protector. An audience is called today at nineteen hundred. . . ."

The general stood at attention while the lightshape of the High Protector materialized. Talion sat up straight behind his immense desk, his gray face relaxed except for tiny alert ripples around his eyes. "It's been quite some time, Ral. How's life on the blue moon? You expect to wrap it up soon, get back down to staff reorganization?"

Acutely embarrassed, Realgar regretted his initial promise, that he would leave Operation Amethyst to Sabas and get himself back to the Palace within a week. It had been four weeks since then. He saw that he faced an uphill fight with Talion.

Realgar cleared his throat. "The first stage is indeed over, my lord."

"Oh? What comes next?"

"My lord, I expected to find here a planet well charted and managed by traders, with native citizens who were peaceful and reasonably cooperative. Instead it's a world of unknown diseases, unpredictable weather, weeds that strangle my equipment, and natives who are insane enough to throw their bodies in front of my troops. It's not a pretty sight, and I'd keep the Palace Press away, if I were you. I need troops and equipment to do this job right."

"An Iridian division and a satellite fleet are not enough?"

"A riot-control unit is what I need. Also prison facilities, to hold a hundred per base. Also—"

"Hold on, there. You've barely a hundred men at each base."

"I need three more divisions, to put a base in every raft system. Only then can we hope to control the natives on a daily basis A one-to-ten ratio: that's standard, for occupation strength."

"But they're just naked women, Ral, not Azurite guerrillas."

"They were crawling at our fence before we gassed them—and they came back for more. They're incredibly dispersed, all around the planet, but if we take one prisoner the whole population is up in arms. And two prisoners killed themselves. Natives willing to die for their own turf are a damned nuisance, whether armed or not."

Talion studied his hands. The pause went beyond interplanetary time-lag. "Troops cost ten times as much to maintain on the Ocean Moon. The expenditure you propose would approach that of the

Pyrrholite campaign. And you say I can't even tell the public what's going on?"

Realgar contained his fury. Expense, public relations—that was none of his concern. It had hardly been his choice to take on this distasteful police job. "How badly do you want to control this planet? Is the 'purple menace' real or not? Siderite will take years to determine anything."

"Oh, not that long." Casually Talion leaned back and stretched his legs. "Months, perhaps." Behind his offhand manner, Talion was watching the general closely. "In fact, Siderite thinks I may have been...premature to send you at all. He finds the natives perfectly cooperative, as far as science is concerned."

The nerve of that lab-aproned trollhead. How had such notions slipped through security? Of course, Talion would have his own spies. And if Siderite had the High Protector's confidence, there was no way to touch him. For a moment Realgar was tempted to throw in the towel, leave this Torr-forsaken planet behind him, forget the whole mess, and get and get back to real soldiering somewhere.

But the moment passed.

Realgar permitted himself a disparaging smile. "Siderite takes six armed guards with him on every visit."

"I see. And that keeps his situation in hand."

"For now."

Talion swiveled in his chair. "Well. Short of outright war, I cannot accept your proposal. As you are aware, several Councilors have already called for me to wipe out the natives completely. They know of course that I can't do that. But the point is, Ral, a war effort does at least raise public support, whereas a covert operation is nothing but a troll on my back."

At last, thought Realgar, they might be getting somewhere. "My lord, a swift exercise of force would be less costly than a drawn-out occupation, and perhaps more humane in the long run."

"One decisive battle?"

"It would certainly speed things up if I could call those natives soldiers."

"To declare war, I need provocation," Talion said. "Usually that's no problem—there's always a terrorist incident, a bomb in a post office or whatever. Do you propose to plant something? Malachite is no fool."

Realgar doubted that Malachite would care, as long as his campaign succeeded. "There is the mental deathblock that all Sharers appear to have. This is a blatant and serious infringement of Patriarchal Law."

"True. Nobody but trained assassins and subversives need death-blocks. What bizarre people those natives are." Talion shook his head. "If they are people. I'm still not convinced. But Malachite is. So you see, Ral, I have to be wary of mass executions of unarmed women—they can't even conceal a weapon, for Torr's sake. It was different in Azuroth, where the guerrilla mamas cooked up explosives in their cottages. I have enemies, you know, ambitious lords who will seize any pretext to accuse me before the Patriarch."

Now Realgar had to commit himself. "Sharers are in fact like Azurite women. They do conceal weapons, biological ones such as the breathmicrobes. They're only biding their time, to gather strength for reprisal."

"Are you sure of that?"

"Consider it yourself, my lord. A defenseless people could never show the fearlessness that Sharers do. They must have something in reserve, and I want my force to be ready to face it when it comes."

For a long while Talion's light-image peered at a point beyond Realgar's shoulder. The image flickered slightly from static in transmission. Realgar gazed back so intently that his eyes began to ache.

Very slight, Talion shrugged. "Suppose I declare war and send two more divisions."

"Well enough, my lord." Two divisions—right away! This was just what he needed. "The Sardish First and Second?"

"The Dolomite Fifth and Sixth. They're itching for another campaign."

"Dolomites, my lord?" Realgar picked his words with care. "They are excellent fighting men, although some do not believe in spaceships."

"They learn soon enough, and they do as they're told. Besides, they mobilize fast."

Never mind; at least the Protector saw the truth now and was willing to back him up. Whatever tricks those catfish came up with next, they would get a good thrashing.

6

An act more unthinkable than death-hastening, so inconceivable that the sea had never named it, was the invasion of a mind. Never named on Shora, by Shora—until now.

At the Gathering on Raia-el, Lystra listened with her sisters as the returned ones shared word of their ordeal. Lystra strained to hear against the buzzing of helicopters, metal arthropods that always hovered near. The will of this Gathering would carry great weight, since so many had come from far rafts to witness at the central solider-place. Even their fingertips were still, and most of their faces showed stark disbelief at what they heard.

Who would believe that any creature could willfully force the door of a mind? That was to violate the very soul of a human, never mind one's physical shell. It was to deny Shora Herself, for every soul is a part of Shora.

"There must be a mistake," someone said. "Clearly you've shared ill treatment—force-fed, trapped in a cage without relief in the sea, bruised and—well, it's all shameful enough. But your mind is your own, sister. Even a lifeshaper can only bring mind-streams parallel—never intercept."

Lystra knew the saying: A mind swims alone, as Shora came alone through the First Door.

But the released one, Lerion Nonthinker, stood quickly and waved her arms for attention. "Why do you think Raessa died after she warned us? She had to, her mind was broken. She told us so: foreign thoughts were put in her had, insane notions about Valans being stronger than Shora Herself. Raessa could have fled the Last Door then, but she waited to tell us. Then she went forever white."

Lystra's fingertips whitened just at the thought. Numbly she stared at the dried weeds before her toes. For some minutes, the entire Gathering was silent in respect for Raessa, who had lived in mind-death just long enough that others might know. Her name would live in ballads for generations to come, if anyone could bring herself to sing this tale of dread.

Something plopped in the dust beyond Lystra's knee. It was a dead clickfly, its legs twisted up, a shriveled husk. Lystra winced and pulled her legs back.

Clickflies were dying all over the rafts, and piles of them mounted around the silkhouses. An unknown infestation was coming closer to wiping them out. Usha sought tirelessly for the source, and surely other lifeshapers around the globe were doing likewise. But in the meantime, a fog of silence blanketed the rafts, isolating the Per-elion cluster. If every clickfly disappeared, learnsharing would be frozen, memory lost, and even time could not be measured. There were other memory banks, of course, memories that could not be lost so long as the last raft remained on Shora. But without clickflies to unlock those memories, life would become impossible.

Yinevra Nonforgiver stood at last, at a hand-wave from Trurl, who balanced would-be speakers with miraculous dexterity despite the size of the Gathering. Yinevra said, "It is time for us to stop sharing ignorance. Anyone with eyes and ears can tell what's going on at the solider-place. Anyone who twice shared poison can tell!"

Murmurs of sympathy rippled through the crowed. Many witnessers suffered lingering effects, and most had grown very angry. Yet confusion was the main thing; there was just no precedent for this problem.

Yinevra went on. "We know that death hastens those who hasten death. And Nisi the Deceiver, born a Valan, says that this is the only stricture that soliders accept. So why not let it happen? Let's share parting with soldiers and go to dwell among the shockwraiths of the underraft. We can manage that, since shockwraiths are far easier to understand than soliders. But when the soldiers come, they will find us both. Then let Shora be the judge of what happens next.

Yes, thought Lystra, let those upstart creatures share their own evil. But she was too much her mother's daughter not to feel a twinge of remorse. You are as responsible for what you let happen as for the actions you share. If Lystra had left Spinel to the fleshborers when he first came, what would that have meant for her?

A much older sister arose, from one of the farther raft systems.

"Nonforgiver, I won't deny that hard measures are called for. But let's not dive into a different sort of ignorance. If Shora Herself will judge the Valans, then why should Sharers act at all?"

"Because *we are* Shora. If we don't act, who else will?"

"Then it is we who share judgment, and the fate of these soldiers. A death hastened is still a death, whether or not you keep your eyes closed."

The words cracked like a shell upon coral. A troubled silence clung. It was hopeless, Lystra thought. She could cast forever for an answer, but the ocean was empty.

Shaalrim observed. "We have to do something. Suppose at first we simply Unspeak the soldiers? When Lalor and I were on Valedon, the Valans didn't begin to hear us until we went Unspoken."

"Well that's the least we can do," Yinevra said sharply. "In fact, I'll Unspeak the Gathering myself if we choose to do less."

"Enough of that," called Trurl. "It's time for us all to stick together, Shora knows."

As it happened, Yinevra's remark brought an enthusiastic response. Unspeech was safe and familiar, a tactic that anyone could understand, although its application to thousands of Valans was a dizzying thought.

Then Merwen arose, and Lystra knew what was coming. "If action is needed," Merwen said, "why Unspeech? Isn't Unspeech just another form of *in*action? If we put an end to sharing, we tie our own hands."

"Unspeech does not end all sharing," Trurl corrected. "We would not let a soldier starve, if it came to that. We can still share our presence, in silent witness."

Someone added to that, "We have to stop speaking. How else can we show them what children they are? You can't talk seriously with infants."

Yinevra said, "We tried wordweaving—I tried as hard as you did, and it got nowhere. Our sisters weren't freed until we witnessed, words or not. Why didn't you witness with us, Impatient One?"

That was unfair, Lystra thought, for once resenting Yinevra. Someone had to stay behind, after all, to share care of the injured. But Merwen said nothing more. Instead, Usha rose, after trying for some time to be heard. "Must we unspeak every Valan who comes in soldier's plumage? One of them has become an apprentice with me. I need good apprentices."

Merwen and Usha seemed to have taken to Siderite. Perhaps they thought they might make a selfnamer of him, like Nisi.

But Nisi herself was skeptical. Nisi said, "The Valans who come to learn lifeshaping do so for subversive purposes. Whatever Siderite learnshares will be used against you in the end. That is why he brings soldiers with every visit."

"A good point, Deceiver." Trurl lifted her chin toward Merwen. "Well, Impatient One?"

"It won't work," said Merwen slowly. "Nothing will work until we learnshare what it is that makes Valans hasten death."

"How?"

She said nothing. Another dead clickfly plopped down, and an age seemed to pass.

Trurl quietly asked, "Will you block our will, then?"

"No."

Merwen's acquiescence startled Lystra. No matter how hard Lystra fought her mother at times, it still hurt to see Merwen back down. Worse than that, it nagged her to think that Merwen might yet be right.

At Raia-el, the Sharers held one great night of learnsharing together, though it was hard with so few clickflies to weave the webs. Then the visitors dispersed to sail off on their long voyages homeward, before clickflies vanished altogether and navigation became a nightmare. This loss of clickflies was an even greater immediate threat than the soliders. Rumors linked the two, but no one knew for sure.

Merwen still wondered about the existence of in-between humans. On Valedon she had seen thick-furred creatures with long tails, creatures half human and half animal. Did they have minds and souls, in-between souls? What kind of souls did Valans have? Only one thing she was sure of: there was no such thing as an in-between hastened death.

The day after the Gathering, Merwen got up early to swim below the branches, watching fish dart in concerted schools and jellyfish drift through the waves and beakfish munching stolidly on coral. It was good to remember the nearness of Shora, to feel herself a part of this one sea of life. Valans and their sickness were merely a bad storm on the surface, so far.

But Merwen emerged well in time to meet Siderite's helicopter as it whined lazily above the water's edge. As usual, Wellen and

Weia dropped whatever they were doing, whether playing games
with sticks or sorting seaweeds for lunch, to crane their necks at
the spindly monster as it descended and shuddered to a halt on the
raft. This time, Merwen caught them both in her arms, urging
them into the silkhouse. "No speaking," she whispered.

"But why, Mama?" Wellen's face wrinkled up with disappointment. "It's just a giant clickfly. What's happened to all the regular
clickflies? Did the giant ones eat them, like Flossa says?"

Somehow Merwen managed to shoo the girls inside. Then she
called Usha up from the tunnels. "Your Valan apprentice is here."
Merwen spread her fingers, a gesture that said, we can make an
exception; I will share it, if you will.

But Usha's hands were closed at her sides. "We both know
what must be done."

The Sharers stepped out through the door and seated themselves
on the raft, just as Siderite came toward them, followed by his six
guards, all potential death-hasteners.

Merwen gripped Usha's hand. She let her eyes defocus until
she stared out to sea, watching the white crests roll and dissolve.
Her soul could dissolve in that sea.

The guards had stopped. Siderite came closer and spoke down
at Merwen. "Share the day," he said. "I've come to..." He
stopped, uncertain. He could tell something was wrong.

Deliberately Merwen continued to look past him. "Usha, we do
not share speech with Valans anymore. We speak only with selfnamers and their children."

"What's the problem?" Siderite squatted, trying to look her in
the eye. "Did the troops rough you up again? Look, I'll do what I
can. I'll even take it up with the general."

Merwen looked past him, almost through him. The waves sparkled in the sun, and she could imagine dots of raft seedlings
swooning into the troughs. She swallowed and spoke again.
"Valans have a choice, Usha: either go home to their Stone Moon
or stay and choose self-names. All else is wasted breath."

Siderite said nothing more. Usha also said nothing; in a tight
spot, her tongue tended to stick.

Merwen's sight blurred, and she shifted her gaze. She hated
Unspeech, it twisted her heart to deny a human call.

The death-hasteners muttered in low voices, until Siderite
spoke up. "No, leave them alone. Let's be off, for Torr's sake."

The blurred Valan shapes receded. Merwen blinked in the sun, then looked to Siderite's back, now covered by soldier's plumage, though his head at least was bare and his hair stirred in the breeze. A sudden thought took her: If Siderite were to turn now, Merwen would smile at him, no matter what any sister thought of it. She squeezed Usha's hand again.

But Siderite was lost among the death-hasteners as they climbed back into their monster, the "giant clickfly" that might have eaten all the little ones.

7

Clickflies were vanquished, and now Jade and Kyril had come up with a new angle. "We figured out what catfish are scared of," Jade told the general. "Metal, rock, gemstone—in short, anything wholly inorganic."

"Stone," Realgar noted. It was hard, empty of life, with a cold light. "But why?"

"It fascinates them, that's why." Kyril beamed, very pleased with himself. "Scares the hell out of some; others can't get enough of it."

"The same ones, you mean," Jade added.

"It's too simple," Realgar objected. "What's the sense of it?"

"Does it make sense for your troops to be scared of purple-skin?" asked Kyril. "Sharers never saw the like of steel or diamond before we got here—not for a hundred centuries."

"So it's foreign. The act of killing is foreign to them, too, but they don't seem to fear that."

Jade shook her head. "Catfish live with death all the time; it's a frontier world, after all. But the very concept of 'metal' has no place in their heads."

He recalled the trade boycott, sparked not by overpricing, in fact, but by the stone trade. It should have occurred to him from the start that stone was a handle, a chink in their armor.

"You can't buy them any other way," Jade said. "Not liquor,

drugs, or women. But stone will get us informants and break the backbone of those Gatherings."

It was shortly afterward that Siderite asked to see the general, a rare event in itself. In uniform now, as Realgar had insisted, Siderite stormed into the office. "I want to know just what those troll-headed goons of yours are up to now. Usha won't even look at me—"

"If you have charges to make, state them," said Realgar. "With evidence."

"Poisoning unarmed women—isn't that enough? You didn't tell *that* to the Palace Press." Siderite's hands clenched and unclenched. The gassing of the native "invaders" must have bruised his sensibilities, but that was well over with.

"The natives use different weapons, that's all," Realgar told him. "Microbes instead of gas. Don't be fooled, Siderite; this is war."

"By the Nine Legions! Must I conduct research on the front line?"

"You've been doing that from the first." Realgar was exasperated. "Those lab warrens *are* the front line. We either get a hold on native lifeshaping or we pull out and let Malachite slap us again next time."

Siderite paused. "Then all your troops are irrelevant."

"In that sense, yes," Realgar admitted after a moment's hesitation.

"Then why not pull out? Pull out, and let me do my job in peace."

Realgar lowered his voice to a hard whisper. "Siderite, you're a damn fool. You don't say a word for us in your reports, yet who do you think assures your access to these lab warrens? The day we arrived for first inspection, Usha was 'too busy' to see you—until Merwen saw we were 'sick'; that is, we showed force. Force is all those natives understand."

Siderite's lips pushed upward. "Maybe so, but they've been incredibly helpful up to now, when all of a sudden they won't give me the time of day. Let me try without the guards, at least."

"No." Siderite was still a security risk, having leaked the identity of the riot control gas. If scientific exchange was to take place, Realgar expected it to run one way only. He called to his monitor,

"Bring in two natives for questioning, Merwen Impatient and Usha Inconsiderate."

Siderite rushed to the desk. "Don't do that. Look, I'll convince them, somehow—"

"You've made your complaint, and it's being handled. If necessary, I'll send you to some other friendly raft. That will be all, Siderite."

The man left in a daze.

When the two natives came, propelled by the guards, they sat on the floor as before. "Greetings, Protector," Realgar began. "Now, Protector, there must be some misunderstanding. What has Siderite done to offend your 'lifeshaper'? Does he cause accidents in your 'lifeshaping place'? You can tell me, I'll set it right."

Nothing. The pair stared like zombies at a point somewhere beyond his shoulder.

"We had a deal, Protector." Softly he tapped the desktop with his finger. "No problems—no prisoners. What's the problem?"

Only their fingers fluttered. Behind the pair stood the blank-faced guards.

"Would you prefer to tell Colonel Jade?"

Merwen's throat dipped as she swallowed. "The Per-elion Gathering has Unspoken all Valan soldiers," she told the spot beyond his shoulder. "As the word spreads, it is likely that many Gatherings will share his will. There is nothing more to be said."

His hand froze. Rage kindled, then quickly subsided into a cold purpose. "You have no more clickflies, Protector. You will travel no more, any of you. And you will hold no more Gatherings."

8

A school of flying fish spurted across the sea and made a playful froth in the distance. From her seat in the rowboat, Merwen stretched her neck and watched their beauty, their dance that was a song in praise of life.

At the prow, Flossa leaned outward, her youthfully smooth elbows perched on the edge, sunshine gleaming from the curve of her back. "Those fish will make a good dinner, Mama; I can taste them already."

Merwen turned back and pulled easily at the oars, in whose wake tiny whirlpools swirled away. The boat shuddered as a raft seedling bumped the prow, a tangle of branches wide as the length of the boat. Only a few seedlings were so large, now, but there would be many more before the swallowers came.

Above the horizon, a helicopter appeared, buzzing insistently. Merwen dreaded the sight of those insects now, for they could disgorge Valan soliders who might snatch her away to face their wordweaver Realgar again, although now they were all Unspoken. Realgar did not understand Unspeech; it only seemed to give him a temper tantrum. Malachite the Dead One had told Merwen that these Valans would share a lesson with her, but so far this one had learned nothing.

The helicopter swooped lower, close enough to alarm her. She watched its wheeled legs as it sailed overhead.

A loud voice blared out of it. "Turn Back to Raft," came the words, Sharer words in a rough accent. "Keep Within Ten Person-lengths of Rafts. All Who Stray Outside Will Face 'Arrest.' Keep Within Ten Person-lengths of Raft. . . ." The one word in Valan made no sense, but Merwen was sure it meant no good.

The helicopter dipped so close that a human face appeared at the front glass. Then steam hissed all around from the sea, and spray drenched the boat.

"Mama?" Flossa's eyes were round, her mouth pinched.

Merwen caught the girl in her arms and covered Flossa's muffled voice. "They're Unspoken."

Merwen breathed deeply. "I can't let you go. You're too young." How could she let this child slip into darkness? How far would the madness take them?"

Out of the helicopter, two soldiers dropped into the boat and pulled Merwen apart from her daughter; Flossa, brave as she was, did not even gasp. Both were swallowed up into the foul gut of the machine, which smelled of oil and stale clothing. An endless nightmare passed, although it could not have been more than minutes, before they were released again, upon the raft.

At the silkhouse Merwen found a group of former witnessers, spread out in exhaustion. But these were the sisters who had just set off for their home many raft-lengths away; a perilous journey without clickflies, only dead reckoning. How could they be back?

"Valans reached us," said one dully. "For a whole day we sped off behind our glider squid—yet the death-hasteners flew us back here in minutes. Think of it, Impatient One."

Merwen nodded. "It is true, in outer space these Valans can outpace the wind. Yet in inner space they cannot cross a web's-breadth."

"But Merwen—we can't just go on like this."

Overhead a helicopter buzzed again and blared, "No Gatherings More Than Five People; Repeat, No Gatherings . . ."

"We will gather tonight, after sharing time," said Merwen.

Lystra caused quite a stir when she made it to Raia-el for Gathering that night. First the Valan creatures had flung her from her boat at Leni-el, then they plucked her from the water where she swam. At last she managed to swim over, hidden beneath a raft seedling.

The news cheered some as they collected in the raft hollow, beneath a night sky still fringed with pink. But Trurl's face was somber, her eyes nearly closed. "It's a black day indeed when dead insects prey on people. When will our live insects return?"

"I'm trying," muttered Usha. "I saved a few clickflies, but they still won't reproduce, and I don't yet have a full structure for the poison molecules. Why did we insist on Unspeaking Siderite? He would have told me."

Lystra said, "Not with six death-hasteners around him."

"Well, what do you expect of me?" Usha was at her wits' end. "I've made a new strain of breathmicrobe; shall we try that? This one will turn them all purple for good. As they should be."

Trurl squeezed her eyes shut as if pained. "*Shora,* no. That would only drive them crazier than ever. Do you know, sister, now they are recruiting the sick ones among us? Sharing stone with the stonesick, and where that may lead . . ."

No one cared to guess where that might lead.

With difficulty Lystra kept her voice level. "Under so much pressure, there are more who will follow Rilwen."

Yinevra had arrived with Kithril, and both sat still as death, though Kithril had tears running down to her waist.

"Whatever we do," said Lystra, "we can't Unspeak our own sisters along with the Valans, not at a time like this."

Merwen said, "I will share care of the stonesick ones. Let anyone who is drawn to stone come to our silkhouse instead. We will share healing, somehow."

Lystra looked away, quite unable to say more.

"We are gathered, Sharers," called Trurl at last. "Let the Gathering grow from our silence."

But as silence fell, the sound of helicopters grew, dozens of them, with a roar that would have drowned out any voices. Then the beasts swooped down, disgorging Valan creatures who stumbled and shouted and started pulling sisters away with them.

Lystra cried out to them, but the Valans had gone deaf. There was nothing but confusion, meaningless noises, here and there a face etched in a flash of horrible light. And all the while it seemed that the helicopters kept coming, and more and more sisters were gone.

The agony wore on, until only a handful of sisters were left. Merwen and Usha—where were they? That was all she could think of.

A numb, stifling rage settled within her. But she gathered close with the few who somehow remained, like the last of a school of fish after fleshborers gorged their fill. She watched the indigo sky, and the stars coming out tranquil as ever, as if this were any ordinary evening. Only humans knew what an evil time this was.

There was a lull in the carnage; the roars died away. Had all the helicopters indeed gorged their fill?

From behind, something grabbed Lystra, twisted her around, and bruised her breast. Blindly her arms swung out and connected the Valan's shoulder; the act made her shudder, but not for long. The Valan reeled backward, then pulled her over in a somersault. She found herself on her back, facing the stars. She tried to get up, but something hit her head, stunning her.

Then the Valan bent over her and tried to do something with his body, the last thing Lystra would have expected at such a time, the thing she had warned Spinel against before. Pain split her insides; she retched and vomited all over her own arm. The pain still throbbed, but somehow Lystra forced herself up on an elbow. Her vision cleared a bit.

The Valan was doubled up on the raft, yelping like a fanwing caught by its tailfeathers. Other death-hasteners surrounded him, waving their metal sticks. "Poor trollhead," said a female voice. "You don't listen to briefings, do you."

It was beyond Lystra's comprehension that someone could mean to use an act of loving to share hurt instead. She gagged again until her stomach squeezed up to her throat and there was nothing left to come out. Then the other mad Valans grabbed for her arms and legs, but they had to stun her to take her away.

9

Merwen spent the night pressed with a dozen others in a cell that stank of urine and had not even enough room to lie down. She stayed in whitetrance, dreading to be caught unawares by a mind invasion before she could stop her own heart. That night, squeezed between a sister's back and the cold sticky concrete that surrounded them on all sides, Merwen felt for the first time what "war" was. Afterward, Merwen would never be quite the same person who had greeted the Valan soldiers when they first came to Raia-el.

In the morning, bruised and aching in every limb, Merwen and the others were dragged out into the light and left to the sea. It took her last strength to swim within sight of Raia-el, where a child out fishing picked her up.

At home, Usha was back from her own ordeal in the soldier-place. Weia clung to Usha, her little eyelids fluttering stark and wide, and would not leave for a whole day. Even Wellen stayed within the silkhouse, subdued and quiet as she helped repair the panels torn by the soldiers. Merwen remembered how that imp had sneaked down to the lifeshaping place to question the Valan death-hasteners. Now Wellen had a taste of the answer.

Usha went back to her clickflies, the precious few that she had kept alive. She was injecting a virus, which would carry certain genes into the cells of the clickfly, to enable it to live and reproduce in the presence of Valan poisons. Sharers maintained libraries of genes for many species, from edible fish and weeds to seaswallowers and shockwraiths. Shora had said that Sharers must share care for all the lesser sharers as for themselves. The ultimate library was kept within raftwood: every living cell of every raft held a library within its genes, millions of units within a cell too small to see.

Like Weia, Merwen stayed with Usha most of the day. As Usha worked, Merwen caressed Usha's arm and leaned her chin in Usha's neck, although she tried not to interfere too much. Her heart pounded with a question she had not dared ask. "Usha, did you see anything of Lystra?"

Usha's face was blank with concentration. Then abruptly it twisted. "No. But I saw many others with burns who belonged here with the lifeshapers."

Merwen looked down at Weia. "The children will grow old before they grow up."

"I grew old that day on Valedon, when that hulk of a malefreak raved at us."

"I grew old years before that."

"Perhaps you were born old."

"I was not," said Merwen a little too sharply.

Usha looked at her, then nodded. "There was Virien, before I knew you. Virien was only one; and now. . ."

Virien, with a twist in her head that nothing could cure. Virien would have let Merwen die, if Yinevra had not come and beaten the death-hastener in such a way that she could not swim again. Yet Yinevra was the one Merwen had never forgiven, because she was sane, and—

Merwen shook her head and squeezed memory's door.

"Only one, then," Usha repeated. "And what good did word-weaving do?"

"Valans are not all like Virien," Merwen said with conviction. "Their sickness is different. For soliders, Death has a 'wage.'" A wage that did not stop with stone and coins, as it did for traders.

Lystra did not return to Raia-el, nor to her new home at Leni-el. Excruciating days passed with more attempted Gatherings and more sisters flown back and forth from the soldier-place, with the burned ones crowding the lifeshaping place, but a few did not return at all.

By the fifth day, things relaxed a bit. Fewer sisters tried to make a Gathering at Raia-el, but the couple of dozen who did collect within the cup of the raft's ridge were not molested by helicopters.

Merwen sat outside the silkhouse, replacing a split beam in her silk loom, when the sound of a motorboat reached her. The boat was weaving in through the branch channels, not very efficiently. When it reached solid raft at last, a lone Valan stepped out. It was Siderite, in his former non-solider plumage, without any guards.

Out of the corner of her eye, Merwen watched Siderite approach her. Blood rushed to her ears and she felt hot all over. Where is Lystra, her heart cried to ask; but to ask would be a failure. Lystra would not want her to ask, to break Unspeech, and she would be right.

Siderite's shadow fell across the loom, darkening the warp strands. He spoke in Sharer. "Merwen, I came without guards. Even the 'general' does not share that I am here. Do you understand?" The voice paused. "I'm sorry for all this. Believe me, I hate this mess as much as you do. I can share a way out of it. Listen: all that the 'High Protector' really cares about is this learn-sharing of mine, with you and Usha. Yes, he would like to control the planet, but it's not worth the trouble. Too 'expensive,' you understand? If you work things out with me, I will—will see to it that the soldiers leave."

Merwen's anger grew as she heard this. Even the best of Valans seemed always to be hiding from the worst. Merwen was sick of it; she wanted nothing to do with any of them. But she tried to keep her mind steady. to Siderite's credit, he had come alone, despite 'orders,' which was a big step for any Valan. If Siderite had even a remote chance of learnsharing further, of taking a selfname, then she had to encourage him.

Slowly she turned her head and looked into Siderite's face. His eyes squinted in the sunlight, and wisps of hair brushed around; his arms hung limp, with fingers flexing nervously. Siderite hungered for a word from her. And Merwen longed to ask what Yinevra had asked Nisi many months before: What is the First Door, The Last Door each enters alone, the Door of your own name?

But Lystra was missing, and Siderite was not ready to tell her where or why. Merwen returned to her loom. A look she had shared; that was all she had in her, for now.

For a long time Siderite stayed, while Merwen waited, and the Valan's shadow inched across the warp strands. At last the shadow fell away. From Siderite's boat, the motor sputtered and groaned, then died away.

Merwen gripped the frame of the loom, almost hard enough to break it again. If only she could know if she had done the right thing. Even Shora seemed to know so little anymore.

10

Siderite's work seemed hopelessly stalled, but the general had planned for that. Not all the native populations were as troublesome as at Per-elion. In fact, one or two company bases reported consistent inspection records and no sign of "witnessers"—in short, their occupied rafts were under control.

The best operation appeared to be run by Captain Theo, a thousand kilometers to the north. So, now that relations at Raia-el had completely soured, Realgar decided to send Siderite out there, where he hoped that the scientist's work might resume.

Captain Theo had her platoons permanently encamped on native rafts, where they could keep an eye on things. She radioed Lieutenant Basil to be ready when the General came out.

"Not *the* General?" From inside the operations tent on Wanli-el raft, Basil stared at his monitor. "Captain, you can't be serious. Why here? Why me?"

"You're just too successful, that's why," the soprano voice squeaked out.

"Thanks a lot."

"Come on, Basil, you can talk those catfish into anything. The General will drop off his scientist, then leave, and all's well. You could even get a medal for it."

"But Captain—"

The monitor clicked dead.

Basil banged his fist on the table, and one of its legs half folded under. Why *now?* Sure, Nira's Gathering went along with things, but lately Basil sensed something cooking; something new was up. Something he might not just talk away this time.

There was good reason why Theo's company base never had "witnessers" from Basil's rafts. Natives could find him right here, any time, and he would talk with them round the clock about the Valan army, and why his superiors were inclined to be "sick," and by the way how were Nira's darling children doing?

Still, his job was no picnic on Trollbone Point. Those medical "inspections"—what a waste of time and holocubes. Basil had to spend an hour every time just apologizing and humoring the native kids and all, or else lifeshaping tunnels would mysteriously "disappear"; and Captain Theo could come up with only so many creative explanations for that.

It certainly had nothing to do with anything he had learned at Iridis Academy for the Protectoral Guard of Valedon. And this was only his first tour in the field.

Basil pulled back the tent flap and stepped out into a clearing, where the troops were being drilled. Sergeant Cerite insisted on that stuff, although Basil foresaw no conceivable action in which to put it to use. Still, it helped morale and kept the sergeant happy. It also seemed to impress the natives, or at least entertain them; there were always a few of them watching, seated still as if mesmerized.

Basil signaled to the sergeant, and the shouting and stamping came to a halt. "Listen, the general's coming out tomorrow. I want this place in shape, you hear?" Whatever that meant.

Cerite came over, a thickset man, slightly balding, with shoulders hefty from years of carrying a pack. "General? You don't mean the Sard?"

"You got it."

Cerite whistled and shook his head. "And these guys can't even hold their guns straight. I'll drill them for the next twelve hours—"

"It's not the troops he wants to see, it's the natives."

"Natives? You mean Nira and her kids?"

"By the way, that's quite a crowd you've got today." Four or five native watchers were not unusual, but now that he looked, Basil counted over thirty of them—mostly elders, at that.

"I don't think they're watching us today. It's you they're waiting for, Lieutenant."

"Me? What's up?" When Cerite did not answer, Basil walked toward the group of natives until he faced Nira.

"Share the day, Nira." He spread his hands to show they were empty. This gesture had a great soothing effect on natives. "For what purpose do I share the honor of such esteemed company?"

"A grave problem has arisen." Nira the Narrowminded was a withered crone, with scars from some seamonster spread across her dusky amethyst skin, and she had as many tricks up her non-existent sleeve as any village mayor. "A problem to concern all sisters, Sharer and Valan alike. We of Wanli-el shared ignorance of it for some weeks because clickflies were gone."

A clickfly was sitting on her head now, placidly cleaning its mandibles. Basil felt his skin crawl. Torr be thanked, Nira did not know who had to spread the pesticides. Orders were orders.

"The death-sickness of your Valan sisters at Per-elion has taken a critical turn. It saddens me to share with you what has occurred, not only unprecedented impoliteness and hastening of death, but also a thing so incredible that we don't have a name for it. It might be best described as a 'rape' of the mind."

The Valan word 'rape' was unexpected. "Mind-rape?" Basil shot a questioning glance at the sergeant.

Cerite spat on the raft. "Use your head, Lieutenant. The top brass are Sards."

Sardish mindbenders—they could extract a man's will and not leave a mark on him. That's what they must be doing to the natives at Headquarters. Basil muttered, "No wonder they have riots on their hands." Then, to Nira, "Listen, I share your distress on this matter. I will send a complaint to the 'Palace.'"

"Does that mean you will share restraint with your Valan sisters?"

Basil chewed that one over. Already he was regretting a promise which could only get himself in trouble. "You know how it is, Nira. With the general, I can only share will his way."

Nira said, "The consensus of many Gatherings is that all Valan sisters, who can fly across sky within hours and share speech within seconds, must be considered as one. We at Wanli-el now share that consensus. Therefore, we must Unspeak all Valans so long as unspeakable acts continue anywhere."

"Unspeak? But the general is coming tomorrow—" Basil broke off, at a loss.

"Then you may share some sense with this 'general.' Meanwhile, our Gathering will share Unspeech by sundown. We're sorry, Basil, but there is nothing more to be said."

"Wait a minute, what about 'inspections'?"

"I am sorry, Basil."

"But 'inspections' are essential to our health and well-being. We'll be ill at our Last Door without 'inspections.'"

Nira said nothing. That meant it wasn't going to work this time, though she was too polite to say so. Basil began to sweat. If the lab warrens "disappeared" for good, there would be the devil to pay all round.

He crouched down so that he could face her at eye level. "Nira, we've got to work something out here. Haven't we all been good friends? Didn't we rescue your cousin's family in that boat caught in the storm?"

Some of the others stirred as if they might speak. Nira said, "We are very good friends, Basil, and that is why we share this for your own good."

An idea came to mind. From his pocket Basil pulled out a holocube and showed it to Nira. "Could you conduct the 'inspection' yourself, Nira? Just press the red dot on one side and carry the cube throughout the lifeshaping place once a week. Then exchange the cube here, without saying a thing. Then none of us gets into trouble."

Nira looked down and thought about this awhile. At last she said, "I cannot do this for you. However . . . I have a granddaughter under twelve who is not yet bound by the Gathering. You may ask her."

"Thanks, Nira, that's a great help." Basil stood up and stretched his legs. "That was a close one, Cerite."

"It still is, Lieutenant. What are you going to tell the general with his scientist tomorrow?"

"I know what I'd like to tell him." What was the point of this campaign, anyway? All the scary science stuff—the company medic privately thought it was a con job, cooked up by the Palace as an excuse for invasion. Who could prove where those new purple strains came from? None of Basil's men were affected, and they practically lived with the natives. And now, this "mind-rape." That Sardish bastard.

11

"Impossible," Realgar shouted when he heard. "We just wiped out the damned insects. And they're *still* complaining about a few mindprobed prisoners. . . ."

Within days the new clickflies had multiplied in swarms never seen before. Clouds of them darkened the sky, and they got into everything, tangling in bedding and mess kits, clogging helicopter engines, smashing into windows until the glass streamed with their juices. Insecticide sprayed into the dark clouds precipitated dead husks like black snow, but millions more remained in the sky.

Day by day, a wall of deafness crept inexorably from raft system to raft system, cluster to cluster. All around the globe, natives were shutting their ears and mouths to Valan troops, Iridian and Dolomite alike. Nothing seemed to break that silence, not shouting, beating, imprisoning.

And then the lifeshaping places began to disappear.

"What do you mean, disappear?" he demanded.

"Just that," said Jade. "Sometimes the tunnels are filled in; or else the walls remain, stripped to bare raftwood, all sign of lifeshaping vanished, even those devilish twisting vines."

If entire laboratories were disappearing, they had to be rebuilt somewhere, but where, and how so fast?

"Imprison the lifeshapers."

"That's fine," said Jade, "except for those rafts where we never found out who the lifeshapers were."

"Never found out?"

"Well, they don't wear white coats and stonesigns."

Realgar slammed the desk. "Stone. What about those stonesick natives you were bribing with gemstones?"

"I was just getting to that. Some informants have let us know where the new hideouts are, and I think that—"

A tone sounded from the monitor: an emergency dispatch had

just come in from a base in the southwest sector. A squad of divers was digging out a nest of natives hidden beneath the raft's underside, when a shockwraith approached. They blasted the thing, but its arms wriggled off in all directions and hit several men with acid. One had just died.

The High Protectoral Guard of Valedon had suffered its first casualty on the Ocean Moon.

Realgar called on the Protector. "As you see, my lord," he told the gray lightshape, "hostilities have escalated. I must have clearance for a full counterattack."

Talion took his time to respond. "The Envoy wants their science controlled, not destroyed. Even Torr needs their knowledge."

"Not yet," Talion reminded him. "Our genetic makeup is foreign to them. It would take them decades to develop a biological threat to us."

Realgar thought uneasily of the altered breathmicrobe strain, but he was loath to contradict Malachite's dogma. Besides, breathmicrobes were not actually harmful. "We can always leave one or two rafts intact, to preserve their science. With the rest of them neutralized, the few that remain won't dare attack us. And if they do, we can isolate the contagion quickly."

Talion frowned and drummed his fingers on his desk. "Ral, I just can't understand how those natives manage to cause so much trouble. So many prisoners, for Torr's sake. Don't the women think of their families?"

"Sometimes whole families go to prison. I'm telling you my lord, they don't think like civilized people. They still don't know what orders are. That's why we have to crack down."

Talion sighed. "Ral, the political fallout from this campaign is getting troublesome. I'd hoped at first it would seize the imagination of Valan citizens to strike out and master an untamed planet, and that this goal in common would help dissolve minor squabbles back home. Instead, the scant news that gets past the censors has only disillusioned the public."

"I'm sorry to disappoint the public." Realgar kept his voice flat. "Would they prefer a daily body count?"

"Oh, no, of course not. Believe me, I'm with you there." Talion smiled apologetically. "You know how people are. What they want and what they think they want are not quite the same. They want heroics, like blowing up those shockwraiths—send some more cubes of that, Ral, it helps your image. If you can suggest native scheming behind the monster attacks, so much the better. Did I send you two more divisions just to put women and kids in prison?"

"Insurgents, my lord; they are insurgents, every one of them. The question is simple: Shall we control the natives or not?"

Talion pondered this for a long while. "Those prisoners," he mused. "They all 'white out' in captivity, do they?"

"Not always. Some stay conscious until interrogation. They all have mental deathblocks."

"Suppose you send me a handful of them, give my Palace staff a crack at them."

Realgar smiled slightly. "Very well, my lord." He would send the hardcore agitators whom he had held when the others were returned. The High Protector would see what they were like, all right. "One is the daughter of Protector Merwen herself."

"A hostage, excellent. Now, to answer your question, Ral: yes, we have to control the natives. Do what it takes to achieve that, whatever it takes—so long as you succeed. Do I make myself clear?"

The message was clear enough. Realgar had better succeed— or else Talion would pick another Commander to pacify the Ocean Moon.

When the thunderclap hit Raia-el, Merwen was astounded: the sky held no clouds, and there was no sign of rain. Again the blast struck, and the raft shuddered at her feet. She lost her footing and covered her ears against the ringing.

Beyond the silkhouse, a column of flames reared and licked at the sky. Somehow the raft was on fire.

Usha and Mirri came running outside. "It's burning, all over the lifeshaping place! At this rate the whole raft will break up!"

From everywhere, sisters rushed with buckets splashing. Still the flames and smoke churned from the tunnels, some of which collapsed inward. Too dazed to think, Merwen swung buckets back and forth, stumbling as her eyes streamed and blurred from smoke. The confusion was worse than when seaswallowers crested.

At last the wormrunners managed to get a hose hooked up to the tail of a starworm, and that began to make a dent in the flames.

As flames receded, the charred sunken surface of the raft looked even more horrible than the fire itself. Black smoke still twisted up and stretched out to the horizon, curdling the sky. A few helicopters kept circling with their maddening drone, surveying their deathwork.

Afterward, Usha picked through the charred raftwood, trying to figure what had been lost. "The supplies: the stocks of every strain of medicine plant, every enzyme secretor, thousands of different ones. I'll have to start over from scratch, from the raftwood genes."

"No, Usha." Merwen held Usha's arm and squeezed hard. "The other rafts will help us. We'll soon be set up again." But even as she spoke, her eyes scanned the horizon. There were black clouds rising above other rafts.

The lifeshaping places of Per-elion were all in ruins, a disaster that no one could have imagined. And the return of seaswallowers, though late this season, could only be days away.

"Do you know, Usha," she mused as she watched the horizon, "I could almost regret the day I brought Spinel home with us."

"Spinel? Merwen, you don't mean that. You still miss him."

Merwen half smiled. "Yes. But for his sake, I bless the day that he left."

12

For weeks now, Spinel had been getting by in Iridis, holding forth as a Spirit Caller amid the crowds on Center Way. He took up with another old Caller, Elaterite of Karias, who rented him half an attic room and bequeathed to him a cowled robe with deep pockets to collect change. Beyond rent and food, Spinel saved every bit he could toward a ferryship ticket for the Ocean Moon.

The coins mounted slowly, and he skimped on food. His breathmicrobes receded until only a tinge of lavender remained in his palms.

Still, business was pretty good, compared to Chrysoport. City folk expected the same thing villagers did, only they talked faster, let him say less, and paid more. City gossip was a bit more lurid —the daily murders, refugee riots, and new trouble brewing out in Azurport—but he soon got used to it. Then came the chilling news that the High Protector declared war on Shora.

Everyone else was thrilled to hear that Valedon would conquer another planet in a crusade for the Patriarch. Half the Spirit Callers on Center Way ran off to enlist.

Spinel was bewildered. "You can't fight a war up there," he told old El. "There's nothing but women and kids."

"What do you know about it?" said El. "The Commander says they're nothing but terrorists up there, concocting secret weapons."

Spinel combed the gutter for a discarded newscube and showed it to El. At a touch, the face of the High Protector filled the cube, going on about the Purple Menace. Next came the Commander, General Realgar resplendent in stones and medallions. The general reported native "assaults" on Valan bases, even at Headquarters. Casualties were light, but many native prisoners had been taken, and "the situation was in hand."

A familiar face filled the cube. Spinel gasped. "It's Merwen!" There were soldiers in the background, and the general spoke with Merwen in an oddly stilted way.

"Greetings, Protector. You must accept the authority of Valedon."

Her lips moved woodenly. "I respect your authority."

Then there were clips of the ocean, of helicopters buffeted by storms and boats entwined by giant octopods. Yet all the while the one face burned in Spinel's mind. "Shora. Oh, Shora," he whispered.

El said, "You look like you've seen a ghost."

"It was Merwen, I told you about her. Did you see the look she gave him?"

"She wished him to hell, I'm sure."

"Not exactly. More like saying, Mister, you're driving yourself to hell." At least Merwen was still there, alive, despite the ill-defined "assaults" and the general driving himself to hell. Was Lystra all right, too? More than anything, Spinel wished he had never left, though he dreaded to think what it must be like up there, ten times worse than with the Dolomites in Chrysoport. He had not yet saved half the fare for the ferryship.

As the next weeks passed, Palace reports were scanty, with little conventional combat, but a lot of shockwraiths blown up, and invidious plagues that beset the troops. There were other rumors, though, spread by men and women home on leave. They said there was no war at all, just a lot of makework and phony patrols and maintaining the bases on a treacherous sea.

"I told you it was crazy," Spinel told El over a cabbage-soup supper in their attic room. "Why'd the High Protector send an army in the first place?"

"It's the Purple Menace, haven't you heard?" El's voice lowered sepulchrally. "A creeping doom will come upon us all."

"Purple nothing. You don't believe that stuff, do you?"

"Of course not. I suppose Talion just wants to keep his troops occupied so the generals don't plot to oust him, the way his own father came to power. That was the year my grandfather lost all his sheep in a snowstorm, and my father came to Iridis to work in a trainsweeper repair shop. . . ."

One day Spinel heard that native prisoners were on display before the Palace. It might be just a rumor, but Spinel ran down the blocks to the end of Center Way to see for himself.

Beyond the courtyard rose as always the majestic face of Palace Iridium, where Malachite and the Legions stood embalmed in mosaic tiles. At the top was the symbol of the Patriarch, whom Spirit Callers were supposed to harken. Spinel himself knew better now, though the "Spirit" he actually called remained elusive as ever.

There was no parade in the courtyard, but the crowd was almost as dense as on the day the Torran Envoy was honored. By now, Spinel was expert at handling city crowds, and he soon wormed his way through.

There was a cage with bars, as if for lions, with a couple of burly guards to keep the crowd at a distance. Inside the cage were six Sharers, dusty and covered in loose prison gowns. Their wrists and ankles were manacled. They sat and stared, lifelessly, unseeing.

Then everything receded except one, shoulders still straight and tall, grimy and sullen and achingly beautiful. "Lystra! Lystra, say something, share a word with me!" The Sharer words rang strangely, here, after so many months.

The guard, a thick troll of a woman, waved a neuralprobe at

him. "What are you jabbering, almsman? Catfish can't talk. You that desperate for a client?"

Onlookers laughed and hooted and sketched starsigns, followed by obscene gestures. But Spinel ran past the guard and clung to the bars of the cage. "Lystra! Lystra, *speak to me, or I'll go Unspoken.*"

Lystra's eyes did not turn, but her lips moved. "Stonetrader. Go join the death-hasteners with Kyril."

She had shared speech with him at last, after all. A rush of joy overwhelmed him.

Another Sharer was scandalized. "Quiet, Intemperate One. They're *Unspoken,* all of them."

"It's Merwen's Valan pet," Lystra snapped. "He *was* one of us."

"Indeed." The Sharer looked out at him with interest. "Have you a selfname, sister?"

The guard caught him by the hair and spun him around. "A miracle," she mused. "A Spirit Caller brought speech to the deaf and dumb."

Spinel winced as his hair tore at the roots, but he dared not risk the neuralprobe. "They're my sisters," he tried to explain.

The guard snorted. "If they're your sisters, I'm the Patriarch." Her huge jaw lifted. "Chains," she called.

Manacles clamped on his arms and legs.

Spinel found his voice. "Hey! Hey, wait a minute—"

"Stop jabbering. You'll tell your tale to the High Protector," the guard flung back at him.

The office of the High Protector of Valedon was the finest room Spinel had seen since the passenger lounge of the *Cristobel,* on his way home with Lady Berenice. But whereas the lounge had been full of cushions and servo arms, this place was sharp and functional. Flat oblong panels pulsed with light behind the massive desk, where sat the Protector himself, a granite-faced man who seemed almost a part of his desk. Spinel's seat was a polished black curve that had risen cleverly from the floor.

The Sharers, still manacled, sat on the floor in a semicircle. Between them and the door, the guards stood stolidly at attention.

The Protector spoke. "So you lived six months among the natives." He paused as if about to pronounce judgment. "A pity we haven't met before."

"Yes, my lord," Spinel replied politely.

"Now. I understand you communicate extraordinarily well with these . . . women."

"Well, I— hope so, my lord."

The Protector said flatly, "Ask them why they cause my troops so much trouble."

Spinel blinked and swallowed. He glanced warily at Lystra. "Um . . . the 'Protector' wants to know," he said in Sharer, "why you share trouble with death-hasteners."

He expected an explosion. Instead, Lystra calmly asked, "Are you a selfnamer yet?"

Spinel recalled what Merwen had said of Uriel. "I'm a 'Spirit Caller.' That's getting close, Merwen says."

"Then see that your children remove these chains."

Embarrassed, Spinel looked to the Protector and wondered how much he understood.

"Unchain them," the Protector ordered. The guards did so. The Sharers promptly slipped off their prison gowns. Nevertheless, the Protector waved away the guards. "Spinel, why do they remove their clothes?"

"Well, I'm not sure." Spinel felt like a hinged door, pulled in both directions at once. "Lystra, why don't you keep your plumage on? It's just polite, on Valedon."

"Because it's filthy and shameful. You share the shame yourself, hiding in a blanket on a day so warm. Your sweat smells stale."

Spinel looked at the Protector again and wondered how he would react if Spinel actually followed Lystra's example and slipped out of his robe. He felt a hysterical impulse to laugh; if only Ahn and Melas could see him now, before the High Protector of Valedon, they would faint away of amazement.

Then he looked more closely at Lystra. Dark welts crossed her arms and breasts, and her legs were torn and scabbed. A chill seized him until his teeth shook. There was nothing to laugh at, here.

"Spinel. Spinel?" The Protector had been calling him. Spinel forced his gaze back. "Spinel, ask her why Sharers do not obey my troops."

He was beginning to understand, now. He could guess where Lystra's welts had come from. His throat thickened until he could barely swallow. "Lystra," he said hoarsely, "why is it that Sharers do not do things that soldiers ask?"

"Soldiers order," the Protector corrected in Valan.

"I don't know the Sharer words for 'order' or 'obey.'"

The Protector said nothing. Apparently he did not know the words either.

Lystra said, "We used to do everything the Valans asked, out of pity for their sickness. Then the death-hasteners sickened worse and shared unspeakable acts. So we Unspoke them."

"What acts?"

"Silence," the Protector ordered. "What I must know is—"

"They took our sisters and put coldstone things around their heads, from which alien thought came and burst the door of self until—"

"Silence." The word cracked like a whip.

One of the guards extended a neuralprobe. Spinel could not tell what the guard did with it, but then Lystra's breath hissed and her muscles pulled into hard knobs. "Until-they-died." Lystra's voice squeezed out as if pressed between rollers. "Then-sisters-came-from-all-over-and-witnessed—"

"Stop it." Spinel lunged toward her. Pain streaked through him, pulling every tendon from the bone. He skidded and fell; the cool floor hit his elbows. The pain dizzied him, and red blotches winked before his eyes.

When his head cleared, the guard was saying, "All it took was a touch on him. What's wrong with *them?*"

The other guard still had her neuralprobe set at Lystra's neck. Lystra went on with her monologue, though her hands were losing color, and Spinel thought, She'll go white any minute and maybe never speak again, but he was too weak to say another word.

"Enough," said the Protector. "I got one talking, at least. So much for Sardish mindbending. Ship the lot back, with the almsman."

So for the third time Spinel crossed the sky between worlds—this time, in the prison hold of an Iridian warship.

13

Once clickflies were hopelessly entrenched again, Realgar changed his strategy. Jade's staff, with the help of a few "stonesick" informants, deciphered the insect communication code. Unspoken or not, Sharers would keep no more secrets from him.

It came as something of an anticlimax to hear, after all, that Talion had gotten the natives to talk.

Jade was outraged. "Trollbones for that. His staff's no better than mine."

"A Spirit Caller did it," said the general. "Got them talking in no time, even the Protector's daughter."

"A Spirit Caller! But that's ludicrous!"

"Yes." His lip curled slightly. "Talion even sent this Spirit Caller back to us, to help us out."

Color rose in her cheeks. "So Talion thinks he got an almsman to do what all my staff couldn't. The nerve of those catfish. That Protector's daughter—"

"Never mind. Now that you've got the clickfly code licked, who cares if they talk or not? At least they can't fraternize with the troops." The troops were getting to be a problem, he knew. Too many Iridians went soft and carried sob stories back home.

The only problem now was that Siderite was without native informants for the time being. There had to be a "stonesick" lifeshaper somewhere on the globe, and Realgar was sure one would turn up. In the meantime, he thought it would be wise to pay a call on the scientist, to smooth his ruffled feathers after the strike on the lifeshaping places. So he went to visit Siderite in his laboratory.

Siderite stood there between his lab benches, with his hair askew and a black apron over his fatigues. He looked more like a mess cook than anything else, Realgar thought. How absurd that the success of this entire campaign should depend upon such a person. There must be an alternative, Realgar told himself for the hundredth time, but he had yet to find it.

To his relief, Siderite accepted his explanations and apologies with equanimity. Relief turned to suspicion; the man must be holding something back. Had Siderite sent covert aid to the enemy again?

Siderite shrugged absently, and his gaze wandered to the ceiling. "There's little I can do about it, is there."

"Of course not. Your understanding is appreciated."

"It will be hard on them, at swallower season . . ."

"But there will be no swallowers this season, at least not in inhabited regions." The House of Aragonite had developed a repellent which would keep the seaswallowers away from all military bases, which meant away from most native raft systems as well. Realgar wondered why the traders had not done so, years earlier. They claimed that the natives disapproved, that they wanted the beasts to come, but that made little sense to him. In fact, it was galling to have to protect natives along with his troops, and he hoped it would not be interpreted as a weakness.

" . . . they will decentralize all the more," Siderite was saying. "My guess is, within a few weeks you'll have ten times as many lab warrens to police as before."

Realgar's attention snapped back. "What's that? Ten times as many?"

"Just a guess, mind you. That's what I would do, if I were them: scatter little lifeshaping places in holes all over the raft. For that matter, plant a few vines in some of the medium-sized raft seedlings, since the seaswallowers aren't coming. Leave spare 'laboratories' floating all over the place." Siderite nodded to himself. "Yes, Usha will think of that."

"What are you saying?" Realgar snapped.

"As it is, every cell of every living raft contains a whole library of all the basic knowledge and skills Sharers possess."

"A *library*, in a cell?"

"A chromosome library. Trillions of bits of data on molecular chains, coiled up so small you can't even see it. In every cell of raft-wood. Billions of cells in every raft seedling, each the seed of an entire Sharer life and culture."

Realgar gripped the lab bench. "Why didn't you tell me this before?"

Siderite wheeled and shouted at him. "I told you the whole

planet was their laboratory! I'd have said a lot more, if I knew what you had in mind. Now get out of my lab and stay out."

Astonished though he was, Realgar waited. He saw that Siderite's hands were shaking, and not just from anger. "You can send me back to Iridis for all I care." Siderite added in an unsteady voice.

The man still feared him, Realgar decided, so he could let the lapse pass. "You will leave when your work is finished, not before." Realgar turned sharply and left without permitting a reply. A library in every cell of raftwood.... What an infernally twisted riddle this planet was.

On a morning two weeks after the lab warrens were hit, Realgar took a hard look at his face in the shaving mirror. It seemed grayer than the usual fair cast of his cheeks and jaw. A jab at the light switch turned the gray to lavender.

His fist crashed on the sink. Of course the breathmicrobes were harmless, the medics insisted over and over. Still, his hand shook as he lifted the razor. Emotions flashed in succession—fear, denial, then a curious sense of release, as if he had yielded something that he had not wanted to win. Then anger washed out everything else. The natives, the damned catfish—*they* had violated him, in an intensely personal way. His pulse throbbed at his temples, and he breathed slowly for a few minutes to get himself under control.

Realgar turned to the monitor plate on the wall. "Get Doctor Nathan, now."

The doctor's voice came on, but he had little help to give. "General, we've done the best we can, but nothing works, so far. At Headquarters alone, nine out of ten men are either purple now or on their way to it soon. Not one of our drugs makes a dent in it. I'm sorry, sir." Nathan sounded decidedly nervous as he finished.

"You mean there's no cure? How far has it spread?" Realgar demanded.

"To over half the bases. The spores are airborne, so they can't be contained."

"And the natives are behind it all."

Nathan hesitated. "I find it difficult to escape that conclusion, sir. It's extremely unlikely that a microbe of this type would develop sudden resistance to the entire range of our antibiotics."

"I'll burn out a few of those rafts," Realgar muttered. "I'll burn them to a cinder."

"Perhaps . . ." Nathan's voice trailed off.

"Speak up, Doctor."

"As far as the medical problem goes, a more practical approach might be to get the natives to produce an antidote."

Realgar was floored. "You mean you have no hope of finding a cure?" This might actually get serious. A purple population on Valendon? Unthinkable. Talion would certainly see it that way; he might even quarantine the Ocean Moon.

Then another thought sent a shock down his spine. "The satellites. Are they also . . .?"

"Some are contaminated, probably all," said Nathan. "We'll get rid of it eventually, General. Not overnight, that's all. It may take Hospital Iridis several years to analyze the strain."

Realgar was barely listening. He dismissed the doctor and put in a top security call to his private quarters on Satellite Amber. Just in time he ordered the visual transmission corrected for his skin tone.

On his viewing stage, lightshape sparkled and sprang into form. The peasant-skirted nanny servo huddled the two children into view. They still wore their nightclothes, and their eyes were heavy with sleep, but they giggled and squirmed at the sight of their father. Elmvar waved furiously with both hands. Cassiter clasped her hands demurely, but the ends of her lips curled into an elfin smile. "Papa, what a surprise! Are you coming home, Papa? Oh, please, will you take us hunting when you come?"

"Not yet, Cassi. Just called to see . . . how you are." He swallowed the tightness in his throat. Already he saw the lavender tinge in her cheeks, just the faintest trace he used to see in Berenice, before the antibiotic had finished its work. But there was no antibiotic now. How would Cassi react once she realized what was happening to her?

Cassiter pouted. "Oh, I'm all right, Papa. Nothing's new at all. It's dreadfully boring up here, without you."

The natives, Realgar thought; they've taken my children. My children are hostage to their microbes.

14

For Merwen, days crawled by with still no word from Lystra. Each day her heart died a little, felt a bit emptier, more certain that Lystra's soul had fled the Last Door and would not come again in the same shape to Raia-el.

The lifeshaping tunnels were rebuilding, slowly. Rafts all over Shora had been hit, but the few lucky ones sent starter cultures by clickfly to everyone in need. And this time Usha built emergency caches into secret places on the raft, to be better prepared for next time.

As Merwen had promised, she took in three stonesick guests, all of whom had been Unspoken by their Gatherings at other rafts and had been sighted at the soldier-place. Shaalrim and Lalor also had moved in, to share the intense care that these guests needed. Often Merwen would stay up with them throughout the night, listening to the endless song of the sea, muffled though it was now with the swamp of overgrown raft seedlings. So long as she stayed close by her sisters, they would stay away from the soldier-place with its gemstones.

On those nights Merwen wondered a thousand times where Lystra was, and where the seaswallowers were, a worry almost as bad as Lystra, for the raft seedlings had to be thinned out, and fleshborers swarmed so thick that one could barely stay in the water. The overcrowded raft seedlings festered and oozed scum that poisoned fish and octopus, while fleshborers devoured what little remained. Then mudworms bloomed and turned the sea brown, without fish to consume them; and fanwings that skimmed the sea for food sickened from the mudworms, until flocks of their bodies drifted on the raft seedlings. The one thing worse than swallower time was the time when swallowers failed to appear.

It turned out that swallowers were traveling northward, after all, but they crowded into narrow lanes, staying hundreds of raft-lengths away from any Valan dwelling. Usha sampled the sea and detected a toxin that repelled seaswallowers.

Merwen was in the silkhouse, reshaping fungal swirls on the wall, when a helicopter came again, hovering and sputtering to a halt outside.

Quickly she sat down with her crippled mother, to reassure her. Ama's hand pressed hers, just a little. "Think of them, Merwen. I never thought I'd see a sister alive more helpless than myself, yet so often, now, they drop from the sky. It's hard not to pity them."

Merwen smiled and thought how a few words from her mother could breed more strength than days of strain wore away.

The Valan death-hasteners came in for Merwen, of course; they never seemed to care for anyone else. As usual she let herself go limp in their grasp, limper even than Ama, who could still flick an eyelid or raise a hand to her dear ones. For the Unspoken Valans, Merwen would make no sign at all with her body, neither to help nor hinder. What use was it, when they could not touch her soul?

Still, it could do her own body no good to be bumped across the raft and into the dead machine until welts swelled all over. Nor was it any better for her soul to be hauled off as if worth no more than a netful of fish. She had to remember, always, that she was in the hands of unfortunates, but the effort drained her will.

Where would she end up this time? The shell of dank, rotting stone? Instead, she found herself in the place of Realgar the word-weaver again, for the first time since Unspeech had begun. Merwen relaxed a bit; the visit was bound to be brief, since she could say nothing. Next to him, though, stood the blond one who committed atrocities against the mind. In both their faces the purple microbes bloomed, and Merwen wondered what that signified. Would the death-hasteners plumb new depths of madness, even as Trurl had warned?

Someone else, in a dusty yellowish blanket, waved arms at her. "Merwen! It's me; I came back, Merwen, to troubleshare again."

She reeled at the voice. Not Spinel, not here. Had Spinel fallen sick too?

"It's *me*, Merwen. Don't you know me?" With a flurry of movement the garment was loosed and tossed in the air. Spinel was free after all, as alive as Merwen's own daughters. She rushed to embrace him, until the soldiers pulled them apart, and her bruises throbbed anew.

"Enough," said Realgar, with a glance at Jade. Jade's metal stick touched Spinel.

Spinel's eyes rolled from the pain, then he tottered and half collapsed. He picked up the blanket again and dragged it over his head, his face a picture of misery.

His pain stung Merwen far worse than her own. Spinel was more than her own daughter; he was a Valan child who had placed himself freely in her hands, her last bright hope for a oneness of Valan and Sharer. Spinel was purple by choice, and the day he had made the choice, Merwen had pledged her life against his pain.

Spinel's throat dipped as he swallowed. "It's...not so bad, Merwen."

Merwen's eyes fell, overcome with the anguish and yet the joy that Spinel was here again as a Sharer. Even his starstone and plumage were that of Uriel, not altogether a bad thing. Deliberately she seated herself on the floor to compose her mind, as if for a Gathering. Spinel glanced at the soldiers, then sat before her.

"Spinel, I want to know," said Realgar, "how long Merwen and the other Protectors plan to flout our rule."

Spinel swallowed again. "He wants to know how long you plan to...not share will."

"Spinel, we may not concern ourselves with what the Unspoken ask to know."

"But I have to, or it hurts," Spinel blurted.

Merwen realized that the young Valan did not know whitetrance and could not control his pain at all. It dawned on her, then: without whitetrance, *no* Valans could properly control their own pain.

She had always known they lacked whitetrance, but she had never drawn this connection. Conscious beings were meant to control pain, to say yes or no to their physical selves, else how could their souls be freed?

"One more chance, Spinel," Realgar warned.

"Please, Merwen—"

"Since you ask, Spinel, we will of course resist until Valans leave or share healing." Valans grew old without learning whitetrance; no wonder they were ill.

"Does she realize," said Realgar, "that many more sisters will die?"

"Do you realize that others will die?" Spinel said hollowly.

"Sharers have died, physically, since the beginning of time."

"But deaths will be hastened," Realgar added. "Does Merwen

wish to have that on her conscience? Does she know that we have her daughter?"

Spinel said, "Do you know Lystra's here? I spoke with her, but she still shares anger with me."

Lystra, alive still. Merwen's hope soared on wings, then plummeted. Lystra, in a stone cell, all this time. "Is she well?"

"No, she's—" Pain from the metal stick twisted his face once more.

Despite herself Merwen shut her eyes hard. "Spinel, this place makes me tired. Why don't you come home with me?" If only Spinel would come home so Usha could share with him the way to hold pain in his fingerwebs. No, he had no fingerwebs, but he did have a soul, and that made all the difference.

"Enough nonsense," said Realgar. "The breathmicrobes. Tell her to get rid of them, or else."

Spinel said, "He wants you to chase out the breathmicrobes."

Merwen opened her eyes again and considered this. "A sad wish, Spinel. If Valans intend to live in our ocean, surely they wish to swim as well as possible."

"Spinel, Merwen knows what Valans think of breathmicrobes, and we know where this new strain came from."

Spinel said, "He thinks you made the breathmicrobes to resist Valan medicines."

"Usha did make the strain," Merwen said. "It escaped from her collection when our tunnels were destroyed."

"Then she can get rid of it," Realgar insisted.

"He still doesn't want to share it, Merwen."

The request was fair enough, Merwen thought. Suppose she offered a "cure," if Spinel were to be freed, and Lystra . . . No, that would mean trading threats, a sick thing to do. She must offer to share the "cure" outright, hard though it was to think of breathmicrobes as an illness to be cured.

Before she responded, Realgar said, "Tell her to get rid of the strain, if she values her children."

Spinel's mouth opened. "Your—your daughters, Merwen," he stuttered. "Something will happen."

Her heart sank. A threat had been made; it was too late to be generous. "Lystra is a selfnamer," she said calmly.

"Her younger daughters," Realgar corrected. "And all the children of Sharers everywhere."

"I think he means Weia and Wellen." Spinel barely forced the words out.

"I hear you, Spinel." There was a pause, expanding as if to fill the room. Merwen stretched herself, her back straightened, and her breasts lifted. "Do you know for what reason sisters become Unspoken? It is because they cry for demands which would only hurt them most."

Realgar leaned forward across his desk. "This is no riddle game. You are ruthless, Protector: you stop at nothing, even infecting our own children. Very well. Every Sharer child age two to twelve will be held as security until something cures this plague."

Spinel said nothing, but sat like a stone.

"Go on, Spinel. Every native child age two to twelve."

Still he said nothing. A shriek split the room; Spinel's eyes stood out from the sockets, his body collapsed and curled up on the floor.

"I hear, Spinel," Merwen whispered, sensing the defeat into which Spinel had unwittingly trapped her.

"Much better. You're talking sense at last." Realgar nodded to Jade, who replaced the stick at her belt. "What do you say, Protector? Twenty-four hours to think it over?"

Her eyes widened with a new idea. "I will do something else for Valans, Spinel, something they all need, very badly; for this, I would share speech again. I will share with them the whitetrance to govern pain."

This only seemed to infuriate Realgar all the more. "You still dare to flaunt your illegally deathblocked minds? What kind of a selfnamer are you? Do you think nothing of your own children?"

"I am a very poor selfnamer, Spinel. I lose patience too quickly. Perhaps my daughters will share more understanding with Valan children than I do."

Spinel was sobbing quietly on the floor, his starstone swung out from his neck.

"No grace period," said Realgar curtly. "Your children are forfeit."

The soldiers hauled her out, without waiting for her to turn white.

Realgar was surprised and gratified at how well Talion's stratagem had worked. That young Spirit Caller really was a key to the

heart of Protector Merwen, her first significant weakness that
Realgar had discerned.

But he would have to follow through with taking the children.
Though it was stretching the letter of the Code, which allowed
hostages to be taken only from key officials, he could fall back on
the official Sharer claim that all their adults were equal Protectors
under their own law. To take their children—an ingenious move:
he wondered why he had not thought of it before. It would not be
long before some one of those mothers cured the Plague.

Beside his desk, Jade still stood, rigid as an epileptic. Her face
and hands were deep violet, almost indigo; it seemed to bloom
worse in women. "I know what I'd like to do," Jade said. "Line up
those little ones and snuff them out before their mothers' eyes.
That would get results."

"Cool down, Jade," he warned.

"The Patriarch's Law wasn't made for catfish, I tell you. Not
for their Protectors, not for their daughters. All those little brats
will spit in your eye as sure as that old cat you just threw out."

15

Around the globe, all the native children that could be found were
hauled in to the Valan company bases. At Headquarters, that
meant over a hundred youngsters were herded into the infirmary
under Doctor Nathan's supervision. The age range eliminated troublesome infants and adolescents, but still they did not settle in
easily. Unless sedated, they would not stay in their beds; instead,
they huddled in corners underneath, as if seeking a tunnel-like
shelter. Finally Nathan had the beds wheeled out and spread mattresses across the floor. That seemed to work better.

Food was another problem, until Spinel was called in to advise
the staff. Spinel turned out to be helpful in other ways; he was
known and trusted by the Raia-el children, and he knew all their
games and stories. Soon he was indispensable to Nathan, as he

kept the girls entertained and in reasonable health. The doctor was relieved to keep some respect for Patriarchal Law, and Realgar was convinced he could keep the little ones until their mothers gave in.

Spinel was kept too busy to think, in the mattress-lined infirmary, with the girls who clamored for a story or the others who had to be coaxed to eat. He felt a warm glow inside. For the first time in months, he thought, he was really doing something to help his Sharer sisters.

Some of the girls still huddled alone, withdrawn, with hollow stares. Spinel winced to see them, the ones who would not respond. But others had recovered their wits quickly, and the older ones tried to arrange some kind of order in their strange surroundings. Wellen mimicked Usha's brisk mannerisms, urging others to sweep off their mattresses and finish the food on their plates, even if it did not taste like the squid steamed at home.

As they recovered courage, the girls began to clamor for their mothers again, more boldly now. Wellen decided to call a "Gathering" to address the problem, since everyone knew that the Gathering had the last word on everything. No one there had a selfname yet, but they could choose them easily enough—the Teasing One, the One Who Won't Go to Sleep, the One Who Spits Up Her Food. Wellen was simply the Screamer, since everyone agreed she screamed louder and more piercingly than anyone else could. Spinel called himself the Impulsive One, and some girls complained they did not know what that meant, but he stuck with it.

They crowded closely into one of the wards; an elbow knocked Spinel's eye when he tried to rearrange his cramped legs. The room was full of wriggling arms and translucent webbed hands, and voices chattering excitedly all at once.

The door to the corridor swung out and a staff nurse poked his head in.

"It's okay," Spinel called out. "Just another game."

The white coat vanished.

"*Quiet!*" Wellen shrieked. She had no idea how to start a Gathering, but this way seemed effective. The girls settled down to a hum of whispering and giggles as they shoved into each other. "All right," said Wellen, "the reason we're making a Gathering is to figure out how to get home."

"Home, I want to go ho-ome," whined Malsha, and she began to cry. Others joined the chorus. Spinel's throat stuck and he thought, Another minute of this and I'll be crying, too. He hugged Malsha and tried to soothe her as she pressed her head to his chest.

"We *all* want to go home. But how?" Wellen's eyebrows furrowed like Usha's.

"Swim home!" piped Weia Who Spits Up Her Food.

"Yes, swim home," others joined, and their mattresses squeaked as they bounced.

Spinel called above their bobbing heads, "The guards will stop you. The guardbeam will reach you and bring death."

"We won't reach for any guardbeam," Wellen said.

"But the beam will reach you anyhow." From the top of the garrison, a directed-energy unit aimed constantly at the sea around the perimeter. There could be no escape by sea.

Someone said, "Let's float away on airblossoms."

"Good idea," said Wellen. "Where do we get airblossoms?"

"We'll send for them by clickfly. My mom will send them."

"Mine, too. . . ."

Spinel sighed. The idea was less than practical, but it would keep their hopes up.

A girl started to moan, drowning out the discussion. "Ssh," said the others, hugging and patting her. But her sister shook her head. "She's tired of gathering. She always does that when she's had enough."

Wellen's eyes opened wide. "We've all had enough. We'll all scream. We'll *all scream*, until they let us go home." She took a deep breath, shut her eyes, and screamed at the top of her lungs.

Within minutes, every girl in the room had joined in. Spinel clapped his ears against the din; then he picked himself up and stepped awkwardly over squirming bodies to reach the door. As he pushed the door open, a nurse and Doctor Nathan came running down the corridor. "What's going on?" shouted Nathan, his voice barely audible.

"It's just a game—" The screams drowned him out; it was hopeless.

Nathan pulled Spinel down the corridor until they could hear each other. "What set them off?"

"They want to go home," Spinel admitted.

The doctor wiped his sleeve across his forehead. His eyes closed, then opened to gaze balefully at Spinel. "What's keeping their mothers, anyway? Why don't they give in and get their daughters back?"

Spinel shrugged and looked at his feet. "Maybe they don't know how." He tried to squelch any thought of what Merwen and the rest must be going through.

"Can't you calm the girls again?" The doctor rubbed his hands anxiously.

Curious, Spinel wondered what would happen if the girls could not be calmed. "I don't think so," he said reflectively. "Once they get started, they'll scream for hours."

Nathan rolled his eyes and sighed. "Torr's name, I'll have to sedate the whole lot of them."

"Oh, no, don't do that." The thought of all those children lying doped sickened him. Already several nurses were at the door with their needles poised. "Wait. Let them outside for a while, that will do it. They need more swimming time."

Nathan looked relieved. "Sure, they can spend the rest of the day in the swim cage."

So the nurses hustled them out to the swim cage, a giant collander with a fence around the edge, set in the water off the deck. Gleefully the girls plunged in, while guards collected at the edge and ran boats around the fence of the cage. Spinel joined the children for a while, diving and splashing and chasing one another.

By suppertime, the girls had to be coaxed back out of the water for their meal in the detested infirmary. In fact, they came more easily than usual, since the exercise had whetted their appetites. Spinel urged them out, promising plates full of fresh fish for dinner, with a long song-story about Shora to share afterward. When the last pair of webbed feet had padded off to the infirmary, he leaned exhausted in the outer doorway, where a wet trail remained as if a caravan of frogs had marched in.

Nathan laid a hand on Spinel's bare back. "I don't know how we'd manage without you. I would have given up long ago."

"Thank you, sir," Spinel began, but something in the doctor's praise gave him pause. "What do you mean, given up?"

"If those girls wasted away to nothing, I couldn't very well keep them here. I'd lose my license."

Spinel was chilled. Did his comfort for the children only prolong their captivity?

"Come in for your supper," Nathan added. "You've more than earned it."

"In a minute, sir."

The door clicked shut. Alone, Spinel watched the twilit sky. A rush of suppressed thoughts welled up in his skull. There were Merwen and Usha and all the families of Raia-el, ground to pieces by the Valan machine. Lystra, he knew, was locked away beyond sight or sound, subject to horrors of which only rumors trickled out on the tongues of Jade's guards. In the midst of it all, Spinel himself had become nothing more than a gear in that machine, making the wheels turn while he enjoyed a false freedom. He was worse than useless here; he would be better off dead.

Spinel found himself walking aimlessly across the windswept deck, toward the perimeter fence. As he reached a gate, his feet dragged to a halt.

The sentry grinned and lunged forward. "Haven't had enough ocean?" Her voice was a gruff contralto.

"I guess not." Spinel forced a careless tone and twirled the starstone on his bare chest.

The gate creaked and clanged. "You come back when my shift's up, and I'll show you a good time."

Spinel's heart pounded as he skipped along the open edge, an arm's-length away from the waves and death from the guardbeam. But there were rafts beyond the horizon, where he belonged. Maybe the land beyond death was like that, a living raft on the infinite sea.

In the watchtower atop the headquarters complex, an alarm buzzed. The guard on duty leaped from his chair where he had slept for the past half hour.

Outside the southeast window, the beam stretched down to the sea, where it ended in a cloud of steam.

The monitor droned that a man without an identity tag had dived off the deck a few seconds before. Place of impact had sustained direct fire; estimated chance of hit, eighty-two percent.

The guard yawned and watched the steam roll over the raft seedlings. Ten to one it was just another legfish plopped over the deck. Unless some poor bloke forgot his tag.

Five minutes passed, then ten. Still the monitor scanned blank. Satisfied, the guard turned away. Even if somebody had dived deep enough to avoid boiling, he would have had to come up for air by now.

In the infirmary ward, Wellen tugged at the white rags of the malefreak that was clearing plates away. "Spinel promised to share a story," Wellen croaked, her voice still hoarse from the screaming. "Where is Spinel?"

"Don't know." The malefreak went on stooping to collect plates, some of which Wellen had stacked neatly, while others had landed face down, spreading greenish sauce over the mattress. No matter how hard she and Spinel tried, they could not get every little sister to share cleaning up. Wellen wished her own mother could share this job once; then she would never complain about her own daughters anymore.

Wellen gasped; for a moment she wanted home so badly that everything went black in front of her eyes. Slowly it ebbed away. It had been worst the first day, when she had waked up to this nightmare of malefreaks in vulturous plumage, flat walls with sharp creases whose length tricked the eyes, nauseating smells and jarring sounds. She had held onto Weia and kept her eyes shut, hoping it would all go away. But it had not.

Then Spinel had come—Spinel, the funny creature who was a malefreak yet was different, somehow. Spinel was the one whom Mama and Mamasister had brought home for a pet, a souvenir of their long journey. Spinel brought good luck, she felt, since Mama had come home safe with him. This time, now, Spinel had not brought Mama back, but he always promised that Mama would come soon, if only the girls stayed brave.

Where was Spinel? Gone to fetch Mama?

In the far corner, Malsha was arranging leftover seaweed on her scalp like Valan headfur. "See," she called to the malefreak, "I'm a Valan now. Can I go home?"

Irritated, the malefreak wiped Malsha's head with a cloth. Wellen giggled loudly to bother him some more. But he just dumped the plates onto a cart and pushed it down the tunnel outside.

Wellen wrinkled her nose at the departing white coat. It was no use; Lystra had always said that you could not get the truth out of someone who hid herself in rags.

As evening wore on, she fretted more. Something was wrong for Spinel to be away this long. The other girls sensed it too, and some started whining for Spinel and his story. Malsha would probably cry all night without a story.

When the malefreak came back to put out lights, the girls chorused, "Where is Spinel?"

"Don't know." He looked away.

Malsha said, "I won't go to sleep, then."

"Me neither, me neither."

"We'll scream again," Wellen warned.

The malefreak turned to her, eyes like pinheads. "Spinel won't come back anymore. He went home. He tells you to stay and be good."

Wellen sucked in her breath. "That can't be. Spinel couldn't share parting like that. I know—he's in the stone-place with Lystra!"

"Stone-place!" Malsha gasped and began to cry.

"Is he there, is he?" Wellen sprang at the malefreak and tore at the white cloth. If only she could get rid of those rags, maybe the malefreak could share truth.

The malefreak slammed her back onto the mattress and uttered Valan gibberish. "Spinel is dead, do you hear? He tried to escape. Let that share a lesson with you. You share any more trouble, you'll die too."

With that, the lights went out.

Dazedly Wellen groped across the mattress. "Weia?" Her sister clung to her, and Malsha crept close also for comfort. *Dead... Spinel... dead.*

Wellen barely slept that night. Someone was always whimpering or sobbing. All she could think of was Spinel, who must be dead, like the old grandmother she had seen once, all shriveled up, her arms crossed in calm before the coral deathweights at her wrists pulled her down through the ocean, with the songs floating after. *Sing for those who dwell on land.* What if Lystra were dead too, by now? What if Mama and Mamasister were dead?

In the morning Wellen stared listlessly at the bowl of breakfast mush.

Weia wrinkled her nose at it. "I won't eat that."

"Me neither," Wellen decided.

The nurse took no notice.

Wellen cleared her throat. "I *won't* eat, at all, anymore. Not a thing, until I go home."

16

By the second week of the hostage operation, Realgar was losing patience. He had not expected the children to fill his infirmary for more than a day or two. Was there not a native mother on this planet who would cure the Plague to get her own daughters back?

At other bases, his troops were a headache. Dolomites seemed to follow orders, but the Iridians who had been up here the longest tended to have trouble "finding" native children on the rafts. Or else the kids would "escape" after a few days. One captain even had the cheek to claim that without birth certificates she could not verify the age range according to orders.

The general issued reprimands, but with resistance so widespread he could not press too far, lest word reach the Palace that his command was ineffective. To replace the troops was better; but how could he do that with the planet under quarantine?

Troop morale plummeted as the Purple Plague spread. Only Siderite seemed to take some hope, even a perverse satisfaction, out of the present stalemate. The day he turned purple, Siderite packed off to Raia-el, put up a tent, and stayed there, having promised that he would get his studies going again, one way or another. Realgar had let him go and detailed a helicopter to drop off supplies and spy on him. Anything was worth a try, at this point.

Today a boatload of natives were detected, approaching Headquarters. This, Realgar hoped at last, was a delegation to sue for terms.

As soon as they landed, however, the natives simply sat before the fence and turned white. Realgar's hopes fell, and his anger kindled. He went out to the perimeter to view this astounding sight: five pallid Sharers facing soldiers awash in dreadful violet, as if the color had seeped directly from one side to the other. No one spoke, except the inescapable voice of the sea.

Realgar strode stiffly past them as if reviewing troops. They were the same five who had come to him for the first prisoners: the Protector, the long-nosed one, the one who had been pregnant, the quiet one, and the guerrilla. All had turned to statues of ice, their lips frozen shut.

They're inhuman, he thought. They are wild things. I would not begin to understand them, even if I cared to.

Realgar barked at the captain, "Get rid of them."

"Sir?"

"Fifty kilometers out. And set the guardbeam on automatic."

"Yes, sir." If the captain recognized the significance of this move, she showed no sign. Any native who came within ten meters of the deck would be incinerated.

Realgar returned to his office. Jade had left a message, and he called her on the monitor.

"General, those clickflies are a gold mine of information, and we just hit pay dirt. Natives have lifeshaped a virus—a Valan-killing virus."

"A what?"

"It says, essentially, 'We here at Sriri-el have lifeshaped a virus to make an end of Valans, and what do you sisters out there think of using it?"

For a moment his throat tightened. Realgar had suspected this all along, that something might have slipped past even Malachite the Infallible. Still, he reminded himself that the lifeshaping places of the most intractable rafts had been smashed open, and nothing worse than mutant breathmicrobes had emerged.

"It's a bluff," Realgar decided. "They know you've cracked their code, Jade, and they're trying to scare us."

"Possibly," she admitted. "There's another good one, about hostages released. I checked and confirmed it: a Dolomite company let all their native hostages go."

"Indeed," said Realgar icily. "There's an explanation, I suppose?"

"'Whereas,'" she quoted, "'the native witch-women bewitched our encampment in the manner detailed below, and whereas Dolomite regulations forbid battle with witches, the offspring of said witches have been released and all further contact is to be kept to a minimum.'"

"The trollheads," Realgar muttered. "What the devil's got into them?" In combat Dolomites were tigers; he had seen them on

Valedon. Outnumbered five to one, a company of them had stormed a Pyrrholite outpost, smashed through its defenses, and held the breach until reinforcements arrived.

"Witches, that's what. Witches to send hailstorms to fell their crops and decimate their sheep herds." Jade's voice was thick with sarcasm.

"You reassured them, of course."

"I invoked every Torr-forsaken authority we've got: the High Protector, the doctors, the scientists—nothing made a dent in their skulls. Witches are witches, as far as they're concerned."

And two more divisions of Dolomites were just settling in. Damn Talion, he should have known better. "Get me Horak on line, immediately."

The Dolomite Major General Horak was responsible for those mutinous soldiers. His lightshape soon appeared in the viewing chamber, broad-chested with huge arms. Horak wore Iridian uniform, as did all the general staff, but he kept his thick beard and his mustache that curved in twin spirals.

"Now, Horak, what can you tell me about witches at Base Eighty-six?"

Horak thrust his jaw forward. "General, I graduated from the Academy, and I know as much as any modern fighting man." There was a slur on the word "modern." "My people have venerable traditions which have guided us since the birth of Valedon. If you so order, I will request the Protector of Dolomoth to send a Spirit Caller of the First Rank, who is authorized to neutralize witches."

"That will not be necessary. Realgar knew what was going on here. Each province had made its own way to cope with the Iridian hold on technology. Sardish lords served Iridis to the letter and received the highest favor in return. Pyrrholites set up a rival center, which thrived until it was smashed. Dolomites rejected "modernity" altogether and cultivated over the years an elaborate counterstructure of myth and mysticism. Their faith in the myths infused their independence with a mulish strength, a strength that could be useful, when it was not a damned nuisance.

Realgar was not about to let a man under his command make a fool of him by invoking a Spirit Caller. "Horak, your troops could use some air-raid drills to dispel the local magic. Alert all bases for mock attacks via satellite, at unannounced times, until further notice. Full response maneuvers will be expected."

Horak showed no reaction, but Realgar expected that his troops would rather deal with "witches" than with unholy lightning from the stars.

Later that day, Nathan reported that the native children in the infirmary were still refusing food. "I think it's a hunger strike," he said.

"A hunger strike? I thought you had the kids under control."

"We did, sir, until that young Spirit Caller tripped the guard-beam. He was like a pied piper with them."

Realgar shook his head. "We've got to tighten security. The troops just don't understand that."

"Yes, sir, it's hard, with no combat for months—"

"We *are* in combat, Doctor, and don't you forget it."

"Yes, of course, sir," said Nathan placatingly, "the troops just can't see it, that's all."

Realgar was tired of hearing it. His own children were still hostage to this Purple Plague. "Let the kids starve. And let their mothers hear about it."

17

After the aborted witness in whitetrance, it took Merwen hours to swim back, picking her way among the raft seedlings. She rested at last with Yinevra on a branch off Raia-el. Yinevra lifted her chin ahead, and her eyes stared past Merwen, lids hooded, lines drawn down from the corners. Yinevra shared Merwen's nightmare, as surely as they sat together, a hand's-breadth apart. The sense of that sharing filled Merwen's mind and touched corners nearly forgotten, across the long years since the time when they had shared everything with each other. Merwen's lips moved, but for a long while she could say nothing. The wind breathed a shrill song past her ears. "It's three days since the last clickfly sighted Wellen." The girls would sicken unless they swam in the sea each day.

"And Lystra?" Yinevra asked.

Merwen swallowed hard. She had heard nothing of Lystra, except words she should have Unheard, from the Valan wordweaver at the soldier-place.

A wave crashed up the branch. Merwen watched the beads of water form on her arms and on Yinevra's legs. Yinevra lifted herself to stand, then offered a hand to help Merwen up. She accepted, and with that touch the old specialness sparked between them. For the first time in many years, for just the thinnest web's-breadth of time, they both reached beyond their names together.

As they walked toward the silkhouse, they passed Siderite's tent, a bit farther up toward the ridge. Siderite's silent presence was a challenge to Merwen. It beckoned her to respond, to accept this Valan who seemed ready to turn purple with Sharers, as Spinel had, and Nisi. Still, a helicopter hovered over him at all times. He was not free of death-hastening yet.

Outside the silkhouse, Usha and Shaalrim were talking in somber tones, while Lalor already sat in white. Merwen walked up quickly and caught Usha's waist. "What is it now?"

Usha's lips hung heavily. "Eight from Umesh-el went to the soldier-place, to witness in white, as we did. Four did not return."

"Caught in stone?" she said faintly.

"Beyond stone." Usha could say no more.

Ishma, the stonesick one, explained, "Columns of light-that-is-death struck from the tip of the soldier-place to the sea. Yes, there will be more death to come, in more unimagined ways, until Shora Herself shall come to an end."

Merwen said sternly, "Death will come until the end of time, what's new about that?" But the news bore down on her like weights of coral. Four more to mourn, and still there was no end in sight to the horrors Valans would share in the name of the wage of Death.

Usha stirred again. "The children," she remembered. "They are starving, clickflies say. They will not eat, trapped in stone."

"See," hissed Yinevra, "our daughters have more backbone than their elders. Those death-hasteners must *go*. Send them a worse plague, Usha, to drive them away. Hordes of stinging mites, perhaps. Even Nisi says it's the only way. I tell you, Merwen, what else can you share with sisters who know only pain?"

There they were, at odds again. "Share more of their pain,"

said Merwen, "until they run dry. An ocean swallows infinite pain."

"But Valans don't belong in this ocean. I insist—"

"Try a pain-stopper, then," suggested Ishma. "The drug we use for children who don't yet know whitetrance. In other raft systems, sisters have shared this drug with soldiers. The soldiers love it, and they bring our children back."

Usha said, "That drug is not healthy; it must be used with care." But there was a hungry question in her eyes.

Sickened, Merwen looked away. Then her eyes widened at a sight by the water's edge. A fishing boat was drawn up, and three Sharers stepped out onto the raft core. One of them was Spinel.

Time stopped; the joy Merwen felt was almost too sudden. Somehow she found herself embracing him, and they held for a long while. Spinel's hair had grown out again, and something hard pressed Merwen's cheek. It was the starstone that hung from his neck. That would cause trouble, but for now it only mattered that Spinel was home. "At last, Spinel, at last you're home again. Did . . . anyone else?"

Spinel shook his head, and his headfur tossed like the fins of an angelfish. "I escaped. I dove way under and swam, until these sisters picked me up. They would not share speech for three days, but I'm not Unspoken, am I? I had to escape, because of the children; they're trying to get out, and—"

"You mean Wellen and Weia? Are they all right, are they?"

The news spread, and mothers came from everywhere to ask after this one or that one. Spinel had to tell many times how the girls were eating, how frightened they were, and whether they might come home soon. But he had nothing to say about Lystra.

By nightfall Spinel was exhausted, his throat hoarse from sharing with the mothers any last shreds of hope for their girls. The swarm of tiny faces he had left behind still haunted him when his eyelids closed. Sharers were turning away now, and some entered whitetrance to mourn for the witnessers of Umesh-el. But not everyone could mourn at once; there were the infants to feed, and airblossoms to harvest, and a shockwraith hunt the next day.

Merwen's silkhouse was full, now, with Shaalrim and Lalor and their infant, and those three strangers whose look pried at him as if something were wrong. The strangers seated themselves between

Spinel and the doorhole, their mute presence telling him that he did not belong there. Spinel was perplexed and impatient. Would he have to plead with them for days, as he had with those other sisters? He was not the children's jailer. Merwen was here, she would explain.

"Merwen?" She stood beside the doorhole, in no hurry to explain. Uneasily Spinel rubbed his palms at his waist.

Merwen walked over and clasped his shoulders, looking up to him now. "We still share no stone, Spinel."

He blinked, "Oh, right." Between his fingers he twirled the starstone, its smooth surface warmed by his chest. "But this is different. It's a starstone, like Uriel's; it's *me*. I'll keep it to myself. It won't hurt anyone."

Merwen whispered, "The choice is not mine alone."

"You mean—" Spinel looked again at the three sullen strangers who blocked the doorhole. He would have to outstare all of them; it was worse than when Lystra had gone sour. "Look, what's the matter with you? It's just a bit of 'rock,' that's all. You got to get used to it."

"Yet it means something special to you, I share that," said Merwen. "It also means something very different to us."

"Well, I don't care what it means." He pushed her arms away. "I didn't come back from Valedon and escape the guardbeam just to argue about a stonesign with *a bunch of stupid catfish.*"

Spinel took off and ran from the house along the water's edge where the branches pleated into channels, as he recalled so well. He trembled, furious at everyone: at his own lost family, at the soldiers who came to crush a planet underfoot, at Sharers who sat by and let it happen while they quibbled over nothing.

A breeze from the sea chilled him slightly. His anger cooled until only a dull ache remained, the emptiness of longing for a home that was not. He had left home to find home and found only death on a dying ocean.

When Merwen appeared he was startled, though he had figured she would come after him. What in Valedon did she want from him? he wondered, not for the first time. He inched away, avoiding her touch.

"Spinel, those who share our home now are stonesick: they have to stay away from stone. Do you understand?"

"Of course I do," Spinel snapped. "Didn't I sit with Lystra on the traders' steps?" he glared accusingly. "What good was that, after all? Why don't you get rid of all Valans for good? Then you'll be rid of stone too."

"I don't want that. I can't want it."

"But how can you let the soldiers—" He threw up his hands at a loss to say what he meant in Sharer tongue.

"We share healing with soldiers, and we tunnel through the barriers that divide us. We must resist their illness as long as we can, or how will they learn? You learnshared these ways before."

"I know your ways. I shared them with my sisters in Chrysoport. But I didn't know that you have 'things' to fight soldiers." Spinel knew a word for "fight," but not for "weapon." "Usha could lifeshape a thing that would make the soldiers die, before they make you die."

Merwen was silent. Spinel suddenly recalled just how forbidden it was, impossible even for a Sharer to think about killing another human person. For a minute he thought that Merwen would Unspeak him, as Lystra had.

Merwen said, "Do you really wish to see me hasten death?"

The thought shook him unexpectedly. Spinel could not begin to imagine Merwen herself taking a life; even to try made him incredibly sad. His hand lifted of itself to touch her cheek, round as a jewel beneath her eye. "I—" He said in Valan, "I don't want them to get you, that's all."

"Spinel, do you remember the ancients, how they lived and died? Their knowledge was so great that they could swim among the stars, as we swim among rafts. Yet a spark ignited them and they burned, until nothing but fire remained, and a few lost ones, groping among the cinders. Only Shora escaped, to a place that will quench fire, will drink of it forever. Can't you see that?"

"I can believe you when you say it," he whispered as if mesmerized.

Merwen looked down. "It's yourself you have to believe. Perhaps Raia-el is not the place for you, just now. Nisi will welcome you on Leni-el."

"Nisi? Not Lady Nisi?" Spinel was astonished. Not that noble lady who had left him in Iridis after his taste of servos and splendor? It was one thing to leave Chrysoport, but Nisi had left a highstreet of Iridis to return to this battered world.

* * *

On Leni-el, Spinel found Nisi working a seasilk loom as she had so often before. Thinner than ever, her bare shoulder blades pointed sharp as a soldier's uniform when she threw the shuttle. She looked up, with little surprise; clickflies had brought word. "So you return, Spinel the non-commoner." Her lips twisted in a smile, but she kept up her speed at the treadle. The defiance in her gaunt face seemed to have crystallized in the wells of her eyes. "And why did you choose exile?"

Spinel uncomfortably traced circles with his toe. "I just came home, or tried to." Home had been swimming with Lystra among the branch shadows, taming the starworms and hunting the shockwraith, or sitting with Lystra on the traders' steps, or lying with her out on an empty raft, just within reach of the sea. What had broken it? The loss rushed at him, and he clenched his jaw to hold it back.

"I'm a double exile, you know," Nisi said. Spinel listened with reluctance, torn as he was by his own sorrow. "Yes," she went on, "that is why I came here from Raia-el." The treadle stopped, then, and she sat back to gaze across the sea. Somewhere helicopters droned, more common than fanwings these days. "Where did we go wrong, my parents and I? We believed in free trade, in the wealth of things to be shared—in a way, I still do. It could be, could have been, if . . ." Vexedly she clasped and unclasped her fingers. "No, it's too late. Shora has only one choice left, and Merwen would rather die than choose it."

"You mean, to fight back? Nisi, Sharers could fight back. Usha can make things—"

"Of course they can, at any time. Malachite was wrong." Nisi shuddered. "It was hard for me to face that fact, I whose House served the Patriarchy since before I was born. But it's true. Sharers could wipe out the Valan force in a week—now, not generations from now."

"So why don't they?"

"Because then they wouldn't be Sharers anymore. Or so they think." Nisi sighed. "They think they're fighting hard enough now. Outside Headquarters, nearly half the bases are letting children go."

"Really? Why?" This was cheering news.

"Annoyance, persuasion, persistence." Nisi flashed a grin.

"Sharers are awfully good at it. They ought to be, after thousands of years of practicing on each other."

"It can work," Spinel exulted. "Even in Chrysoport, we held off the Dolomites with nothing. We could have thrown them out, if only—"

"No. Not in the long run. Soldiers don't work like a Gathering. Generals run wars, and generals mean to win. And Ral—he's a Sard in the end." Nisi's voice faltered, and she twisted her head back until the tendons pulled straight on her neck.

Spinel said, "I think Merwen means to win, too."

Nisi's sudden glare startled him. "Win what, Spinel? Don't you know why Merwen brought *us* here? To convince Sharers everywhere that Valans are human, *humans who can't be killed.* Better for them if we had stayed where we belonged."

"It can't be like that. There has to be something else," Spinel exclaimed, trying to convince himself. Nisi's shuttle was already flying again. But it had to be more than plain foolishness that had brought Merwen to weave in the shadow of the firemerchant's door.

18

In the wake of the latest outbreak of death-hastening at the soldier-place, the Raia-el Gathering met yet again. They met with a sense that many sisters had swum to the end of their patience with Valan horror—and with startling reports from distant rafts where whole Gatherings had done the same.

Scattered plantlights echoed the evening stars as sisters settled within the hollow. Between Merwen and Usha sat Flossa the Reckless One, nursing a plantlight before her crossed legs. Flossa and most of the older girls had chosen selfnames exceptionally early, after seeing their younger sisters wrenched helplessly away.

This evening, selfnamers waited a long while to reach oneness with Shora. The distant waves rumbled, and clickflies stuttered fragments of news long delivered. Yet these sounds only thickened the stillness of the Gathering, and no one seemed eager to stir the surface.

"All right," said Trurl at last, "if anyone can suggest a way out of the mess we're in, it's high time she shared it. Otherwise we might as well go back to our silkhouses." Trurl was brusk, even harried, and her nose cut a grim outline against the yellowish glow of lights.

Someone called out faintly, "What can we do now, except just go on?"

"I just want to understand, first," said another. "We know why the seaswallower comes, and what the fleshborer is about. But why do Valan *people* share this horror? How does that feed the web?"

"That's the question," said Trurl dryly. "Even our 'Skycrossers' have yet to share an answer."

Merwen contained herself, for she was tired of wearing that name. Instead Lalor rose, a little shyly, keeping a hand on Shaalrim's shoulder. "I can't answer why, except for one thing: Valans don't learn whitetrance, and they can't control their own pain. So how can they control anything else? Their souls are trapped by their shells."

"Perhaps they've lost their souls altogether," Trurl reflected.

Startled, Lalor quickly sat again.

Yinevra got up and strode to the middle of the Gathering. "Valans have lost their souls, and more. They have regressed, devolved, into a lower state of life, lower than human." Yinevra paused to let this sink in. "We have ample proof of their regression. Not only Sharer children and survival are threatened, but all the other creatures of Shora, the lesser sisters, seaswallowers, fanwings, rafts—from snail to swallower, not one is untouched by the Valan pestilence!" Her voice had risen to a cry. "We are protection-sharers; as Shora protects us, so we must protect Her heritage. When the balance tips, when the web stretches—who remains to balance life and death, if not us?"

A hushed tension flowed and stretched among the selfnamers. Yinevra's wish was well known, but there had never been such a compelling argument for it. Merwen felt again the fatalism of her first Gathering upon return from Valedon. She knew the current of her heart, and that she would follow it still; but she was drifting, not swimming, she realized with dismay.

A defensive note entered Yinevra's voice. "I know better than to expect the decision from this raft. But there are other Gatherings at other rafts, and other lifeshapers. Clickflies have come from Oon-elion, where a virus was shaped to reduce the Valan pestilence. They will soon choose to release it."

So this was what Sharers had come to, isolated as they were now, without the daily farsharing of the starworm's song to bind them together in strength. Merwen had crossed the sky thinking she alone could set an example for Sharers everywhere to forestall this day. Perhaps that was her hubris. Certainly she had not counted on the stifling of the starworm's song, and the fragmentation that bred despair.

"Already it may be too late," whispered Usha to Merwen. "That lifeshaper should never have made such a virus. If it escaped by accident, what then?"

"Speak up," Merwen urged.

"I can't anymore. My strength left with Weia and Wellen. I feel drained as an empty whorlshell."

Merwen's pulse raced; she longed to deny it, to say—but there was nothing to say, only the end of this sad hour to share. Afterward, if there were a dawn beyond the dark, she could no longer see it.

Trurl said, "It is highly unlikely that the Gathering of Oon-elion would release such a terrible thing without the consent of all Gatherings of Shora. That is why we must respond at once."

"Death hastens those who hasten death," someone murmured. "What other response can there be?"

"Exactly," said Yinevra. "That is why the death-hasteners must die. As humans, in spirit, they have already died. Their race has regressed and decayed."

Many voices stirred and murmured, "I share that." Yinevra's wish was so easy, as seductive as waterfire.

From behind, Ama's fingers brushed Merwen's arm. Immediately Merwen gestured to Trurl, and she and Usha raised Ama's shoulder between them, so that her voice might carry farther. Ama said, "Before we hasten to hasten death, let us at least share the word of that one of the Valan race who has taken a selfname with us."

There was a shamed hush, with furtive glances at Nisi, who still came to Raia-el Gatherings though she rarely spoke. Nisi stood now, a stark, haunted figure, her cheeks sunken. "You ask too much of me. I would rather throw myself into a seaswallower than keep Sharers from doing what they must, that Shora may live."

Merwen listened with bitter sadness, as if a storm had washed out in a day a raft she had nurtured for a generation. Trurl still cast about for further words for Valans, and there were few. At last, Trurl's eye fixed on Merwen and gazed for some time. "Impatient One, I hear the sorrow in your heart; but if you will not speak, share a sign at least."

Merwen lifted herself, and for a moment she felt lightheaded and waited to steady herself. "It was I who first said that Valans are more terrible than any creature we have ever known. I said also that they are one with us. What I've heard tonight only confirms my belief."

For many long minutes nothing spoke except the sea and the keening breeze that carried clouds past the stars. Then Yinevra rose again, a tall silhouette against the plantlights. Merwen could not see her face, but her voice broke with anger. "You," said Yinevra. "I never thought even you could twist things so, to set our lives and the lives of our children worth no more than Valan bestiality."

"Then say what you mean, Yinevra. Are Valans human or not? Go on, say it. In the name of poor Virien, I dare you to say it." Her heart was beating too fast, and red streaked before her eyes; she sat down hard on the raft before she would collapse.

"Go on, then." Yinevra's voice had fallen an octave. "Yes, send clickflies to every raft in the sea: tell all our lifeshapers to tie their hands lest they shape death instead. But for myself, I say this: I will return to the soldier-place, again and again, and the first day I spend in Valan hands will be my last. I will not share an ounce of will with those degenerates that crossed the sky just to putrify our seas."

Merwen's anger rushed at the notion that she herself shared the will of those sick ones. Even so, Yinevra's bluff had been called: she knew in the end that Merwen was right. And with such a vow, Merwen thought bleakly, Yinevra will not last long. She is my sister, and I cannot bear to lose her.

19

At headquarters, the guardbeam ran haywire one morning and scorched a patrol boat, killing three of the crew. Realgar immediately called off the beam until the glitch could be fixed. It turned out that a native had actually climbed up into the boat from the water and her unauthorized presence had set off the beam.

To improve troop morale, he ordered war games maneuvers—sea battles between fleets, and satellite raids. These were explained to the Palace as "preparations for assault," though Talion pointed out that combat was expensive enough without footing the bill for both sides. Realgar swallowed his disgust at the complaint; it was simply incompetent of the Palace bureaucrats to send him on a campaign they were not willing to pay for.

He still had to stare at his own livid face every morning. And now that doctor was nagging him about the children again. "I have to tell you, sir," Nathan said, "that I can't maintain these hostages much longer under present conditions."

"Can't you force-feed them?"

"Their stomachs won't hold it. And intravenous nourishment is inadequate for growing bodies. There's the Law to think of, sir," he finished hurriedly.

"Kids spring back fast. Just keep them alive, that will do."

Nathan's mouth drew into a knot. "As a doctor, sir, I can't allow—"

"What's your alternative? Would you prefer to execute their parents?"

"I only know that *this* alternative is outside the Law. As is Colonel Jade's alternative, sir."

This remark startled the general. It startled Nathan himself, too; his eyelids fluttered, and his hands shook as if the words had slipped out by mistake.

There were rumors, of course, that the chief of staff had gone beyond useful mindbending technique in her treatment of the adult prisoners. Realgar was inclined to let her try whatever might work, even primitive methods. But now that the doctor had voiced an objection, he thought he should at least find out what was going on.

He called Jade to his office. "Any progress lately on the mindblocked prisoners?"

Jade's complexion was still dark, except for her pale lips, but she seemed to have gotten over the initial shock of the Purple Plague. "That's hard to say. A prisoner may crack rather suddenly after a long, gradual tightening of the screw."

"Which means they haven't cracked yet, after three months. I'd like to take a look at these hardy creatures."

She hesitated. "I wouldn't advise that, sir. My program of sensory deprivation would be interrupted."

"You must be set up for remote observation."

Jade called to the monitor for transmission to the viewing stage. A glimmer of a lightshape appeared, and she switched off the room lights for a clearer view.

Out of the darkness a corner of a prison cell projected, outlined in sallow monochrome. The figure crouching in the corner emitted a halo of body heat, typical of an infrared image. At first, the figure looked like a monkey asleep in a cage. Then Realgar saw that it was in fact a native prisoner, shriveled and shrunken with the knees folded up to the chin. The limbs were wasted to the bone and twisted like rubber sticks. Between fingers and toes the webbing was torn and stripped, something equivalent to fingernail extraction, Jade said. She enumerated the various chemical and physical treatments, and the duration of each.

Jade showed in succession six more native prisoners. All looked about the same, except that they lay in different portions of their cells. None moved or made any sound. Jade concluded with the most notorious one, who had dared even to talk back to Talion: the daughter of Protector Merwen.

Realgar cleared his throat. "Are they ever conscious?"

"They go in and out," Jade said. "When one wakens, I administer drugs and electrostimulation, in various scientifically devised sequences. Until she reaches the brink of self-termination, in whitetrance; then I pull back. Eventually I'll catch one again in that in-between zone, where the mind is vulnerable yet not completely lost."

Yet all this time not one had cracked, not since the very first prisoners taken, before they had known what the mindprobe was. Realgar frowned with vague unease. "Natives can suicide by throwing a mental switch. So why do they hang on in the face of this... pressure?" He was reluctant to name what Jade was doing, and his reluctance annoyed himself.

Jade said, "Only mental invasion triggers the deathblock. Physical pain is endured until the brain itself breaks down."

"Then you haven't touched their minds, all this time. You haven't reached them at all. How can you break a man to obedience without reaching his mind?"

With a slight shrug, Jade whispered to the monitor. The office filled with flat, normal light that jarred unexpectedly. "Indirect methods take time," Jade added.

Realgar knew it could take months or years to break a professional mindblocked agent. But natives knew nothing of that sort of game. They had nothing to hide except their own free will.

The shapes of the twisted primates persisted in his vision well after Jade had departed. They summed up the appalling uselessness, even irrelevance, of any physical threat to native minds. In the evening, Realgar dined with Jade as usual, though neither was inclined to speak much. Upon finishing, Realgar could barely recall what he had just eaten. He shook himself, straightened the sleeves of his loathed Iridian uniform, and stood abruptly. "Let's get some air."

The two of them strode out to the narrow strip of deck beyond the perimeter fence. A fine spray dampened Realgar's cuffs, and the sea moaned with a hollow sound. From the livid sky came a breeze, sweeter than usual, while below, the rotting seedlings seemed to be dispersed. Perhaps the lifeshapers had finally done something about it.

It shook him to realize how easily he assumed that natives were in control.

The planet is their laboratory. ... If that were true, what could any commander do about it? What could one throw at the sea that the sea could not swallow?

There had to be something, and Realgar would find it, but he needed time.

He stopped and faced out to sea, folding his arms tightly, though he was not all that cold. Jade halted at his elbow. He counted waves as they rolled in and crashed up the side, until the tenth one had passed. "Jade," he said without turning, "I want those prisoners out, kids and all."

"Yes, General. I formally request transfer from—"

Realgar caught her arm. "I don't want your damned transfer, do you hear?" When his breath came easier he went on. "All I know is, whatever we've done so far has failed. Maybe Sharers just can't obey, it's not in their vocabulary. Maybe we have to kill them off one by one, or by the hundreds, or—" He broke off.

"Then why blame me? If I've lost your confidence, send me back to Sardis where at least my career won't hit a dead end."

"Hold on, Jade. We've been through too much together."

"Yes, we have. We've stormed burning camps where children lay in the dirt with their guts hanging out, and the dogs cleaned them up. You've seen enough to turn your hair gray. What's shook you up now?"

"You knew those catfish would never give in, no matter what you did to them."

"What do you know of my methods? You've always detested what I do, as much as you need it. You think I get off on twisting catfish?"

"Nonsense."

"I do hate them, as a matter of fact. They made their nasty bugs to screw up my system, so that I don't even know my own face in the mirror." Jade's lips pulled back harshly in her shadowed face.

"That's unprofessional."

"Is it?" Jade breathed. "For a strategist, you mean, General. You could use a little more hatred in those lower echelons that let the children go."

There was no answer for it. It dawned on Realgar that he had known all along what Jade would be doing to the prisoners. He only grasped at the knowledge now as an excuse to himself, a rationale to back out of the impossible corner he was in, between diehard natives and troops gone soft.

Sharers had neither the strengths nor the weaknesses of ordinary soldiers. They slipped through his fingers like the slimy fish they were. *Know your enemy.* . . . It was hard enough to fathom the Dolomite mentality. How much harder it would be to bridge the gulf of Shora.

20

Usha labored without stopping in her resurrected lifeshaping place, whose walls still smelled of freshly dug raftwood and coral. In the daytime, Flossa and Mirri and a dozen others helped her, preparing substances to retard growth of raft seedlings, parasites to curb the rise of mudworms, nutrient supplements to help fanwings grow back strong. Clickflies hovered constantly, chattering from distant lifeshapers, since all their efforts to heal the sea must mesh as intricately as woven seasilk. With luck, the web would hold.

But Usha kept on not only through the day but all night long as well. Merwen found her alone there, one morning before sunrise, standing and staring into her tangle of vines. Merwen sighed and leaned into Usha's back, curving an arm about her waist. "You never sleep anymore. You don't even swim in the sea. Come out with me, for just a while."

Usha's fingers lifted, then fell again. Merwen pressed her a little tighter. Merwen knew what Usha was going through; it was worse than ever, because the Gathering had closed without action and would have to meet again. Every day without Wellen and Weia was another inch of death. Yet one had to cling to life; there was Flossa to think of, after all.

"Do you know why I don't swim anymore?" Usha's voice was parched. "I dream that one time I will simply turn downward and swim forever to the floor."

Merwen's voice hardened. "Then you're coming away, right now. You must come, Usha."

Usha turned reluctantly. She must have known she would get nothing else done, if she tried to ignore her lovesharer.

Out on the raft branches, thousands of green stalks extended buds from whose tips peeked spots of orange. The cycle of seasons was only too willing to try again. Merwen dipped under, keeping Usha beside her, enjoying the cool shadows among bows of coral, though she still kept an eye out for fleshborers. So far the only fish that streaked past were harmless, brilliantly colored and spotted, their only thought to evade the clutch of a bloated red squid.

Usha looked so beautiful with her pearled inner eyelids, and her swimming was grace itself. Merwen could have watched her for hours on end. Yet even a Sharer has to come up for breath some time, and when Merwen did so, her lids retracted just for a moment to scan the sky.

There were three helicopters, bearing down toward the raft core.

Usha surfaced and gasped. "It's Flossa—they're coming for Flossa now." She plunged and sped back toward the silkhouse. Merwen followed, and by the time they had pulled themselves out of the water, Flossa was outside the door seated in whitetrance, as she had learnshared, while soldiers were pouring out of their monster machines. But others were coming out too: Sharers, little ones—

With a scream Usha ran to gather her two girls. They were emaciated and very quiet, and Weia showed little recognition. Merwen huddled with them, and Flossa kept whispering anxiously, "It's all right now; don't you remember me?"

A hand fell on Merwen's shoulder. "Merwen," said Lalor, "there are others. . . ."

Around her, neighbors were gathering quickly for this long-awaited return of their children. And adults had returned, too, in far worse shape than the children. They were deformed almost beyond recognition. One of them could not have been Lystra. But she was.

The most ravaged ones were hastened to the lifeshaping place, where Mirri and Flossa fitted them with vines of healing substances and immersed them in water-wombs. Lystra rocked slowly within her transparent shell, where she might have to stay for days, perhaps longer. Sharers crowded everywhere, helping the lifeshapers and exclaiming about their loved ones who were home at last. All the while Merwen watched Lystra, barely believing Lystra was here now, and still not quite able to believe her condition. The hands fixed her gaze, Lystra's fingers with the webbing so badly ripped between each that Lystra would not swim for a long time. For a while, nothing else existed for Merwen, as all the sorrow and anger she had shared for Valans was overwhelmed by one question: What sort of mind was it that could willfully share what had happened to Lystra's hands?

An age seemed to pass before Merwen remembered something, and she tore herself away. Outside the silkhouse the sun was setting, and liquid red dribbled down the waves. Merwen went straight to the tent where Siderite had stayed Unspoken for three weeks.

Merwen paused at the folds of the entrance. Inside, Siderite was sitting with his legs crossed and staring at a box full of jumping lightshapes. He blinked to see Merwen, and the box turned black.

Her tongue pressed back in her throat, but she made herself speak.

"Come. You must share this."

Siderite clumsily picked himself up, and the loose folds of his trousers wrinkled like Lystra's skin against her bones. Merwen led him down to the chamber where Lystra and the others were healing.

When the Valan entered, footsteps and chattering ceased. Mirri paused with instruments in hand, her face puckered in a questioning frown. Others stared, and only Usha seemed too busy to notice.

"Our sisters are home at last," Merwen told him.

A smile glowed on his face. "I share your joy," Siderite said.

"Then share this also." Merwen took him by the hand and led him across the chamber, passing the prone figures of weakened children wrapped in blankets. She nodded at the water-womb which enclosed her daughter. "Lystra. You remember Lystra?"

Expressions flitted across his cheeks and lips as if several people struggled inside. Then he wiped his hands back over his head, through the hair that surrounded a bald patch. "I'm sorry," he said, averting his eyes.

"Why?" Merwen asked. "Why is this?"

All around, Sharers watched, fierce enough to pounce on the answer. Siderite reached out to touch Lystra's shell, and hairs lifted on the back of his hand. His lips worked unsteadily. "Fear. They share fear of you, that is all."

Soldiers feared Sharers, as Sharers feared them. Yet the sickness of the soldiers must magnify their fear and twist it into something beyond imagining. Only this pattern could begin to account for what Merwen saw.

Usha came forward and eyed Siderite critically. "What's all this standing about when there's work to be shared? Hurry up and draw out those enzymes with Mirri." Usha was brisk and competent once more, as though this were just another load of refugees from the seaswallowers.

21

On Leni-el Raft, Spinel was overjoyed to see the children back. They were amazed and even frightened to see him after they had heard he was dead. "No, I escaped," he boasted. "I swam under all the way to Sayra-el," which was only a slight exaggeration. "How did you get out?" he asked Mirri's daughter.

"We stopped eating." The girl's voice was small, and her eyes huge and staring. She lay thin and listless in Mirri's arms. Spinel's excitement receded then. Still, he told himself, if only there were a few kids as brave as that back home, Chrysoport would be a different town, probably a free one.

To Nisi he said, "See, we're winning. What kind of general is he, to let a bunch of kids get the better of him?"

Nisi stood at the water's edge, as she often did, pensively watching the horizon, her mouth a dry chiseled slit. For some reason the return of the children alarmed her more than anything. "I can't believe it's the end, for Ral. What his next move is, I can't say, but it will come."

Chilled, Spinel went away in a thoughtful mood. Then everything was forgotten when two clickflies alit on his arm: *"Lystra is home. . . ."*

He jumped and would have dashed off right away to Raia-el. But Lystra was injured, the clickflies said, too badly injured to see anyone. And besides, Merwen's stonesick guests would only bar the door to him again. And Lystra would agree with them.

Spinel flicked the dark stone on his chest, and its sparkle pierced his eye. How easily he could swing it over his neck and toss it to the waves. It meant nothing practical now; he would never need a stonesign again. Yet for just that reason he clung to it, to the one last trace of his Valan self. He could not throw it away without throwing himself after.

Lystra could not have loved him without knowing what he was, a shaper of stone. Or could she have? Was that why she had rejected him, once she saw what he was?

He tried to teach a clickfly to send a love greeting, but it sounded awful no matter how he put it, and besides clickflies were too prolific to trust with something private. So every day he waited with his heart pounding to hear how Lystra was progressing, and whether she was out of her water-womb.

As soon as word came that Lystra was out, Spinel set out for Raia-el. He let the glider squid race ahead at reckless speed, but when he reached the outer branches he released the squid and paddled in slowly, and slower yet when Merwen's silkhouse appeared, its deep blue concave surfaces cupping the sky like webbed fingers. He pulled in the oars for a moment, and he touched the shallow scar on his ankle, reassuring himself that it was still there, that Lystra really had pulled him from the shockwraith once. Suddenly he needed Lystra so badly that it filled his skull and threatened to explode. Again his fingers strayed to the stone on his chest; but he clenched his fist around it until it dug into his palm. Spinel thought, I'll only hate myself, and her too, if I give this up. I'm a Spirit Caller, and a stonecutter's son. I will not deny my fathers.

He tied the boat to a branch, then walked up quickly, light-headed, nearly stepping on the flat things sunning themselves before they slithered down the sides. Ahead, the silkhouse looked about the same as the last time, with the greener sections behind, above the reconstructed lifeshaping tunnels.

Someone was sitting on a low stool beside the doorhole, pulling seasilk between pronged cards and packing the fibers into bundles to be spun. Was she one of the stonesick ones? Spinel stopped. She held her head the way Lystra had, and her elbows swung and her chin nodded to her work, just as he remembered. But this could not be the Lystra he had known.

His mind flashed to the last hour they had shared alone, when he had asked something that she would not give. At that time, she had exuded physical strength, her shoulders and legs shaped by long swimming and wrestling with starworms. Now her limbs had wasted away by half; but the strength was still there, transmuted into something else, a presence that he feared to touch.

"Lystra?" His voice cracked. He glimpsed the scars all over her, even on her breasts. His anger flared, and he wished a soldier had been there so that he could have beaten him to a pulp. But the thought was gone, as soon as a spark on the sea. Lystra was here, now, alive. There was only that huge invisible wall that rose between them.

Spinel sat in front of her and tried to catch her look, as the cards grated past each other. In his ears his pulse drummed, louder than the waves at the water's edge behind. "Lystra. I came back for you. I need you more than anything, and if you won't listen, I won't speak anymore, or eat anymore, or *anything.* Do you understand?"

The cards slowed and she laid them down. Lystra's eyes lifted then, thrilling him with a touch of flame. Her gaze swept down his chest. Then she took up the cards and tossed them on top of the mounded seasilk, picked up the basket, and turned to the doorhole.

Spinel scrambled to his feet. "Lystra, you've got to share this. I gave up everything I could to come back here, but I can't give up my starstone. It's part of *me....* " Despairing, he called after her, "You said you loved me, didn't you? Can't you love *all* of what I am?"

The basket thudded, and fibers were strewn out. Lystra wheeled to face him, her eyes wide and dark. "And you? Could you ever love me, *as I am?*"

His tongue stuck; there was nothing that could begin to say what he felt. His arms went around her, and she held him as hard as ever. The rush of warmth was almost too much to bear, and Spinel thought he would faint from her nearness. He was sure now that Lystra was meant for him, no matter how "different" she was.

Yet now he was frightened, and he found himself shaking with hot tears that fell and rolled down Lystra's back. Gently she cupped his forehead in her hand to look at him. Spinel said, "I—I don't know what will happen to us. I don't know if I can do what I have to, if—" He stopped and swallowed. "Nisi says the soldiers will come back."

Lystra spoke in a voice he had never heard from her. "I learned two things, when I was held in stone. One is that all the stone of Valedon can't touch the will of Shora. The other is that it would be far better for us all to pass Death's threshold in a day than to share the deathhasteners' sickness." She paused. "But it will not happen. Because you are a Valan, and yet a Sharer with us. We will share healing, Spinel."

22

For the first time in weeks, the general heard from Siderite. The scientist appeared on the viewing stage with the roof of his tent slanting behind him. His violet features were full of excitement. "General, I'm back to work again, full steam ahead! And what's more, I've got the cure for the Purple Plague!"

"What?" Realgar started from his chair. "Get back here with it, immediately."

"Oh, no, sir. I can't leave now; I'd lose my credibility. Even talking with you—" Siderite leaned off to the side as if looking for eavesdroppers "You're still 'Unspoken,' you know. But I'll leave samples in the pack for the helicopter to pick up."

"Hold on, there. Where did you get this 'cure,' and how do you know it's not some trick? You haven't 'cured' yourself, I see."

"I don't intend to. I want to stay as native as I can, while I'm here. I worked out the cure with Usha, and we know it works because—well, breathmicrobe biochemistry is well studied, to keep natural mutations in hand, and to maximize oxygen efficiency—"

"All right, send it back." Realgar allowed himself a smile. "If it works, I'll recommend a medal for you."

Siderite said, "There's something else you could do for me that would immensely aid my work in the long run."

"Yes?" Realgar keyed his monitor for a memorandum.

"Pull all your troops out, now. Just let my work go on."

Stung though he was, Realgar thought carefully before replying. "Siderite, how long will they help you, once my troops are gone?"

"As long as I'm here. I'm an apprentice lifeshaper, remember?

In fact, as soon as that damned helicopter stops buzzing around, they'll let me share a selfname with the Gathering."

"I'm not so sure that's a good idea." A "selfname" was what Berenice had taken, before she went off the deep end and caused that dreadful scene with Talion.

Siderite sat up straight. "General, I am a loyal subject of the Patriarch and of Valedon. I have an exemplary record at the Palace, if I may say so. In any event, with or without soldiers on my back, you have no choice but to trust my work."

That was true. Still, Siderite had his weaknesses: Usha, for instance; he had grown quite partial to her. Yes, Siderite could still be controlled. "Pull out, you say. That's easier said than done."

"Is it?" Siderite was relaxed again. "You're in command. Why can't you just declare you've won and go home?"

Realgar laughed shortly and felt better than he had in weeks. "Stick to science, Siderite, and get that plague cure over here." He signed off, then alerted Nathan that the cure was on its way. Good news at last, he thought, with immense relief.

The whole picture was changed now. And the more he thought it over, the more sense he saw in Siderite's suggestion. Of course the Guard would not pull out completely; a token force would remain, with all the satellites, to keep an eye on things. With the plague cured by the natives themselves, Realgar could say in effect that the natives had capitulated. As for lunar developers and their native problems, that was none of his concern. In the end Talion would decide, and while Talion liked to keep the support of the great Houses, he detested costly inconclusive campaigns.

Realgar told Jade what was on his mind. To his surprise, Jade was quick to agree. "I'm all for it, sir. I said from the first we didn't belong in this cursed swamp." But her gaze was absent, and Realgar knew what she was thinking. The natives would remain, especially Protector Merwen, unyielding, unscathed, uncracked.

"Jade, what else could we do here?"

"Look at it this way. Would you war with cockroaches according to the Law? No, you'd hire an exterminator. Catfish aren't human; they're vermin, and that's how to treat them, if only the High Protector gets up his nerve."

"And if Malachite so orders." Malachite wanted something else, and there had to be a way to get it, to break the Sharer will. Realgar would never find it now.

Jade shrugged. "A few loose ends, before we go. Remember

that Valan-killing virus I heard about? Well, they canned it, not because the children went home, but because clickflies swarmed from all over to oppose it. Shocked as schoolmarms, they sounded. If it was just a ruse, somebody sure took it seriously."

"A charade, that's all." Realgar wished he felt as sure as he sounded.

"This other item from the clickflies looks more promising. There's a possible Valan traitor living among the catfish."

"A Valan traitor?"

"Could explain a lot, couldn't it? No wonder they know how to make so much trouble."

"You mean Siderite?"

"No, sir. A nominal Sharer who has lived here for some time. Her name I translate, appropriately enough, as 'Nisi the Traitor.'"

23

It was the season when waterfire should have filled the sea at night, as phosphorescent diatoms multiplied in the wake of the seaswallowers. Instead, there was only a tinge of green light in the waves for a night or two. As if to make up the lack, Merwen dreamed night after night her own cryptic version of the fire that consumed water and sky alike.

Their daughters were home safe, that was the main thing. Even Lystra was recovering faster than Merwen expected: a week under one roof together, and already they had fallen into their first quarrel.

"Mother, what's the matter with you? Was it I who brought Spinel here in the first place? It was smooth swimming, so long as he kept his place like a sandturtle for the children to play with; but as soon as we get serious, you tread water."

Merwen clapped her hands to her head. "Lystra, how can you *say* such things?"

"I'm furious, that's how." A smile wavered on her lips. "I always say things like that when I'm furious."

"Will you go on earning your name forever?"

"Don't you name me, Mother. If you've outgrown your own name, why don't you choose another?"

Merwen said nothing. Lystra fidgeted from one foot to the other, and her toes curled around knobby seams where the torn webbing was knitting back. "All right, I'm sorry." Lystra's voice fell. "I just want to stay here awhile with—with the family. I was alone so long in that place."

"I know, and I want you here too," Merwen said. "I wish you could stay here always, and Spinel also. You can't know what a joy it is for me to see you both happy together."

Lystra spread her hands helplessly. "Then why do you ask us to leave?"

"For one thing, you and I will always quarrel under the same roof." The truth tasted bitter, but was better out.

"Only when you ask crazy things, Mother."

"Lystra, you know how hard it is for our stonesick sisters to face Spinel with the stone. It's a starstone, and I know why he kept it, and I'm gladder than I can say. But Ishma—"

"Well, it's high time our sisters stopped running away from themselves. They will never be free until they face it."

Very angry now, Merwen kept her voice to a low monotone. "There are more kinds of courage than that of swimming to the soldier-place. What courage does it take for a stonesick one simply to live through each day normally? How soon you've forgotten."

"I have *not* forgotten!" Lystra shouted. "How could I, *when I was just as sick as Rilwen?*" She drew back and went on more quietly. "I fought harder, that's all. Through work, and through hatred. I shared more hate with stonetraders than anything, until Spinel came. When Rilwen died, I nearly died with her; but afterward, it was easier, without her example to drag me down. And Spinel helped me then."

"Do you think I don't know all this?"

Lystra shuddered. "I suppose you do. What you don't know is that in the soldier-place I spent three months totally surrounded by stone. It was so dark I never really knew what the place looked like. It was like hanging alone in space, without even stars. And in the end, for me, stone was just that—just nothing at all." Lystra paused for breath, and the drone of a helicopter was heard outside.

"So you see, Mother, we can't hide anymore, especially from ourselves. I know I sound crazy, but certain things have to be said."

"I'm used to you. I've shared your life for twenty years."

"And I've lived with you for those years, Mother."

They smiled then and hugged each other. Still, Merwen knew, nothing was changed. Lystra was right, but her stonesick sisters were right, too.

Outside, the helicopter rumbled louder, until it sounded like a pair of raft trunks knocking together very fast. It was not for Siderite; it was too close.

Merwen met Lystra's eyes and squeezed her hand once. Without a word they both stepped outside to stand before their door. Merwen recognized the soldiers by now, the ones who always came when Realgar wished to see her. She was so relieved that it was not Lystra they came for that she went herself to meet them at the helicopter.

"Go with Shora, Mother," Lystra said to show she was not afraid. "When you return, we'll have supper waiting for you."

As usual, Merwen was hunched into the floor of the helicopter, and she fought to keep her stomach settled. Even so, she wondered if this might be a good time to begin sharing speech again. The Gathering should properly decide, but she could listen and consider whether the Valan wordweaver might be ready to share a gesture of goodwill.

The soldiers tossed her as rudely as ever onto the floor where Realgar hid behind his desk. "You hear me," Realgar said in distinct Valan, louder than usual. "I know that, and it's good enough. I want the Lady Berenice of Hyalite, whom you call Nisi the Traitor. I give Nisi twenty-four hours to surrender herself here. In the event that Nisi fails to appear, every Sharer in Per-elion will die."

Merwen's first response was incomprehension. Every Sharer would pass the Last Door some day, no matter what Nisi chose to do. But of course by now Merwen knew what the death-hastener meant, or what he thought he meant.

Merwen had known all along that hiding was useless, especially from one's lovesharer. Merwen herself had avoided this truth, while Nisi passed test after test yet shunned the only true test of a Sharer. Would Nisi survive it now? Nisi, who had shared love with this hastener of death?

Long ago, Virien had asked Merwen, Will you share my love? This Valan wordweaver now was something much harder than Virien, an ocean of malevolence beyond understanding. Somehow, though, Merwen would have to reach that understanding. To what lengths must she go, and must Nisi go? What a deadly thing it was to share love among Valans.

Nisi was weaving at her loom and squinted as the sun reached to her eyes, low as it was on the horizon. A boat wandered in and Merwen stepped out. With a wave, Nisi jumped from her seat and embraced her. "Merwen! It's been so long. I can't believe all our sisters are back. How are the girls doing?"

"Stronger by the day, devouring their weight in squid." Merwen's smile flashed only briefly. "Nisi, I have a bad choice to share: I have to bend Unspeech, rather than hide a truth from you."

Nisi's hands dropped to her sides. "Yes?"

"Your lovesharer asks for you."

Nisi blacked out, then caught herself again, as red streaks receded from her vision. "He asks ... for me?" No place to hide, not anymore, now that Realgar had found her. "What else, Merwen? What else does he want?"

Merwen was silent.

"What else, do you hear? You're hiding from me."

"In his distraction, he speaks of hastening death for all other Sharers of Per-elion."

So that was the ultimatum. Nisi could actually breathe easier now, knowing the worst. In a sense she could breathe easy for the first time since "Lady Berenice" had ceased to be.

"A shameful thing to threaten," Merwen added. "Yet children talk biggest when they share the most fear."

"What? Merwen, he will do it, I know him well. And if I give myself up, do you know what they'll share with me? A fate ten times worse than Lystra's."

"Then stay here."

"Nonsense. We'll all die then." Even as she said this, Nisi rejected both choices. She would never give herself up, never give them the satisfaction of putting her on trial. As for Realgar, he would kill as many Sharers as he had to, whether she surrendered or not. Vengeance would be just another excuse.

There was only one way left for Sharers to survive, all of them. "Merwen, when Usha taught me whitetrance, I learned that it is right to hasten one's own death for freedom, for a free mind."

"Yes."

"If that is true, then I believe it is right to hasten a few others, that Sharers may live in peace once more."

"A contradiction many times over. To hasten death, one must share death, and the death of another can't be shared until one dies."

"Yes, but what if every Sharer had to die all at once? When the hastening of Valans could prevent it? Just once, Merwen, to save Shora."

"To save what? Which is worse, to die having lived or to live having died?"

"Merwen! We can't afford such sophistry now. We're facing thousands of Viriens all at once."

"And you would hasten them all? And you tell me Shora will survive? Nisi, all Valans are not Virien, even among death-hasteners. We can share with them, share ourselves with their selves, until they see themselves for what they are."

"You only postpone the inevitable. I know soldiers, and I say this: in the end, either they die or we die. You can't just give in."

"It is you who give in. Why Nisi? What words did I share that brought the poison?"

"I learnshared your whitetrance, and I'll do what I have to, but I will not die just to save them the trouble of hastening me!" Nisi turned and rushed into the silkhouse, pulling at the doorhole so it whooshed shut behind her.

All she could think was that she had to act before Realgar did. Sharers would do nothing, but Nisi still had her explosive pack. If she had to pass death's door, at least she would take a few soldiers with her. Perhaps her act would even shock some sense into other sisters. Merwen had said one could not share death *unless* one died, first. If Nisi blew herself up, along with Planetary Head-quarters . . .

A sense of unreality descended on her. It was absurd to think that she herself would commit a singlehanded suicide assault on the Valan fortress. Nisi shook her head to clear the haze, to focus on what must be done. She dug out the explosive from her hiding place in the tunnel below. Vaguely she wondered how strong it was, since the figures on the package meant nothing to her. It made little difference, since she had no choice left, only one path ahead. Realgar had foreclosed all others.

Nisi rubbed herself all over with fleshborer repellent. Then she went out to the water's edge. The sight of the horizon caught her unawares. Clouds stretched into velvet mountains, lined with molten cinnabar that streamed downward into the ocean, mountains of a heavenly country that could be seen and yearned for but never touched. It was as if the Patriarch had allowed her one last glimpse of how the world could be if only His pure wisdom were obeyed. But I will never find it, thought Nisi bitterly, not in this world where men are deceivers ever.

She plunged and swam out beyond the branches, not daring to take a boat, which guards might detect. Fortunately the sea was calm this evening, and she could reach Headquarters without exhaustion. The package strapped to her waist scratched softly as she kicked. In the sky, red and green headlights twinkled, and ahead at last loomed the hulk of a space freighter with a deck built out around it, where Realgar would have—

Nisi choked and sputtered, and she clung to a dead branch of raft seedling to catch her breath. Don't look back, she warned herself; you've made your choice for dead and free.

On the deck there were many points of light, and they cast long arcs of feathery red onto the ripples. Nisi wondered how close she could get undetected. The best thing, she figured, was to dip under and trust to her breathmicrobes the rest of the way.

Blackness closed over her, except for the faint streaks of searchlights above on the surface. She swam on, whether for five minutes or fifty she could not tell. The surface light grew brighter, and she feared she would be seen; but then it suddenly trailed off again. She swam upward slowly, until her head bumped something hard. This must be it, the underside of the deck. Nisi took the explosive and pressed it up. It's seal broke, and the plastic molded and stuck.

It sat there, inert. What in Torr's name was wrong with it? Was there another catch, or had it simply gone bad over these months?

Once doubt cracked her senses, instinct flooded through. I am a survivor, her mind screamed, I'm still alive, and I will live. She swam blindly, gasping for air, heedless of anything except to get away, away from darkness and death. How far she swam, she had no idea, until the blast ripped the night sky in two and showered the sea with flame. The Headquarters towered behind, a jagged silhouette against the flame.

From everywhere helicopters swarmed and dove at the sea, and loudspeakers called. Lights were all over. Something caught Nisi and choked her as she thrashed about to kick herself free. Half conscious, she felt someone drag her across the slimy deck of a ship, whose oily odor gagged her stomach. She was shaken until her ears rang, and stark leering faces whirled above her.

"Bastard catfish," she heard from one, his lips stretched taut against his teeth. "If that's your doing, by the Nine Legions you'll pay for it."

"Say, you're an odd catfish." Someone squeezed Nisi's hand and pried apart the fingers and jabbed under her nails. She cried out sharply.

"It squeaks, too."

"A halfbreed, that's what; a filthy halfbreed."

Abruptly the soldiers fell back, their attention diverted. Nisi raised herself on an elbow and looked past the booted legs. What caught their attention was something else hauled from the sea: a corpse, gouged to the white bones by fleshborers.

Someone whistled and said, "The wounded don't last long in this swamp, do they? I'd burn your head off, halfbreed, only it's too good for you."

They took her into Headquarters, where the flames had been quenched by now. Her head was stunned and she could barely keep her feet, dragged before one officer, then another. And then at last a familiar face came into focus.

It was Realgar, oddly out of place in his Iridian uniform. Incredibly, she felt relief, gladness that he was here and alive after all. She had loved him too hard and too long.

Realgar stood rigid, every muscle tensed to keep himself in hand. After all those months of mourning, to find her like this, shameless before all his troops and thoroughly in league with his enemy. How had those natives twisted her mind?

"Go," he told the guards. He was alone with her now. "You did it, didn't you?" he asked, cursing himself for the hope that it was all a mistake somehow.

Bernice straightened, pulled her arms in, and lifted her chin in her old defensive way. "You would have killed us all, Ral."

"Did you really think I'd waste two thousand civilians just for a damned fool like you?"

"You told her so. Aren't you a man of your word?"

His hand cracked across her face, and she slammed to the wall. She raised her arms slowly, leaning against her palms as she faced him. "Berenice. Do I have to knock sense into your head?"

"Yes...perhaps you do," she said thickly, her lip swelling. "Oh, yes. I understand you, much better now."

Realgar frowned, uncertain how to take her words. "When I heard you were here, all I wanted was to get you back quietly, so it wouldn't get out, and I could send you safe to—"

"To a sanatorium."

"*Yes,* by Torr. The best in Iridis."

"How thoughtful of you."

"Instead, you sabotage my base, and my troops drag you in here shameless as a field whore. Berenice—I'm the Guard Commander, and you're a traitor in wartime. What can you expect of me?"

She shook her head slowly. "Nothing. I want nothing from you, ever again."

"What do you mean by that?" Realgar's voice became low and harsh. "You're one of them, is that it? Did you take a woman lover, too?"

Her lip curled down on the unbruised side. "I wondered when it would come down to that. The one thing you always liked about me being here was that I was cloistered among women." She tilted her head in a ghastly flirtation. "Suppose I had loved a woman. I can have a child, Ral; they fixed me up long ago. I don't need you; I never did."

The blood pounded in his temples, until he thought his head would burst. But the moment passed, his breath slowed to normal, and with it the world changed, shifted gears. Berenice was nothing to him anymore, Realgar told himself. She was worth less than nothing. "So that's how it is. Well, then, I'll send you back to stand trial. But first, you shall witness the execution of your co-conspirators."

Her eyes widened. "I had none."

"Sharers never act alone. All decide for one, and one for all."

"I acted alone, I tell you. You said you would not kill civilians over me."

"What civilians? They, and you, are responsible for the deaths of twenty-three of my troops, at latest count. Oh, I see: too good for killing, the natives are, but they'll look the other way when you do it."

"Merwen begged me not to do it, I swear!"

"Merwen will die last."

She threw herself at him and clasped his arms. "Ral, all I ever wanted was for them to be free. Didn't you betray me by leading this senseless invasion? Don't punish someone else for what I've done. I'll go to the sanatorium, I'll—"

He knocked her to the floor, then pulled her up by the arm and whipped his hand across her face, back and forth, knuckles cracking as they connected bone. At last she fell, limp and still. Realgar breathed heavily and rubbed his numb fingers. His tongue tasted nausea as a buried memory rose: his father with his mother, and himself a child whimpering in the corner. . . .

Then he stared, and his toes curled. Berenice lay crumpled, with her head swollen unrecognizably, yet an unmistakable otherworldly whiteness was seeping into every pore of her skin.

24

In the morning helicopters buzzed over Raia-el again, five all at once. Soldiers swarmed out to tramp through the houses, pulling people out for what mad reason none could guess, and dragging them, not to the helicopters, but of all places to the central cup of the raft. Before, soldiers had forbidden Gatherings; now, they tried clumsily to make one.

Merwen lifted her head wearily, with Weia's last screams still ringing in her ears. Around her, sisters wandered uncertainly, while soldiers pointed their coldstone wands and ran about in a curious crouching position as if they expected the sky to collapse on them. Radio chatter barked from all directions.

Trurl leaned over to help her up. "Thanks, sister," Merwen said. "Shora, what is this new madness?"

"Just another fit of the old." Trurl sniffed disgustedly. "There was an accident, I hear. Part of the soldier-place caught fire. It seems to have inflamed their minds as well."

With a shudder, Merwen turned away. "Let's go home." Others were already walking away from the desecrated gathering place.

A streak of flame cut across their path. The raft hissed and smoldered where it touched. When the smoke cleared, two Sharers were splayed out, a mangled gash cut through them. Someone cried out, and everyone collected at the spot. Merwen gagged at the scorched odor. Usha huddled over them, but one was charred through to the ribs, and Merwen knew already it was useless.

The horror of it overloaded her senses to the point of detachment. Yet again the death-hasteners had cursed themselves, this time here, in the gathering place of Raia-el. Death paid a wage, for a hastener; but was it more than a trader's wage, in disks of coldstone? If only she could answer that question.

A death-hastener grabbed her again and dragged her to a site where a row of poles had been erected. There were Sharers tied to the poles: Trurl, and Shaalrim, and Lalor, and last Yinevra, all the staunchest of witnessers. Merwen noticed, as if outside herself, that she herself was being bound to one of the poles. Several death-hasteners faced her, including Realgar and Jade, and also Nisi in whitetrance with someone propping her up. At the sight of Nisi, Merwen breathed a sigh, for she could guess what had happened now. It was true; Nisi's fate would be ten times worse than Lystra's.

An amplified voice blared Valan speech past her. "This is the Commander of the Valan Guard. As you are all aware, last night your traitorous sister launched an unprovoked attack on Headquarters in which twenty-four troops died and eighteen are missing. From now on, the slightest infraction of Valan orders will be met with execution on the spot. To demonstrate our intent, the Protector and four of her Councilors shall be put to death."

Merwen barely heard the last part. Nisi had set the spark; Merwen knew that, and it would have sickened her if she had any room for feeling left. What had become of Nisi, after sharing Merwen's home for so many years? If only she could understand that, she would have the key to everything: Realgar and his insane demands, even Malachite the Living Dead.

Fear was the cause, and the wage for one who hastened death. Fear was the same wage for traders, who feared to starve if they ran out of stone. Valans might imagine other wages and desires, but in the end, they *killed* because they *feared being killed;* they hastened death because they feared it, yet they feared it more, the more they hastened. That was the final paradox left to her.

A flame sprouted, a column of yellow and black, crackling,

shooting to the sky. There was an odor of cooked flesh again. It took Merwen a minute to realize that Trurl had been tied there.

Fire and fear. The ancestors had perished in flames; or was it fear of the flames that had consumed them? *Fear bred fire, and few were the Doors that remained. . . .*

Another flame sprouted, this time where Shaalrim had been. Trurl and Shaalrim; they were *not,* anymore, and half Merwen's life seemed to slip away.

Then sisters were crowding all around her, and around Lalor and Yinevra, sheltering them with their own bodies. The death-hasteners pulled them away, burning some, but others came; it was a feast of fleshborers, and it was not long before the flames licked Lalor. And all the while Realgar stood there, unmoved, the word-weaver who did not care to share words anymore.

Yinevra was still alive. Her torso rose above those who surrounded her, though her arms were lashed tight behind the stake, her stare fixed ahead, set in the deepest lines of contempt that Merwen had ever seen. But something stopped Merwen there: she had to stay Yinevra's death, Yinevra who had saved her from Virien, although Merwen had never forgiven how it happened. Now Merwen would act to save Yinevra, even though Yinevra would never forgive her if she succeeded.

"I have something to say." Merwen looked directly at Realgar as she broke Unspeech, in Valan, a double shame. "I have something to ask of you."

Amid the smoke and shouting, and the natives underfoot everywhere despite the troops pulling them back, Realgar caught the movement of Merwen's lips. She had said something, and she was staring at him. She had broken Unspeech. Realgar knew the significance of that. The Sharer Protector herself had cracked.

Up to that point, Realgar had been irritated by the turn this spectacle had taken. He had expected the natives to sit by passively, as usual, while the five were executed, a scene he could send back to show the Palace how decisively he had dealt with native terrorists. Instead, they had interfered, interposing their own bodies and necessitating extra killings, too disorderly for the recorders.

But then, Merwen had spoken: Protector Merwen, she who had stolen Berenice from him. Her life represented all that thwarted him on this Torr-forsaken Ocean Moon. Had she decided to yield at last and convince her sisters to obey? Or would she simply beg for her own life?

"Cease fire." Realgar walked toward the stake, and the soldiers cleared a path. The sounds and confusion all receded from his mind. He halted a few paces away. Merwen looked at him, her eyes and cheeks flat, her old scar trailing up her neck and scalp.

"I know your wage, Death-hastener. But who will pay, when none are left to die?"

The Valan words knifed and twisted. Blindly he slashed her face with the end of his firewhip. Realgar struggled to shake off the dread she unleashed, in her challenge that every Sharer would die before one would yield. If it came to that, before Malachite returned, Realgar would have lost, failed completely.

Was there any way out? Could he let them all die?

An inspiration came to him. What Malachite really wanted was Sharer knowledge, knowledge of lifeshaping. That knowledge would remain, even with Sharers extinct: a trillion chromosomal libraries in every raft, even the raft Realgar stood on now. Malachite could find some way to tap those libraries.

His breathing slowed and his head cleared as he realized that he could exterminate the catfish if he had to. But he was not done with them yet.

Realgar nodded at Merwen and the other one. "Remove them to Headquarters, and let's clear out."

There was still a chance he might break them. He could turn their own psychological weapons against them, in a way that Jade was too conventional to try. If Merwen had broken Unspeech under pressure, then she had fallen, as judged by her own code, and that fall was the first step toward her defeat. She would live to see her planet die.

Part VI

THE
LAST
DOOR

1

Raia-el was quiet now, except for the wind, whose thin sorrowful cry swept the ridge. High cirrus clouds splashed the sky, and the sea was a blue mirror. Spinel looked into the sea and thought he heard Merwen whisper again, What do you see? But when he turned, she was not there.

Lystra and the other adults were all in whitetrance, mourning the souls departed in haste the night before. Spinal was left alone with his thoughts, or rather non-thoughts, not-thinking about flames charring raftwood, not-thinking about those whose ashes were mixed in. He thought of his family again, for the first time in weeks. Beryl had told him he would never understand what they had undergone in Chrysoport. Now it ripped through him, what Beryl must have felt when Harran was killed, and he knew why Chrysolite villagers would suffer anything to keep the peace, would submit with equal resignation to Protectors or to Dolomite occupiers so long as peace held.

Yet Sharers would not. Was Spinel a Sharer yet? The knife of that question only twisted deeper.

A touch at his elbow startled him. Lystra had come out, her finger-tips still white. Her arm curled around his waist, pressing warmth into him, her muscles leaner than they had been once but growing tough enough for the starworms again. Her cheek pressed into his, and Spinel closed his eyes to let all the ache drain from his head. Her breast was full at his side, and it was easy to float away with her breath as it brushed past his face. Only there was no time to rest. "Lystra, what are we to do now?"

"Feed the next starworm."

Lystra's matter-of-fact tone surprised him. Spinel turned and blinked at her.

"Without Yinevra, who else will make sure it's done right?"

Lystra did not reply right away. "Mithril will always be welcome here," she said at last.

So Leni-el raft was not going to make it, after all the sweat lost in digging tunnels and implanting starworms, and the Sharers would be refugees again scattered throughout Per-elion. His vision blurred, and he wiped his eyes. "What then, Lystra, after we feed the starworms?"

Her lips twisted. "A Gathering, today."

"Oh, I'll come this time." Sensing her hesitation, Spinel added, "I'll learn whitetrance, too. It's my right, isn't it?"

"That depends. Are you like Nisi still, or have you grown up?"

Anger filled him, until he saw Lystra's hands shaking and realized what an effort it took her to say that. "You know what I am," he told her. "Whatever that is, it has to be enough."

In the lifeshaping place, Usha was sitting across from him an arm's-length away, with the mindguide curling down from her fingers like a sleepy spider. Spinel shrank from it at first, but after all, he thought, it could hardly be any worse to turn white than to turn purple. The mindguide settled lightly on his head.

His mind rushed out like a train speeding through a tunnel while the wind screamed past. He blossomed out into the vastness of Shora's ocean, then watched it curve into a blue bauble and slip away to a speck smaller than the moon ever seen from Valedon. Valedon, too, and even the precious sun receded as his mind pressed outward, crowding the stars in his grasp. Illusion, it must be, some sort of conjuror's trick. Or could every mind hold a universe all in itself?

Then memory coalesced and paraded behind him, while he stood at the lip of the Last Door and realized how amazingly simple it would be to slip through. All it took was to linger long enough at the Door, to feel how meaningless was fear, how useless any threat to the mind. And yet . . .

When he returned to himself, Spinel stared at his feet for a long time, until the patterns blurred and left opposite colors in his eyes. He stretched his arms and glanced at Usha again. Usha tilted her head expectantly. "Well? You took a long time to come back."

Spinel shivered all over and hugged his arms. "I could have stayed there forever. Why does anyone come back?"

"Well, why did you?" Usha sounded satisfied as she picked up the mindguide, which had fallen from his head, and patted it into a neat bundle.

For no reason, Spinel thought, except perhaps that a life worth dying for is worth living a little longer.

Before the Gathering, Wellen and Weia would not let Usha leave them alone in the silkhouse. Weia screamed and hung fast to Usha's leg, while Wellen more politely insisted, "We have self-names, Mother, we chose them at the soldier-place. We have to come." Then Mithril's daughter clamored to come too.

Usha relented at last, but Lystra was scandalized. "They're too young; it's just not correct."

"These are highly incorrect times," Usha replied. "Merwen would have thought this best."

Lystra wanted to cry out, Don't talk about Merwen as if she were already dead. She made herself think of the Gathering and of what must be done. Whether or not they yet lived, the Gathering would have to act without Merwen or Yinevra today.

And without Trurl to sift the speaking; Trurl was not there, would never be there or anywhere again, no matter how automatically Lystra looked to the center of the gathering place where Trurl always sat. She could not imagine a Raia-el Gathering without Trurl's good sense, or without Shaalrim and Lalor, always optimistic despite their rough adventures on the Stone Moon. Only their infant Laraisha survived, now nursing at Elonwy's breast while her lovesharer cradled their own toddler. And the raft carried blackened scars.

In the air clickflies still hummed the mourning songs sent from other rafts. Farther above, a lone helicopter hovered against the clouds.

The selfnamers shared greeting in subdued voices. Only Flossa and Mirri seemed happy, as they cuddled together; a romance had sprung up between them in the lifeshaping-place where they spent such long hours together. Lystra sat with Spinel and wished that her stonesick guests would get over their nervousness about Spinel and his starstone. Another headache to add to the rest.

An almost unbearable silence hovered among them all. Lystra doubted she was alone in her voiceless call; Shora, where are you now?

Usha was staring pensively at the weeds beyond her crossed legs, as if all the answers might be found there. She looked up and around at the gathered Sharers. "We all know why we are gathered here. How are we to go forward this day, after . . . what has happened?"

Hands and fingers stirred, and a voice said, "Somehow, Valans have to share healing."

"What if they can't heal?" asked Elonwy as she patted Shaalrim's child, now her own. Her voice dragged with weariness. "Consider Nisi the Deceiver."

Usha looked down, and Lystra thought she might be too overcome to go on. *Merwen, Mother, where are you? Are they prying the skin from your fingers?* The empty cry escaped Lystra's mind, reaching past the raft and its branches full yellow with blossoms, dissolving in the sparkling water.

Usha said, "We share great sorrow for the Deceiver, but we can't judge from one case."

"Yet one is all we have left."

"We have Spinel," Lystra said abruptly, pulling him closer. "Spinel is one of us."

Elonwy sighed. "That's what I mean."

Lystra thought hard. "Nisi was never wholly one of us, not inside where it matters. That was why she called herself Deceiver."

Usha looked at her. "Suppose Spinel fails too, someday. Will you say the same of him?"

"It's not the same." Shaken, Lystra cast a stricken glance at Spinel, who blinked at the unexpected turn. "Are you a Sharer or not? Tell us."

"You know that I am," Spinel said in a low voice, his shoulders hunched as if to hide the stone that accused him. Even Nisi would never have been so brazen as to wear a stone at a Gathering.

Then Wellen piped up. "Spinel already has a selfname, like us. We all made a Gathering at the soldier-place. Spinel nearly died to help us escape."

A sigh rippled among them, and Perlianir said to Spinel, "Will you name the Three Doors?" So he stood beside Lystra and named them, the Sun, the Last Door, and his own name, Impulsive One. He sat down again quickly and Lystra hugged him, amazed and relieved that it had come so simply. If only Merwen were here to see—she jammed her eyes shut; it tore her apart every time she had to think of that.

Kithril spoke up suddenly. "Merwen believes that even the

death-hasteners may yet share healing, and that is why she and my lovesharer are still alive."

Startled, Lystra looked up at Kithril, who rarely spoke at all when Yinevra was with her. Kithril stood tensely, snapping her fingerwebs. "Merwen never did want to Unspeak them," Kithril said. "So she spoke at last, spoke straight to their fear. It was then that they stopped the—"

"They never listened before," someone countered. "Why should they listen now?"

"They heard Merwen, more than once," Usha said flatly. "That is why Merwen is still alive."

"But she might be better off dead." Elonwy shook her head. "I'm sorry, Usha, it has to be said. There are worse fates than an early death. So far, all the doors I see ahead are worse." The infant Laraisha started to wail. Usha stared on into the sun as if she had not heard.

Ama was trying to speak, and Lystra helped her raise herself. "We have rarely spoken *for* the Valans, from the Gathering," Ama said. "Always we sent selfnamers to ask after our own sisters and daughters. Merwen asked the soldier, What will become of *you?*"

There was a pause. Someone demanded, "What else can we share that we have not? Whitetrance is what Shaalrim said to share: where is she now? The Deceiver shared whitetrance, and what became of her?"

"Nothing left but ourselves," said Ama. "That is all, in the end: to keep on sharing of ourselves, until the day comes when Valans see our eyes in the ocean of their own."

"And if we die again at the soldier-place?" Elonwy's voice was harsh and uneven. "Isn't it just as shameful to die hastened as to hasten death?"

"Not if we reach beyond death," said Perlianir. "We will show that a death-hastening is no answer to fear. That's what Merwen tried to share with the death-hastener."

Lystra froze, knowing what must come next.

"I will go first," said Perlianir. "My lovesharer is dead, my daughters are grown; if I must go, I am ready."

"It's not right." Lystra stood quickly. "This Gathering can't send one of us to a certain death."

"No one sends me. I send myself to share with the death-hasteners."

"Then I'll go too."

At her feet Spinel gasped and said, "No, Lystra."

"No," said Perlianir very quietly. "You don't want to go, yet; only to share my choice. But this choice can't be shared."

The truth tasted bitter. Lystra wanted no more of death or soldiers or their coldstone cells. She had had enough; all she wanted was to live here forever, with Spinel and their daughters and daughters of daughters. Though forever was impossible, and she could not shake off the dread that she would yet suffer for not wanting to die.

Usha said, "No one wants to die. But someone has to tell these people in a way they can share that we will never join their madness. I can't ask you not to go, Sharer."

Ama called faintly, "I will go, after you. Even a death-hastener can't share fear with someone in my condition."

Others volunteered, and each name cut with a knife of ice until Lystra shivered from the cold. This could not go on. What would Shora be, when there were no Sharers left?

Spinel's steps dragged as he walked back with Lystra and Usha. "It's no use," he said dully. "You'll never make a Sharer of a Sardish soldier, not in a million years."

Usha said, "It's not a matter of making, but of finding what is lost and buried."

Spinel had no answer for that, although it seemed to him that he had known the answers long ago and lost them. He looked out to the sea and thought again, What use, when even the ocean world is not to be spared? The web of life had still not recovered from the missed seaswallowers; certain weeds were hopelessly overgrown, stifling the silkweed groves, and fanwings were still scarce. What would happen the next time swallowers were due, just three months from now?

At the door of the silkhouse Siderite was waiting. With raucous giggles Weia reached up at him to pull at the material of his trousers, just as she used to tease Spinel. "What is your conclusion?" Siderite asked Usha, while he tried to unpry Weia's fingers.

"More sharing," said Usha. "Share on, until the ocean overflows."

Lines tensed around Siderite's eyes. He looked at Spinel, and briefly they shared an outsider's perception of helplessness. Spinel only gripped Lystra's hand tighter. He had no explanations; he only knew which side he had chosen.

"Usha," Siderite asked, "how can you hope for mercy from the Guard, after all that has happened?"

Usha frowned over the Valan words. "I'm not sure that 'mercy' is, but sharing is what we want. Sharing works something like this: Think of those living molecules which you know so well. As molecules grow colder, very cold, fewer levels of energy remain that can bridge the barrier between them. But no matter how cold it gets, molecules never lose the lowest level, the zero-point energy. At zero point, they tunnel through the barrier to share electrons. Sharing between souls works like that; there is always a last door to tunnel through."

Siderite might have known what Usha was getting at, but Spinel had only vaguely heard of "energy levels," in atoms of stone where they absorbed light and spat it out again in colors. He scratched his toe on the raft and wished that Usha knew as much about stone atoms as she did about "living" ones. Then maybe he would get less trouble for his starstone.

"A last door," Siderite repeated to himself. "Do you realize that the Commander now has a 'last chance' policy? That is, it's your last chance to give up before you all die."

"Each of us dies someday," Usha said. "Like most children, Valans tend to forget this."

Siderite opened his mouth to add something, then changed his mind and switched tongues. "Usha, we must share parting. Many thanks for all the learning we have shared; but it must end, before this learning can be used against you."

Usha nodded. "Perhaps that is best. Some learning is too dangerous for children. But you could still stay with us, and learn whitetrance, and take a selfname."

"And end as Nisi did?"

For long minutes they contemplated each other, then Siderite turned and plodded heavily back toward his tent.

Spinel watched in dismay. *I won't end like Nisi,* he insisted to himself. *Yet how can I know what I'll do when the soldiers come for me, or for Lystra.*

2

At headquarters everything was under control. Siderite's plague cure had done the trick, quarantine was lifted, and most of the troublesome Iridians and Dolomites had been sent home, replaced by Sards. On the home front, news of the attack had ignited public sentiment. Talion's councilors called for a stunning counterattack: "Boil off their ocean," said one. In fact, twenty Sardish divisions had been promised, of which eight had already arrived.

There were enough troops and submarines now to cover every woman and child on every raft, around the clock. Once the new regime settled in, every raft would become a prison.

Of course, it was ridiculous to keep a hundred thousand troops to guard a prison camp. Realgar's staff was devising a plan to concentrate the natives in a more convenient facility, once their spirits were broken. That was bound to happen, sooner or later; around the planet, hundreds were dying daily, just for getting caught away from their home rafts. The Sardish machine was in control.

After the public executions on Raia-el, two prisoners had been taken, of whom one had died in whitetrance the first night. So much for the future guerrilla leader of Shora. Protector Merwen, however, was still alive. Realgar had her put on critical life support and made Doctor Nathan personally responsible for her survival.

Within a week of the new regime, a response developed, if one could call it that. Each day, two or three natives from one of the Perelion rafts would swim out to Headquarters, from deep underwater to postpone detection until they climbed onto the deck to be gunned down. Their motive would have been opaque, except for the clickfly missives that spread their purpose everywhere. They intended, quite simply, to convince the soldiers to stop killing and go home.

Realgar started to laugh but caught himself. Whatever else

348

Sharers were, they were not stupid. He had to watch out for their ways of seduction and stamp out the first signs. At least his Sardish troops would not put up with nonsense.

Still, it was such a murky business to deal with Sharers. Even Berenice had barely begun to figure them out. Berenice remained under guard at Satellite Amber, available for interrogation, though Realgar had persuaded himself that Jade would have little to gain from it. Berenice . . .

"You know, Jade," he reflected, "if she had not pulled that trick last week, we'd be back in Iridis by now."

Jade shrugged. "As I see it, she only saved us the trouble of staging an incident."

Perhaps Jade was right. It would have saved time and lives if he had staged an incident at the start. At any rate, he was back on course, with a corps of Sards behind him. Nothing could stop him now.

Siderite asked to see the general, for the first time since the crackdown. Realgar could guess what was coming. It was time to pull out the diplomatic stops again.

"You're looking well, Doctor," Realgar told him, though Siderite had perversely kept a purple cast to his skin, long after his curative formula had been adopted by the entire Valan corps. Siderite accepted the chair that slid up from the floor. "Your recent work is remarkable. I'm greatly impressed." That is, Doctor Nathan was impressed. Realgar himself comprehended less and less of Siderite's findings, but he considered this a sign of scientific progress. "So tell me, what can I do for you?"

Siderite cleared his throat. "General, I regret to inform you that I am resigning as Research Director of Operation Amethyst."

Realgar was angry at first, then just annoyed. "Siderite, I'm as sorry as you are about the recent turn of events, but what can I do?"

"You agreed to pull out."

"Circumstances have changed, beyond my control. Now tell me, Siderite, is Usha stalling again? Does she refuse to—"

"No." After that firm word, Siderite added, "I find present conditions intolerable for my work."

"Indeed." It was clear that Siderite had let the natives seduce him, just as Berenice had. This time Realgar would come down hard. "You're here to do a job, Doctor, not to set conditions. You will stay here and do it, until you're discharged." He paused. "Or stay here and not do it, and suffer the consequences."

Siderite's gaze defocused as he stretched back in his chair. "Circumstances have changed, have they," he muttered and clasped his hands behind his head. "Beyond your control, and mine. Who controls them, I wonder?"

Realgar's hands tensed on his desk. "What are you getting at?"

"General, have you noticed how often the natives call us 'sick' or even 'living dead'?"

"What of it?"

Siderite stared up at the ceiling, then down at his toes. "Just speculation, of course, but—"

"*Enough speculation.*" Realgar paused, regretting the lapse. Somehow this pudgy civilian could touch his nerve every time.

"Very well, sir. Am I dismissed?"

"No."

With a shrug Siderite sat up. "Call it a thought experiment. Let us suppose that you, sir, are an immensely powerful entity, powerful as a Torran Envoy, for example. You face a pair of planets isolated in space. One of the pair is familiar, predictable, snug under your thumb, so long as you snuff out a city once in a while. The other is unknown and uncontrollable, with potentially lethal powers. What action do you take?"

Realgar said carefully, "The danger is not immediate."

"For the sake of argument, let's assume the opposite."

Realgar showed no outward sign, but a wall of denial was crashing down. If he went on, it was to admit that his worse fear might come true. "Send a deathship from Torr," he said, barely moving his lips.

"As a general, yes, you would do that. But a Torran Envoy is a statesman as well as a general, and even a scientist too."

"A statesman would at the very least have to quarantine the planet, isolate the contagion before destroying it."

"But Shora *is* isolated. Except for Valedon. What would the scientist do?"

"What would you do?" Realgar asked ironically.

"I'd set up an experiment, of course. I wouldn't want to destroy the people until I had analyzed their powers and acquired them for myself. So, put them in a test tube with the 'reference' planet, Valedon, boil them up together, and check back after ten years."

Realgar's thoughts raced. "Do you dare to say Malachite lied to us?"

Siderite shrugged noncommittally. "It is standard practice to mislead experimental subjects so that they can't prejudice the results."

"Where's your evidence to back this up?"

"Only my own estimate of Sharer abilities. And the 'Purple Plague,' of course."

"Sharers themselves carry breathmicrobes," said Realgar. "They don't consider it a plague."

"And it's about time you realized that. Sharers never take *any* action toward you which they would not gladly accept for themselves."

This turn of logic confused him. "If they can make lethal strains, why don't they use them to retaliate?"

"They retaliate, in their own way. Why else were you all set to pull out, last week?"

Realgar frowned. "Because they're a damned nuisance, that's why. Off the record, they're not worth wasting good money and troops on."

"And why is that? Bloodless 'invasions,' fraternization with troops, 'haunting' Dolomites—those natives work hard at being a nuisance. Alternative methods: alternatives to killing. Now, what sort of people are likely to develop methods of confrontation which exclude violence?"

"People who have no weapons."

Siderite waved an impatient hand. "The first tools man invented were knives and arrows. Think again."

Who were the Sharers? Vestigial Primes, whose empire had collapsed centuries ago. Some of the dead planets were radioactive, others not, though all were shunned today. Except Shora. "A people whose weapons are too deadly to be used."

"Quite possibly." Siderite was vexingly offhand.

Realgar shook himself. "It's absurd. If Malachite had known that, he would have blasted the planet on sight."

"Not if he wants it badly enough. Though it's true, the Patriarch has tended to steer clear of advanced life-science: it's too hard to control, as I keep telling you. You can't just snoop around with a Geiger counter to check what's going on." Siderite leaned forward and rubbed his hands together. "Now comes the 'living dead' part. Suppose that Sharers take our threats seriously. They could spread an infection which would lie dormant within us for years, only to mushroom into disease and wipe us out—unless Sharers are still around to halt it. Or the latency period could be generations; then we'll live, but our children's children will share their extinction."

Alive, with his grandchildren doomed? Realgar's flesh crawled as his worst fears multiplied. "Impossible," he barked. "If natives could do that to us, then—then why didn't they get rid of seaswallowers and fleshborers long ago?"

"Those are too useful. Swallowers keep the raft population in check, so the ocean doesn't turn into a swamp. Fleshborers keep down the swallowers. And both take their toll of Sharers, whose numbers remain level without an overload of oldsters."

Realgar blinked. "They really think like that?"

"Sharers see themselves as part of the web. Every creature has its niche, its function, but what are *we* trollheads good for?"

Now Realgar saw Merwen's challenge in a new light. *When none are left to die. . . .* Merwen had warned him of a fear that would not die with the last of the Sharers. "Why in Torr's name would Malachite want us to provoke them?" he wondered.

"The experiment, remember. Force their hand. Try to make them show what they can do—now, not a generation from now."

"To loyal Valen citizens." Realgar looked hard at Siderite. "You realize, of course, that you speak treason."

"I was waiting for that." Siderite sighed. "You always end up calling me a traitor."

"This time I'm serious. I'll turn you over to Jade."

For a moment Siderite looked faint, then his eyelids fluttered and he relaxed. "Yes, it had to come to that. A bearer of bad news, and all that. A fool shares gold with a stranger. What of it? I've nothing to hide."

Already Realgar was thinking that even if Siderite were on the level, Realgar himself could not know how valid his speculations were. Only Sharers knew. Merwen knew. He would wrest the truth from her. He had won the first round by getting her to speak at all. Once talking, Sharers were not very good at deception.

3

When Merwen first arrived, she had been thrown into a cramped, dry prison cell, with no light, no water, and no change to break the tedium except for the flames that rose ever higher in her feverish imagination. Then fire receded to leave a maelstrom of despair, swirling deeper than any she had ever known. To flee those sucking waters she passed into whitetrance and for the first time felt drawn to stay there. The physical universe left behind seemed one immense boulder, bigger even than the cliffs outside Spinel's home on Valedon, a rock of emptiness, a vacuum of life. Though somewhere a stone might yet have a star in it—perhaps every stone, if one looked hard enough. Merwen was tired of looking.

Still, there was that strand of life she had snatched from death, for herself and Yinevra. That silken strand tied her to Usha, and Lystra, and Spinel, with his tantalizing promise of hope. Merwen was far from giving that up yet.

She was rescued by Nathan, the primitive lifeshaper. Nathan's place was at least well ventilated, and amply lit with a cold white light. Salves were put to her peeling skin and edible food was shared. Curious odors passed her nose, some bitter, others fresh. Merwen was expected to lie on a platform of spongy material, disconcertingly raised off the floor so she had to remind herself not to roll off. One time she did get off and wandered among the bizarrely furnished rooms, but then the primitive lifeshapers were greatly upset, gesticulating quaintly with their limbs whose white drapery exaggerated every gesture.

Nathan warned her about the medical instruments, which she had not recognized as such. She tried to figure them out: boxes in rhomboid array, with lighted dots like scattered pearls; a shelf with a roll of loosewoven bleached material, next to a canister of long metal sticks with curved points.

"The boxes," Nathan explained, "are intracorporal monitors to show what goes on inside you. On the shelf are surgical scalpels and bandages."

Merwen was confused. "What is 'surgical'?"

"For precise incision, to repair internal organs."

"Cutting? To repair?" Merwen saw that he was serious; his forehead was wrinkled as deeply as the creases of cloth at his elbows. "Why not program a virus to tell the cells how to heal?"

Nathan looked away. "You don't use bandages either, do you?"

"Oh, yes, we do. A gash must be bound and contained, and then—" Her impatient fingers danced in the air. "You know. The kind of fungus that spreads a protective shield around the wound while secreting growth factors."

"Siderite tells me." Abruptly Nathan left the room. As for Merwen, she wondered if she might actually be safer cramped in the prison cell.

The next morning, Nathan told her she was to see Realgar again. Her pulse quickened; perhaps she could go home?

"Don't remove the electrodes," Nathan reminded her, pointing to the bits of colored tape stuck to her head and chest, related somehow to the "intracorporal monitors." "And please, Merwen, don't try anything...rash. If anything happens to you, it will go badly for me. Do you understand?"

So Nathan's life was yet another linked to hers. Merwen squeezed her eyes shut against anguish. "I will try not to earn my name."

In the office, Merwen sat herself down at the side, on the soft carpet with its fantastical animal shapes. She looked up at Realgar. He sat in a chair apart from the desk, so that he faced her unhidden except by his clothing. His legs were crossed above the knee, and a wide boot jutted at an angle. Merwen could not help thinking of long toes bound up excruciatingly inside, although she knew that Valans had stunted toes. She forced herself to look farther up, into his blue eyes as distant as polar icecaps. Distant, but perhaps not unreachable.

"Greetings, Protector," Realgar said. "Will you not have a chair?"

Annoyed, Merwen asked him, "Why do you call me that, 'Protector'?" The unearned title had pricked at her for a long time.

"Are you not the Protector of Shora?"

"You say that I am." Merwen paused. "I share protection as far as I can, as does any Sharer. My proper selfname is Impatient One. It is your privilege to remind me of this failing."

"Very well, Impatient One. Why do you never sit on the chair?"

Merwen glanced aside to the molded seat that extended from the floor. "It is wise to sit as close as possible to the ocean, to be reminded of Her wisdom. It is impolite to sit on a work stool, unless there is manual work to be shared: spinning or carding, perhaps."

"Among Valans, Impatient One, it is never polite to sit on the floor."

If this Valan would share words better, Merwen thought, she might as well sit on the chair. She got up and lowered herself into it, feeling highly selfconscious. Her toes twitched nervously, and her fingers itched to hold a spindle or the oars of a boat.

Realgar asked conversationally, "Impatient One, why is it that you have remained alive, whereas Yinevra has not?"

Yinevra. Gone after the others, spindrift on the wind. Bright streaks crossed her retina, and Merwen found herself sitting down on the hard floor, her head clearing as blood rushed back. *My next day in Valan hands will be my last,* Yinevra had said.

"Why, Impatient One? Are you afraid of death?"

"I swim a different stream. Do you suppose that all Sharers think alike, just because we smell the same when we burn?"

"Of course not. Now you're talking sense, Merwen. You know what's at stake better than most of your sisters do. Why don't you accept the Patriarch and live in peace? Hundreds of diverse planets have accepted his rule. Pay taxes, a mere token for people of common means, and follow some basic regulations, and in return you earn the universal protection of the Patriarch."

"Protection from what?"

"From yourselves. From the irrational forces which inevitably corrupt all peoples. And from foreign invaders like myself."

"I doubt I can protect this Patriarch from you, and from Sharers there is no need. I tried to share this with Malachite the Dead One. Malachite was afraid, but we refuse to share that fear."

Realgar's hand stilled, though his face stayed calm. "And why was Malachite afraid? What have you done to us?"

"What have we done?" Merwen echoed. "We try to share healing." And failed, dismally.

"And will the next generation of Valans die out, from a disease you spread among us?"

"You are dying already inside, from the sickness you call 'killing.' If you would only stop trying to share death, which can't be done, then we could help you learn to share life. Then you wouldn't need fear anymore."

Realgar seemed caught up in his own thoughts, as he rose from his chair and paced across the room, then back, his boots clicking on the floor.

"Do you trust this Malachite so much?" Merwen asked. "Malachite told us that Valans would come, to share learning and pain. Pain there has been in abundance, but when will the learning begin?"

Realgar stooped in midstride. "What was that? 'Share learning' —is that what the Envoy told you?"

"I have shared as hard as I can, but it takes two to try."

"Then you must learn from us," Realgar said slowly. "What would become of Sharers if we taught you to kill?"

Merwen blinked. At first she did not understand; then she realized what he must have meant. "We would be like animals again." She nearly added, Like you.

"Humans are animals, with animal needs."

"Humans are that, and more. Humans are aware of the universe, and self-aware."

"You still have to survive. Your sisters are dying, hundreds every day. They break our rules, swim to our boats and our bases, and they are executed. How can you let this go on?"

"My sisters know what they are doing." But she was thinking, Hundreds hastened. Who would house the next souls to be born?

"You know that we will go on killing your sisters, until you obey—or until you kill us."

This was what Nisi had learned from her lovesharer. Merwen was struck with a rage so full that some minutes passed before she could speak. She flexed her swollen tongue and said in a monotone, "If we kill, we lose our will to choose, our shared protection of Shora, our ability to shape life. Our humanity would slip away, beyond even your own." Her patience had evaporated, and she let her fingers bleach. Fortunately Realgar put up no fuss but let Nathan lead her away. As she lay again upon the elevated sleeping-place, she stared numbly past the primitive medical implements, and her eyes defocused as she thought, If only I had died many years before at the hand of Virien rather than live to see Shora die a slow death.

And yet, this Valan wordweaver had left Merwen her life once for a word; and of words, Merwen had plenty more. Alerted, now, she would not lose patience again.

4

Realgar was sure he had the key now, the key to unlock the Sharer mind. Siderite's story confirmed it; just to double-check, he had Jade run the man through the mindprobes.

"He's on the level—almost," Jade reported. "Siderite believes the catfish could wipe us out, or hold us hostage to some latent disease, but that they are psychologically incapable of it."

He fisted his palm. "There's the answer. It's what the Envoy must have expected of us from the start: to teach the Sharers to kill."

Jade raised an eyebrow. "A novel approach. Where does that get us?"

"Don't you see, the Sharer mind is constructed entirely around *not*-killing. If you break that, everything else breaks down. Merwen herself admitted they'd be too scared even for lifeshaping; it's too dangerous, in the hand of killers. And Merwen—Protector or not, the whole damn planet listens to her." He had read enough clickfly messages about Merwen. If she fell, countless others would follow.

"It won't be easy," Jade warned. "Catfish are good at mind games, if nothing else. They've had generations to practice on each other."

"But they have one weakness. They have a limit to the stakes they will play, whereas I have none."

* * *

Only one event marred the steady campaign of attrition by the Sardish troops. Two soldiers lost since Berenice's attack on Headquarters showed up on Sayra-el raft, wearing native seasilk blankets but otherwise alive and well. The native lifeshapers had nursed them back to health.

Realgar was infuriated. The last thing he needed was any possible excuse for native sympathizing. He grilled the pair closely. "Why did you stay so long in enemy hands? Why did you fail to get in touch with us?"

"We tried, sir," Lieutenant Colonel Adrian, a special assistant from Jade's staff, spoke with impeccable correctness. "The natives risked their lives to inform the troops. Three of them were shot."

Realgar eyed her coldly. "You expect me to believe that?" He cursed the words as soon as spoken; of course, it was just typical insane native behavior.

"They couldn't do enough for us," said the other excitedly. "On the night of the explosion they fished us from the sea. I'd been stripped to the bone by fleshborers, but the natives pulled me through. In one of those lab warrens, they grew this sort of green film all over me—it was weird as the devil. But my flesh grew back underneath, see?" In his eagerness, the man pulled his sleeve back to show the skin, mottled with a slightly shadowed texture. A glance at the general's face shut him up.

"You will keep quiet, both of you," Realgar ordered. "Not a word of this will get out; is that clear?"

Officially it was put out that the two had survived despite barbaric conditions as prisoners of the natives, who had returned them only under pressure from Valan forces. Even so, some of the troops had got the idea that any native who approached them might have a rescued man to deliver.

To put a stop to it, search teams scoured every lab warren they could find for others "rescued" since the terrorist attack. Sure enough, two missing guards and a construction engineer turned up in the tunnels of Umesh-el. Doctor Nathan was sent out immediately.

On the general's viewing stage the missing men appeared, each encased in a greenish cocoon that bristled with vines and trailers, while native lifeshapers bustled about as fretfully as ants disturbed in their nest. Realgar was repulsed, but Nathan assured him all was well. "A living bandage covers the patient almost like another skin, to promote tissue regeneration. Their prognosis is excellent," said Nathan as he bent over one of the cocoons.

"I hope your follow-up confirms that assessment, Doctor."

From their partly exposed faces, the men appeared healthy, and one was awake enough to be debriefed, even exchanging wisecracks with members of the search team.

Nathan's face turned up toward the camera. "Another week, sir, and they'll be out and ready for duty, the lifeshapers say."

Realgar had heard enough of what lifeshapers had to say. "Good; ship them back to the infirmary."

"Oh, no, sir, I wouldn't move them. They're progressing fine here. I'm not sure I'd have the know-how to maintain those bandages properly."

A lifeshaper stared boldly at the camera and nodded for emphasis. Blackmail, thought Realgar, and his jaw clenched. "You propose to leave them hostage in enemy territory?"

Wrinkles deepened in Nathan's forehead, and he wiped his hand back over his scalp. He looked away as he said, "I simply can't guarantee their recovery if they're moved."

"Can you guarantee it if they stay?"

Nathan swallowed once and laid a hand on the cocoon, pressing it as if somehow to coax an answer to his dilemma. The doctor had aged fast during this campaign, Realgar thought. Did Nathan, too, suspect what Siderite had told the general—that native life science might already be potent enough to spell disaster for Valedon?

The man in the cocoon opened his eyelids wide and stretched his lips to speak. "Please sir; I'll be all right here. I looked like mincemeat when they put me in, but I'll be strong as a troll when I'm done. They promised. I'm not afraid, sir; I'm lucky to be alive."

The natives must have brainwashed him. "Nathan, I will not leave prisoners in enemy hands. Return them right now for intensive care in your own facility. And I want a full report on their state of health—physical and psychological." That was that, as far as Realgar was concerned. No native witch-doctor was going to make a fool of him.

5

Days passed, each marked by which one of the seven rafts—only seven, since the abandonment of Leni-el—sent witnessers to the soldier-place. None had yet returned, not even to Sayra-el, where soldiers rescued on that night of death had been nursed back to life. To heal in body is not always to heal in spirit.

The steady trickle of deaths bore down on Lystra, worse than having her own fingers broken one by one. She swam out to other rafts to share the sorrow of loved ones left behind, though she risked being caught; boats could not even get safely out of the branch channels. Around the ocean, clickflies white-eyes for mourning brought similar tales from every cluster, though few were as hard-pressed as Per-elion, where the Valan sickness was most acute.

The only Sharer whom clickflies had sighted alive at a soldier-place was Merwen. Many requests came for Merwen: had she survived and come home yet, and did she still believe that Valans were human? Lystra was surprised to see how important her mother's judgment had become to distant sisters who had never touched a branch of Raia-el. Merwen was just Lystra's mother, yet to others she seemed to be almost a legend. Faintly annoyed, Lystra caught herself wishing she had an ordinary mother living at home, rather than a legend dying in hell.

However impossible things got, starworms were there to keep her busy, and Spinel to share some comfort. Spinel even swam strongly enough to help her and Elonwy tend the starworms, raking their hide and their mouth filters, and refitting their bindings with new shockwraith sinews. Spinel had let his hair grow out about a thumb's length, and it waved underwater like an anemone. There was always something new and cheerful about Spinel, as well as the everpresent hope that he might yet provide an answer to the scourge from Valedon.

A rainstorm came over, not hard enough to send everyone down to the tunnels, but enough so that the family crowded together in the silkhouse for supper. Wellen and Weia were grumpy because they kept knocking elbows. Flossa and Mirri huddled together, whispering as if to shut out the rest of the dismal world. Lystra pulled her fingertips through Spinel's hair and remembered when he had hair before, in his early time here that had ended with the day he faced the breathmicrobes in his skin. That had not been easy, any more than for Lystra to survive the cage of stone.

Ishma was telling Usha, "We can't let the seaswallowers pass us by again. Stripeweed would strangle the silk groves, legfish would overrun the raft, and what next? The balance must be restored before it's beyond hope." Ishma spoke stiffly, in the tone she always used when Spinel was there. It vexed Lystra no end, but she could not help it if the stonesick ones Unspoke him.

"The swallowers will return," Usha replied. "Nira the Narrow-minded of Wan-elion has analyzed the toxin from the soldier-place and lifeshaped a microbe to consume it. She sent me the strain, and I think its efficiency can be improved a hundredfold; if released, then it will solve the problem. Mirri and Flossa will share this task."

"Can they bear such a crucial burden?"

"I hope so. I myself won't be around forever."

Lystra was stricken. Surely her mothersister did not intend to follow Merwen to the soldier-place?

Usha looked up from her plate, where seaweeds were tangled, uneaten. "We also need some new leaders for evening learnsharing, Spinel."

Startled, Spinel sat up and shook the hair off his forehead. "Who, me? I'm no good at learnsharing. I never learned a thing in school."

"You're a good learnsharer," Usha insisted. "You must know so many useful things: about Valedon, for instance."

"About Valans," suggested Flossa. "About why they—" She did not finish.

Spinel looked stricken.

"What more can Spinel know about that?" Lystra demanded. "*That* seems to be the only thing anyone ever wants from him. I have a better idea, Spinel. Share with us what you know about stone."

At that, even Wellen's eyes widened with interest. Ishma stiffened and turned her back, but she did not leave the room, as she could have.

Usha nodded. "On the nature of stone, an whether its atoms are alive or dead. That would make a good lesson."

"But—but that's forbidden." Disconcerted, Spinel looked back and forth between Usha and Lystra, and the icy star flickered on his chest.

"No learnsharing is forbidden."

"Oh, but I can't, that's all. I don't have any chipping tools, or even different kinds of stone, to demonstrate."

Lystra snapped, "All right, so you don't want to." Disappointed, she glanced across the cluttered table to Wellen, who was stretching her arms and lazily fluttering her fingers although she ought to have cleared the table by now. "Wellen, if you don't finish cleaning up I'm going to sit outside in the rain until you do."

"If you do, I'll go to the soldier-place tomorrow."

All around, shocked eyes stared at the child. Wellen pulled a ferocious frown, but she got up and stacked plates with a clatter.

Lystra could not bear it any longer. She escaped down into the tunnels, where the patter of rain was shut out and she was alone except for a few apprentice lifeshapers still at work in their vine-filled chambers. After a minute or so Spinel found her, since he knew her favorite paths. He caught her waist and rested his chin on her neck. "Come back," he whispered in her ear. "You got everybody upset."

"I'm tired of it all." Too many hours wrestling the starworms. Every bend in a tunnel seemed to open into the gut of such a beast.

"You have to come for the singing, so we can sing the song for the—for 'Those who dwell on land.'"

"Is that all we can do for them?" Lystra shuddered violently. How could she go on living, while so many were dying? Trurl, Perlianir, Grandmother Ama; in the dim phosphorescence their faces rose to beckon her.

Lystra dreamed she was back in the stone cell with her skin tearing off, a nightmare that often cursed her sleep. She awoke with a start. Light was seeping in, and the raft was still. The rain must have spent itself overnight.

On the mat beside her, Spinel was still curled up in his blanket, his furry head turned away. Lystra pressed the hair gently, careful not to wake him, and thought, This might be the last time.

Lystra stole outside and blinked in the light of the sun, which blazed at the far edge of the ocean. She clucked her tongue until a clickfly appeared and stuttered out what the time was. Then she walked slowly down to the water's edge and sat in the damp weeds. It would not be long now, before the two soldiers came for their stroll, as they did every morning, regular as the sun.

Suddenly each remaining moment became infinitely precious, full of meaning beyond sharing. A leaf tickled her foot, and a millipede crawled to the green tip, then fell off. The leaf sprang back, and droplets of water spattered Lystra's skin, each one with a spark to it, as round and expectant as a door. Each moment was a door that opened into the next, and even the Last, when it came, would only open into the First again.

Two dusty figures took form in the distance, as they approached along the water line. They grew into malefreaks, swinging their rust-feathered arms.

Lystra rose to her feet and stepped deliberately, one foot ahead of the other. The malefreaks stolidly kept up their approach. One was actually a "normal" female, Lystra saw, not that it made any difference. Their faces came into focus, four flat blue eyes with black pinhead pupils.

One of the figures slowed, and their steps broke synchrony. "What do you want, catfish? You got one of us hidden in the raft?"

Lystra spread her hands. "What have I to hide? Do you hide yourself behind your skin?"

Boots ground to a halt in the mud. "Catfish, if you get lost I'll pretend I didn't see you."

"Why hide truth behind words?"

"I'll have to kill you," said the blue-eyed face.

"And why kill?"

"It's my duty, that's all." The face looked away, as if impatient.

"I know what your 'duty' is," Lystra said. "Your 'duty' is to protect mothers and children, not to kill them."

"The devil take you." A silver stick flew at Lystra's head, and that was the last she recalled.

* * *

Her eyelids flickered open. Her arms were so heavy they might
have been weighted with coral, yet she dimly realized that she was
not quite ready to sink to the ocean floor. As her mind cleared,
Lystra saw Spinel leaning over, his forehead as wrinkled as silk-
weave with a pulled thread. His hands clenched tight over his starstone.

With an immense effort Lystra pulled herself up, until her head
spun. "I—I'm still here. The death-hasteners came, and they..."
There were only the bootprints sunk in the mud, to track all around
the raft.

From behind, Usha said. "They left you alive. It's a good
sign."

Usha's casual tone startled her. Lystra blinked and twisted herself around.

"Well, what do you expect?" Usha demanded. "At this point I
couldn't even stop Wellen from throwing herself into the fray,
much less you. I know it's unfair of me, but just remember all the
same who will blame me for whatever trouble you share."

Lystra shut her eyes. "Unfair you are, Mothersister."

A kiss touched her scalp as Usha whispered. "She would be as
proud of you as I am."

With a sigh Lystra sat up straight, her head throbbing though
her mind had cleared. Spinel cupped her head in his hands.
"Lystra, why? Why didn't you tell me?"

She winced at the pain in his voice. "For that which can't be
shared."

"Well, you're still alive, and I won't let you go again. I won't
leave you alone until you promise."

She relaxed in his hands, still dazed at the wonder of it, that she
was still here, that once again the Last Door had shut in her face.
"I do what I have to. And so will you."

For answer, he pulled away and scooped something up in his
hand to show her: five brittle shapes of stone, one clear and sharp,
the others polished round. "I found *these* outside the door this
morning. How do you suppose they got there?"

Lystra laughed wearily. That Ishma must have squirreled away
a few of the forbidden objects, all this time. "Well, stoneshaper,
you have your work cut out for you."

"A stonecutter," Spinel muttered in Valan, "to teach what stone
is made of. If only my father could see me now."

6

In the evening, plantlights cast flickering beams among the sisters gathered for learnsharing. Sheets of clickfly web stood tall, covered with glowing symbols and diagrams.

With help from Lystra, Spinel had programmed one section of clickfly web. The insects spun out some simple crystalline diagrams of the sort that Cyan once made him memorize. Spinel was determined to show the Sharers that there was nothing about "stone" that could not be explained in rational terms, that the "dead atoms" of stone were just the same as the "living atoms" that made up living things, no matter what the traders said.

Lystra looked back over her shoulder. "You've collected quite a crowd tonight."

Spinel turned to see. Besides Usha and the girls, and the stone-sick ones, there were various neighbors and cousins from other silkhouses of Raia-el. At least they did not all sit in the back, the way Spinel and his classmates used to do in the schoolhouse; that would have been unbearable. Instead they pressed together close, and perfume wafted over from some of them. Spinel found himself wondering who was going to start off the learnsharing; then he remembered there was no one else but him. He cleared his throat and wondered where to begin.

Then a sharp glint of light caught his eye, and he froze. The light reflected off the firewhip of a soldier who stood back in the shadows with his arms crossed.

Spinel lost his balance and gripped Lystra's arm. "Lystra, why don't we do this tomorrow instead?"

"What? Spinel, you're not going to back out just because there's a craven death-hastener standing behind us all, too shy to come up where he can see." Lystra jabbed at one of the diagrams that glowed in the clickfly web. "What are all these dots and circles, stacked in a cube? What's that supposed to mean?"

"That's a salt crystal." Spinel's voice sounded thin and shaky in his own ears. "Like when seawater dries, and salt grows out in little cubes. The atoms pack together, alternating sodium and chloride." He looked to Usha, hoping he had gotten the names of the atoms right in Sharer.

"Those are the main atoms in seawater," Usha agreed.

"Well, stone grows up in the same way."

Someone asked, "Then why don't we have stone here? There's plenty of seawater."

"You do have stone, but it's heavy and falls to the bottom." Where the dead dwell—Spinel hurried past this. "Other kinds of stone formed when the planet was young, when it just came from the sun and everything was liquid as water. So stone is just as 'alive' as the sun is."

A few chins lifted at that, and the listeners muttered among themselves. "I don't believe it," said Ishma. "I've never seen a piece of stone grow or change at all."

Spinel was disconcerted. How could you run a class if the pupils talked back like that?

Lystra demanded, "Do you accuse an untruth?"

"Of course not." Ishma was scandalized. "I just can't share the concept of it."

Spinel said, "It takes high heat and pressure. On Valedon, in a 'factory' with lots of firecrystals, you can grow stone, even diamond." He held up the diamond, a sparkling clear gem, one of those he had found that morning outside the silkhouse door. "Diamond is the hardest stone there is. It's just plain carbon packed together in pyramids." He pointed to another diagram. "Carbon atoms, each glued tight to four others." Everyone knew carbon, the most basic atom of living things. They had to see, now.

"Where do the colors come from?" someone asked.

"Oh, that's from trace atoms that absorb light in different ways. In my starstone, for instance, a few iron atoms make it blue."

"But iron makes blood red."

Usha said, "That's all right, it depends on the oxidation state, and how the electrons swim around. How are the iron atoms arranged, Spinel?"

"Well, the stone is made of oxygen and 'aluminum' in hexagons, layered like a sandwich. Here and there, iron takes the place of 'aluminum.' And then, if you get tiny needles of 'titanium oxide' mixed in with the hexagons, they reflect light in a sixpoint

star; but you have to cut the stone just right for it to come out."
Then Spinel wanted to tell about the cutting and polishing of stone,
how gems were shaped to make them sparkle, since this was what
he knew best.

But someone wanted to know, "What are these things called
'aluminum' and 'titanium'? Are they regular atoms?"

Now he was trapped. Spinel had only the vaguest notion of
what distinguished different elements. "Well, those atoms are
heavier than carbon; 'titanium' is almost as heavy as iron." He
turned to Lystra and said in Valan, "It's no use; I told you I never
learned much."

Usha asked, "Can you say how many protons they have?"

Spinel squeezed his eyes shut and tried to remember.

"Twenty-two," called a deep voice. Spinel's eyes flew open.
"Titanium has twenty-two protons," the soldier said, "and aluminum has thirteen."

Attention shifted, and the learnsharers went still and tense.

"Is that right," said Usha, unruffled. "I know what aluminum
is, then. Some plants need it. But I've never detected the atom of
twenty-two protons."

"It exists all right, lady. I should know; I was a metallurgist in
Sardis, before I signed up." The man sounded casual enough, but
all Spinel could think was, What the devil is he here for? Spying?

Usha asked, "are there other atoms, too, between titanium and
iron?"

Vanadium, chromium, and manganese." He listed their proton
numbers.

"Manganese, yes, that's essential for plants. How very curious." Usha turned to her sister to explain in Sharer about these
elements and how they fit in.

The soldier turned to Spinel. "You sound like a stonecutter."

Somehow Spinel found his voice again. "My father was, Cyan
of Chrysoport." He kept glancing at the shiny weapon that hung
from the man's belt.

"Well you can call me Jasper. I don't want my name and rank
getting around, see. Listen, can you tell me, are any of those native witch-doctors around? I've had this hell of a back pain, the
doc says it's all in my head, but I used to ease it with a moon
medicine, before trade collapsed. You still trade gemstones around
here? I've got some real pretty ones the gals will like."

Stonetrade, of all things. Spinel was shocked and embarrassed.

Before he could recover, Lystra stepped boldly in front of the soldier. "You'll have whatever medicines you need, if you share with us something equally crucial: you must join our learnsharing every night from now on."

Jasper blinked at her. "Lady, I risked my neck just to come once."

"So do I, to talk with you."

"So what do you want soldiers hanging around for?"

"We like sharing with soldiers," Lystra said coolly. "It helps us feel 'protected.' Isn't that what soldiers are for?"

Jasper scratched his head. "Maybe I can stop by every week or so."

"That's not often enough."

"Twice a week, if my back gets completely better."

"Done." Lystra extended her hand to shake on the deal. Not for nothing had she shared with traders for all those years.

7

Realgar had Merwen brought to his office again. As usual she had not a stitch on except for Nathan's electrode monitors taped to her scalp. Merwen sat crosslegged on the floor, with all the brazen equanimity of a street beggar. Realgar laced his fingers upon his knee as he faced her, relaxed. "Impatient One, have you any idea of how many Sharers have died at our hands in the past month?"

Merwen considered this. "Even one is too many."

"Forty thousand, across the globe," Realgar emphasized. "That's over a thousand a day. You do the arithmetic: how long can that keep up, before no Sharer remains?"

"That depends on how soon soldiers stop trying to share death."

Realgar laughed shortly. "It's not like you to delude yourself. 'Killing' is the proper word, Impatient One. Killing is a soldier's business."

"So is 'protection.' Clickflies assure me that many have already learned to share protection instead of death."

So that trollhead of a doctor had let her pick up *clickflies* outdoors. She must know damned well how many natives were dying —and how many were spared. Realgar wondered in fact what the actual figures were. It was hard to check out the reports of his officers. At any rate, Nathan would suffer for this, and as for Merwen, she had breathed her last fresh air. "Do not expect to brainwash us all, just because you succeeded with a few victims of your terrorist attack. We're on to that trick now."

"'Brainwash'? What is that?"

"You know very well what it is. The sort of mindbending for which whitetrance is a defense."

Merwen looked puzzled. "Whitetrance is the most vulnerable state of consciousness. On Shora, with such small rafts to dwell upon, it is hard to find solitude. Whitetrance gives each Sharer one place alone with her soul. And that aloneness is just a whisper away from death. If you learn whitetrance, you will see how it is."

For just a moment he was tempted, out of curiosity; then he was furious with himself. "Your sisters are dying by the thousands," he told her coldly, "and you, Impatient One, are responsible. A word from you could prevent their deaths."

"Which word is that?"

"A word of submission to the Patriarch."

"Should I exchange one sort of death for another?"

"You'll have to fight back, then. Is that why your lifeshapers plan to inactivate our seaswallower repellent? To kill my troops?" Swallowers would be a nuisance, all right, but if natives were to blame for it, his troops would would be a lot less softheaded two months from now.

"Seaswallowers threaten us as much as you, except that you do not dwell on proper rafts. You are welcome to share our rafts when the time comes."

"Yet a few deaths are unavoidable."

"Without seaswallowers, the entire life web would collapse, and Sharers would starve."

"That's just the point, Merwen. Unless you kill us, you can't stop us from killing you, all of you, to the last soul. So why should you not 'hasten' a few deaths, a brief epidemic? That would give Talion pause for thought. He might pull us out altogether." Realgar watched her closely.

Merwen shook her head slightly, as if the answer were obvious. "There is a difference between seaswallower and human. A human sees herself in the mirror. I am human, and so, inescapably, are you."

"But you are desperate. How can you refuse to kill those who threaten to exterminate you?"

"How can I not refuse? I am a selfnamer; that is, I know myself not only in the mirror of ocean, but in the mirror of every living pair of eyes. If I were to kill, my soul would die. If Sharers took to killing, we would surely exterminate ourselves." Merwen paused. "Our situation may be desperate, but we do not despair. You, perhaps, are trapped in chronic despair. Berenice pulled out of it, for a while, but she fell back in."

His muscles knotted, but he kept his voice calm. "Why?" he asked slowly. "What pulled her back after she became...one of you?"

"She shared your love, and your despair."

Realgar thought he should have hated the Sharer for daring to say such a thing. Oddly, he felt only a numb weight on his chest. Perhaps by now he had exhausted his capacity for hatred of her. "Sharers don't love men," he observed dryly. "Is that why you are immune to our despair?"

"No one is immune. My own daughter nearly fell into despair, yet love for another brought her back—love for a young man from Valedon."

"So you might yet become desperate enough. That is why Malachite requires us to control you."

"Why pull us into despair? Instead, let us help you *out*. Once you understand our way, you need never share fear with Malachite again."

Realgar felt his pulse quicken. It was a seductive promise, never again to fear the dreadful power of Torr. But the promise was pitiful illusion. "It is only wise to fear Malachite."

"And to be feared by him?"

"Impossible. How could any mere Valan threaten the Envoy of the Patriarch?"

"Only in the way that Sharers seem a threat...by immunity to 'orders.'"

His voice rose. "Do you think we disobey orders by killing you? Do not depend upon the mercy of Malachite. You are declared Valan subjects, and we may discipline you at will, even wipe you off the planet." Realgar paused, then reflected in a silken tone, "That would be a pity, for such peaceful people." At the press of a button, a guard stepped in to take her away.

Afterward the general took a brisk walk out on the deck to clear his head. The sea crashed and sprayed against the side, while in the distance new raft seedlings bobbed upon the sparkling waves. The persistent scent of raft blossoms was depressing, and overhead clickflies chattered as if to mock him.

He should have ignored the issue of Berenice, Realgar told himself, since it betrayed personal weakness. More insidious was Merwen's strain of resistance to the Envoy, a resistance that was quixotic yet startlingly attractive. Realgar himself admitted resentment against the Envoy who had leveled Pyrrhopolis, made the High Protector bow and scrape before him, and left Valedon the subject of a cold-blooded experiment, if Siderite was to be believed. But then, envy of one's superiors was only the natural order of things. Merwen was naive indeed to propose an alliance against Torr.

The three men removed from native care in the lab warren did not fare well. Their "living bandages" grew out of control, rooting parasitic fibers into their flesh, and none of Nathan's skill could save them from a lingering, excruciating death. Realgar expressed official regrets and laid the blame for the tragedy on the barbaric treatments of native lifeshapers. Like Malachite, Realgar accepted the fact that his duty required decisions painful to his subordinates.

8

While daily witnessers at the soldier-place still met death, on the rafts it was different. Soldiers out on patrol would leave a Sharer stunned or simply ignore her. At night on Raia-el, it became common for soldiers to drop in on learnsharing sessions, either out of curiosity or to "trade" for medicines. From what Jasper said,

Spinel gathered that medicines from the Ocean Moon had cost a mint in Sardis, even in the best of times, and were no longer to be found since Operation Amethyst put a stop to trade. Jasper came often, and he brought holocubes to depict the fabrication of metal and stone, many things even Spinel did not know.

Swallower season was almost upon them, and Sharers were fixing up their lifeboats again, when one night Jasper approached Spinel, along with a pair of important-looking officers. "Listen, son, could you help us out? The colonel, here, wants to talk with the Protector's wife."

Spinel blinked, at first not comprehending. Jasper was sweating and hunched his shoulder uneasily. Was it because of the colonel? Both the colonel and the lady officer behind him wore cloaks to cover their stonesigns.

"Protector's wife?" Spinel repeated. "You don't mean Usha?"

"Yes, that's right, Usha." Jasper shifted his feet, clearly wishing he were somewhere else.

Spinel hurried down to the lifeshaping place to find her. At first Usha would not leave her work, and Spinel had to persuade her of an emergency, that a sister might be lying mortally ill.

Usha appeared outside, her face etched in moonlight. "I am Usha the Inconsiderate, lifeshaper of Raia-el. Where is the sick one?"

Jasper asked, "May I go, sir?"

"Dismissed," snapped the colonel, "and keep your mouth shut."

Jasper was gone in an instant.

The colonel turned to Usha. "First of all, if our purpose here tonight were uncovered prematurely, we would be shot. Do you understand?"

"Yes," said Usha without irony. "I am sorry to hear this."

" A number of officers are concerned about the direction of this campaign. We are aware that plans have been drawn, and approved by the Palace, for comprehensive directed-energy bombardment of inhabited rafts. We are convinced that the High Protector and the Commander of the Guard intend nothing short of full extermination of your people. Do you understand?"

"I hear you," said Usha.

"It is in clear contradiction of Patriarchal Law for one planetary population to exterminate another. That privilege is reserved for the Patriarch alone. If His Envoy should return to find Shora empty, he might well destroy Valedon in turn, or at the very least destroy Sardis, if Sardish troops were found to be responsible. The Iridian High Protector claims, of course, that Shora is a dangerously rebellious province under his protection. Frankly, I consider that claim preposterous. There is no rebel force here, and Talion knows it. Talion wants to trap us, so that Sardis will take the blame when the Envoy returns, and Iridis will be left with one less rival city to control."

"I am very sorry to hear all this," said Usha, although Spinel suspected she had no idea what the colonel was talking about. Spinel knew only too well, and the blood pounded in his ears.

"It is unfortunate," the colonel went on, "that our respected Commander has allowed his ambition to supersede his better judgment in this matter. Nevertheless, enough key officers are ready to rise and demand a cease-fire—if a statement of noninterference is obtained." He paused, then added, "You must promise complete noninterference with Valan interests on Shora."

"Interests? Does that mean traders?"

"Lunar developers. We have their tacit support already. The war has meant costly delays, and every week lost marks red ink in their books."

The lady officer added icily, "A fool's war it's been, with no army to fight and no land to fight for."

"There is ocean," said Usha. "Traders share harm with the ocean."

The colonel frowned. "Your very existence as a people is at stake, remember. Once we cease fire, you can negotiate whatever you want, including our withdrawal and the return of your Protector. A statement of principle is all we need now."

Usha thought awhile. "The Raia-el Gathering will consider this."

"When? We need an answer tonight, before it's too late. That is why we came to you."

Usha clearly was baffled.

Spinel blurted out, "There is no Protector of Shora."

The colonel stiffened. "Adrian, is this raft Raia-el not the 'capital' of Shora?"

"It's the closest thing to it," said the lady officer Adrian. "I've decoded enough clickflies to know that other rafts will go along with Raia-el. What Protector can ever guarantee his provinces completely?"

"I know, but the field officers won't join without a statement."
He turned to Usha again. "We'll give you twenty-four hours to
decide. I warn you, every minute of delay risks blowing the whole
deal open."

The two officers bowed formally, then marched off. Minutes
later, the engine of a helicopter roared off in the distance, briefly
covering the sound of the sea. Then it was gone. Spinel thought
surely he could only have dreamed it all, that a Sardis colonel had
come and bowed to Usha the Intemperate One.

9

After three months of attrition, natives still insisted on showing up
every day, not just at Headquarters but at regional bases as well.
Realgar could not understand it. What were they, automatons? To
keep his troops from getting restless, he ordered more maneuvers
at sea and staged satellite attacks, and tried to ignore the inevitable
Palace complaints about footing the bill. One could not expect to
subdue a planet cheaply.

Despite his efforts to boost morale, his troops were slacking
off. Just how badly was hard to tell, with the patrols spread so
thin, but it was clear that troopers were neglecting to shoot natives
on sight; they would stun them or simply look the other way, as if
imitating the passive resistance of their opponents. The men were
disciplined when caught, but it was not possible to watch everyone
at every moment, not when even line officers turned a blind eye.

To be sure, some of the troops had grown inured to their task,
as Realgar had expected. Unfortunately they got out of hand, and
the resulting atrocities had further depressed morale, while sprouting ugly rumors back on Valedon. The polarization had reached a
point where a number of regiments should have been replaced, but
it would be unthinkable to approach the Palace with such a re-

quest, now that he had the Sardish corps he had pressed for so hard.

So long as natives were dying steadily for their incalcitrance, plain arithmetic showed they would have to give in soon. But with deaths tapering off, how could he hope to persuade any of them, let alone Protector Merwen, that the game was up?

He was left to the last resort: satellite targeting of the rafts. Now he wished he had started off with that, right after the "terrorist attack," when the political risk would have been lowest.

Then Jade brought stunning news. "General, I've uncovered a mutiny in the works, a plot among the staff."

"A mutiny? What the hell do you mean?"

"With native collusion," Jade went on crisply. "The deal was for the natives to back off long enough for the troops to make a decent exit and let Talion do as he liked thereafter. To be frank, sir, they think Talion has overstepped his mandate, and that you—"

"Yes, I know what the trollheads think." Realgar himself knew better, he knew what a lethal threat those natives were; but how long could the troops believe in a threat they could not see or feel? Until this was settled, a satellite strike was out of the question.

Shock swept through him as the news sunk in. Mutiny was unheard of, except perhaps in a battalion cowed by a ninety-percent casualty rate. Everything was turned upside down in this campaign.

"I've got the situation in hand, General," Jade assured him. "With the leaders captured, the insurrection died as swiftly as it arose."

"Execute the leaders. Torr's name, who were the damned leaders?"

A printout spat from his monitor, a list of officers, mostly colonels and lieutenant colonels from the first, third, and fourth divisions. At one name, he slammed the paper down. "Jade, that Adrian had to have been brainwashed. Why the devil did you keep her on?"

"General, I probed her inside out and she read clean. Her stay in that lab warren gave us invaluable intelligence about—" Jade stopped short and bit her lip. Lines worked in her cheeks, an unusual lapse of control. She must have thought what Realgar was thinking: If even Jade could no longer depend on such a trusted assistant, then who could the Commander himself count on?

* * *

In his office Realgar paced back and forth between his desk and the throw rug with its tigers and antelope stitched in fine russet wool. His thoughts were far from Sardis now.

Time had run out on his crumbling campaign. To be sure, the revolt had been quashed without Talion's hearing of it, but it was a matter of days, a week at the most, before Palace spies would get word somehow. He could still order a satellite strike, but was it worth losing control of his own corps? Not while another option remained.

The Natives might yet yield—or strike back with a blow that would galvanize his troops once more. This was it, the last chance for Protector Merwen.

Behind him, the door hissed open. Realgar turned and stood at attention as Merwen entered. "So, Impatient One," he began without letting her sit down. "What do you have to say for yourself? Your sisters have thrown themselves defenselessly before the onslaught of my troops, a psychological device that may soften the heads of a few men but only hastens the final day of reckoning."

Merwen looked more awkward standing than she did seated. Her cheeks sagged beneath her eyes, and her skin had a grayish cast, for she was never let outside now. "Your words puzzle me."

Realgar laughed. "You are more coldblooded than I gave you credit for. You've used defenseless citizens, even grandmothers, as weapons. There is more ice in you than in Jade."

Merwen hesitated, and her fingers twined at her sides. "It is true that one who watches one's sisters die without lifting a finger is in danger of losing her humanity. One's soul may drift away, almost imperceptibly, like a raft without starworms. Still, there is hope for you."

"Don't hope to hard. Your subversion of my soldiers has only convinced me to let the satellites finish you off. And Raia-el will go first—today." Realgar paused to let this sink in. "So now is your last chance to quit."

She was silent.

"You disbelieve me?"

"I learned a year ago on Valedon how dangerous your kind can be. Nothing you have shared surprises me."

"You did not answer my question," Realgar said with forced quietness. "Do you believe I will erase your people from this planet?"

"You will not, she said, too quickly. "You fear the final end to us even more than you fear us alive."

He did fear, and he could have strangled her for it—fear of Malachite's judgment, fear of what hidden plagues might already have doomed him. "So you depend on fear, even as we do."

"No, no; we don't share fear by choice. Fear is your ultimate weapon, not mine. Mine is sharing: to share my own soul with yours, until the mask falls from your eyes. When you come to see that your survival is inseparable and indistinguishable from mine, then we both will win."

"Nonsense. Death is the ultimate weapon. Once you all die, that will be the end of it."

"Will it? How can you be sure? If even one lives to know your shame, you will fear, and your fear will consume you."

Realgar's fists tensed. "Your raving will make no difference. You will be dead, and so will your children."

Merwen stepped closer. "How can you stand there and tell me you're not human? Don't you hear your own voice and see your own eyes? What do you see in the mirror?"

He saw the shaving mirror again, that first morning when the purple tinge appeared, and the mornings afterward as it deepened, dark as the face below him now. His fury heightened. "What in hell tells you I'm human at all? What makes you so damned sure of that?"

Lines tautened under her chin, and the silence lengthened into minutes.

"So you doubt us." Realgar sensed a ghost of a chance. "You doubt that I am not human."

"Not at all."

"You're afraid to say why, though, which amounts to the same thing. What is it? What makes you sure?"

No answer.

His voice filled with contempt. "Where is your honesty now, Sharer, the frankness you are so proud of? You fear me far more than I fear you."

"I fear for you. Some kinds of truth are too dangerous for children. Answer this first: Whose eyes do you see in mine, and whose in the mirror?"

With a will of its own his arm lashed out, connecting with one cheekbone, then the other. Merwen reeled back against the wall, but kept her head up without covering her bleeding face, still gazing from eye sockets beginning to swell.

Realgar turned and barked at the monitor for a guard. Intensely discomfited, he could almost feel her stare pressing at his back before she was led away. Already he regretted his mistake. In one instant of anger, he had lost sight of what he most needed to know, just when it came within his grasp. He had to regain the advantage now, before time ran out.

10

Merwen pursued her deadly game with the Valan wordweaver, as doggedly and perhaps as blindly as she had with Virien so many years before. In between, down through those years, how many countless gatherings and unspeakings and troubled souls had shared at least some healing from Merwen's wordweaving, yet today it was Virien all over again, with thousands of lives and rafts at stake beside her own.

They did share a common goal, she and Realgar. Each intended to reach an agreement, an understanding, with the other. But where Merwen tried to elicit healing, Realgar offered only sickness, which he wished her to share in order to lessen the shame of his own living death. Against that current Merwen had made slow progress.

Merwen did not blame him for striking her. She knew she had asked for it the moment she slipped and let herself share his fear, instead of reaching for his soul. After that, his own fear rose to such a pitch that it had to come out somehow. And then, his act was a sign to her: when a wordweaver acts, it is usually because one has run out of words.

Merwen thought over these things as she sat crosslegged upon her elevated sleeping-place, her swollen face uplifted to Nathan, who examined her bruises with his blunt Valan fingers. Nathan asked, "Are you sure you won't take an injection? The swelling will go down much faster.

"No, thank you." Perhaps unfairly, Merwen had resisted Valan medical treatments as far as possible since the deaths of those poor men withdrawn from the care of Sharer lifeshapers.

"The general wants to see you again," Nathan added. "I told him you are in critical condition, but he is very insistent."

Merwen eyed Nathan sternly. "Why did you share an untruth?"

At that the would-be lifeshaper left in a hurry, and Merwen was suddenly alone. She thought of her daughters, and of the untold suffering that went on outside, until anguish possessed her and screamed from her mind: *The sea . . . give me back the sea. How long must I dwell on land?*

A dark shape entered the room. Merwen struggled to focus her eyes, which stung beneath her hot eyelids. The shape wavered, then fixed.

It was Realgar. Merwen had never seen him come to this place before. Realgar watched her calmly, his arms at his sides with the fingers closed, his mouth small, his eyes clear and wide. Then he sat down and crossed his legs on the floor.

Immediately Merwen slid off the sleeping-place and fell hard on the cold floor. She seated herself to face him, and her pulse raced as though a wild fanwing had come to roost at her feet. The Valan looked so odd, though, with his flat-bottomed boots poking awkwardly from his legs and the creases stretched in his plumage. Nervous laughter welled up in her throat, but she clenched her teeth against it.

"I regret that I shared injury with you. It will not happen again." His words flowed in Sharer, for the first time since Merwen had come here.

"I saw your anger," Merwen said, trying to relax, to slow the blood that swelled her veins. "A Sharer so angry would have Unspoken me for a year. That would be much harder to bear."

Realgar took time to choose his words. "Do you know why I was so angry? It is because I saw my face in the mirror at the time when it most resembled yours."

Merwen sighed and her eyes half closed. If only the Valan could grasp the full truth of his own words. "And why? A hundred times why, why should that make you angry?"

"Because the choice was not mine. You insisted then that I was 'human' enough to share your breathmicrobes; yet you will not share with me why you know that I am human."

She remembered suddenly when Nisi had first brought her Valan lovesharer to Shora: a male, as strong and proud as Yinevra, one who rarely spoke but showed a dry wit when he did, his eyes hard as coral except when they reached to Nisi. "I knew, when I saw the love you shared with Nisi."

"Nisi." The name came reluctantly from him. "I share nothing with Nisi. In fact, I will have to hasten her death."

Then Nisi was still alive. Merwen glowed with the pleasure of it. She had been so sure that Realgar would not let Nisi live, despite his love. Merwen thought, How little faith I have.

"Does it please you to hear that the one who betrayed you will die?"

"I rejoice that she may not die, that you still have a chance to share life with her. To *not-kill* her." Not-killing—in Valan terms, that was the lesson Merwen had to share.

Merwen thought. "There was Siderite."

"Siderite betrayed you with every word he shared. All his learnsharing was intended to control, to share defeat with you."

"If that was his intent, then we indeed betrayed him. Do you suppose that Usha would share the most crucial of her skills with a frightened child?"

Realgar said nothing, and the silence expanded, a wave rippling outward. The silence called to her, shamed her more than any words could to share the last truth. Feeling lightheaded, she did so, knowing that she committed herself to fate.

"Spinel," she whispered. "Spinel may be Impulsive, but he will never share betrayal."

"The young Spirit Caller?"

"Spinel was like you, as a child. On the day we first met in Chrysoport, he urged me blindly to share the will of those who carry deathsticks, as you do. Yet now he is healed. That is why I still share hope with you."

"Perhaps it's time we had a reunion with . . . Spinel."

The next day Merwen was led again to Realgar's office. He was sitting carelessly on his desk, in relaxed conversation with another soldier—

Spinel, in full red plumage down to the black boots, toying curiously with a death-stick in his hand.

Spinel turned his face, and he gasped, and the death-stick clunked on the floor. He stepped forward, reaching out. "Merwen, it's you at last!"

But she shrank back to the wall, every inch of her skin rebelling at the shape he had taken, her tongue arching with nausea.

Spinel stopped, puzzled. "It's okay, Merwen. They wouldn't let me in without getting dressed. Anyway, I've come to share taking you home." He glanced uncertainly at Realgar, then back to Merwen.

Realgar said, "He learned to use the firewhip."

"What? Not really, only just now." Spinel kicked the death-stick away from him.

"Didn't you? You've become one of us now."

"I did not." Blinking furiously, Spinel began to see the trap he was in. "I did not, I tell you! *You tell her I didn't!*" He grabbed insistently at Realgar's arm.

Realgar shook him off. "Come, now, is that any way for a Sharer to behave? It's no use; you're one of us now."

"I . . . am . . . not . . ." Spinel slumped down against the desk, his head at an angle. Gradually his face and hands turned olive-green as on the first day she saw him, devoid of violet.

"Damn." Immensely irritated, Realgar shouted at a plate on the wall, and a guard came to drag Spinel away. Then Merwen regretted that she had not shared a word at least, that she had let the shock repress her. But this time, she thought, he knows white-trance; he must be safe.

Realgar was cordial again. "Of course, Spinel was too shy to perform for you, but we have a recording of his service with us."

The room darkened, except for a luminous cube above the viewing stage. A simulation appeared, a three-dimensional mirror of life as miraculous as the ones shown by the first traders. There was blue sky, above the deck of the soldier-place, where Spinel stood in his soldier's plumage, strangely impassive. The sound of ocean rushed in, and a stray note from a clickfly: *today was a daughter conceived by Aia of Umesh-el. . . .* Beyond Spinel sat two sisters of Sayra-el, come in their turn to witness unto death.

The cloth creased and stretched behind Spinel's shoulder as his arm rose, and at his hand the stick glinted, and then the witnessers gave up their life-blood.

Spinel. Spinel had died in life. Yinevra was right; the Valans were no better than servos. Let the flames consume them, and let Shora's ocean bury them forever.

But the Sharers of Shora would never know.

Already her surroundings were telescoping into one dark hole, but her last words escaped. "Hear this, however long you live in death: Though Spinel has shared my betrayal, you, Realgar, shall not."

Then her soul flew out, and the galaxies swirled away to sunspecks on water. Farther and farther her senses expanded, more distant than she had ever flung herself before, until all the universe was just a faint haze in the dark behind her, a shockwraith slinking away. She reached out to the Last Door and stepped through.

Dreams came, too vivid for whitetrance. All those she saw in her dreams were dead by now: Mother Ama, Trurl, Yinevra glowed whitely before her. Their bodies were youthful, all barely out of girlhood, as Merwen had not seen them for decades. Yinevra's forehead was as unlined as on the day they first had kissed and murmured of a future together, a future unknowingly foreclosed in bitterness and pain. Only there was no pain here. "Yinevra. Forgiven."

Yinevra smiled, the small knowing smile that Merwen had leaned upon before she had learned her own strength. "Almost too long you waited, Patient One. Come in, now, and close the door behind you."

So the Last Door remained open; she still had to close it. For some reason Merwen hesitated. *Today was a daughter conceived* . . . "Yinevra, what are you doing here? Why hasn't your soul found a new home?"

Yinevra's shape flickered and fled. Ama loomed above her, erect and tall, large as if Merwen were still a child. "My daughter, we can't go back yet, because there are too few infants to take us in. Too many deaths hastened, too soon."

Then Merwen understood that Mother Ama wished her to go back, to somehow find a way. "It's too late, Mother. I would only fall sick." The sickness unto death—Merwen would not share that betrayal.

The dreams evaporated, and all was still. Out of the stillness, through the Door, came a regular tapping sound, and she strained to catch it. It was the sound of her own heart beating.

Someone or something outside in that distant blot of a universe must have kept her heart going when she had willed it to stop.

Could it be Nathan, the primitive lifeshaper? Perhaps his Valan skills were good for something, after all.

Curious now, Merwen stilled her own breath. Within seconds it started up again, despite her absent will. It must be Nathan, she thought, and the thought of a Valan actually shaping life for a change gave her a peculiar joy. What else could Nathan shape? The pressure of her blood, its pH, its sugar level; all these she willed out of balance, in turn, and each was soon restored. When she altered her endorphin secretion, that failed to return, so she restored it herself and continued to probe Nathan's skill. Merwen was in no hurry to close the Door, nor to return and face the impossible existence she had left behind.

11

In the infirmary Realgar looked down on the frail Sharer head, which was white as the sheets around it except for blue veins tracing around her neck. Realgar himself felt drained from mental fatigue, his neck tense and sore. The day before, it had taken more out of him than he expected to face Merwen here, for every ounce of his will rebelled against the submission of sitting on that floor.

But the gain was well worth it, since he had stolen the last of her secrets. And now, despite her defeat, the doctor had kept her alive. "Nathan, you've done well."

"Yes, General." The doctor's chin shifted as if he meant to say more, but he looked down instead.

"What's that? Something wrong?"

Startled, Nathan looked up again. "Nothing, sir, only... given our previous experience, I'm surprised I kept her against her will."

"Perhaps you have more at stake this time."

But Realgar knew better. He had seen the despair sink into Merwen, and he had heard her last threat, "Though Spinel betrayed me, you shall not." Merwen knew she had to kill him to keep him from betraying her; she had accepted the unthinkable.

And despite that, she lived. She had lost her will to die, at the last minute, just as Berenice had done.

Broken, now, Merwen could go home to share her defeat with her sisters. At long last, the will of Malachite had been done.

From what Merwen had said, even Siderite had never learned the true extent of lifeshaping power from his precious Usha. Those treacherous lifeshapers had played with the scientist all along, tossing him harmless tidbits of their skill, just as Realgar had predicted but Talion refused to see.

And sure enough, reports came in that his seaswallower repellent was not working as well as the first time, even as clickflies had forewarned. Swallowers were starting from the north pole and already had caused some nuisance at the northernmost bases. Realgar ordered the dosage raised tenfold; if that did not do the trick, they would have to hunt down stray swallowers by helicopter, and his troops would have good reason to curse the natives again.

Another swallower season, already. . . . He would never have believed that Operation Amethyst could spin out so long.

There was still Berenice to think of. What could he possibly do with her? *You still have the chance to not-kill her.* That insidious voice. . . . Torr's name, he was glad to be done with the Impatient One.

Abruptly his monitor came to life with an alert: trouble had erupted on the deck outside. A scuffle had broken out between a couple of guards and threatened to spread among the troops. The captain soon got things in hand, but Realgar was concerned enough to go out and assess the situation.

Out on the deck, a brisk wind whistled from the hard blue sky. There was a knot of guards who straightened into rows as the general approached with several aides in tow. Three men and a woman were under restraint, one badly bruised, their hair disheveled and tossing in the breeze.

"What's up?"

The captain saluted. "Quarrel started over a native, sir."

"A native?"

"Here, sir." The captain pointed.

"Here? Why wasn't she shot?"

"I don't know, sir."

Realgar stared hard at the captain, then followed her pointing arm.

A young native sat near the edge where the waves splashed up, her small-boned arms glistening in the sun. In her arms she cradled the tiniest infant Realgar had ever seen, nursing calmly as if there were nothing else going on in all the world.

His mind faltered, and there was a flash of yielding, a sense that he had already lost a struggle somewhere. It faded swiftly, leaving only a dull apprehension. Realgar shook himself free of it and faced the captain again. "What happened?"

"Barite and Zircon started the quarrel, sir."

"*I* would have wasted them," Zircon shouted hoarsely. "That's the orders."

"Go ahead, why don't you," challenged the other. "Sniveling childkiller."

"They're *catfish,* I tell you, slimy sneaking things that crawl into wherever they're not wanted, like maggots. And I'll squash them like maggots, like we're supposed to, until the whole planet's clean of them."

"Treason, you swine—in the name of the Patriarch."

Everyone froze. Only the ocean beyond rumbled on, pounding up against the deck, while the troops awaited the judgment of the general. What was treason, and what was not? When was a suckling infant a soldier?

"Captain, confine the troublemakers to barracks, all privileges suspended. Everyone else clear out."

"Yes, sir. And the native—"

"I'll handle it."

"Yes, sir."

In short order the troops were dispersed. "Stay here," Realgar told his aides. He strode quickly to the native girl, hoping the sea would mask their voices. He looked down at her sternly. The infant was sleeping now, and she leaned her head over it, rocking gently, while her eyes watched the general.

"If I let you stay, tomorrow I'll find a hundred of you."

She thought it over. "I'll come alone. With Laraisha," she added, hugging the child.

"Very well; but one more, and you're all dead."

"But why? Won't you stay and tell me . . . ?"

Realgar had already returned to his staff. "She'll stay, and no others," he told them. "It'll help public relations." Behind the terse remark, Realgar knew he had about reached the end of his rope.

With his troops demoralized, half under the spell of the natives, his hands were tied.

But the seaswallowers were coming, brought by those natives; and there was still Merwen, who would return to tell her sisters they had to fight back. As soon as the first hint of their next plague came, his troops would rally again, and then his satellites would strike.

12

A dozen strands of life now linked Merwen's body to the Valan lifeshaper with his primitive skill. Still she lived, her thoughts dancing about the rim of that dread that blocked her return, a cloud blacker than vacuum.

Come back, Merwen, come back to go home. A voice called across the vacuum, a child's voice, Nathan's voice. Home... an odd thing to offer, for here she was, at the lip of her own final home.

Was it just possible, though, to shrink that dreadful vacuum, to wear it down to something she could handle again?

The question was, had Spinel in fact shared betrayal or not? Before her own eyes Merwen was convinced he had, yet his denial, and her own knowledge of him, equally convinced her he had not. How could she resolve such a paradox?

Home, Merwen. You will go home. I promise. Nathan again. Merwen glimpsed that other home now, behind the black void, the place where Usha and Lystra struggled to swim on among the living. Perhaps she could make it back—if only she found the truth first.

As her eyes opened, they were pierced by a bright light overhead. With an enormous effort Merwen sat up on the mattress and pressed the sheet aside. Long filaments like dead vines adhered to several places on her limbs, but Nathan soon removed them. Merwen stretched her arms and smiled. "Thank you for keeping my life."

Nathan looked away. "It was you who kept mine."

"Thanks, too, for that privilege." Merwen paused. "Nathan, let me see Spinel."

He turned his white-cloaked back toward her as he fiddled with instruments on the shelf. "There won't be time. You'll be home within minutes, Merwen."

Alarmed, she sat up straight. "I can't go home; I'm not ready. Let me see Realgar, at least, just for a moment, whether or not he speaks—"

The wall broke open, the door-piece swung back, and two young soldiers came in. Nathan said, "Your helicopter is waiting."

Carefully she lowered her feet to the floor. Then she caught Nathan's sleeve and twisted herself around to look up into his face, saying in Sharer, "Can a recorded picture share untruth?"

His lips quivered and a scalpel slipped from his hand to clatter on the floor; his eyes were the very image of terror. Cruel though it was, Merwen could only feel pity for Nathan, and a deeper pity for herself.

On Raia-el the sun-warmed soil pressed her soles, and so many sisters came to greet her.

"Merwen, you're back at last; oh, everything will be right again."

"Even airblossoms will grow faster, now that Merwen's home!"

"How you've wasted away . . . but you'll get better soon."

"Mother, I know, I know how it was, but you can't just hold it all inside, you have to share it out, it's all right now, everything's fine."

Only nothing was right yet, and Merwen was not ready to share speech at all.

13

Fate was fickle, Lystra thought. Just when Elonwy and Laraisha had been spared to witness at the soldier-place every day, the Valans returned Merwen in such a state that she went alone to a raft offshoot. Unspeaking the Gathering. The thought of what Merwen must have undergone was enough to bring back nightmares of Lystra's own agony in the place of stone.

Now the clickfly missives mingled joy and sympathy, and they whispered, Merwen the Impatient is silent because she is too ashamed to admit she no longer thinks Valans are human. That was sad, but by now too many soldiers had proved themselves human by "not-killing." After all, who ever heard of a fleshborer that learned not to hasten death?

Spinel had not been seen on Raia-el since the helicopter took him. A visiting soldier said that Spinel had been sent up to the dreaded Satellite Amber.

Lystra's heart felt heavy as a deathweight to drag her under as she swam among the corals. Only the everpresent demand of the starworms kept her up from the floor of the sea.

The first seaswallower was sighted by Flossa, who yelped with glee and dragged every sister within earshot to see. Flossa was beside herself, since she had helped shape one of the microbe strains that now consumed the toxin from the soldier-place and let the swallowers come.

Lystra was not pleased for long; seaswallowers, however essential, were nothing to laugh about. Grimly she peered at the horizon, where the white spiral grew and came near. Raft seedlings were sparse, since fewer than usual had sprouted after the foul blight of the last season. So the starving seaswallowers would nibble away at the rich branches of Raia-el, despite the deterrent of fleshborers. Even the soldier-place, though not a raft, would attract swallowers to its organic effluents, and what would the soldiers do about it? Lystra wondered. Well, they had plenty of warning.

By the end of the week, the churning whirlpools were coming near enough so that an outlying branch strained and broke off. The jolt of it shuddered and quaked across the raft. Lystra, at work on an escape craft, lost her balance and fell. Dazed, she picked herself up, recalling that Merwen was still out on an offshoot, Unspoken.

Lystra stomped down to the lifeshaping-place to confront Usha. "Enough is enough, Mothersister. When will you share sense with her?"

Usha did not look up from the seed pods that held her microbe cultures. "Am I Shora Herself and the sun and stars besides? I have nothing but patience to share with the Impatient One."

Lystra stomped back up and shoved a rowboat into the branch channel, as fleshborers snapped and squirmed below. Eerily, this act recalled her last day with Rilwen, the day she had set out to bring her lovesharer home and returned with only Spinel. Rilwen's agony was something Lystra at least understood, but Merwen's was beyond knowing.

Beyond the network of channels, a lonely bit of windscraped raft stuck out of the sea. Lystra pulled her boat up, walked over to her mother, and sat down obstinately beside her. "Mother, I won't leave until you do. And this time, Spinel isn't here to pull me back."

Merwen sat in silence for a minute or so, calmly gazing past Lystra out to sea. Then the corner of her lip twitched, and her head tossed back with a quick laugh. "Come, let's go." She rose to her feet.

Dumbfounded, Lystra scrambled up. "That was easy."

"I knew I had no choice, with you."

"You were just ready to come, that's all."

"Perhaps." Merwen stepped into the boat.

Lystra started to pick up the oars, then she dropped them and turned on her mother. "Mother, what did they do with you at the soldier-place? They hurt Spinel—that's it, isn't it? Where is he, what became of him?"

"He became a soldier."

A chill shocked Lystra and her breath came fast.

"He denied it, but I saw," Merwen added.

Lystra drew a deep breath. "It's a lie, I tell you, I don't care what they made you see! A lie, like all the traders' lies I ever shared."

"Why are you shouting so?"

"Because you believe it, don't you?"

"Lystra, you're right, it must be a lie. But you didn't *see* what I saw in the picture cube. That moment when Spinel held the fire-whip was totally real, for me. I have to come to terms with that, do you see?"

I don't." But Lystra was uneasy. After all, Spinel had tried to share the soldiers' way more than once, before he took his self-name. What would become of him now, in that sky-place with the mind-twisters? "Mother, you have to trust someone."

"You have to trust everyone, in order to draw out what truth is in them. Even Kyril shared valuable truth with you. Spinel I trust absolutely now, because I have to. It's all right, Lystra; I am content."

"Content, you say," Lystra muttered as she picked up the oars again. "Content, when we're all headed for extinction?"

Merwen cocked her head toward the sky. "Oh, I doubt that. Billions of galaxies are out there, and how many planets full of souls?"

"Mother! You can't start thinking like that."

"I'm tired, Lystra, much too tired." She looked tired, Lystra realized suddenly, despite the bright words. Merwen had aged a decade in the Valan prison.

14

Realgar had heard traders' tales of the seaswallowers, but he tended to discount them. Certainly he had never imagined anything quite so powerful as those whirlpools that now sucked hungrily on all sides, some broader than the Headquarters itself. And when one fountained, so high that the spray took several minutes to come down—it was breathtaking, as though the whole ocean had turned into a great primeval monster.

To the north, a battalion headquarters was swamped by a fountain.

After that, Realgar suspended everything except attacks on swallowers. The guardbeam hit whirlpools that approached Headquarters, producing masses of steam that the beasts sucked down until they choked. Submarine homing missiles got others. Even so, three more bases were swamped, then a fourth, as the population crested past.

Realgar surveyed the sea with growing apprehension and wondered what more could be done. At this rate, there would be dozens of bases to clean up by the time the swallowers were through.

As the crest peaked, Lystra and Merwen were checking the escape craft, where food and medicines were packed and the children were safely ensconced, Weia playing finger games with Elonwy's toddler. To Lystra's astonishment, Elonwy herself emerged from the water, gasping and heaving, while Laraisha clung like a limpet to her neck. "Elonwy! You didn't lose your boat?" Lystra caught up the infant to give her a rest.

"The soldier-place—its' washed away! I was sitting on the edge, as usual, and a guard had just asked me if Laraisha was teething yet, and the next minute I was swept away."

"But you got back—"

"I don't know how, Lystra. I just swam and swam, and Laraisha hung on, and I guess Shora didn't want me lost yet. But Lystra, those Valans: they can't swim at all."

Lystra drew back, and her heart congealed.

Merwen said, "Take this boat. With four of you pulling oars, you'll manage. Wellen, get the girls out and into the next boat."

"We can't, Mother," Lystra protested. "The whole raft could break up, any minute now."

"The crest is past; we're safe enough. I knew Raia-el raft." Already Ishma and two others were settling into the boat, to hunt for survivors. Merwen leaned on the boat frame as if to test it. "Lystra, with your strong arm you'll all make it."

Lystra muttered, "I have to tend the starworms."

Merwen stopped to look at her. "What are you saying?"

"Why should I bring myself to help another one of those creatures ever again? After all the weeks I wasted away, and the months as they hastened our sisters without a thought, and their last gruesome trick with Spinel? Why, Mother? I say, let it be. Let Shora Herself share Her own justice."

"Have you learned nothing since your selfname?" Merwen's voice held a rare snap. "Never mind, time wastes us all." She flung the last words over her shoulder as she jumped into the boat herself.

"What? Mother! You can't go, in your condition—"

But Merwen had her back turned and of course would not listen. That was just too much. Lystra picked her up like one of the children, then stomped into the boat herself, sitting down so hard the others jumped. "All right, Mother! I won't have *your* death on my soul, do you hear?" With an oar she gave a furious shove at a raft branch, and the boat slithered out into the channel.

So the seasilken boats went out, one after another, to pull survivors from the tormented sea. Since the soldier-place was thoroughly swamped, the Valans were brought back to the raft. Some needed quick treatment to live, while others just stretched out on blankets to dry.

Realgar found himself stranded on the raft, left without clothing, weapons, even a radio to summon assistance, as if the natives had seized the last chance they would get to mock him. And it was their last chance, he swore as he watched them saunter shamelessly past the blanketed men; their last, before the satellites got them.

But the first thing was to get back to Headquarters, and how was he to do that without contact? Not a helicopter was in sight; was his whole corps in disarray? Or had his officers mutinied? He felt suddenly cold, and his hair stood on end. Cut off in one instant from the vast machine he ruled, he was alone, as alone as in the Sardish wilderness.

He caught sight of the captain of the perimeter guard, amid a group of blanketed troopers. The familiar face brought him somewhat to his senses. He got up and walked over, wrapping his blanket tighter, swallowing embarrassment. "Captain. Anyone manage to keep a radio?"

The captain pulled her arm out from a fold of seasilk to salute. "Yes, sir, we did." A noncom was fiddling with a waterlogged instrument, which produced nothing but static.

As the others crowded and swore at the radio, a webbed hand fluttered among them, a youngster of Merwen's household. "I'll send a clickfly for you." The girl had a clickfly perched on her head which rubbed its lopsided mandibles and clucked with maddening cheeriness.

A man turned to her hopefully. "Sure, kid, why don't you—"

"Shut up," said the captain. "You know the rule."

The man's face turned pale. The rule was still to burn on sight any native who acted "forward," without exception. He looked at his empty hands as if expecting an order to strangle the girl.

The captain grabbed the girl by the arm, twisting it behind her back, and the startled clickfly flitted up to escape. "Where are our weapons? Brink them back, or it's lights out for you."

"The death-sticks are on their way to the sea floor," the girl replied without blinking. "Those toys are too dangerous, even for me."

The captain shoved the girl away. She seated herself at a distance, with the watchful look of a nanny at a playground.

Realgar tensed with fury, every tendon stretched to breaking. He would rather face torture, interrogation, even a shot in the back—anything rather than the appalling sight of that girl. He hated every inch of her and her web-fingered kind who dared to fish his troops from the sea. Even if he were to strangle them, their faces would show only pity as they died.

Then his hatred subsided, leaving a headache and a weariness that would not vanish even when a helicopter appeared at last in the sky, and he snapped out commands to gather the survivors into some semblance of order. The campaign would be won despite this setback, but Realgar sensed an indefinable loss of spirit that would take him a long while to recover.

Out of the helicopter stepped Jade, smart and trim as ever, with a brisk salute as if it were all in a day's work.

"Jade, you made it! I should have known. You'd live through the flooding of hell itself. What's left of Headquarters?"

"The framework is intact, though it needs a big cleanout. Casualties are uncertain, since we're still picking survivors off the sea. Though by the looks of it, most of them ended up here." Her gaze took in the scene, the troopers wrapped in ludicrous seasilk, the natives wandering around. "Imagine, those catfish still hope to capture our sympathy. I can't wait to turn on the satellites."

"Since nothing else worked?"

Jade's mouth snapped shut; then she turned and started spouting orders at the helicopter crew.

Realgar's temper had flared because Jade had no business taking over and telling him what to do next, and also because she had stated his own thought aloud, in front of all the natives, where the mockery of it was obvious. What a hollow triumph it would be to destroy all the rafts just because Sharers could not be ruled.

15

While his troops worked feverishly to rebuild damaged bases in the wake of the swallowers, Realgar faced a grilling by the High Protector.

Talion's lightshape glimmered above the viewing stage behind his monument of a desk. "General, by the Nine Legions I want to know just what in hell is going on out there."

Realgar cleared his throat. "My lord, it's just bad luck with the season—"

But Talion already was speaking again, not deigning to wait for the general's reply to reach Valedon. "Didn't I give you everything you asked? A corps of your own compatriots, twenty divisions' worth, and what happened? They melted away, as far as I can tell. They're a disgrace, even a laughingstock. Everywhere, citizens are clamoring to know why a whole Sardish army can't control a few women and children without resorting to brutalities that would shock the Patriarch." Talion leaned forward across the desk. "To top it off, your own officers mutinied—and you actually tried to keep it from the palace. It's beyond belief, Ral." He paused, his wrath spent for the moment.

Realgar knew he was finished; but Talion must want something from him still, or he would have simply replaced him, without this harangue. "The insurrection was put down, my lord, before it posed a real threat."

Talion's palms slammed down. "No real threat! When your entire force is essentially out of control?" He sat back, lacing his fingers, and his eyes narrowed. "You aren't that incompetent, Ral. The truth is, you share the sentiment of your treasonous officers. You dare question my authority to order what must be done to Shora."

Realgar hid his alarm and disgust. Of course he detested Iridians, but that was a personal matter. "My lord, I swear to you, in the name of whatever honor I possess, that I never have and never will intend anything but full obedience to the High Protector of Valedon."

With a businesslike air Talion sat up, saying, "In that case, I'll give you one more chance. You shall activate the satellites to burn out the entire native population of the Ocean Moon. To the last mother and child—do I make myself clear?"

The turnabout wrenched him off balance. "Every last one?" he said guardedly. "Not even a handful left, to satisfy the Envoy of Torr?"

"Unnecessary. Their knowledge will remain, encoded in those rafts. That will have to do. Even one native left behind could unleash all sorts of plagues in revenge." Talion shook his head. "You had your chance to get them under control, as you swore you would. Now you must wipe them out—and take full personal responsibility."

There was a trap, his instinct warned. "Since I clearly have lost my lord's confidence, I offer to resign."

"As you wish."

Realgar tensed, and his chin jerked up. He saw it now; the order would still go out, under his own name. Valan citizens, already aroused against his campaign, would be shown a release of the Sardish Commander explaining why the people of the Ocean Moon had been extinguished—whether or not Realgar himself was actually responsible. Whether or not he resigned, there would be such an outcry that his banishment was assured, his life worth nothing.

It made cold sense, for the High Protector. Talion needed someone to take the blame for a slaughter of innocents—preferably someone not Iridian. Realgar's officers had been right; he himself was the perfect scapegoat. When Malachite returned, nine years hence, Sardis would fall before his wrath, just as Pyrrhopolis had. And Iridis would be left with one less rival.

There had to be a way out.

For some reason he thought of Siderite. Talion had not quite heard the last word on that. "Are you aware that your scientist's mission was useless from the start? That the natives never intended to reveal the extent of their powers?"

"I thought as much. But we had to humor the Envoy."

"Did you think Malachite such a fool?" He saw Talion's eyes flash open, and his breath came faster. "Didn't you ever wonder what Malachite really had in mind? He was playing with us; he set us up, just to provoke those creatures into striking back, to test their power."

"General, do you realize what you're saying?" Talion's voice lowered, became smooth and deadly.

Realgar felt the sweat on his palms. He had to go on, there was no turning back, and what was another treachery on top of so many? "Siderite was convinced of it. In fact, he believes we are all hostage to lifeshaped pathogens, already 'living dead,' contaminated with the seeds of our own destruction—which only *they* can cure."

"And if they die, we die, is that it?" Talion clenched his fists. "I saw no such report. You'd damn well better back this up."

"Of course, my lord; Siderite was mindprobed. Surely you heard from your spies."

"By Torr, you Sardish bastard, you've been holding out on me!" After the outburst, Talion cooled down somewhat, running a hand through his thinning hair as he shook his head. "How could even a Sard hold back a thing like that, a threat to the entire planet? Ral, do you really think I follow Torr like a servo, or that I even give fool's gold for the Envoy and his grand designs? We're men of *Valedon,* live men on a planet with some life to it, not just a machine world like Torr. Valan survival is what counts."

Realgar was amazed, and by the end of Talion's speech his hands were shaking. "Then why do we have to bow and scrape to the Patriarch's servo every decade? And allow *it* to snuff out a city at *its* own calculated whim? If every planet in the Patriarchy refused to be ruled, *we all would be free.*" Even as he spoke, alarms screamed inside his head. He was finished for certain.

But Talion only grew very calm, even reflective, as the general's words reached him across space. The pause lengthened beyond timelag. "And then would Sardis and Dolomoth, too, refuse to be ruled?" he mused, half to himself. "Would children cease to obey their fathers; would hands no longer follow the brain?" He shook his head slowly. "How little keeps our world intact, safe from the law of the jungle. Always, in every age, a few strong men bear the burden of civilization. I had thought, Ral, that you were one. But you disappointed me." A hint of contempt entered his voice. "Or perhaps you were, once, but you listened to *them* for too long."

So Realgar was relieved of his command. But one piece of unfinished business could not be left to his successor: Berenice.

Though still alive, Berenice had not uttered a syllable since the night of her capture, a scene almost too painful to recall. He had left her alive, but now, what the devil was he to do with her?

At Satellite Amber, he found her alone in her sparse quarters, where she sat crosslegged on her bed, her back to the door. Her pose was so unnervingly Sharer that he nearly turned and left; but she was clothed, after all, in a demure white talar with the blue and gold nested-squares border stretched out around her knees.

"Berenice. I'm leaving. I've been recalled; my successor will be here within the hour." Realgar paused, then hurried on. "Talion wanted the Sharers wiped out—completely. I refused. Does that mean nothing to you?"

Berenice did not even turn her head. It was hopeless, but still Realgar could not bring himself to leave her in the hands of his Iridian overlords. There was one alternative: to leave her to those whom he hated more. "Berenice, you'll be sent to Iridis soon, and you know what that means. Unless . . . I set you down on Shora." He added, "You'll be taking your chances there. Talion still hopes to—"

She wheeled, leaning her arms on the bed, her face stricken. "Shora?" she whispered hoarsely. "You'll leave me . . . there? After what I've *done?*"

It was actually Sharers that she feared, more than Talion, for by their standards she had betrayed them far worse. How would they punish her?

But she had melted at last, that was all that mattered. Realgar took her by the shoulders, saying, "I won't leave you. I'll take you back to Sardis in secret, and we'll retire in the backlands. We'll have Cassiter and Elmvar, and every luxury you need. I'll protect you—"

Pulling free of him, Berenice swung her legs over the bed and stood, her face turned to crystal again. "I don't want your protection, Ral," she said distinctly. "Only forgiveness, though I deserve it even less from you than from *them.*"

In her own hard way she was asking him to forgive, but she refused his protection, and in that she rejected him. Berenice must have known that, if she knew him at all. His heart congealed; he could never say he forgave her.

At the observation dome of the transport ship, Realgar stood with his children, who watched with wide eyes as the Ocean Moon curved and shrank away to a fine sickle against the stars. Cassiter squeezed his hand. "Papa, can't we stay long enough even to go for a swim? You promised to take us, sometime."

"It's too late, Cassi. The ship has left orbit."

"Then order it to turn back."

Realgar could not bring himself to tell her he could not. He was alone: no monitors to break in with a call, no emergencies, not even paperwork to command the attention of a deposed commander. It had been years since he had felt so powerless, so insignificant.

"You'll take us back someday, won't you, Papa? I never did get my whorlshell." His children would share his exile; they had yet to learn what that meant.

His past flooded back over him: the battlefields strewn with corpses, the control rooms, the promotions, all to dissolve here on a slippery bit of ocean between seaweed and seafoam. How had it happened? Those webfingered creatures were fiendish tacticians. So many times they nearly drove him out, with their bloodless "invasions," the Purple Plague, the uncanny bewitchment of his troops, no matter how many of their own deaths it cost.

But was it more than tactics? In the end, Sharers actually forced him to set their world free—but why? Why had he done so, when he did not believe Siderite's warning, any more than Siderite himself? He had learned too well what Merwen really meant by the *living dead.*

And Merwen had said, *You will not betray me.* How could she have known? Had he played out the lie just to spite his superiors, or was he in awe of something else, a mystery beyond the dread of lifeshaping?

Time. Sharers had lasted for millennia before the Patriarch arose, and something whispered to him that they might endure even after Torr had blown to dust.

With a shudder he turned impatiently away from the empty stars. The glass door of the observation deck did not open at first, and his own shadowed reflection faced him.

Whose eyes do you see in mine, and whose in—

His fist swung out and crashed; a white spiderweb leaped into the glass. Behind him his children gasped at the shattered door. Shaking all over, he clasped his knuckles to stop the blood and breathed deeply to get a grip on himself. Somehow, he would never see a glass again, or look into the eyes of a cornered bear, without knowing that the wildest thing he ever hunted still swam beyond his grasp.

16

Seaswallowers passed as they always did, leaving the waters clean and clear but for white tongues of foam. This time Per-elion did not lose a raft, Shora be thanked, but clickflies brought work of distant rafts to be sung for.

In a few days waterfire bloomed again, a lovely biolumine-scence that etched the waves for seven nights and kept everyone awake dancing in its brilliance. Another strand of the living web was rejoined.

At the soldier-places, Valans kept to themselves, and many dis-appeared to the sky. And with their departure, a remarkable thing happened: the song of the starworm began to penetrate the far ocean again. Soon the deep rumbling tones could be heard from one end of the globe to the other, more clearly than they had since the first sky-crossing traders came to settle. Once more, all the Gatherings of Shora could share will together within the period of a sun's flight across the sky.

Merwen thought of all these things as she sat at her spindle, touching strands of yellow to the head as it whirled, and the yellow strands grew like the beams of the sun just edging above the ocean. The smell of night things still clung, and Weia and Wellen had not yet uncurled from their sleeping holes to swim out chasing through the branch channels. But for Merwen, the day was already long and old. Sleep was coming hard to her, and she found herself rising earlier and earlier, to listen to the roar of the sea and to calm her troubled hands with silk-spinning by the light of the Stone Moon.

Shadows were still long when Spinel came out to sit beside her workstool. A helicopter had returned him to Raia-el, the week after the rescue of the soldiers from their flooded base.

Spinel cleared his throat and said, "Merwen—don't you think we have enough spun silk for a while? Especially the yellow stuff, it's only used in thin lines. . . ."

Her eyes turned toward him, while her hand still fed the spindle. Though he sat flat on the raft with his feet tucked under, his eyes were nearly level with hers; he was as big as Lystra now, big and black, not like the timid brown child who first approached her and Usha on the Valan shore, so long ago. And except for Usha, she realized, he was the only one who ever approached her nowadays, when she was like this.

"It's been a long time," Merwen said, "since I could afford the luxury of useless work." Taken aback, Spinel looked away a moment. But then he looked up again, his eyes bright with eagerness. "Did you hear they're all leaving for good? Death-hasteners, traders, all of them; I heard it from the trawler deckhands, lined up at Dak's moonferry. The High Protector says they can't come back, ever. So we're rid of them, Merwen."

"Yes. That is why I spin yellow silk."

"What makes you so sad? No one else is."

No, only Usha understood, and no one could tell when Usha was sad. "And what are you glad for, stoneshaper?"

Then his face crumpled, and Merwen was sorry, though at least he never brooded for long. "You knew I didn't, didn't you?" he asked.

Merwen paused to finish off the spindle. "I thought at first I had betrayed you, that I had asked you to be something you never could be."

"Oh, no, never."

"Not even when your palms first turned color? I asked too much of everyone, even of my own daughter."

"No. When you ask, we simply find we had more to share than

we thought." Spinel swallowed. "You only ask too much of your-self, Merwen."

"Shora asks," she whispered.

"You did the best you could. I always wondered why the death-hasteners in Chrysoport left you alone at the tree, and I sure found out."

"So did I. I thought they showed respect for whitetrance; but it was only fear."

"Fear of your fearlessness."

"What good is that, without understanding? How few of them ever shared understanding, from my words or from the patterns I wove that spoke more than words. As for myself, I tried so hard to learn, to share the Valan thinking. I even became a trader, trading a bolt of seasilk—for you. And at the last, I could well have become a death-hastener, and then Death would have sailed the waves from one pole to the other. It was only for love of you that I did not."

She saw him wipe a tear from his cheek and thought, This time I've gone too far, but I have to make certain he knows his own mind. "Are you quite sure you want to share our lot, Spinel, now that you know it's forever?"

"You know I am."

Merwen paused a moment. "Then go share the news with Nisi. She may not be sure."

Nisi the Deceiver had come back unexpectedly, just before all the other Valans started to leave. She promptly Unspoke everyone and withdrew alone, and for that she won respect from the Gather-ing.

Spinel remembered how Nisi had stood up for him, when he first came to Shora and everyone seemed to hate him. "Merwen says I should tell her," he told Lystra.

"Someone has to tell her," Lystra agreed. "It's right that you should."

The next day, Spinel and Lystra approached Nisi on her isolated offshoot raft. Nisi hugged her knees and did not acknowledge the visitors. Like Spinel, she had let her hair grow out, and the strands knitted over her forehead.

Spinel knew that Nisi was determined to make no sign. Her crime still weighed heavily upon her, and that was right. But sup-pose she really did want to go back? To lose Valedon forever—the thought was so awful that Spinel himself had not let himself think of it yet. On Shora he had Lystra, and that was what mattered. But it was hard to say what mattered most for Nisi. "Nisi, you have to hear this, just once. Valans are leaving, all of them, to come no more. It's your last chance; do you understand?"

Nisi made no sign.

Suddenly he added, "Nisi, speak with me—or I'll go Unspoken."

Startled, Lystra stared at him. Why should Spinel care to share Nisi's withdrawal?

Spinel himself was scared, and not sure just what he had intended. He watched Nisi anxiously, but she kept still. "Look, I didn't mean it; that is—"

Lystra's expression was scandalized. Spinel had to follow through on his impulse.

"Berenice!" He rushed to her, kneeling on the raft to look into her face, pouring out in Valan, "Lady Berenice, you can't do this to me. You know I couldn't keep quiet a whole year: I'd die for sure. Please, Lady Berenice."

Her gaze descended perceptibly, and a smile tugged at her lips. "Spinel, you're still a commoner, after all."

"Well," he said shamefacedly, dismayed at how quickly he reverted to his old ways. "I can't change what I am overnight."

"Nor can I. And yet, one can't stop changing, either." She took his hand and laced her fingers with his, as only Valans could, and Spinel felt ice tickle down his spine. Nisi looked up and past him again. "If Ral had only asked me to *share protecting*, I would have gone back with him. What else is love for? But it's too late for us. Here," she said, and handed him a whorlshell of exquisite pink and yellow swirls. "It's for his daughter; I promised, once. When you return to Valedon, will you . . . ?"

"I will."

She withdrew from him, then, to her silence.

Lystra pulled him roughly away. "Spinel! You didn't say you're going *back?*"

"I—I don't know." A sense of loss overwhelmed him. The tide lapping in the harbor, the towering limestone cliffs, even the spurt of a ripe tomato on his tongue, and the feisty old market vendors, and his father and mother: all of it he would never see again. "I just can't bear not to go back, even to visit. Oh, why does it all have to be so impossible?" The day he turned purple, he was sure that he would never face such a terrible choice again. But now, when he might never see home again, it seemed that he had yet to really make that choice.

"You're one of us now," Lystra insisted. "You've said it, and you know it. Why should you return to that ocean of despair?"

"I'm a troublesharer. Merwen never expected me to stay here. She wanted me to share learning on Valedon, as she did: to weave words like a Spirit Caller. Yes, because all they really need is a spirit to call on—the spirit of Shora, not the Patriarch. This is what I can share."

"Have you lost your head? What do you expect to *do* with such barbarians?"

"I can do more than sing for them."

"Spinel, of all the Valans who've come here, how many shared? Stay here and be safe. Help raise our daughters; yes, we need daughters so that the departed souls can find new homes. That's what Merwen brought you here for."

Spinel was so overcome that he could say nothing at first. To think that even Lystra would want to share his blood, for all his hated lineage, to make a child that might have hair or lack webs between the fingers. His hand brushed her scalp. "But Lystra, are we really safe, even here? Will our daughters be safe?"

For that Lystra had no answer.

"Death-hasteners say they won't come back, but they could change their minds, especially when Malachite returns. We can't rest until every one of them shares healing."

Lystra turned away. "Well, then, do what you have to."

"You could come too, Lystra."

"Who, *me?* To that dry bone of a planet?"

Back at Raia-el, they talked for long hours, until the sun was gone and the half-moon of Valedon had risen high in the sky.

17

Spinel leaped out of the boat and tied it to a post at the former traders' raft. Lystra followed, warily. Ahead of them rose the moonferry, with the same old creased fins and crackled insignia. Spinel had the feeling it was bound to collapse after just one more trip.

Captain Dak looked much the same, several days unshaven, his brow etched with deep herringbone wrinkles that belied his easy grin. His breath came sour, and he was sure to have a bottle hidden away somewhere.

"Hey there, Dak; how's business?"

Dak's jaw shifted sideways. "It wouldn't be half bad, if I'd earned a pension from ten thousand years of service. And yourself, starling?"

"Oh, all right. Listen, how much would a pair of tickets come to, one-way?"

"The same as always—and there's none *but* one-way." His body shook with laughter, then abruptly he was serious again. "Might I ask who they're for?"

"Why, us, of course. You know Lystra, don't you?" Spinel put his arm around her. "Lystra the Intemperate One."

"Pleased to meet you, ma'am. Uh"—Dak kneaded his bristly chin—"no offense, but you folks do plan to put something on, don't you?"

"Well . . . I guess we figured we could get clothes when we reach Valedon." Spinel looked uncertainly at Lystra, whose frown was thick with distaste.

Dak waved his hand dismissively. "I can scrounge up an old shirt for you."

"Gee, Dak, thanks a lot."

"I don't know what for. I'm ferrying you to certain death."

Spinel stared at him.

"Don't you have *ears*, starling? Haven't you heard how it is? Valans don't want the least thing to do with catfish anymore. They'll shoot you on sight."

Spinel put his hands at his hips. "You can't scare us, Dak; we know all about it. We just won a war."

"Then why start another? Listen: maybe you could make it back, if you clear up that skin of yours, but your lady friend can forget it. Not another passenger would even board my ship with her on it."

"What?" Spinel's mouth hung open with dismay. "That's outrageous."

"It's plain fact." Dak lowered his voice sympathetically. "Starling, of all the planets I've known, you're standing on the coziest one right now, do you hear? The only one free of the Patriarch. Whatever do you want to *leave* for?"

"We can't ever be safe here, not so long as Valans are all out there."

"And you aim to set them straight, is that it?" Dak nodded. "And once that's settled, you'll move on to Arcturon, and Sol-Rex, and even Torr itself, I suppose."

"Well . . ."

"You'll never be 'safe' otherwise," Dak assured him. "The whole universe'll blow up, anyhow, in another hundred billion years; you plan to solve that one too?"

"You got to start somewhere."

Dak shook his head. "A fool shares gold with strangers. Look." He thumbed at the door of his ship. *"I'm* still available to whoever wants the Ocean Moon. It takes two to 'share learning,' starling."

"And one to start. . . ." He turned to Lystra—

She was gone.

The bundle of herbs and medicines for the ferry ticket sat on the raft, but Lystra's craft was a dark shape shrinking across the sea behind her glider squid.

"Lystra!" Spinel's cry set off a flock of clickflies swirling in surprise, but Lystra was too far away to hear. He skipped back to the edge of the dock and stood there, dazed.

Lystra had left him alone. Alone to think it out, for the last time, and here he was stumbling through it. Was Dak right, after all? Why had Spinel left Chrysoport the second time, if not because his own people stopped their ears to what he tried to share?

Patience . . . he had more of that, now, but still infinitely less than the Impatient One.

Lystra's craft sped on, and his heart strained after it, taut as the charness of the glider squid. Could he bear to stay here, a freak for the rest of his life? What did that matter, if Lystra would carry a child in whose veins his own blood swam?

With a sudden thought, he reached into his package for the seashell that Nisi had given him. Then he walked back toward Dak. "You know, if you think it's so great here, why not come back after your last trip? You're more than welcome on Raia-el."

"Who, me?" Dak's voice deepened. "I'm too old, starling. Seen too many planets come and go."

"Shora is even older than you are."

"I'm too young, then. Too young to settle down." His grin twisted.

Spinel smiled sadly, knowing that the old man was sure to end his days planet-bound, one way or another. "Just don't say I never asked. Could you do me one last favor?" He handed Dak the whorlshell. "Send this to the Commander, the one who got sent back to Sardis. Tell him it's from Berenice, who still loves him."

Dak blinked. "Whatever you say, starling."

There, he was quits now; and who could say what might come of it? "And if you're ever in Chrysoport, Dak, you can tell them—" His throat ached too much to swallow. "Just tell them the door is still open." Spinel hugged Dak hard, and the man's stubble scraped his cheek. Then he spun around, sprinted to the water's edge, and dove, his starstone dancing on the chain as his body knifed the waves. He plowed outward, fast as he could swim, his head lifting every few minutes to spot the speck of Lystra in the distance, where a friendly fanwing dipped and soared overhead like a hand beckoning, Come, lovesharer, come home.